PURPLE HEARTS

Arthur Archambeau

Arthur Archambeau

Copyright © 2021 Arthur Archambeau

All rights reserved

The characters and events portrayed in this book are fictitious. Any similarity to real persons, living or dead, is coincidental and not intended by the author.

No part of this book may be reproduced, or stored in a retrieval system, or transmitted in any form or by any means, electronic, mechanical, photocopying, recording, or otherwise, without express written permission of the publisher.

ISBN-13: 9798475914991
ISBN-10: 1477123456

Cover design by: Art Painter
Library of Congress Control Number: 2018675309
Printed in the United States of America

For Bunky, the little cat who could. You charmed us with your kind, gentle ways. Why couldn't you have just lived forever? In our memories—our hearts— you will. See you at the Rainbow Bridge, pal.

CONTENTS

Title Page
Copyright
Dedication
Chapter One: The Nine Lives   1
Chapter Two: Someone Saved My Life Tonight   11
Chapter Three: The Midnight Ranger   39
Chapter Four: The Debutante and the Mutt   60
Chapter Five: Hard To Say I'm Sorry   78
Chapter Six: I Knew You Had A Pretty Name   93
Chapter Seven: Our Time In Hell   100
Chapter Eight: The Good Thief   113
Chapter Nine: Take My Whole Life, Too   135
Chapter Ten: Yes, Hope, There Is A Santa Claus   154
Chapter Eleven: The Frankenstein Sweater   161
Chapter Twelve: The Hello Kitty Onesie   176
Chapter Thirteen: Out of the Mouths of Babes   187
Chapter Fourteen: Doctor Mike   202
Chapter Fifteen: War Story   218
Chapter Sixteen: Crazy For You   230
Chapter Seventeen: You're John Candy   249
Chapter Eighteen: Luke's Love Emporium   264

Chapter Nineteen: Fix You	274
Chapter Twenty: Redemption	280
Chapter Twenty-One: Bunky	295
Chapter Twenty-Two: Cat's In The Cradle	301
Chapter Twenty-Three: Works In Progress	307
Chapter Twenty-Four: Victim's Statement	316
Chapter Twenty-Five: The Final Bell	333
Chapter Twenty-Six: The One	339
Epilogue: Charlotte's Song (This Medal You Gave)	345
About The Author	351
Books By This Author	353
Books By This Author	355

CHAPTER ONE: THE NINE LIVES

He was worried that their food would freeze before they had a chance to eat it. It was supposed to get down to single digits, around seven degrees, with a chance of flurries.

January in Baltimore. In the crime-riddled neighborhood surrounding Fulton Avenue, the area known as Mondawmin. Nearly as unsafe as the streets of Bagdad or Kabul, it was the East Coast's version of the Wild Wild West. The most dangerous neighborhood in America's *most dangerous city.*

On this Monday night, Luke Matthews set out seven Styrofoam bowls in an alley adjacent to a liquor store and a porn shop. A couple of lights on the outside walls of those buildings provided a bit of illumination to work with. He opened seven cans of cat food, in a variety of flavors. Gary, Bunky, and Samantha liked the turkey. Lola and Daniel Striped Tiger enjoyed the tuna. Sassy favored the kind that combined beef with little chunks of cheese. And Basilone, well, Basilone wasn't picky. He would eat anything.

Seven lives. Seven souls. Insignificant to the rest of the world, but not to Luke. To him, they were his babies. They were the *Mondawmin Seven*, as he called them.

He wore a pair of blue jeans, white sneakers, and a heavy, purple Baltimore Ravens satin jacket. But he was still cold. *Probably should have swallowed my pride and worn a stocking hat and a pair of gloves, but I don't really look good in stocking hats and gloves make it harder to open the cans of food and dish it out.*

1

He used a stainless steel fork to transfer the food from can to bowl. Then he called the crew. He whistled. "Okay, guys, dinner is served. Come and get it."

Luke was thirty. He had jet black hair and glacier blue eyes. He was tall, about six-feet-three-inches. And he was thin, roughly a hundred and seventy pounds. By anyone's standards, he was a good-looking man. He looked a lot like a young Elvis Presley, so much so that his Marine Corps nickname had been *Elvis*. He walked with a slight limp, favoring his left leg, the result of being wounded in Afghanistan some ten years earlier.

He clapped his hands to alert the feral cats that dinner was being served. From his jacket pocket, he pulled out a bag of cat treats and shook it, as the cats had grown to associate the sound with mealtime.

A set of eyes, glowing in the dark, peeked out from behind a dumpster. Tentatively, a cat emerged. It was Bunky, a smallish gray and white longhair. Luke guessed that he was only about six months old. He'd probably been born the previous summer. They were all feral, but Bunky was the one that he thought might one day be tame enough to become a housecat. Bunky immediately went over to the bowls and picked out one of the ones with turkey. He began to inhale his food. One-by-one, they all came out and ate.

Gary was older and solid grey. Basilone, a gray tabby. Samantha, a gray and white short-hair. Lola, a black and white long-hair. Daniel Striped Tiger, a marmalade tabby. And, finally, Sassy, a very large black and white short-hair. She was easily the most stand-offish of the colony. Bossy with the other cats, she was not above swatting at anyone—human or feline—who violated her space.

As they ate, Luke gently talked to them. "That's right guys—eat it before it freezes."

He smiled and felt relieved that they were all there. All safe and accounted for. At least for that night.

The cats scarfed down their food, constantly looking around, scanning their environment as they ate, on guard for any sign of trouble. After they finished their canned food, he prepared to give them some treats.

A vehicle slowly drove by the alley and spotlighted him. He put the treats back in his pocket and his arms up to shield his eyes from the light. Then the light went off and the car stopped. He could see that it was a white car trimmed in blue, with a reflective emblem on the side. It read—*Baltimore Police*. Below that was a picture of a police badge. And below the badge were the words—*Integrity. Fairness. Service*. The car turned into the alley. The cats scattered. He shook his head in disgust. *Great. Now they're not going to get their dessert.*

Once the police cruiser got to within about fifteen feet of him, the spotlight came back on and it was again pointed directly at him. Again, he shielded his eyes.

He walked out of the spotlight and towards the vehicle, stopping roughly five feet from the driver's side door. The window of the cruiser came down. He saw that it was a female officer. Her coal-black hair was up in a bun. He guessed she was in her late 20s. She wore trendy eyeglasses with black frames. Her black leather service jacket was unzipped. He thought she kind of looked a little like Demi Lovato. *She might actually be better looking than Demi.* There was chatter coming over the vehicle's police radio.

He bent down to see her better and smiled. "Hey, how you doing tonight, officer? You all chipper and full of life, are you? Keeping nice and warm in there? It's a cold one out here tonight, right? Don't know about you, but I'm ready for spring." He pointed to her glasses and blew into his hands. "By the way—I like those glasses. They look really good on you. They *become you*, as they say."

The cop ignored his small talk and compliment. Instead, she barked out orders—"*Do not* come any closer. And put your hands up where I can see them."

He put his hands up and waved them from side to side. "Everybody put your hands in the air. Everybody put your hands in the air," he quipped.

He laughed. She didn't.

"That, ah, that was just a little attempt at humor but, ah, really, I'm just feeding the cats. That's all."

She turned off the ignition, put on her navy eight point police service hat, and stepped out of the car. She was short but had a nice body. *Damn. She's really beautiful.* He thought her blue uniform went well with her dark hair. *She can protect and serve me anytime.* She pointed a heavy duty black flashlight at his face.

He kept his hands up but squinted to avoid direct exposure to her light. "Can you, maybe, not point that directly into my eyes, ma'am?"

"Who's in charge here, huh? Me or you?"

"Well, since you have the gun, I guess you are, ma'am."

"Hey—don't you patronize me. I'm not *ma'am*. I'm not *babe*. I'm not *honey*. I'm not *darling*. I'm not *sweetheart*. I *am* Officer Kennedy. You understand me?"

"Yeah. Sure. But I wasn't patronizing you. I didn't mean any disrespect. Where I come from, *ma'am* is a respectful way of addressing a woman."

She finally turned her flashlight off and hooked it to her duty belt. "Uh-huh. Save your bullshit. I've been a cop for three years now and the biggest jerks are the ones who start out calling you *ma'am*."

"Can I put my hands down now?"

"Yeah. You can put them down so you can give me your ID."

"Why do you need to see my ID?"

"Because you're out here, at night, in a dimly lit alley located in a notorious drug neighborhood. And it's freezing cold. And the only reason someone would do that is if they're participating in a drug deal."

He put his hands down, retrieved his driver's license, and handed it to her. "You've got it all wrong. I'm not a criminal."

She examined his ID. "So, Mister Luke David Matthews of Roland Park—are you a buyer or a seller? Huh? Because you have to be one of the two. You live in a good neighborhood, so the only reason you'd come out here to Dodge City is to either buy or sell. I just want to know which it is."

"It's neither. I don't buy or sell drugs. I told you—I don't commit any crimes. I'm here to feed homeless cats. I volunteer with an organization called Recycled Love. It's a cat rescue, a no-kill cat rescue. We try to find homes for our residents. And we take care of feral colonies."

She looked around. "I don't see any cats."

"Well, of course not. They're feral. You scared them away when you pulled into the alley. They're probably hiding behind the dumpster."

"Yeah, and are you aware of the new city ordinance? Ordinance number three-five-seven-five."

"I know about it, yes."

"So, you know that it prohibits anyone from feeding stray and or feral cats, right?"

He nodded. "Yeah. I'm fully aware,"

"So, why are you out here violating my ordinance?"

"Because the cats are hungry." He turned sarcastic. "Plus, I love to visit this part of the city. It has great medicinal properties for me. See, I have allergies." He sniffed the air. "And the scent of the bums' fresh urine on the sidewalks helps clear my sinuses. It must be the ammonia."

She emphatically pointed her index finger at him. "Don't you be a smartass to me."

"Look—I'm here for the cats, okay? They need help. Life on the street gets pretty rough. After all, they didn't ask for this fate." He used his hand to make a sweeping gesture. "And they shouldn't have to live in this…this…this *mess*. I'm just trying to put a little bit of food in their bellies, that's all."

"Uh-huh. And you think you're special, do you? Oh, yeah. Mister Luke David Matthews is special. Everyone else in Baltimore has to follow the law, but Luke David Matthews can just do whatever he pleases. Even if that means violating my ordinance."

"Doctor King once said that an unjust law carries no moral

weight. And that we have a responsibility to disobey such laws. To peacefully disobey. So, that's what I'm doing."

"Oh. Doctor King. Quoting Doctor King. I'm impressed. What a smart guy you are. I have me one learned, educated perp. Well, you know what happened to Doctor King, don't you?"

He just stared at her.

"They shot him in the head. Which is exactly what's going to happen to you if you keep hanging out in dark alleys of drug-infested neighborhoods."

"I'm just trying to make a difference. I'm trying to help the cats. They need help. We all need help sometimes."

"Oh, yeah. I'm sure. You're just here to feed the cats. Uh-huh. And O.J. really *was* at McDonald's with Kato during the murders. Now, put your hands on the hood of my cruiser and spread your legs."

"What—am I under arrest?"

"Not just yet. But if you don't comply, you will be for failure to obey a police officer's lawful order."

He hesitated.

"Come on. Do it now. I haven't got all damn night. I need to frisk you to find your drugs. Unless you just want to hand them over."

He threw his hands in the air. "I do not have any drugs."

She ignored his plea of innocence. "Come on, creep—up against my car. Now!"

He walked over to the hood of the vehicle and placed his hands on it. It was still warm. *Well, in the spirit of looking on the bright side—at least this kind of warms my hands a bit.*

She barked at him. "Come on—spread those legs!"

He spread his legs so that they were a few feet apart.

Shortly thereafter he felt her hands on him. Inside his jacket, his pants pockets, down his pant legs. When he felt them on his buttocks and groin area, he snickered. "Hey, if you're going to touch me in those places, you should at least have to buy me dinner first. A movie might be nice, too."

"Shut the hell up. I am not in the mood for your bullshit."

"I'm sorry. It was just a little joke. By the way, is this where the phrase *copping a feel* comes from?"

He could tell she was talking through clinched teeth. "I told you to shut up. You're getting on my nerves with these bad jokes. You're not even funny. You're very unfunny, in fact."

He shook his head. "Dang. Talk about a tough room. I feel like I just wasted some of my best material on you, lady. I swear, you're quicker with the hook than the Sandman from *Showtime at the Apollo*." He chuckled.

She kept searching him, but asked, "The *who?*"

"Nah. Never really got into The Who. I've always been more of a KISS fan. I guess that's because I really do want to rock and roll all night. And party every day."

"Idiot."

"Uh-oh. Sounds like somebody's got a bad case of the *Mondays*."

She finally finished frisking him. "I guess I got here too late. You're obviously a dealer who's already completed his transaction."

"I told you—I am not a drug dealer or user."

"You can take your hands off the hood now. Step back about five feet and keep your hands where I can see them. No hands in pockets."

He rolled his eyes but nonetheless did as she ordered.

"I'm going to get into my car so I can run your driver's license information. Do not move."

"Fine. Whatever. Do what you need to do."

He saw her get into her patrol car and type on her onboard computer. His feet were starting to go numb from the cold.

After a few minutes, she emerged from the car and handed him back his ID. "You don't have any warrants so I'm going to let you go. Now—get out of here. Go home. But pick up these damn bowls first. Since you claim you were the one doing the feeding, you can clean up."

He put his ID back in his wallet. "I was going to pick them up.

I always do. I don't litter. I was just waiting until I was finished. You see, the cats haven't had their treats yet. And they really look forward to those. Tonight, I have some shrimp-flavored Temptations. And those are a real delicacy to a cat, and—"

She cut him off. "Look, buddy—do you realize that, technically, I could arrest you right here and now for admitting to me that you were feeding these animals? You want to go to jail? Spend the night in City Jail? Oh, they'd just love a pretty boy like you. You wouldn't survive two hours in that place."

"Why are you so angry?"

"I am *not* angry. I *am* doing my job."

"Don't you feel bad for these cats? They're just trying to survive. Just like you and me. Don't you like cats?"

"No. I do not like cats. Okay? I do not like them."

"Why not? They're wonderful. I have two at home. Animals are a gift from God, you know? There's an old saying—*God made the cat so that humans could know what it's like to caress the tiger.*"

"It's none of your damn business why I don't like them. I just don't. And spare me your stupid quotes and your stupid religion."

"You know, cats have been scientifically proven to have a positive impact on your health. Yeah, it's true. They've done research on it. Turns out that just petting a cat lowers your blood pressure. Did you know that? And you seem like someone who might have a little hypertension going on because, I swear, even though the lighting here isn't the best, I thought I saw those little veins in your neck popping out."

"If my blood pressure is up, it's because I have to deal with people like you every damn day, pal."

"Listen—these cats are all spayed and neutered. All vaccinated. We used humane traps to get that done. So, they're not going to reproduce. They're not going to spread disease. Please, Officer Kennedy—there's *nine lives* in this cold, dingy, dirty little alley right now. Yours, mine, and those seven cats. I'm no mathematician but I believe that makes nine, ma'am—

oh, excuse me—*Officer Kennedy*."

"Pick up the bowls and get the hell out of here before I change my mind an arrest you. And, from now on, stay out of my district. You do not belong here. Tonight, you were lucky that I drove by before the street gangs did. And I certainly wouldn't want to see you get shot or stabbed or whatnot. Because that would cause me to have to do something that I really hate—paperwork."

He shook his head in disgust. "You know, when I first saw you, Officer Kennedy, I thought you were gorgeous. Drop-dead gorgeous. Easily, one of the most beautiful women I've ever seen. Hell, I might have even entertained the idea of asking you out." He glanced down at her left hand and pointed to it. "I mean, I don't see a ring on that finger. Well, now I know why. Because I can see that, on the inside, you're a very ugly person. And, for me, looks can't make up for a black heart. A heart of darkness. You're beyond redemption, lady. These cats won't get their treats tonight, and that's the one thing that they have to look forward to. The one thing that makes this existence a little less miserable. I hope that you can live with yourself knowing that. *Officer Kennedy*."

He thought for a moment, and pulled the cat treats back out of his pocket. "You know what? I don't care what you say. They *are* going to have their treats." He turned the bag upside down, emptying the contents onto the pavement. He smiled mockingly. "There. How do you like that, Officer Kennedy? Huh? They're still going to get their treats. After we've left, they'll come back and eat them."

She glared at him. "You defied the law."

"I defied heartlessness." He threw up his hands. "And what are you going to do about it, anyway? Huh? You going to arrest me? Go for it. I certainly won't resist." He shook his finger at her. "But I'll tell you something right now—this city's full of crime. Real crime. Violent crime. That said, it doesn't reflect well on the Baltimore Police Department that it chooses to focus its efforts on people who are feeding hungry cats. You're being petty. You're a *petty* officer. And, as a former Marine, I can tell you that in the Navy, petty officers are the backbone of the fleet. But on the police force, they just drag the entire city down."

She stammered. "Just—just—just get out of here. Okay? Get out of here. Pick up your damn mess and leave."

He picked up the bowls, turned and walked away, back towards his car which was parked on Fulton Avenue.

She screamed to him. "And what makes you think I'd want to go out with you? Huh? Never! Don't flatter yourself, honey, because I'd never go out with you. And don't you dare show up in my district ever again. Or your ass will go to jail. I'll find a reason. Do you hear me? I'll find a damn reason! Stay in Roland Park, with the rest of the yuppies."

He briefly turned around, emphatically pointed his index finger at her and shouted, "You know what your problem is, lady? You're not likable. That's what the focus group would say…if…if there was a focus group here in this alley. Anyhow, you're *likably-challenged*, that's what you are. Hell, if nastiness were an Olympic sport, your picture would be on a box of Wheaties." He turned back around and started walking again.

As he walked away, she again yelled at him. "Oh, yeah? Well, I wouldn't be the least bit surprised if one day *your* picture ends up on a wanted poster. You're a jerk, Luke David Matthews, of three-one-five Roland Avenue, Roland Park. You're a first-class jerk. There. I got the last word in."

Without even turning around, he yelled back at her: "You know, someday, this is gonna make for one helluva Daddy-tell-me-about-how-you-met-Mommy story." He chuckled and added, "*I* got the last word."

CHAPTER TWO: SOMEONE SAVED MY LIFE TONIGHT

one week later

Hope Kennedy took a sip of her coffee as she patrolled eastbound route forty in West Baltimore. It was still cold, only about twenty degrees. The forecast called for an overnight low of eleven. And the heater in her police cruiser wasn't working properly. It was putting out a little heat, but not much. She wore her black leather service jacket but was still cold. Shivering, she shook her head in disgust. *The largest police department in the state and it can't even afford to fix the damn heater in a patrol car.*

It was almost 9:30PM. She was about halfway through her shift, which had started at 6:00. It had been a slow night so far. She'd issued a few minor citations for traffic violations. Then she responded to an alarm at a little ma and pa grocery store in Pigtown. Turned out that mice had activated the alarm. They were eating the homemade fudge that sat on display near the register.

Somewhere in this damn city, somebody's breaking the law. Have to find some action, something to get into. Something to make the time pass. A nice drug bust sure sounds good. Or a DWI. That would work, too.

Then she saw it. A late model, blue Chevy Equinox. It had a red bumper sticker with a gold Marine Corps emblem on it.

The SUV traveled slowly, about twenty-five miles per hour in a fifty-five zone.

Drunk. Drunk driver for sure. Either that or running drugs. All paranoid about the cops, so he's trying to keep his speed way down, thinking that he won't get pulled over. Idiot. Doesn't he know that's one of the red flags that we look for?

She hit her emergency lights to initiate the traffic stop. The SUV immediately pulled over onto the shoulder. Hope pulled her cruiser in behind it.

She called in the stop to the dispatcher over her radio. "Thirty-five-one, traffic stop, eastbound forty, near Bennett Lane. Blue Chevy SUV, Maryland registration, Michael one—four—zero—six—nine—eight." There was a beep after the transmission.

A female voice came back over the radio. "Copy you thirty-five-one." Another beep followed.

She put her hat on and exited the vehicle.

Slowly, she approached the driver's side window. Her left hand rested on her holstered nine millimeter service weapon.

When she reached the window, which was already rolled down, she peered in and saw him. It was Luke Matthews. He wore a black leather jacket and a pair of blue jeans. He smiled at her and casually worked some chewing gum.

She shook her head in disgust. "I thought I told you to stay out of my district, Mister Matthews."

"*Aw.* You remembered my name. That's sweet. I'm flattered, Officer Kennedy."

"I always remember the jerks."

"I think you look really nice tonight. And I think I already told you this but it's worth repeating—I love your glasses."

"You think you can sweettalk your way out of trouble? Turn off the damn ignition."

He shut the engine off. "Trouble? What am I in trouble for? I'm not breaking any laws."

"Why are you driving so slow? The limit here is fifty-five. You're going, like, twenty-five."

"What—is there a minimum speed here?"

"It's highly suspicious. My experience tells me that people who drive that slow are either drunk, high, or running drugs. And because they're so paranoid, they think that if they drive super-slow, they won't get pulled over. I guess you people think cops are stupid, huh?"

Shaking his head, he told her, "Not at all. I think you're probably a highly intelligent person."

"Do not be a smartass."

"That was sincere. Geez, lady, what the hell is wrong with you?"

"I need your license and registration."

"You just ran my information last week."

"I need to run it again. That was for suspicious activity. This is for a traffic stop. Two totally different interactions."

"Fine." He reached into his back pocket, pulled out his wallet, and then his ID. He handed it to her. Then he turned on the cabin's overhead dome light and reached over to the glove box.

She again put her hand on her firearm. "Stop! I did not tell you to reach into your glovebox."

"That's where my registration card is."

"Fine. But open it very slowly. And keep your hands visible to me at all times."

With great deliberation, he slowly, carefully opened the glovebox. A large, clear plastic bag full of a fine, green, grass-like substance fell out onto the passenger's side floor.

"Stop! Stop right there. Do not move." *Pot. He's got a bag full of ground up pot. Probably grinds it to extract the kief. Looks like a quart bag and it's full.*

He complied.

"Is your passenger's side front door unlocked?"

"Yeah. It already is."

"Keep your hands where I can see them and do not move. I mean it."

He put his hands up.

She walked over to the passenger's side, opened the door,

and retrieved the bag. She walked back over to the driver's side and held it up for him to see.

"Well—well—well. What do we have here?"

"Catnip," he matter-of-factly told her.

She laughed and shook her head. "You think I'm stupid, don't you? This is dope, dope that's been run through a grinder. I've seen it before, you know. You potheads like to grind it up so it's easier to smoke. Plus, you can extract the kief, and use it to season your doobies, so that they're more potent. This isn't my first day on the job. I've made plenty of drug busts in my three years on the force. And this is a big-ass bag, so you're probably dealing." She placed the bag in her jacket pocket.

"Test it. It's catnip. I don't use drugs. I don't sell drugs. I'm out here tonight looking for a kitten. Our shelter received several calls that there was a tiny little kitten, an orange tabby, darting in and out of traffic. That's why I'm going so slow. I'm trying to spot him."

"*Bull. Shit.* You're a drug dealer. I knew you were the moment I first saw you. That was my very first instinct, and I was right."

"My first instinct when I saw you was that you were going to be a nice person. Maybe that's just what I hoped for. I wanted you to be as pretty on the inside as you are on the outside."

"In your dreams, pal. In your dreams. Don't start with that crap again. I don't date drug dealers."

"I told you—test it. Please. I swear it's not marijuana."

"Oh, it'll get tested. Eventually. But right now, I'm calling in the drug dogs. You like animals? You'll love these guys. They'll tear this SUV apart—literally—to find the dope. You want to just tell me where the rest of it is? You have a secret compartment? All drug dealers do."

"I don't have any secret compartments. There's no drugs in this vehicle. Look—I'm worried about this kitten. He could get hit by traffic."

She screamed at him. "Enough! Enough about the cat. I don't want to hear it. If you think I have some soft, sentimental side —you're wrong. I don't fall for that shit."

"Pardon me. I thought maybe you had a human side."

"Yeah, well, I don't. I have a cop side. That's it."

"Boy, somebody really ruined you, didn't they?"

"Shut up. Shut the hell up. I do not need you to psychoanalyze me, Doctor Phil."

"Fine. Whatever."

"Give me your keys."

He handed them to her.

She keyed the mic of her two-way radio that was clipped to the collar of her jacket. Nothing. *Damn. It's dead. I thought I charged it. Maybe I didn't.*

"All right. I'm going to have to step into my cruiser for a minute. Stay right where you are. Do not move. Under no circumstances are you to move. Understand?"

He nodded. "Yeah. I understand."

She walked back to her patrol vehicle and called the dispatcher on the car radio. "Thirty-five-one, I'm going to need a K9 unit at my location. Traffic stop yielded suspected drugs. I believe there's more in the vehicle."

"Ten-four, thirty-five-one. ETA on the K9 is approximately ten minutes."

"Ten-four," she replied.

She started walking back to the SUV. She was walking along the driver's side of her car.

She saw him quickly exit the vehicle. He advanced towards her. His gait was a combination of a run and a hobble.

"Get back in your vehicle! *Now!*" She screamed.

But he kept coming.

She reached for her gun.

He met her as she unholstered her weapon. The collision of their bodies caused her to drop the pistol. It fell to the pavement and discharged a single round.

He scooped her up, shambled for a few strides, and dove off the shoulder of the road with her still in his arms. They ended up in a drainage ditch, with him on top of her.

A split second later, she watched a white van careen along

the shoulder at a high rate of speed. It never attempted to break or even slow down. Then she heard that horrible sound of metal forcefully meeting metal. The van clipped her cruiser, in the location where no more than a few seconds earlier she'd been walking. Her vehicle was propelled forward, ramming the back of Luke's SUV. The van briefly righted itself, missed Luke's vehicle, but again drifted onto the shoulder. It ran off the road, ahead of the SUV, coming to rest in the ditch, about seventy-five feet from where Hope and Luke lay.

He looked down at her. "*Whew.* The fact that I don't run so good anymore made that too close for comfort. I saw it in my rearview mirror, driving on the shoulder. I knew it was going to hit your vehicle. I just knew it...are you okay?"

She didn't answer but instead shook her head, as if to clear the cobwebs.

Her glasses had fallen off. He found them only six inches from where their bodies came to rest. One of the lenses had popped out. He held them up, looked at them, and declared, "Aw, they were such nice glasses, too. Here. One of the lenses came out, so you'll have to be *three eyes* instead of *four eyes.*" He tried to put them back on her face.

She swatted his hand away and tried to rabbit kick him in the stomach with her small feet. "Get off me, jerk."

He climbed off her. "I just want to know if you're all right. I want to make sure you're not hurt."

She held her ribs. *God. I'm in pain. I think I broke some ribs or something. It even hurts when I breathe. But I can't let him know that.* "I'm fine. And if you think you're going to get off scot-free because of this, you're wrong."

He laughed and shook his head in disgust. "You're really a piece of work. If someone holds the door for you at the post office and you don't say *thank you,* well, that's just mildly impolite. But when someone saves your life and you don't say *thank you*—that's just plain ignorant, lady."

She ignored him. Gingerly, she got up, retrieved her pistol, and holstered it. She winced and again grabbed her ribcage.

"You *are* hurt, aren't you?" he asked. He tried to put his hands on her side.

She again swatted his hands away. "Leave me alone, for God's sake."

She slowly walked over to her car. The radio had been smashed by the impact and was inoperable. But her cell was sitting on the passenger's side floormat, undamaged. She used it to call in the accident and asked for backup and an ambulance. *I think I need to go to the hospital. At least to get checked out. It hurts like hell.*

She and Luke walked up to where the van came to rest. She pulled her flashlight out of her duty belt and focused it on the driver's side door. The door opened and several beer cans fell out, as did an empty bottle of Thunderbird. A very short man with thinning gray hair emerged, stumbling. The impact had activated the van's airbag and horn. The horn was sounding nonstop. It played *Dixie* ala The General Lee from the *Dukes of Hazzard*. The motorist had a disheveled appearance and reeked of alcohol. He looked to be in his late 40s. He wore a pair of white painter's pants, and a black shirt which identified him as being a special agent of sorts—*FBI: Female Body Inspector.* He had no shoes or socks on. His hammertoes featured long, yellow toenails. She watched as he placed the tobacco end of a cigarette in his mouth and lit the filter end. It burst into flames. "Oh. *Fuck. Me.* And pardon my language, Chee-suss," he said as he dropped the smoke. It landed on his bare left foot. He did a dance, a little jig, and further announced, "Oh, snap, homeboy —burned my fuckin' toes."

The drunk surveyed the accident scene. He checked out the vehicles that were now twisted chunks of metal. "Merrrr-ceeee sakes alive! Look what I did. Little ole me did all that?" He dismissively waved his hand. "Nah. Impossible."

Hope pointed her flashlight at his face. "What do you have to say for yourself, douchebag?"

The man held up five fingers on one hand and four on the other. "Two beers, au-cif-fer. That's all I had. I know you're gonna ask. So, I figured I'd just be real upfront and honest with you right from the get-go. Two beers." He staggered forward.

"Two beers, huh?"

He shook his head but still said, "Two beers. Just two yummy beers. I swear to Chee-suss."

Hope looked down at his feet. "Where's your damn shoes, bud? Huh? It's freezing cold. You're going to get frostbite."

"My feet were sweatin' so I took 'em off." The drunk hiccupped.

She retrieved a pair of cheap, black bobos from the van and handed them to him. "Well, here—put them back on. I don't want to get the blame when you have to have half your toes amputated. Not only that, but your nasty feet smell like Limburger cheese. I can smell them even over the alcohol."

He tried to put the shoes on but fell down. "Whoa, Nellie! The damn earth keeps movin' on me. We must be havin' an earthquake." He put his sneakers on while he sat on the ground. "There. I got my Air Jordans on. Now, I can dunk." He laughed and stood back up but was a bit wobbly.

The drunk sang Gospel. "Whaaat a friend we have in Cheeee-suss."

Hope had her phone in her back pocket. It rang.

The drunk stopped singing. "Cuse me, friends. My phone's ringing." He pulled a pack of Marlboro reds out of his pants pocket and placed it to his ear. "Hello? Hello? Who's this?" the drunk said into the cigarette pack. "Where am I? I'm out here on route forty, hanging with my friends…huh? Say what? Have I been drinkin'? Oh, a wee bit, I suppose. Thunderbird. What's the word? Thunderbird. How's it sold? Icey cold. What's the jive? This Bird's *alive*. Hey— listen. Listen! Is Jody Biffle still sittin' outside his trailer, huffin' gas and so forth? And, if so, is he seeing those pretty pink dragons that do The Macarena? That's what I always see…huh? What? What did you just say to me?" He paused for a couple of seconds, listening intently with the cigarette pack pressed to his ear. Finally, he resumed his rant. "Well, screw you, too! And don't call back. You called me. I didn't call your sorry ass. You're makin' me all uncomfortable, now. And I got all my scruples about myself, too. So there." The drunk gave the pack of cigarettes the finger. "And I'll tell you something right now—I can either be the Angel of Light or the Angel of Darkness. You decide which you'd rather deal with. Do you even recognize what I'm talking abo—"

Hope snatched the cigarettes away from him. "Phillip Morris will call you back later, asshole." *Damn. Not only is he talking into a pack of cigarettes—he's getting answers from it. Having an argument with it and whatnot. He has to be more than just drunk. Probably a combination of alcohol and PCP. A drunk dipperhead. The worst possible combo…oh, God. My ribcage hurts.*

The drunk briefly got sentimental and misty-eyed, announcing to no one in particular, "I'm the hero this crazy world needs but doesn't deserve."

The drunk loudly passed gas. "Fire in the hole!"

Luke laughed.

Hope shot him a dirty look.

He shrugged. "Sorry. I know drunk driving isn't funny. It's the post-accident comedy routine that's killing me." He placed a hand on his ribcage. "And I almost literally mean that because when I laugh, my ribs hurt like hell."

Hope shook her finger at Luke. "Yeah? Well, you don't have anything to laugh about anyway, mister. The two of you are going to be cellmates by the end of the night. If you're enjoying his standup act, he'll be playing another set later at City Jail, but he probably won't be as funny sober. They never are."

The drunk looked her up and down. "Hey, you're purr-tey, girl. Real purr-tey. Better looking than the girls down at The Pussycat Club. Way better. They're all hard looking. You're all soft looking. Look, I'm a very open, honest individual. I say what I think. And I think you're probably a real slut in bed. So, why don't we forget about this little misfortunate incident and go back to my place. *And screw.* Huh? What do you say?"

Luke grabbed him by the collar. "She's not a slut. Don't you dare call her a slut. Take it back." Luke shook him. "Take it back!

Now!"

The drunk looked at Hope. "What? This your boyfriend? Your boyfriend looks like Elviz. Elviz Pess-ley. He liked chee-boogers. And peanut butter and nanner sam-itch-es." He laughed and did an impromptu Elvis impression. "Thank ya. Thankyaverymuch." Then he belched and passed out. He slid to the ground and Luke let go of him.

She gave Luke the evil eye. "What the hell are you even doing?"

He shrugged. "Just trying to help."

"I do not need nor do I want your help. I can fend for myself, thank you."

"Look—I was...I was trying to defend your honor."

"My honor? My *honor*? How do you know that I have any honor to defend?"

"Forget it. Just forget it. Next time, I'll let them talk however they want to you."

"There won't be a next time. You're going to jail. And we are never going to see one another again. Except, of course, at your trial."

"So, then we *do* have a date?"

She just rolled her eyes and shook her head.

The backup arrived. Four Baltimore cops and one Maryland state trooper. They had to shut down the right hand lane of eastbound route forty to clean up the mess and conduct the investigation.

An ambulance arrived to transport her to Mercy Medical Center. The EMTs who assessed her at the scene suspected she had at least one fractured rib.

As she got into the ambulance, she retrieved the bag containing the suspected drugs from her jacket pocket and handed it to the trooper. "I got this bag of drugs from the guy's vehicle."

The older, pudgy trooper asked, "Which guy? Elvis or the drunk?"

"The good-looking one," she barked. *Oh, shit. That just kind of slipped out.*

"Okay." He turned his head and yelled out to the other cops, "Hey, the drugs belong to Elvis." The trooper chuckled and added, "Some things never change. Elvis still likes them drugs, don't he?"

"Yeah. Whatever. You guys can sort the rest of this out, right?"

"Yeah, we got it, Kennedy. Just get to the hospital. Get those ribs taken care of. Fractured ribs are nothing to mess with. And they'll give you some real good and perfectly legal dope for that, too. So *en-joy*."

He slammed the ambulance door shut. Hope lay down on the gurney and closed her eyes. She grimaced in pain. *God. On a scale of one to ten, my pain is a twelve.*

As the ambulance sped through the streets of Baltimore, she closed her eyes and wondered. *Why the hell would a guy who's dealing drugs save a cop's life? Doesn't make any sense. None at all.*

Two in the morning. She got a ride back to the Western District Headquarters with Corporal Coffey, who had been at Mercy following up on an accidental heroin overdose death from earlier in the night.

After x-rays and a CT scan, she'd been diagnosed with a broken rib.

Slowly and deliberately, she walked towards her locker to retrieve her purse. Her supervisor, Sergeant Harris, walked into the locker room. Roberta Harris was a fifteen year veteran of the Baltimore Police Department. She was an African-American woman in her early 40s. And she was pretty. Despite the fact that she had a supervisory desk job, she kept herself in excellent shape. She ran marathons, went to the gym every day. The whole nine yards. Her uniform was immaculate. Her service oxfords highly shined. Her black tie—as straight as could be and just the right length. She was one squared away cop.

"How you doing there, Kennedy?" Harris asked.

"All right, all things considered. One of the ribs, on my left side, is broken."

"I know. I talked to the hospital. You in any pain right now?"

"Right now? Just a little. But not too bad. They gave me a big fat shot of Dilaudid. That was a while ago, though. It's starting to wear off. It made me pretty loopy, too. It's the first time in my life that I've been on an opioid. It hit me pretty hard. It took away the pain all right but made me real loose-lipped. I told the doctor that he needed to trim his nose hairs. Which he did. And I told one of the nurses that her boobs were implants. Which they were."

"Uh-huh. And did they give you a script for a painkiller?"

"Yeah. They gave me a script for Percocet."

"Okay. When you're finished here, Coffey will run you over to the all-night pharmacy on Greenmount Avenue so you can get it filled. Just be careful with that stuff. You're a very petite woman and opioid painkillers pack a wallop."

Hope rolled her eyes. "I know that. I'm a cop."

"Anyone can get addicted. I'm not saying you don't need to be on them. Just be careful. Okay?"

"Yeah. Okay. Fine."

"You're going to be off for two months," Harris informed her.

"Two months?"

"Yes. Eight weeks."

"Why?"

"That's the amount of time the protocol says you have to take off for a broken rib."

"I don't need eight weeks. I don't even need eight days. Maybe, like, two or three days. That's it."

"Take it up with the union. They're the ones who negotiated the contract. Plus, you know how city government works—always paranoid about getting sued and whatnot."

"Oh, God. Two months? What am I going to do with myself for two whole months?"

"Oh, I'm going to give you some homework."

"Homework?"

"Yep. Since you're not in any significant pain right now, you and I need to have a talk. In my office, Kennedy. *Now.*"

Oh, shit. This probably isn't to tell me that I've been selected as Officer of the Month.

They walked into Harris's office and she closed the door. Hope sat in a chair directly across from the sergeant, who sat behind a desk made of oak. There was a small American flag on the desk, next to a computer. Off to the side, was a small silver boombox which was playing some easy listening music. But the two most prominent items on her desk were two pictures. One was a framed photo of Martin Luther King Jr. The other, a picture depicting Jesus on the cross.

Harris clasped her hands together and began. "So, Officer Kennedy, tell me about what happened out there tonight—out on the street."

"Not much to tell. I stopped a perp who was driving suspiciously on route forty. He had drugs in the vehicle. While I was waiting for the drug dog to arrive, a drunk plowed into my patrol car, which in turn, plowed into his SUV."

"Mm-hmm. Is that all you have to say?"

She shrugged. "I guess." Then quickly added, "Oh, wait—was my car totaled?"

Harris nodded. "Yes. And it was never *your* car. It was the *taxpayer's* car. But, yes, it was trashed. And according to the accident report, it sounds like Mister Matthews' vehicle might have been, too."

"Did that Matthews character go to jail?"

"Let's talk about Mister Matthews, shall we? Because that's really why you're in my office right now."

"What's the problem? He had dope in his vehicle. A fairly large bag, in fact. One of those Ziploc quart bags, and it was nearly full. That's a helluva lot of pot, indicative of someone who's most likely dealing."

"Did you test it?"

"No. I know what dope looks like. I've been a cop long enough to know that."

"Uh-huh."

"I mean, it *was* dope, wasn't it?"

Harris nodded. "Oh, it definitely gets them high, all right. Gets them all strung out and whatnot. Makes them act crazy, in fact."

Hope emphatically nodded. "Right. Dope."

"Yeah. When they tested it, it, ah, it came back as *Nepeta Cataria*. That's the scientific name for it."

Hope shrugged her shoulders. "Is that a new one? Because I haven't heard of it."

"No. It's been around for centuries. Very popular in this area. Readily available, too."

"What's the street name?"

"Catnip."

"Say again."

"Catnip. Cat. Nip."

"That has to be some new, cool street slang for it. Has to be."

"Nope. It's catnip. Run-of-the-mill catnip. Meow-juana. Ray and I buy it all the time at the pet store for our cat, Cleo. She loves it. And, yes, it gets her high as a kite. Now, granted, it can bear a resemblance to pot that's been through a grinder, but a simple field test would have told you it wasn't. But you decided to be cocky about it."

"I'm not getting Officer of the Month, am I?"

Harris emphatically shook her head. "You're not even up for Officer of the Second."

"*Shit.*"

"Let's talk about your encounters with Mister Matthews. And I know for a fact that you've had two of them."

"How do you know I've had two?"

"We'll get to that later. For now—suffice it to say that, after fifteen years on the force, I know a little something about how to conduct an investigation. I've done my research, my due diligence. And I know. All right?"

Hope nodded.

"Now, why did you approach Mister Matthews a week ago?"

"Did he complain about me? Is that how you know?"

"No. He didn't complain. Not at all. Now—what I need from you is your reason for approaching him. Answer me."

"Fine. Yeah. I approached him. He was suspicious. He was in this dark alley, the one right next to that porn shop. He was out of place. He lives in Roland Park." Hope threw up her hands and shrugged. "I, I thought he was there for a drug deal."

"Did you find any evidence of drugs?"

"No. But he *was* feeding feral cats, in violation of city ordinance number three-five-seven-five."

"Right. And you know what Commissioner Davis had to say about that, don't you? You got the memo. I know you did because you electronically signed off on it. But allow me to refresh your memory—the commissioner specifically states in said memo that enforcement of that ordinance is not to be a point of emphasis in our patrol duties. And, in fact, that officers only need to address violations in the event that complaints are made. In other words—we have better things to do with our time. And were you, on the night in question, responding to a complaint regarding those cats?"

"No."

"So, why did you harass Mister Matthews?"

"I didn't harass him."

"You *did* harass him. I saw the bodycam footage."

"What made you look at the footage?"

"We'll get to that. Just remember, Kennedy—I'm like a good lawyer. With every question I ask, I already know the answer. It would behoove you to keep that in mind."

"You got anything else for me or are we done?"

"Oh, get comfy because we are not even close to being done."

"Okay. What else?"

"Why did you stop Mister Matthews tonight?"

"What difference does it make? He's a creep. He is a perp. He's up to *something*. So maybe that wasn't dope that he had tonight, but that doesn't mean he's not a bad guy."

"You have diarrhea of the mouth, woman. You open your mouth, and the shit just spews out. Like a damn river. Now—why did you pull him over tonight? What was your probable cause?"

"He was driving, like, twenty-five miles per hour on route forty."

"Is there a minimum speed on that road?"

"No. There's not."

"So, why then? Was he driving recklessly? Disobeying traffic laws?"

"No. But it's dangerous. Driving that slow can cause accidents. The average speed on that road is—I don't know—sixty-five, maybe even seventy."

"But the limit's fifty-five."

"Right. But people typically do at least sixty-five."

"Okay. *Sooooo,* instead of pulling over the folks who are over the speed limit you pull over people who are under the limit? Because it's just their own fault that they're not breaking the law like everyone else? Is that it?"

"Yeah…I mean—no. I mean—you're twisting everything around on me. Just like those damn defense lawyers do in court. Besides, he gave me this BS story about trying to rescue a stray kitten."

"Uh-huh. There was a kitten out there tonight. An orange tabby. I know that because we got at least ten calls from concerned motorists who saw him darting in and out of traffic. We referred them to Animal Control. Some of them probably called the cat rescue where he volunteers."

"How do you know he volunteers at a cat rescue?"

"We'll get to that."

Hope winced and spoke sheepishly. "Did…did you see the bodycam footage from tonight yet?"

"Yep. That's the first thing I looked at. And that's standard procedure anytime we have an incident like this, a crash involving a patrol car. And, as I'm sure you know, all I have to do is download the video from the server. Takes a couple of minutes. So, yes, I saw your entire encounter with Mister Matthews tonight as well. You ought to be ashamed of yourself, Kennedy. I'm ashamed to be your supervisor right now. I am."

"Hey—I'm a damn good cop."

Harris leaned forward and intensely glared at her. "No. You're not. Tonight, you were a bad cop. Tonight, you were the stereotypical bad cop. And it's not your technical knowledge. I know you can do the job. I know you're smart. But it's your attitude. Your arrogance. You were so sure that what was in that bag was dope that you didn't bother to test it. That's where you fail. Your mentality. You're not there to *protect* and *serve*. You're there to *threaten* and *intimidate*. You're the reason that people in this community won't talk to us about what's going on in their neighborhoods. You're the reason people flip us off as we drive by. You're the reason that folks are more afraid of us than they are of the damn drug kingpins. You are the reason that people—the very people we're sworn to serve—see us more as an occupying army than as their protectors. Yes, Kennedy, you are *that cop*. The sad thing is that you weren't always *that cop*. As recently as two years ago, you were a good cop, on the fast track to a leadership position."

"The reason I haven't been promoted is because I'm a woman, sarge. The good old boy network is still alive and well in this department."

"I can't sit here and say that sexism doesn't exist. But I can tell you, for a fact, it has nothing to do with your not being promoted. Do you want to know why you haven't made corporal? You really want to know?"

With attitude, she replied, "Yeah, sarge, *I wanna know*."

Fine. I'll be happy to show you." Harris picked up a Manila personnel file off her desk and waved it in front of Hope's eyes. "Right here, Kennedy. Here you go. This is why. Your file is full of LOCs—letters of complaint. Let me read some examples. I'm sure you're already familiar with what folks have had to say about you. But, nonetheless, I'll give you a little representative sampling." Harris put on a pair of reading glasses, opened the file, and sifted through its contents. "Here we go—*Officer Kennedy disrespected me….Officer Kennedy cursed at me… Officer Kennedy has a negative attitude towards the citizens…Officer Kennedy seems to have anger management issues.*"

"Bogus. What else are perps going to say? They're just pissed because I locked them up."

"Maybe some of them. But not all of them. I know, for a fact, that a lot of these complaints have merit."

"Sure, Sarge, take their side."

"It's not a question of taking sides. I like to think that I'm on the side of truth and justice. But I'm not sure you are any more. It seems to me you've become a hater."

Hope rolled her eyes. "Oh, Jesus Christ. I am not."

"You. Are." Harris pulled out a Bible from her desk drawer and held it up. "And this book, this Good Book, says that hate will destroy you. And it will."

Hope raised her voice to her supervisor. "You don't know what it feels like. Nobody does. Unless you've been there."

"You're right. I don't know. And I'm sorry that you do. I am so very, very sorry that you got—" Harris abruptly stopped.

"Say it. Say it, sarge. Come on—say it. I got raped. *I. Got. Raped.* Nobody likes to use that word. It's a disgusting word, isn't it? It's a dirty, filthy word. But it's a dirty, filthy act. And it's what happened to me. So, I call it what it is. I refuse to clean it up and call it *sexual assault* so that people don't have to hear *the R word.* And you've only read the reports. Words on paper. Well, here's the firsthand account—two years ago, my ex-boyfriend, Jason, broke into my house, all drunk. He was pissed because I broke up with him. And he injected me with Ketamine and raped me. And, while I was knocked out, he used an ice pick to stab my cat to death. And Desi's body was the first thing that I saw when I woke up. Jason put him right there on my chest because he *wanted* that to be the first thing that I saw. He wanted that seared into my memory. And there was blood everywhere. And Desi's mouth was all open and so were his eyes. His lifeless eyes. *God.* I'll never forget those eyes. How his eyes looked after Jason murdered him. It was like he couldn't believe that anyone could have been cruel enough to do that to him. And it was like he couldn't believe that I *let* someone do that to him." Hope paused and her lower lip quivered. "*Desi.* My best friend. The only male figure in my life who ever treated me like I was worth a damn. And you have no empathy whatsoever for any of that."

"No. You're wrong. I have empathy in spades for you and those like you. Why do you think you haven't been disciplined for all these complaints? Huh? There are enough complaints in your file to merit at least one suspension. I've got LT breathing down my neck. Every time another one of these complaints comes in, I get an email asking—w*hy are you not disciplining Officer Kennedy? Why do you continue to allow her to get away with her BS? Why is she skating by?* I'm serious. I get those emails. And it gets harder and harder to justify. Bottom line —this job is not the place for you to vent. You can't use this profession to lash out and release your inner rage. Maybe you need to vent, but this job isn't the appropriate forum for that. I want to help you. I do. But I'm not an expert in this stuff. I'm not a mental health professional. And as much as I want to help—and as much as I sympathize— I have a duty to the citizens of Baltimore, more than half a million people. And it's my responsibility to make sure that the officers under my supervision exhibit good judgement and are truly there to serve. Look—I know there are plenty of scumbags in this city. But you've gotten into the habit of assuming that everyone is bad.

"As cops, we have power. Real power. Power to take away someone's freedom. Power to take away someone's life. With that power, comes an awesome responsibility. And we can't bring our personal issues to work with us, regardless of how serious and legitimate those issues might be. Now, your attitude, demeanor, and lack of professionalism is unacceptable. Tonight, it's finally come to a head. And I can't continue to coddle you and hold you to a lower standard. It's not fair to the other officers who *are* getting written up and suspended for misconduct. And, most importantly, it's not fair to the citizenry because regardless of what happened to you, you can't just treat people like shit. Among other things, it embarrasses the department and damages our credibility."

"You have no idea how hard it is to live with those memories. You don't know. I'm sorry, but I can't just count my blessings that I didn't get pregnant and move on. Do you know that I have triggers? Yeah. I do. My ex, he had a tattoo, on his left shoulder. It was a big Cobra, coiled and ready to strike. How appropriate. So, now, I don't like men with tats on their shoulder. And he wore an earring in his left ear. So, now, men with earrings make me uneasy. And he was originally from Georgia, so he had a Southern accent. And now, men with southern accents bother me. And I think I'm ruined forever. I don't know that I'll ever be able to have a normal relationship with a guy. And even though he's most likely in prison for the rest of his life—that's not enough. He should have gotten the death penalty. Hell, I would have thrown the switch on the electric chair myself. He took something away from me that I might not ever be able to get back. And, yes, I hate him for it. And before you start lecturing about the sin of hate, try to put yourself in my shoes. Because if it happened to you, you might just hate, too."

"Maybe I would. I'm not going to sit here and play holier than thou. But you are a young woman. Not even thirty. You most likely have at least another fifty years on this planet. But if you don't do something soon, the hate and the rage and the bitterness and the hurt will keep growing. Like a cancer. It'll metastasize and take over. Take over your very soul. Hell, it basically already has. You need to heal. But you're not even trying. *You. Are. Not. Even. Trying.* That's the part that's inexcusable. And that's why I'm losing my patience with you. The department psychologist said you need to be in counseling."

"Yeah, well, I went. It didn't help."

Harris rolled her eyes and threw up her hands. "You went to two sessions and quit."

Hope yelled at her boss. "*It didn't help!*"

"You never gave it a chance. Two sessions isn't going to make everything fine and dandy. It takes time to heal."

"What. Ever. Are we done now? Can I go?"

"Nope. Now, we're going to talk some more about Mister Matthews. I think you need to know a little about this *bad guy*, this *perp*, as you call him. I did some research this morning. So, here's the dossier on your *perp*—in two-thousand and ten, he enlisted in the Marine Corps. In two-thousand and eleven, he was discharged be—"

Hope interrupted and emphatically pointed her finger at Harris. "Ah. Ha. He was only in for a year. My cousin was a Marine. The standard enlistment is four years. If he was discharged after only one, he screwed up. He did something, that's for sure."

"Oh, he did something all right. He went to Afghanistan and fought for your disrespectful little ass. He saw combat and was wounded. And I'll bet that's why he has a slight limp. He was a medical discharge. He has a Purple Heart. And a Bronze Star for valor. And while you were still playing dodgeball in high school gym class, he was dodging bullets. Real bullets. And some of those boys who he fought next to came home wrapped in the American flag. My cousin's son, Gary, came home that way. You are *not* the only one who has had life deal them something less than a royal flush."

Hope started to get up. "I've heard enough."

"Sit. Down. Sit your ass back down. You're going to hear more."

She sat.

"Now, he's the head carpenter for Homes For Heroes. That's a local nonprofit organization that builds houses for disabled vets. They build homes all over Maryland and even into DC,

Delaware, southern PA, and south Jersey."

"So, this Matthews guy has a job—so what? As Shania Twain would say—that don't impress me much."

"You're unreal, Kennedy. Do me a favor—don't even look at me. Look down at the floor while I talk to you. After tonight, you don't have the right to look at me. I'm a good cop. And I've worked hard to be a good cop. And cops like you don't have the right to be eyeballing cops like me. I'm dead serious. Look. Down."

Hope hesitated. "What? This shit's right out of day one of the police academy."

"Well, that's about where you are in my eyes right now. Now, I said—eyeball the floor, not me."

Hope looked down.

Harris continued. "And he also is a volunteer at Recycled Love. And the number of feral and sick cats in the community has dramatically gone down because of that organization's spay, neuter, and vaccination efforts. Me and Ray adopted our cat from their shelter. It's a very nice facility. They're nice people. Yeah, this guy's definitely a cross between Charlie Manson and Ted Bundy, huh?"

Hope shrugged. "What? You want to run him for God or something?"

She heard Harris emphatically pound the desk with her hand. "Don't you be all blaspheming in my presence, girl! I don't want to get hit by that lightning bolt intended for *you*."

Hope rolled her eyes and under her breath muttered, "Oh, good Gawd."

Harris continued. "And now that brings me to the highlight of the evening. This man, who barely knows you, risked his life to save yours…and you didn't even have the common courtesy to say thank you."

Hope started to look up.

"Don't you be eyeballing me, girlfriend."

She quickly put her head back down.

"You were ready to shoot him."

"He was charging me. I didn't see or hear the van. How was I supposed to know he was trying to get me out of the way?"

"And you were only in that situation because of the bogus traffic stop."

"It was *not* bogus."

"Oh—and then your firearm discharged. How nice."

"I didn't pull the trigger. He knocked it out of my hands, and it went off when it hit the ground."

"It doesn't matter, Kennedy. That stray bullet could have *killed* someone."

"But it didn't."

"And even when you realized that he'd just saved your life, all you could say was—*get off me, jerk*. Your exact words. You're disgusting. You're a victim—I get that. But, tonight, you made someone else a victim." Harris paused for a few seconds before continuing. "Someone saved your life tonight. And another Someone, Someone beyond this world, was looking out for you."

"I don't believe in that God bullshit, if that's what you're talking about. Used to. Not anymore. Never again."

"Yeah? Well, you're blessed. Because He evidently still believes in you. And He put an angel on your shoulder tonight, soul sister. And that angel has a name and a phone number and an email address. Here. Take this piece of paper. *Take it*."

Hope kept her head down but reached out and took the piece of paper. She looked at it. It was a yellow Post-It note with a phone number and an email address written on it. "What is this? What am I supposed to do with this?"

"It's Mister Matthews' contact information. That's your homework. Before you return to work you are to reach out to him. Either via phone or email. If you're more comfortable with email—that's fine. And you can even use your departmental account. But either way, you will A. apologize for your unprofessional conduct and B. thank him for saving your life. I *will* follow up on this. If, by the time you return to duty, I find out that you have not reached out to him, it'll be a three day suspension without pay. And you can kiss your chances of making corporal anytime in this decade goodbye. Understand?"

She nodded but said nothing.

"And that brings me to my final talking point. Now, I'm taking my badge and stripes off. I'm not talking to you as Sergeant Harris anymore. I'm talking to you woman-to-woman. Understand me?"

Hope nodded.

"This guy likes you, Kennedy. And I'm not trying to sound all seventh grade over here, but he *likes you likes you*."

"That's bullshit."

"It is not bullshit. I saw the bodycam footage. I saw the look in his eyes after it happened. He was more concerned about you than he was about himself. Do you know he suffered two fractured ribs?"

Hope looked up. "He did?"

"I *did not* say you could eyeball me. Put that head back down."

Hope quickly looked back down at the floor.

"Yes. He did. I got the hospital report. Your foolishness not only got yourself hurt—it got someone else hurt, too. Now, listen to me—I've seen that look in a man's eyes before. It's a look that no player could ever fake because it comes from the heart. From the soul. When I broke my leg ten years ago, long before you joined the force, I ended up in the ER. And Ray came in and he looked at me just the way this man looked at you. A combination of concern and adoration. Absolute adoration. And I have no idea why this man would like you. You've given him no reason to. Maybe he's crazy. Maybe that's his thing. But rest assured, he *does* like you. And he's single. I know that for a fact, too. And he's only two years older than you. I ran a comprehensive check on him. Never arrested. No legal issues whatsoever. Two speeding tickets on his record, and those were more than ten years ago. Real easy on the eyes, too. Looks a lot like Elvis, young Elvis. And I still can't believe you told him he wasn't funny. As I watched the bodycam footage of your encounter with him in the alley, he had me in stitches. I'd totally pay to see him do standup. That line about the Sandman was priceless. And during my research this morning, I also found him on social media. Now, I'm going to get on my computer here right quick, and I want to read you something from his Facebook page. This is what prompted me to view the bodycam footage of your first encounter with him, by the way." There was a brief pause. "Now, this post is dated a week ago and it was right after he was harassed by you that first time. Here's what he wrote about *you,* lady, after you were a total jerk to him—*I met a woman tonight. A very beautiful woman.*" Harris paused to tell her, "The word *very* is in all caps, by the way." She continued to read from where she'd left off. "*She's a cop and that means she has a tough job. She wasn't real nice to me. I'm not sure why. I'm not a criminal. I just feed homeless cats. I told her she had a black heart, a heart of darkness. But I'm sorry I said that. I don't think she's a bad person at all. On second thought, I don't think she has a black heart. I think she must just have a purple heart. A badly bruised, wounded heart. And I know something about purple hearts. I have one myself. So, Officer Kennedy, if you, by some miracle, ever read this—please know that I've been thinking about you a lot. And maybe two purple hearts can come together, and, somehow, help one another heal. PS—I'd really like to know your first name. I'll bet it's pretty.*"

Hope closed her eyes and cried.

She again heard Harris pound the desk. "Don't you cry on me, woman. Do not sit there and shed those salty tears on my oak desk. This desk cost the taxpayers a pretty penny and you will not soil it with your salty tears. Stop. Crying. You haven't earned the right to cry. And you're only crying for yourself, anyway. I'll let you cry in this office when you start crying for someone else, like that fifteen-year-old kid tonight who died from an overdose right down the street. That, by the way, happened while you were tied up harassing the man who's a cross between Mister Rogers and Captain America. Yeah, big, tough Officer Kennedy. Five foot nothing, barely a hundred pounds, but she stomps around here like she's Godzilla and the Western District is her own personal Tokyo. *Now*, she wants to bawl her eyes out. Well, you'll not do it in my presence. Stop it right now. Stop it. You put me in a difficult position, but I cannot and will not handle you with kid gloves anymore. Especially when you make no effort whatsoever to help yourself. So, stop your bawling."

Hope sniffled. "Are you just trying to make me feel like shit?"

"Nah. You make yourself feel like shit. I'm just pointing it out to you."

For a few seconds there was silence. Finally, Harris added, "Do you know how many women would love to have a guy say those sweet things that this man said about you? And you don't deserve any of it. There are women out there far more deserving of hearing those kind, gentle words than you. You want to know what I think, Kennedy?"

"What difference does it make? I'm sure you're going to tell me anyway."

"You're damn right, I am. This is my office, after all. I worked hard for it. And I say what I want within these walls. I'll speak truth to power, and I'll speak truth to weakness, too. And I'll leave it to you to guess which of the two I'm addressing right now. So, here goes—part of me thinks that this whole incident is just the result of your own folly. Your own anger, bitterness, and rage. And poor Luke Matthews just had the misfortune of getting caught up in the middle of your hot mess, your meltdown. But there's another part of me that believes that maybe, just maybe, there's something more at work here."

"Like what?"

"Like maybe this is The Man Himself trying to make it right for you. Maybe He's trying to take everything that was wrong and make it right. I don't know why He would. You don't deserve it. Hell, I don't know that I would do it for you. But I'm not Him. His ways are different from mine. He gives to those who don't deserve. He gives anyway. That's kind of His thing.

And that's the Beauty of Grace. And I learned that as a little girl at Bethel AME Church. Yes, I did. But here's the thing— He can only put you in that moment in time. What you do in that moment—that's up to you. You've built up all these walls, Kennedy. You've shut out the rest of the world. You've shut out the bad. But you've shut out the good, too. And I understand why. I do. But at some point, the walls have to come down, and you have to expose yourself. That's part of being human.

"You know, I'm an old Army brat. My father was stationed in West Germany when the Berlin Wall fell in eighty-nine. And it came down because of *freedom.* Doctor King worked to bring down walls in the name of *freedom.* Maybe one day you'll tear down your walls. Because you'll never be free until you do. There. I said my piece. Coffey will drop you off so you can get your pain meds and he'll take you home. Don't come back for two months. When you do, have a doctor's note saying you're fit for duty. And reach out and apologize to—and thank —Luke Matthews. Or else. *Luke Matthews.* That's a good name. He has half of the four Gospels covered right there. Middle name's *David*, so that covers the Old Testament, too. Plus, he's a carpenter. Good job. Honorable job. Because, once upon a time, a carpenter changed the world. A simple carpenter divided all history. Because he went from a wooden manger to a wooden cross. Yes, he did. Anyway— get out of my sight. Be gone."

Hope got up and started to walk out the door, head still down.

"Oh, and Kennedy—one more thing."

She turned around but still looked at the tile floor.

"Look at me, Kennedy."

Hope spoke meekly. "You said not to eyeball you."

"Now, I'm telling you *to* eyeball me. Look me square in the eye, woman."

She looked up.

Harris changed her tone and spoke tenderly. "Kennedy... *Hope*. Why don't you try living up to the name your mama gave you? It's a pretty name. A beautiful name, in fact. But you're

not doing it justice."
　　Hope turned back around and walked out the door.

CHAPTER THREE: THE MIDNIGHT RANGER

By three-thirty in the morning, she was home. Home was a nice townhouse in the Mount Royal area of Baltimore. It was a safe neighborhood, a hodgepodge area. A mixture of yuppies, blue-collar types, and students from two nearby schools, the University of Baltimore, and the Maryland Institute of Art.

Her house was neat. She was a neat freak. Everything had to be in its place. The floors were hardwood. The furniture, modern. Her walls were adorned with photos of her deceased cat, Desi, a handsome gray tabby. On one of the walls in the living room, hung a fancy oil painting of him she'd commissioned from a photograph. On the mantle, above the fireplace, sat a golden urn which contained his remains. Right next to it, on the adjacent wall, was a large poster that was inscribed with the Rainbow Bridge poem.

The house smelled of Angel, a chocolaty, gourmand fragrance. It was her go-to perfume. She'd also found the scent available as an air freshener. *God. I love that scent. Can't get enough of it.*

She sat on the black leather sofa in the living room. Exhausted, she hadn't bothered to change out of her uniform. Her bulletproof vest had been removed when she was at the hospital, and that was the only part of the uniform that was truly uncomfortable. She did remove her hair clip and shook her head. Her silky, shoulder-length black hair came cascading down. It got in her eyes, and she brushed it aside. Next, she unbuckled her duty belt and draped it over the back of the couch. Finally, she removed her black uniform tie, unbuttoned the top button of her shirt, and tilted her head back. And she thought. She thought about her conversation with Harris. It was the first time in a long time she'd talked to anyone about the assault. It was the first time she'd even made mention of it since her last counseling session, nearly two years ago. It was hard to talk about, after all. *How do you talk to someone about rape? How do you even broach the topic? Most people don't want to hear it anyway. It makes them all uncomfortable. They have no idea what to say. The whole topic is so embarrassing.*

She thought about what Harris had said about walls. *Could I ever be with a guy again? Could I ever kiss a guy again? Kissing? Yeah. I think I could. I don't think that would freak me out. Jason didn't like kissing. It wasn't his thing. But sex? I don't know about sex. I'm scared of intimacy, yet I still crave it. Does that make me crazy? To be scared of something but want it, too? Is that just nuts? I wish I could not want it. But I guess humans are just wired that way. We're programmed to seek intimacy. And that's why I hate Jason. He took from me part of what it means to be human, to be a woman. He took it. My feelings about him are justified. I'm not going to feel guilty for hating him. I'm entitled to it. It's completely within my rights*

She walked over to the painting of her cat, stared at it, and talked to it. "Oh, Desi, I'm sad. I miss you so much. You were the best boy. And those were the best of times. I pretend that I don't like cats. Do you know that, kiddo? Yeah, it's true. I do. I know that's crazy, right? But it's easier this way. Because *like* is only one step removed from *love*. And love is only one step removed from pain. When you love something, it just ends up leaving you, one way or another. And I wouldn't be a very good Mom to another cat anyway. I wasn't a good mom to you. I didn't protect you from that monster. I didn't deserve you. I don't deserve anything. I don't deserve love." She kissed the palm of her hand and pressed it against the painting. She whispered to the portrait. "But I do love you, boy."

She stood there for another minute and debated some of her recent decisions. *I was hard-hearted towards Luke Matthews and those feral cats last week. Why was I that way? Why do I do things like that? I could have just allowed him to feed them without hassling him. But people interpret kindness as weakness. And I have to protect myself. Don't I? I have to keep up the front. Right? Better for people to think I'm a heartless bitch than think of me as vulnerable. Vulnerable. Isn't that the worst thing anyone can be? I don't know. I just don't know. I'm confused. I feel so lost. I hate feeling this way. If there is a God, why won't He help me?*

She got out her phone and went to YouTube and looked at a video in a series that she was gradually working her way through. The title was *Rainbow Bridge Cats Volume Seven.* It was a simple photo montage of cats who had one thing in common—they were all dead. They'd all gone to the Rainbow Bridge. The photos were set to music, to the Beatles' *In My Life.* Some of the photos were obviously quite old, from the pre-digital era. She thought that that added additional poignancy, for some reason. With each photograph, there was text on top of the picture, a message from that particular cat's person. The slideshow started with a smallish all black cat—Little Man. *Mommy loves and misses you.* A Ragdoll—Napoleon. *Gone from my life but never from my heart. Waiting to hold you again, my sweet boy.* A cream-colored Persian—Alfie. *You were my life, my everything. It's been nearly forty years since you left me that day in 1982 and it still hurts like it was yesterday. I never got over you and never will.* A pretty gray tabby—Elsa. *You were my best friend. I love you!* A long-haired dilute tortoiseshell—Dada. *Dear little friend. Why couldn't you have just lived forever?* A solid gray cat—Brandon. *My beautiful son. You saved my life.* A Calico—Dilly. *I'm an old man and have no one except YouTube to tell how much I miss my cat. I love her and miss her so much. She defined my life.*

The combination of the images, messages, and music made her cry again. She found herself wondering about each cat in the video, about their lives, about how they died, about what made each of them special. And about the people who posted those messages, messages that oozed both love and pain. *Did they ever get another cat? I imagine some of them did. Most of them probably did. What about Brandon? How did he save that person's life? That must be quite a story. I wish I knew. And what about Alfie's person? The cat died in nineteen eighty-two and that person still hurts, all these decades later. Alfie must have been very special for his death to have left that kind of hurt, that kind of void.*

She walked back over to the couch and sat down. The Dilaudid she'd been administered in the hospital had completely worn off, and she was again feeling significant pain. She opened the bottle of Percocet and tapped out one of the blue disks. A can of soda was sitting on a brown coffee table next to the sofa. She popped the pill in her mouth and took a swig of the soft drink. Then she waited. She waited for that warm, fuzzy feeling to kick in. That *there's-an-asteroid-the-size-of-Texas-headed-straight-for-my-house-and-yet-I'm-still-happy* feeling to kick in. After about fifteen minutes, she was there. And the pain wasn't. *Oh. Yeah. Hell, yeah. I can totally see why people get addicted to this shit. It feels so good.* She talked to herself aloud and slurred her words a bit. "Oh, Lore. I ont know. *Shit.* Maybe I should jess go to bed? Nah. This is a legal high and I'm going to enjoy it."

She was in The Zone. Mellow. Happy. Carefree. The sadness that had plagued her earlier was gone. She turned on a radio that sat on a mahogany end table, next to the sofa. She tuned it to 104.5 FM. *The Midnight Ranger Show* was on. And it was her show. It was a lonely hearts call-in program. A combination of Doctor Phil, Dick Clark and Howard Stern, the host was Baltimore DJ legend, Ronnie Nixon, The Midnight Ranger. He took requests from insomniacs all over Charm City every Monday thru Friday, from ten at night until six in the morning. Most of the folks calling were the lovelorn. They'd call and tell The Midnight Ranger their stories and he'd play their requests. Sometimes, he'd dispense advice, with the caveat that he was "not a licensed therapist." There were always a lot of sad songs played. A lot of breakup songs. Hope listened faithfully every night for a couple of hours after she got home from the swing shift.

But she'd never called in. Never even had been tempted. Always just listened. But this night was different. *Maybe it's just the drug but I want to call.*

For the first hour and a half, she resisted the urge. She knew she was high, slurring her words. She wanted to wait until the most pronounced effects of the painkiller had worn off. She practiced her speech. Eventually, she was able to coherently say, "rubber baby buggy bumpers." *There. I'm good. I'm intelligible. It's safe to call now.*

She picked up her cellphone and dialed the show's toll free number. When it started ringing, she lost her nerve and quickly hung up. But a few minutes later, she dialed again. *I'm going to do it. I'm not hanging up this time. Tonight, I'm going to talk to The Midnight Ranger.*

The show's producer, Stormin' Greg Norman, picked up the line and placed Hope in a calling queue. It was a busy night. There were lots of lonely insomniacs who wanted to dedicate songs.

After nearly a half-hour in the queue, The Midnight Ranger himself picked up. Hope put him on speaker. She liked speaker mode because she frequently made hand gestures while talking.

"Okay, caller, the first thing I'm going to ask is that you turn down your radio please because I am getting nothing but feedback. Can you turn down your radio, please."

Oh, shit. Yeah. I have to turn the radio down. Duh. I should have known that. She turned the volume down until the feedback dissipated.

"That is so much better. Thank you, caller. And to whom do I have the pleasure of speaking to this fine morning?"

"I'm...I'm Hope." *Maybe I should have used a fake name. Agnes. I should have been Agnes. Oh, what the hell. There have to* be hundreds of Hopes in Baltimore. Too late now, anyway.

"Great to have you aboard, Hope. Where you calling from?"

"Baltimore."

"Where abouts in the city?"

"Mount Royal."

"Okay, we've got Hope from Mount Royal joining us. What's on your mind, Hope? What can The Midnight Ranger do for you?"

"Well, first, I just want to say thank you, Richard Nixon, for having me on the show."

The Price Is Right losing horn sound effect played. The Ranger laughed. "Oh, Hope, I love you already, sweetie. You just promoted me from late-night DJ in a mid-major market to the Presidency. I'm the leader of the Free World, damnit."

Producer Greg keyed his mic. "Free World's in trouble."

The Ranger added, "By the way—I am not a crook, though the folks at the tax office may beg to differ. I mean, I told the IRS I'd give them an IOU, but evidently that wasn't good enough because now they're garnishing." A laugh track played.

"I meant to say Ronnie Nixon. Thank you, *Ronnie* Nixon."

"We know what you meant, honey," The Ranger assured her. "Just having a little late-night radio fun, that's all. We like doing that here at 104.5."

"Yeah. Anyway, I'm a first-time listener, long-time caller."

The Ranger again laughed out loud and the sounds of hands clapping in the background could be heard. "I *love* it. Now, you see, we get lots of folks on this show who don't listen worth a damn, but that doesn't stop them from calling and talking, voicing an opinion. Talking their crap and whatnot. At least Hope, here, can admit to it. She doesn't listen. She just freaking calls. I love it. Love. *It*."

"No. I, I meant to say that I'm a long-time listener, but first-time caller."

"We know, honey. Just having some fun with you. Not laughing at you. Laughing with you. That kind of thing. You're a little nervous, huh?"

"Yeah. A little."

"Look, Hope, pretend it's just you and me having a conversation over coffee, okay? Forget all about the fact that roughly seventy-five thousand of our closest friends, from all over the state, are listening in, all right?"

Greg chimed in. "Our ratings just went up, so it's probably more like eighty thousand."

The Ranger said, "Basically, same difference. It's a lot of folks, but don't let that intimidate you, okay, Hope?"

"Uh-huh. Kay."

"So, what can I do for you?"

"I want to send out a song to someone."

"Okay, *well,* that's kind of what we do around here. But you're going to have to be just a *wee* bit more specific. Songs have been around since the Cro-Magnon era, you know. Oh, and, by the way, here's a little piece of trivia for you, gang—first song in human history? It was when a caveman stepped on a hot rock and screamed. Then he rolled around on the ground in agony. And that, folks, is how rock n' roll got started." He laughed along with the laugh track.

Greg added, "Yeah, the songs of the Cro-Magnon period— they still play them on the oldies stations."

The Ranger and Greg both laughed.

"An Elton John song. I want you to play an Elton John song for me." *And can't you guys be serious for just a minute? Damn.*

"All right. Better. Better. EJ. Sir Elton. The Rocket Man himself. One of the all-time greats. Can never go wrong with Elton. But the man has a pretty major body of work. So, I still need something more specific."

"Can you play *Someone Saved My Life Tonight*?"

"I can. But here on *The Midnight Ranger Show,* it's not just the songs that interest us. I mean, I'm going to grant your request. I'm going to play the gosh darn tune for you. Don't you worry about that. But what we really like to get into is the story *behind* the songs. We're nosy around here. We just are. And, Hope, I've been doing this a long time, and something tells me that there is quite a story behind this request."

"Yes. There is."

"Hope, I'm going to come right out and ask—did someone save your life tonight? Did they, sweetie?"

"Yes." She cried. "Look—maybe I should just hang up."

"No–no—no. Please. Do not hang up. Please don't do that. We have to hear this story. All of sleepless Baltimore, sleepless Maryland, now wants to know. Can you tell us about what happened tonight? How did your life get saved? How did it go down, Hope? Tell it to The Midnight Ranger, sweetie."

"There was a bad accident on route forty, in Mondawmin. A drunk driver hit a vehicle that was pulled over on the shoulder. Well, that vehicle was mine. My car was pushed forward, and it hit an SUV that was also pulled over. Anyway, I was walking on the shoulder when it happened, and I never even saw the van coming. And this guy…this guy picked me up at the last possible moment. He carried me in his arms and dove into a ditch along the shoulder. And the van clipped my car, right where I had been walking, just a few seconds earlier. The van was going pretty fast, too. If…if he hadn't picked me up…I would have died. I know I would have. And that's how my life was saved tonight."

Greg weighed in. "I saw that accident when I was on my way in tonight. I had just stopped at Royal Farms to get some fried chicken." He launched into a quick testimonial for the convenience store: "Royal Farms. *They* offer the best because *you* deserve the best. So, next time you get a hankering for some chicken, make sure it's Royal Farms chicken that your pickin'." With the impromptu commercial over, Greg continued, "Anyhow, it was a bad accident. They had eastbound forty shut down for a while. Police cars everywhere."

The Ranger tentatively inquired, "Hate to ask but…any fatalities?"

"No."

"Great. Injuries?"

"Yes. I have a broken rib and the guy who saved me has two fractured ribs. The drunk wasn't hurt at all."

The Ranger observed, "Ever notice—the drunks never get hurt? They always walk away unscathed. I think it's because, at impact, their bodies are so relaxed or something like that. I think I heard that once on *Myth Busters*. Did the bad guy at least go to the slammer?"

"Yeah. He went to jail."

"Good. Good—good—good. That's where he belongs. Now—getting back to *this guy*, as you call him—does *this guy* have a name?"

"Yes."

"What's his name? Tell us, Hope. We need to know. We have to know."

"Luke."

"Luke. Okay. *Luke.* So, is Luke a friend of yours?"

"No. I hardly know him. He's just an acquaintance. Barely an acquaintance, in fact."

Greg interjected. "Oh, hell yes. Hell. Yes. This is getting good. This is like when you turn on an episode of *Friends* and it's the one where Ross bleaches his teeth so that they, like, glow in the dark, and you're all like—*oh, yeah. I have to watch this from start to finish. This is a good one.* I am *so* getting that vibe here."

The Ranger chastised him. "Then shut the F up, Greg, and let her tell the GD story. Please and thank you. So, let's get back on track here—now, you don't really know this guy and yet he risked his life to save yours?"

"Yes."

"Wow. Wow. And Wow. Just *wow*, Hope. Do you know anything else about this hero? Because that's what he is, by the way—a hero. So, what else can you tell us about Luke?"

"He's a former Marine."

The Ranger whistled. "Hope, this story gets better every time you open your pretty little mouth, sweetie. A Marine. And you never really stop being a Marine. There's an old saying—*once a Marine, always a Marine.* You're always a part of that brotherhood, you know? Not that I would because I never made it beyond Cub Scouts. But, ah, what else? I speak for all of Baltimore right now—we want the four-one-one on this guy because I can tell you he's already bigger than Ken Bone."

"Oh, *a lot* bigger," Greg added.

"Well, um, he fought in Afghanistan. And was wounded, so he has a Purple Heart. And a Bronze Star, too." Hope started crying louder.

"It's okay, Hope. It's okay, honey. It's okay to cry. I'm almost crying myself. And I'll bet you dollars-to-donuts that quite a few listeners are, too. I, I have to tell you, folks—this is freaking compelling radio. That's what this is. This is why I do what I do, okay peeps?"

Greg noted: "Ain't bad for the ratings, either."

The Ranger countered, "To hell with the ratings, Norman. This transcends ratings. This is about the freaking human condition, okay? This is like the guy who saw the Hindenburg crash and was all like—*oh, the humanity*! He had a crazy sounding voice, by the way. The guy who announced the Hindenburg crash, that is." The Ranger paused and asked, "Any-who, so what does this guy look like? I think our listeners of the female persuasion would like to know."

Greg asked, "Who persuaded them to be female? No way anyone could ever persuade me to be female. You have to sit down to pee. And then there's the whole period thing." A laugh track played.

The Ranger said, "Do me a favor. I love you, dude. But shut the F up. You're not bringing class and dignity to this show right now, okay? You're making *my* show sound like a frat boy roundtable. Now, pa-leese, let the woman answer. So, what does he look like, Hope? Tell us."

"Elvis. He looks just like Elvis. But he's a nice guy. He isn't into skanks. Skanks need not apply. So, they can just forget about it." *Even though I hardly know him, I'll bet that's true.*

Greg laughed. "Oh, *Me-owl.* And *hiss—hiss*. I think Hope's claws came out a little right there. I think she was basically, in so many words, saying—*I'm first in line for this one, beeotches. And there's no cutting.*"

The Ranger said, "That's how I would take that if I were a woman. Finders, keepers. Only fair. And this guy sounds like a keeper. God gave him to her, after all. Anyway. Looks. Elvis. Presley or Costello? Because Costello ain't nuthin' to look at."

"Presley."

"Young, Thin Elvis? Or Jelly Donut Elvis?"

Hope giggled. "Young Elvis. Exactly like young Elvis."

The Ranger exclaimed, "Ding—ding—ding! Jack-freaking-pot. He would still be a hero even if he looked like Howard Cosell or Julia Child, even if he looked like Jabba the Hutt or whatever. But Elvis? Young Elvis, no less? Come on, people. This is the All-American Hero. Everybody's All-American. Right here. Luke. I'll bet you anything when this guy takes a dump, it's red, white and blue. I know—it's disgusting but that's the first thing that entered my mind. And this is live radio. And it's freaking zero dark thirty. So, it's out there now. Live with it, gang."

Greg said, "This guy's a hottie and a hero."

The Ranger agreed. "Totally, he is. And I'm not the least bit gay, but I want to take a long walk with him on a moonlit beach and hold his hand all the while, okay? I can only imagine what women would like to do with him. Know what, Greg?"

"What's that, buddy?"

"I think we should appoint this guy emperor for life. I think he would be a kind and benevolent ruler. I can*not* see this dude going all Vladamir Putin on us. Can't see it, peeps. I think he'd be like The Lion King, like Mufasa. I'm going to write him in for President next election. I swear I am. Luke For President. Yeah—that's the ticket."

Greg laughed. "Just *Luke*, huh? What if he wins? How are they going to know who to give the keys to the White House to if all we know about him is that his first name is *Luke*?"

"We'll cross that bridge when we get there, man. The guy's only at twenty percent in the polls right now."

Hope laughed. "You just started his campaign ten seconds ago and he's already at twenty percent?"

"*At. Least.* I am an influencer, Hope. When I say I'm for something, people get on board with it in a hurry. Believe you me—by the time we leave the air this morning, he'll have the Electoral College all sown up. President Luke. By midday, he'll have his second term secured. All thanks to The Midnight Ranger. All right—enough silliness. Enough jocularity, as Father Mulcahy would say. Let's get back to the story. This *compelling* story. Now, what I want to know is—why was Luke out on route forty in West Baltimore? Because West Baltimore is not Mayberry, okay? You're not going to see Andy, Barney, and Opie sitting out front of Goober's Filling Station, drinking Cherry Coke and eating Moon Pies, waving to everyone who walks by, calling them by their first name and so forth. West Baltimore is gangs and murders and drugs and muggings. We all know that. And if West Baltimore wants to file a class action lawsuit against me over that statement—*fine*. Because it ain't slander if it's true, folks. So, why was Luke on the mean streets of Tombstone tonight, sweetie?"

"He…he was trying to save a kitten who was darting in and out of traffic. See, he volunteers at a cat rescue."

"Hole. Lee. Shit. And, yes, that's a fine. Fifty bucks. The station fines me a Grant every time I say, on the air, one of those seven words that George Carlin always talked about. You know, the seven words that you can't say on radio or TV. But it all goes to charity, so I'm totally cool with it. They call it The Midnight Ranger Cuss Fund. Special Olympics of Maryland—the check's in the mail, babes."

Hope laughed.

The Ranger elaborated. "This…this…this guy. He's a war hero. He's pretty. He saved Hope's life and was in a position to do so because he was trying to save a kitten. This dude isn't just Luke, okay? He's either Saint Luke or Archangel Luke, whichever is higher. I don't know how that hierarchy breaks down. I'm not sure what the pecking order is in Heaven. I'll have to email Father Flannagan on that. Any. How. He was trying to save a kitten." The Ranger's tone turned serious. "And that's special to me. And here's why—I have a thirteen-year-old daughter named Nicole. And I've never told Nicole's story on the air because I don't want to exploit her, don't want anyone to be able to say that I used my daughter to garner ratings and so forth. But, tonight, I feel compelled to tell this story. So, here goes—Nicole has severe Spina Bifida. She will never know what it's like to ride a bike. Or dip her toes in the ocean. Or go ice skating. She won't. But she has a cat. A cat named Sunny Boy. Big, orange tabby. That sucker must weigh twenty pounds. Part of our family, he is. Sunny Boy has his own stocking for Christmas, all right? Nicole can't do a lot of things, but she can pet her cat. He sleeps with her at night. She reads these YA books to him. She sings to him. She sings *You Are My Sunshine* to him. Okay, people? Sunny Boy is her world. Her reason for getting up in the morning. So, last summer, we were watching the girl's version of the Little League World Series on ESPN. It was the softball version. And Nicole looked at me, looked me square in the eye, and asked—*Daddy, when will I be able to play Little League*?" There was a brief pause before The Ranger continued. "And goddamn, people. Just...just...*goddamn*. And that's another hundred bucks out of my paycheck. And Jimmy cracked corn and I don't care. What does a parent say to their child in that scenario? If someone out there has the answer, I want you to call in and tell me because I need to know."

Hope could tell that The Ranger was crying. Nothing was said for several seconds. Hope cried into her phone. *God. I've seen murders and suicides and drug overdoses. And I haven't cried over any of them. And now I'm bawling my eyes out over a little girl who won't ever be able to play Little League.*

Finally, The Ranger's voice came back over the airwaves. "Okay. I'm back. I'm good. I'm good now. That was just a little story about why I love cats and why I love the people who love them. Because that cat is one of the great joys of Nicole's life. So, Hope, what, ah, what did you say to this hero when he saved your life?"

She continued to cry. "I'm not sure I want to go into that."

"Did you at least thank him?"

"No."

"No? *No?* Why not? Why, why, why didn't you thank him, Hope? You might get a little heat from our listeners for that. You might. Just a little. *A little bit*, as Bobby De Niro would say. He saved your life, for God's sake."

She talked through her tears. "I know, he did. But I'm messed up in the head. I'm messed up real bad. I have a lot of pain and anger inside me. Deep inside me. And it's not his fault. But I took it out on him. I feel so bad about how I treated him. I was so wrong. I was so wrong about him. I don't know if I can even face him anymore. I don't know if he'll forgive me. I don't think I can talk anymore tonight. I'm tired and I hurt, both physically and mentally."

"It's okay. This is a real complex scenario. I can sense that. But let me tell you something—we've been joking around a little and we probably shouldn't. This is a serious situation. It's about two lives. And, I think, Hope, if this guy is the real deal, and I believe that he is, he'll forgive you for your transgressions. Whatever you've done, he'll forgive you. Know why?"

"Why?"

"Because it's what the Gospel According To *Luke* says. It's in there, sweetie. Read it. It's all about forgiveness."

"Do you think so?"

"I do, honey. I do. And you should, too. Hope should have hope. Will you do that for me? Will you try to have hope? Will you try to live up to your name?"

She sniffled. "Uh-huh. I'll try."

"Could you talk some more tomorrow night?"

"Um. I guess. Maybe."

"Okay. I'm going to do something I've never done in the fifteen year history of *The Midnight Ranger Show*. I call it the nuclear option. Folks, I am going to have our producer,

Stormin' Greg Norman, give Hope the direct line number to this studio. So, that when Hope, hopefully, calls tomorrow, she can get right through to us. No waiting in a queue for Hope. Hope's a star. And stars do not wait in queues."

Greg announced, "The phone lines are on fire right now. Texts are flooding in, too. So are the emails. And they're nearly all about Hope and Luke. That's what folks want to talk about. Tons of interest in this story. *Tons.* This is going to bleed over into *The Big Bad Morning Show.* They're still going to be talking about this as we go to sleep this morning. I have to say—I don't recall experiencing anything like this before, and I've been your producer for ten years now, Ronnie. I'm just scrolling through the emails and it's impressive, especially considering the time of day. And all the emails are about Hope and Luke. Well, all of them except the spam emails advertising porn. Unreal. Un-freaking-real. A present just fell into our lap tonight. Thank ya Gee-suzz. Thank ya, Lard. And I'm Jewish."

Greg and The Ranger both laughed.

Hope laughed, too. "You guys are making me laugh and laughing hurts my ribs."

"Okay, Greg, enough of your cornball jokes. They're bad for Hope's health. And we can not have our little starlet in pain. She's going to put our kids through college with all the revenue she's going to generate for this station with this story. T-shirts. Bumper stickers. The book. The movie. And there *is* going to be a gosh darn movie. We already know that. Seriously, if they can make *Magic Mike XXL,* they can make this. They just can. And it'll be called *The Miracle at Mondawmin.* Which is so ironic because Mondawmin might literally be the worst neighborhood in the United States. Yet out of this cesspool of crime and vice comes this beautiful, beautiful happening. And it's like God's telling us—*it's still My Universe, peeps. I'll work My Magic anywhere I damn well please, including Mondawmin.* And the film, if it's done right, will win Best Picture. Bradley Cooper will be Luke. He'd be the perfect Luke. Rugged yet sensitive. And, I'm going to say...Melissa Benoist as Hope. Oh, my God.

Melissa Benoist. Greg, have you ever heard her version of *Moon River*? Good God, man. Makes me cry. I bawl like a baby when she does that song. Makes the hair on my arms stand on end."

Hope rolled her eyes and shook her head at The Ranger's hyperbole. *Yeah. Sure. They're going to make this into a movie and Melissa Benoist will play me. This guy's such a bullshitter... I think Jennifer Lawrence would make a much better me. And if Bradley Cooper's going to be Luke, then Jennifer Lawrence would be the natural choice because she and Bradley had great chemistry in Silver Linings Playbook.*

Greg laughed. "You really need to shave that arm hair. It kind of gives me flashbacks to the old WWF and George the Animal Steele. Remember him? Dude had tons of hair everywhere—everywhere except on his head." They both laughed along with the laugh track.

The Ranger told her, "Okay, sweetie, we're going to let you go and get some rest. And we're going to take some of the reaction calls and read some texts and emails. But we so look forward to your call tomorrow. Promise me that you'll call in tomorrow. Because you have struck a chord in this community. In our fair city. In Gotham. You and your story resonate with people, girl. So, we have to have you back. Promise me you'll call back."

"Kay. I will. I promise. After all, I'm off work for quite a while with my rib. So, I have nothing but time."

"Great. Wonderful. Stay on the line, honey, and Mister Greg's going to give you that special number that you'll use tomorrow. And, for being such a great caller, we're also going to send you an official *Midnight Ranger Show* coffee mug. It's a nice mug. Very stylish yet supremely functional. Do you drink coffee, Hope?"

"Ah, yes. Yes, I do."

"Beautiful. See that? It's the perfect gift. Greg will get your address and get that right out to you. Kay, babe?"

"Kay." She got the direct line number, gave Greg her home address, hung up, and continued to listen.

The Ranger was quick to rate her call. "Wow. What. A. Call.

What a freaking call. Lord have *mercy!* Greatest caller of all-time. Right there. Hope from Mount Royal. Hall of Famer. First ballot Hall of Famer, no less. She was better than the guy who called in and had the dog, the Boxer named Julius. Remember him, Greg? He could play *Memories* from the musical *Cats* on the piano. I found it ironic that a dog was playing a tune from *Cats,* but he was awesome. There's a video clip of that on our YouTube channel, if anyone cares to view it. Have a box of tissues handy, though, because Julius' sensitivity to the nuances of that piece of music *will* move you to tears. Anyway, I have to tell you—I was dragging when I came in here tonight. Didn't really want to be here. It's cold. It's January. All bleak and whatnot. January in Baltimore. But now I am jazzed. All over this whole Hope and Luke saga. Mark my words, peeps—this story has a sprinkling of gold dust on it. And I find myself not being able to wait until tomorrow night. I'm already counting down the hours. It's like looking forward to Hope and Luke, round two, is going to get me through the day today. And I have a root canal scheduled for eleven this morning, by the way. And we're going to flesh this thing out even more tonight. How cool is that, huh? And what would be uber cool would be if we could get the man of the hour himself on the line. If we could get Luke on the show—gold. Ratings gold. Actually, it's already ratings gold. Luke on the show with Hope would be ratings platinum. Greg, can you look online for this guy. Just type *Luke —Baltimore* and see what comes up, man, because the son of a gun has to be out there somewhere. And here's the thing, too— she's not making this stuff up, folks. This is not some WWE storyline, all right? She's not exaggerating at all. At. All. I have no doubt that everything she said was legit. Some people call in and—bottom line—they just want to be on the radio. They want their fifteen minutes of fame. Like the chap who called in six months ago—Harvey from Catonsville—and said he had every single line from every episode of *The Brady Bunch* memorized. And I called BS on that real fast. He didn't even know the *porkchops and applesauce* thing, okay? But Hope?

Hope's the real deal. And I know that because you cannot fake the emotion in her voice. Can't do it, peeps. Best actress in the world couldn't do that. Jennifer Lawrence couldn't do that. Now, she could do *me* if she wants. But not that. Impossible. And I'm kidding about the whole JLaw thing. I've been happily married for nearly thirty years and have never cheated on my wife. Never would, either. *Love* that woman."

"I totally concur with what you said about Hope being the real deal," Greg told him.

"Of course, you do. You're my Ed McMahon. You're contractually obligated to concur with me."

Greg ignored the comment and said, "And I think there's a lot more to this story than she's told us thus far."

"Oh, definitely. For sure. She's not showing her entire hand just yet. And I like that. I admire that. I respect that because that makes the story even better. She's just feeding us these delicious little morsels, these little dollops. But she hasn't put out the main course yet. And here's what I think—I think there's a strong romantic element to this that she hasn't even broached yet. In fact, being the keen observer of humanity that I am, I can say that I am certain that there is a romantic dimension in play here. I think she's in love with Luke. There. I said it. I'm putting it out there for your consideration, Baltimore. And, by the way, I think Hope's a hottie, too. Oh, yeah. I can tell from her voice. Totally. She's a THH, a Total Hottie Hope. And since I just mentioned her name—how great are the names in this little soap opera, huh? Okay, we've got *Hope.* What's the one thing this crazy, messed-up world needs more of? Hope, right? It needs more hope. It just does. And then you've got—*Luke.* This is, like, freaking Biblical, people. Of Biblical proportions, as they say. This is like the chapter of the Bible that God wrote but was all like—*this stuff's too good for them. I'm just gonna save it for Myself, for now.* And it's like somebody in His inner circle got all pissed because He allowed *Toddlers and Tiaras* to get picked up for another season and decided to leak it. One of those deals. For sure. For. Sure."

"So, you think Hope is already in love with this guy?" Greg asked.

"Absolutely. I totally believe in love at first sight. I think she already loves the man. And I'd be willing to wager a year's worth of *your* salary on that, Stormin' Greg Norman. It's like that first time I saw Angie. I peered in through her bedroom window, and she looked at me. And it was just love at first sight...once we got past the whole restraining order thing, of course." He paused for a few seconds, and the crickets chirping sound effect played. Finally, he said, "Kidding. Just kidding. Please, peeps, no need to start a change dot org petition to get me fired. It didn't really happen like that, but, seriously, I have great instincts for these things. My gut feelings are never wrong. Never. It runs in the family. Did you know, Greg, that my grandfather had a dream about the bombing of Pearl Harbor?"

"Did he alert the authorities?"

"Nah. He didn't have it until December eighth."

They both laughed and the laugh track played.

"God, I hate being your straight man, you nut. I love you, though. And that thing you said to her about The Gospel According to Luke—that was freaking beautiful, man. That made me misty-eyed. I haven't felt that way since the last time I watched *Brian's Song*."

"Yeah, I hope that there's something in that Gospel about forgiveness. I just kind of picked it because that's his name. It just seemed so right. I rolled with it. Maybe I should have checked first. I don't know." He paused. "I'm kidding. Just kidding. It is in there. Luke's Gospel definitely talks about forgiveness. Have faith, Hope. We're rooting for you, kiddo. And I don't like to preach. I don't go to church much. Not a big church-goer. On Christmas and Easter, we go to Saint Jude's for Mass and whatnot. So, I do believe in God. And I don't apologize for that. I think only fools are atheists because if you're wrong—you're screwed. So screwed. Now, if you're a believer and you're wrong—no real penalty for that, you know? And I'm not trying to offend any atheists out there. Truly, I'm not. But I'm not trying to *not* offend them, either, okay? They pay me to speak my mind, so I do. This is woke-free radio, gang. If you don't like it, tune me out. Angie does all the dang time. But, anyway, this story—Hope and Luke—this is like a small miracle. People won't even hold the door at McDonald's for each other anymore. And yet this guy risks it all to save someone who he really doesn't even know. And the best part is—there could be some romance, real romance, there. It doesn't get any better, ladies and gents. I think this is going to end in wedding bells. I think these two are riding off into the sunset together. And a chorus of angels will sing *What a Wonderful World* as they do. I really believe that. Again, it's just my intuition. And we'll all cry our eyes out. And if they do get married, I think it'll be live streamed on YouTube and more people will watch than watched Harry and Meghan get hitched. And I honestly think that this little Gift was given to us tonight by The Big Guy Himself. Like He was saying—*you all need a reason to have faith. So, behold—I give you Hope and Luke.* I think that's what this is all about, folks. And I would really dig it if they'd name their first kid after me. Ronald. Even if it's a girl."

Hope took a sip of her soda and giggled. *God. This guy's jokes are so cheesy but for some reason, right now, everything he says is hilarious. Maybe it's just a residual effect of the Percocet. But maybe it's not. Maybe I'm actually alive a little bit again. I haven't laughed like this since before it happened. And maybe The Midnight Ranger is right, about his gut feelings.*

Finally, The Ranger announced, "Luke, buddy, wherever you are—thank you for bringing a much-needed piece of Heaven down to earth tonight. And for giving us all *Hope*. So, without any further ado—from Hope to Luke—Sir Elton John, nineteen seventy-five, back when EJ still had a little bit of hair—*Someone Saved My Life Tonight*. And you're listening to *The Midnight Ranger Show*. Hope and Luke. To. Be. Continued, folks. Be sure to tune in tomorrow to 104.5 Lite FM, *thee* greatest station in the nation."

The song played. Afterwards, The Ranger played the *Marines' Hymn* to honor Luke's military service.

Hope nodded. *That was a nice touch. Thank you, Midnight Ranger. You're a good guy. You tell bad jokes, but you're still a good guy. I guess there are some good guys left in this world.*

She stretched out on the sofa and slowly drifted off to sleep, to the sounds of sleepless Baltimore discussing Hope and Luke.

CHAPTER FOUR: THE DEBUTANTE AND THE MUTT

Tuesday afternoon. It was snowing. Two to four inches were expected before dark. Luke looked out the window of his Roland Park home. He lived in a stone and siding Center Hall Colonial with red shutters. It was a big house for only one person. One person and two cats, to be exact. Only two because the Roland Park Homeowner's Association limited the number of pets to two per household. There was a black cat named Bobby. Bobby was overweight, had a severe underbite, and was missing part of his left ear. He'd been a street cat. Luke brought him home one night eight years ago, when he found him roaming around Camden Yards, near the baseball stadium. Kids were throwing rocks at him.

The other cat was Hannah, a brown tabby. He'd adopted her two years prior from the city's high-volume kill shelter. The cat had been on the facility's pull list because she suffered from epileptic seizures. She required daily medication.

He sat in a brown recliner in his living room, wearing a red sweatshirt bearing the Marine Corps emblem and a pair of blue jeans. The television was tuned to the *TV Classics Network*. He was watching *Seinfeld*. The show was just starting but he immediately recognized the episode. *This is the one where Kramer impersonates a doctor. Oh, yeah, this is a good one.*

His ribs were hurting badly. But he was still trying to avoid taking the opioid he'd been prescribed. Then he sneezed. *Oh, damn. That hurt. Okay. Enough is enough. I'm not going to feel guilty about taking a legally prescribed medication as directed.* He tapped out a Vicodin from the bottle, popped it in his mouth, and washed it down with some bottled water.

Bobby jumped up on his lap and started purring and kneading. The cat drooled on Luke's jeans as a result of his underbite.

Ten minutes later, the doorbell rang. *Just when we were both getting comfortable.*

"Sorry to have to do this to you, Bobby." He gently picked the cat up and set him down on the hardwood floor. Bobby mewed his displeasure over being evicted from the warm lap. Luke stood up and found that even getting out of the chair produced some discomfort.

Gingerly, he walked to the door. He opened it and standing there was his best friend, Dean *Dino* Cavanaugh, 34. He was holding a pizza box and a six pack of soda. Dino wore an expensive navy blue business suit, a white shirt, and a red power tie. He was good-looking. His hair was black, and his eyes were grey. His features were soft, even delicate. He was nearly as handsome as Luke.

"What's up, dude?" Luke asked with a smile. They shook hands.

"Nothing much. Lockheed let us go home early today because of the snow. Since you're newly injured, I thought I'd bring you some late lunch. Or early dinner, however you want to think of it." Dino walked in.

"You old Air Force boys are so soft. Seriously, bro, two inches of snow? Lockheed shut down over two inches? Us Marines would be humping in a foot of snow. Two feet, in fact. Three, even. Because failure was not an option"

"Not my fault I was smart enough to get into the Air Force."

Luke corrected him. "You mean the *Chair* Force."

"We fought just the same as you guys. It's just that once we did our fighting, we went home to a warm bed, cold beer, and clean, dry socks. Oh, and porn flicks. Softcore. No hardcore. Hardcore wasn't allowed. So, you know, there had to be an actual storyline, some kind of romance and what have you. We didn't care as long as we got to see the good stuff."

"Uh-huh."

They walked into the living room. Dino set the pizza and soda on a brown coffee table that sat between the recliner and a blue sofa. Luke sat back down in the recliner. Dino sat on the sofa. They each grabbed a soft drink and pulled the tab.

"I was down at Baltimore-Washington International for a little while yesterday. They had an angel flight touch down while I was there," Dino announced.

"Oh, no. Really? Who?"

"A kid from the city, from Waverly. I can't remember his last name, but his first name was Paul. An Army SF guy. Syria."

"Wow. And most of America probably doesn't even realize that we have boots on the ground in Syria."

"I know, right? Anyway, from what I heard this guy was twenty-one. He had a chance for a full football scholarship to the University of Maryland but chose to join the Army instead. Then went Special Forces."

"You have to respect that."

"Yeah. Respect. It's a shame he wasn't afforded the proper respect."

"Why? What happened?"

Dino shook his head. "Just a couple of creeps. Have you ever been on an angel flight?"

"No. Never."

"Well, it's like this—still on earth but almost in Heaven. What they do is wait until maybe a half hour before they touch down to announce it to the passengers. The captain will get on the PA and say something like—*today we have the honor and distinction of being designated an angel flight. We're helping a hero make one last trip home.*" Dino started to tear up as he told the story. "You know—they don't want people to freak out when they land and see all the lights from the emergency vehicles. And then they do the whole water canon salute thing. And they ask that passengers wait, in silence, while the military honor guard makes the dignified transfer. Only takes five or ten minutes. Then passengers can exit the plane just like normal. Well, a couple of assholes at BWI didn't want to wait. They didn't have connecting flights either, from what I understand. Just didn't want to wait. They wouldn't give that kid five minutes. Not five damn minutes."

"We just did, though, Dino. We did. That's all we can control."

"Amen."

Luke held up his can of soda and proposed a toast. "To the returning hero. Welcome home, lad. Rest easy."

Dino raised his can, too, and they clinked them together. Dino added, "Welcome home. No more trips to foreign lands for you, son. Rest in your native soil. Forever."

Luke shook his head. "Still can't believe those passengers. I swear—I like cats more than most people. Seriously, people can be total jerks."

"And speaking of jerks—let's talk about your run-in with that cop last night. And this was the same cop who hassled you last week, correct? The one who you mentioned on Facebook, right?"

Luke nodded. "Affirmative."

"Yeah, well, when I read your email, I couldn't believe it. It pissed me off, is what it did. How are you feeling, by the way? Your ribs and all? You should be suing Baltimore PD over this—you know that, right? And I know a great lawyer—my little sis."

"I'm doing okay. It hurts. I'll be off work for a while. But I'm not suing anyone."

"That incompetent cop almost got you killed, buddy."

"It wasn't her fault."

"Wasn't her fault? It was totally her fault. Why are you making excuses for that witch?"

"Don't call Officer Kennedy a witch. Please. Don't do that.

She's not a witch. And it was the drunk's fault—that's whose fault it was."

"Well, if Officer Kennedy's not a witch, I guess no one qualifies to be a witch anymore." Dino threw up his hands. "I guess that whole category of person has been eliminated. I guess now it's politically incorrect to shame those who are just plain bad people, huh?"

"Look—it makes me feel bad when you call her mean names. Just humor me, all right? Don't call her any bad names. Please. If not for her, do it for me."

"Oh, I definitely won't be doing it for her."

They opened the pizza box, and each took a slice. The topping was sausage.

"You got any plates around here?" Dino asked.

"Since when do you need plates for pizza?"

"Kaitlyn says it's rude to eat without a plate."

"*Kaitlyn says*, huh?" Luke laughed and shook his head. "Kaitlyn's not here. So, let's be Neanderthals. What do you say? Besides, I don't have any paper plates. And if we use real plates, I'll just have more dishes to wash. I won't tell Kaitlyn. I promise. Plus, once you start using plates for pizza, the next step is using a knife and fork to cut it up and eat it. And you don't want to become one of *those* people."

"Okay. Fair enough. We'll forgo the plates."

They both took a bite of their pizza.

Luke took a swig of his soda. "Thanks for bringing this by, pal. I appreciate it. It's a nice little treat."

"Sure thing. It's the least I can do."

"So, what's going on with you?" Luke asked.

"Not much. Job's good. Family's good. Everything's good… for the most part."

"What about the least part?"

"I had a bad dream last night. About Afghanistan."

"Welcome to the club."

"I know, right?"

"Was it that recurring dream about that one sortie you flew

where you accidently dropped your bombs on the friendlies, on that team of Navy SE—"

Dino interrupted. "Yeah. That one. The one where I dumped my thousand pounders on those Navy SEALS. And killed three of them. That one. I had to watch the video on *CNN*. Now, I watch it in my dreams."

"Not your fault, buddy."

"It was my B Fifty-two. And they were my bombs." A tear rolled down Dino's cheek.

"No, man. They screwed up. Even SEALS can screw up. They called in the wrong coordinates. It happens in war, in the fog of war. And from forty thousand feet, everybody looks the same. And I had my own *fog of war* moment, too."

Dino nodded. "Right. I know. I know you did. And that wasn't your fault, either."

"Yeah. I keep trying to tell myself that, bro. Every day I try telling myself that." He paused for a moment before continuing. "Listen, I know I break your balls about being in the Air Force, but you boys in blue were always there for us infantry guys. Sangin was bad. And they were all over us. They were close enough that you could tell what they'd had for dinner when they burped. They all had that crazy look in their eyes, too. I swear, they were coked-up or something. And we had to call in *London Bridge Is Falling Down* because they were preparing their final attack. The *coup de grace.* The one that was going to finish us off. And you flyboys showed up. Carpet bombing, man, carpet bombing. The great difference maker. It saved our asses that day. God Bless the United States Air Force and the Boeing Corporation."

"Amen."

"Anyhow, you did good. Look at you—you parlayed that Air Force experience into a consultant's job at Lockheed. Nice house. Great house, in fact. Nice car. I like Cadillacs, too. They're classy. I might get one someday. I want one of the old-school ones though. One from, like, the mid-nineties, when they were really land yachts. Now, it seems like even the biggest Caddy isn't all that big. I guess that's just the fashion." Luke shrugged and continued. "But most of all—you have someone to share it all with. I know I kid you about Kaitlyn domesticating you and so forth, but she's a great woman. Not just a good one. A great one. A guy could get places with a woman like her by his side. Wish I had one like her. I get lonely, man. In the night. You know that's the worst time for the flashbacks. In the darkest part of the night. I have this thing now where I'm actually afraid of the dark. I swear, at night I feel like they're sneaking up on me. The Taliban, that is. Trying to slit my throat and so forth. I'm thinking about actually getting a nightlight. Seriously, dude— a freaking nightlight. Hard to find them for adults, though. I found a Barney nightlight at CVS the other day, but that was the only kind they had. I have Bobby and Hannah. They help. A lot. I don't know what I'd do without them, in fact. But it'd be nice to have an actual human being here, too. Someone to talk to. Someone to hug and hold. Someone to say—*I love you* to. I don't have that. You do. I envy you."

"Yeah, well, that's kind of part of the reason I came over today, actually."

"It is?"

"Yeah. I want to talk to you about something."

"So talk."

"You know my sister, Gretchen, right?"

"Yeah. We've met a few times."

"Yeah, well, newsflash—she digs you, buddy. Big time. Big. Time."

"I...I dig her, too. I like her. I do. I don't really know her too well, but she seems nice enough."

"Look—not to sound all seventh grade here, but she *likes you likes you*."

Luke nodded and opened his mouth. "Ooooh, *that* kind of like."

"Uh-huh. *That* kind of like. She's a great girl, too. A year younger than you. Twenty-nine. Her best years are still ahead of her."

"Yeah. I'm sure she's terrific."

"So…what do you say? Want to go out with her?"

"Oh, gee, I don't know."

"Why not? I shouldn't say this about my own sister—but she's hot. Shoulder-length brown hair, honey-brown doe eyes. Great smile. High cheekbones. She's five-seven, weighs a buck fifteen. Perfectly proportioned. Works out several times a week. Nice skin, too. No skin issues whatsoever."

Luke nodded. "Yeah. She's pretty, all right. Can't argue that. She's a real looker."

"Well, of course she is," Dino said as he pulled out a slip of yellow legal paper from the breast pocket of his coat jacket and glanced at it before continuing. "Um, she…has a killer body. Her breasts are large and succulent. Th…th…thirty-six double D. And…and a…a tight…round…bubble butt. *Whew.* There. I said it." Dino nervously smiled.

"I don't think you're supposed to be saying those things about your sister, dude. I think in some states, you can literally go to jail just for saying that stuff about your sister."

Dino held up the paper. "This is the list she wrote for me. She wanted me to lay all these selling points on you, bro. And I know you love big boobs. I know it for a fact. I'll bet you anything if I looked at the browsing history on your computer right now, there'd be some searches like—*Kate Upton topless.* Come on, now. I know you, fella."

Luke sheepishly agreed. "Yeah. *Busted.* Pun intended. I do like big boobs. That's true. I once went so far as to actually sit through an entire episode of *Keeping Up With The Kardashians* just to see Kim in a low-cut top."

"You had to sit through an entire episode to see that? Normally, they play that card in the first five minutes."

"It was a *very special episode* that focused primarily on Scott's myriad of issues. Anyway, what are Gretchen's other selling points? I'm just curious."

Dino again looked at the list. "She just made partner at

Donaldson, Cohen, and Jenkins. Her annual salary is now almost a quarter mil."

Luke shook his head. "That's not important to me."

"It should be. It means she's successful and stable." Dino tore up the list. "Listen, this list was a stupid idea. I told her as much. But she didn't want me to forget anything. Here's the deal—she's a great girl. Maybe I'm a little biased, but she is. Beyond her looks, she's sweet and nurturing. Has a nine-to-five job. So, she'd be there at night, and on weekends. Holidays, too. Plus, she's religious. I know that's important to you. And you're both the same religion. She actually teaches Sunday school at Saint Mark's Church."

Luke wagged his finger and shook his head. "No. Technically, not true. We're not the same religion. I'm Roman Catholic. You all are Episcopalians."

Dino shrugged and threw up his hands. "Same difference. It's the same thing. We're just Catholic lite, dude. Henry The Eighth wanted a divorce, and the Pope wouldn't grant it. So, dude started his own freaking Church to get around it. Must be nice to be that powerful." Dino thought for a moment and added, "Of course, there was that sweet episode of *Sanford and Son* where Fred started his own church when he found out that churches don't have to pay taxes." Dino pumped his fist. "Yeah, Fred—stick it to The Man. Anyway—Catholic and Episcopal—it's the same religion. But we Episcopalians only have half the guilt."

"I've always heard Episcopalians like to drink."

Dino grinned a shit-eating grin. "Well, where you find three or four of us gathered, you generally find a fifth. Thanksgiving is always great when everyone gets all liquored up after dinner. And you have these precious little moments of truth, okay? And we have this one uncle—Uncle Nate—who gets all drunk off his own little private stash of Crown Royal Regal Apple and gives the big speech about how if you didn't vote for Trump, you're a pinko communist. Then he starts smashing things. Sometimes with a golf club, no less. And then he tells us all how he never really loved us, anyhow. By eight, he's passed out on the couch with his hands down his pants ala Al Bundy. At that point, I take his picture and post it on Facebook. And that, my Catholic friend, is Thanksgiving in an Episcopal household."

Luke laughed. "That's cute."

"But look—Gretchen doesn't drink. She's a total teetotaler. And she's a great lawyer. She got her undergrad degree from Harvard. Then, she graduated Summa Cum Laude From Yale Law School. Other lawyers do not want to tangle with her, either. Because she's a winner. She wins. It's what she does. Victory runs through her veins. Very competitive, that little gal. They call her *The Tigress* because she's so ferocious in the courtroom. But the moment she steps outside the courtroom, she's June Cleaver again. She could be Maryland's Attorney General one day. And from there, maybe Governor. You could be the First Gentleman of Maryland, dude."

"*First Gentleman?* Is that what they call a female Governor's husband? Oh, I don't know about any of this."

"She likes you, buddy. Really likes you. She'd be good to you."

"I'm sure she would, but I remember from your Christmas party last month that she has that crazy high voice. And I hate to sound superficial, but I'm not sure I could ever get used to it. It's higher than Kristin Chenoweth's."

Dino shrugged and nonchalantly said, "What? Would you rather she sound like someone giving a *Sixty Minutes* interview who's part of the witness protection program? Besides, the high voice just means she's good in bed."

Luke shot him an incredulous look. "*What?* What did you just say? I seriously don't think you're supposed to be speculating about how your sister is in bed."

"Look, it's not particular to her. All women who sound like Mickey Mouse are good in bed. Hey, that's common knowledge, dude."

Luke shook his head. "Never heard that one. And I thought I heard all that stuff in the Marine Corps. For example, I always heard that redheads are really wild and kinky. And you know what they say about petite women, don't you?"

"No. What's that?"

"That they're like Ebenezer Scrooge."

"Ebenezer Scrooge?"

Luke raised his eyebrows. "Yeah, you know, they're...*tight*."

Dino laughed. "In the Air Force, I always heard that you should never have sex with a woman who has a cold."

"Yeah, well, that makes sense. Sex is intimate contact. You could conceivably catch her cold."

"Nah. That's not why, man. It's because she could *conceivably conceive*. That's why. See, the germs responsible for the common cold also render birth control ineffective."

Luke dismissively waved at Dino. "No. You're way off on that. It's an urban legend. Just like the one going around that says Mister Rogers was a Navy SEAL in Vietnam and he wore that sweater to cover a *Born To Kill* tattoo."

"Yeah, well, urban legends aside, let's get back to my little sis. I want someone who'll be good to her. Guys hit on her all the time, but they're ones who just want to get into her pants. With you, I wouldn't have to worry about her getting cheated on, or abused, or disrespected. I want someone good for my little sis. I don't want her to end up with Carlo from *The Godfather,* all right? I want her to have a good guy. The best, in fact. Is that so wrong?"

"No. Of course not. And I'm flattered that you think I might be that guy."

"It's such a no-brainer, man. It's a win-win for everybody. If you guys ever got married, we'd be related. How cool would that be? Two best buds, two comrades-in-arms, together every holiday, hanging out on the weekends. Watching sports together and so forth. It'd be good. I can't understand why you're not totally on board with this. You need to get on the Gretchen train because it's at the station waiting."

"We're already like brothers. Besides, your sister doesn't know about my issues."

"I talked to her about it a little. Not in a lot of detail, mind you. But a little. And she wants to help. She is so nurturing. Give her a chance. What have you got to lose? She adores cats, too, by the way."

"This just feels like some arranged marriage. Am I supposed to give you a milking cow and a year's worth of my corn crops or something like that?"

"Exactly. And as soon as I get the cow and the corn, I'll drop her off here at your place. No refunds—no exchanges."

"What kind of dowry is she bringing to the marriage? Any gold? Gold would be outstanding. I'd really dig getting some gold that I didn't have to dig."

They laughed.

"Seriously, just go out with her."

"I don't know, Dino. I'm kind of not over…"

"Over what?"

"Over the…the cop."

"*The cop?* The cop who almost got you killed? The cop who thought catnip was dope? The cop who threatened to arrest you for feeding homeless cats? The cop who almost shot you because you were trying to save her life? Which wouldn't have needed saving in the first place if she was even remotely competent. You don't need to get *over her*. You were never under her. Nasty shrew."

"I asked you not to talk that way about Officer Kennedy."

"*Officer Kennedy.* That's it exactly. That's precisely my point. You don't even know her freaking first name, dude. What are the wedding invitations going to say—*Officer Kennedy and Luke cordially invite you to celebrate their undying love for one another?* And the priest is going to be all like—*do you, Officer Kennedy, take Luke to be your lawfully wedded husband?*"

"So, I don't know her first name yet. So what?"

"What does this woman look like, by the way?"

"Beautiful, just like I said on Facebook."

"Yeah, but I need a comp."

"Demi Lovato, circa twenty-seventeen, when she did the *Tell*

Me You Love Me music video." Luke whistled a catcall. "Hubba, hubba. What a dish. But this woman's prettier, in my opinion."

"Say what? Prettier than Demi in her prime? Is that even possible?"

Luke emphatically nodded. "Yeah. In my humble opinion, she is."

"What about boobs? Bet you she isn't thirty-six double D."

"She might be, actually. It's kind of tough to tell with cops because they wear the bulletproof vests. But I know for a fact she's got something going on up there. I could tell that much."

"What about her butt?"

"Total bubble butt. Better than JLo in her prime."

"Damn. Lord have mercy! That is significant—I'll give you that."

"She's tiny, too. I like petite women. And she's maybe about five-feet, weighs about a buck. Little tiny thing. Cute. Cute—cute—cute."

"Five-feet tall? She's a freaking Munchkin."

"Yeah, but she doesn't know that. It's like she's oblivious to her lack of size. It's very adorable. Kind of like a Chihuahua who thinks she's a Rottweiler."

"But she called you a jerk. You said that yourself in the email."

"She did say that, yes. But my theory is that when women say stuff like that, they actually like you. Especially when they invoke your middle name, which she did. Middle-name-invocation equals true love. Every time. Except, of course, when you were a kid, and your mom would call you by your middle name. That generally meant you were in trouble. But in virtually all other cases, it's a sign of interest."

Dino emphatically shook his head. "Nah. You're overanalyzing, man. More often, they really do think you're a jerk."

"I think there's a reason why she's like that. I think something happened to her. Something bad. And I think she's hurting. Just like me."

"But you're not an asshole to people."

"Different people process it differently."

"Forget about her, will you? She doesn't like you. Gretchen, on the other hand, is crazy about you."

"It's just that I think Officer Kennedy and I—well, we're both mutts."

"Say again?"

"We're both mutts. Both blue-collar types. Both non-pedigreed. Your sister went to all the right schools. Hell, at your Christmas party last month, I remember her talking about the fact that she went to finishing school. I didn't even realize that finishing schools still exist. I thought they went out of style with poodle skirts and bouffant hairdos. And she went to Harvard. Then Yale."

"What? You don't like that she's been successful?"

"No, that's not it. It's just that I was a grunt. Infantry. We rolled in the mud. Didn't bathe for days on end. We were either too cold or too hot. We smelled. And we saw the face of war—up close and personal. It looks different on the ground, dude. A lot dirtier than it does at forty thousand feet. It sucked. And we embraced The Suck. Because a grunt can take it. A grunt can take anything. And there are things seared into my memory that I'll never forget. And Dino—there's something seared into this woman's memory, too. I know it. I just do. And maybe we need each other to heal. Maybe I can help her heal. And maybe she can help me heal, help me get beyond that day in Sangin."

"Nah, bro. This isn't a movie. That stuff only happens in movies. Movies and novels."

There was a long pause as Luke mulled it over. Finally, with a sigh, he admitted, "Yeah. Maybe you're right. Maybe I'm just seeing what I want to see."

"*Exactly*. That is exactly what you're doing. Come to the Ravens game with us on Sunday. Four tickets on the fifty-yard line. In a luxury skybox. Courtesy of Gretchen's law firm. Me and Kaitlyn. You and Gretchen. It's the playoffs, dude. And the Steelers are in town. Another perk about Gretchen—you'd be going to any sporting event you'd want to attend. Terps. Orioles. Ravens. Concerts, too."

"Come on, man. That's not a good reason to be with a girl, for sports and concert tickets and such."

"Not in and of itself. Just one more thing, though. Gretchen checks all the boxes. The Kennedy chick checks none of them. Well, none except the bubble butt box. And maybe the boob box, pending seeing her without her bulletproof vest on. And you'll never get that far with her. This shouldn't even be a choice, man. You're a fool if you pass on my sister. She wants to be there for you. You know, she offered to come over here and take care of you while you're dealing with these ribs. My sis is the real deal. Officer Kennedy's a figment of your wishful thinking."

"I'm in pain, bro. I'm not sure about going to the game with my fractured ribs. I just…I don't know."

"Well, if you don't go, let me ask you this—are you still going to watch on TV?"

"Of course. I'm a diehard Ravens fan. No way I'd miss it."

"So, how would it be any more painful sitting in a luxury skybox at M andT Bank Stadium than it would be sitting on your couch here at home?"

He shrugged and threw his hands up. "I guess it wouldn't. You got me. I'll concede that point."

"Right. So, you pop a couple Vicodin and you're good to go."

"But it's supposed to be cold on Sunday. Around twenty-five degrees. For a high."

"Yeah. And you'll be in a climate controlled skybox. At the game but out of the elements. And if it does happen to get drafty in there, Gretchen will keep you warm. She said to tell you she loves to snuggle. My sister is all about you. Officer Kennedy, on the other hand, thinks you're a jerk. What do you want to do? Huh? You need to start thinking a little bit with your head, buddy, instead of your heart. That's going to get you hurt. And I don't want to see my buddy get hurt. Let my sis help you. She wants to. Let her. Let her make it better for you.

Let her make it right. I love my sister, my only sibling. My only blood sibling. But you are as a brother to me. And I love you like a brother. And all I want is for the two people who I love to love each other. Is that so wrong?"

Luke again thought for a moment. Finally, he announced, "No, man. It's not. I'll...I'll go. I'll go with Gretchen. I guess it'll be the debutante and the mutt."

"She will be so psyched. So, it's on?"

"Yeah. It's on. But it's just one teeny, tiny little date. That's it. Don't start printing the wedding invitations just yet."

"But you do like her, right?"

"What? Do you have a little slip of paper with two boxes that says—*do you like me? Check yes or no.*"

Dino reached into his coat pocket and pulled out a sheet of white paper and a pen. He unfolded the paper and handed both items to Luke.

At the top of the expensive rag stationery was the letterhead —*Donaldson, Cohen, and Jenkins. Attorneys at Law. 304 Saint Paul Place. Baltimore, MD.*

Dino pointed to the paper. "Just check the *yes* box. All right?"

Luke stared at him in disbelief.

Dino shrugged and nervously laughed. "What can I say? She's a lawyer. Likes everything in writing. Always tells me— *Dino, always get it in writing. If it's not in writing, it doesn't exist.* Yep. That's what she says, all right. Uh-huh."

Luke flashed Dino a scowl but nonetheless checked the *yes* box and handed the paper back to him.

Dino surveyed it and immediately handed it back. "Ah, I need you to sign it at the bottom, next to her signature. Notice, too, that she has that super cute, girly handwriting."

"Uh-huh." He signed it and handed it back.

"The pen. I need the pen, Luke. I have to sign it, too."

"Why do you need to sign it?"

"I'm the witness to your signature."

Luke rolled his eyes and handed the pen over. "Good grief. I'd hate to see what I'd have to sign to actually have sex with her."

"She's drafting that one as we speak. It's a multi-pager. It's going to take a while. It might be ready by Sunday, though." Dino raised his eyebrows, smiled, and nodded. He signed the document and placed it back inside his breast pocket.

Dino took another piece of pizza and got up. "All right. Mission accomplished, as we used to say in the Air Force. All set. We'll pick you up at ten in the morning on Sunday. Oh, and we'll be taking a limo. That's courtesy of Gretchen's firm, too. How about that? Ever been in a limo?"

"Yeah, I shared a limo with some folks in Vegas once. When I was on boot leave from the Marines, right after I graduated from Parris Island."

"Who'd you share it with?"

"Three Frank Sinatra impersonators and Andy Dick. Oh, and also, a Sammy Davis Junior impersonator. He was good. The Sammy was a good one. He had a glass eye and everything. And he sang this absolutely soulful rendition of *Mister Bojangles*. It brought a tear to my eye. Yes, it did. I'm not too proud to admit it."

"Wow. There has to be a great story in that."

"It'd take at least two hours to tell. One thing I will say—Andy Dick lived up to his name. Total dick."

"Well, that's unfortunate. I've never really heard anything good about Andy Dick, to be honest. Kimmel had to literally drag his ass off the show for groping Ivanka Trump…any-who, we'll see you at ten on Sunday."

"Why so early? The game doesn't start until one."

"Gretchen likes to tailgate before the games. Another plus for her. Great cook, my sis. Wait till you taste her mac and cheese. She seasons it with Old Bay. That's her secret. Bet the Kennedy chick can't even microwave a TV dinner."

"Yeah, well, I don't know about her culinary talents. But, hey, listen, thanks for taking me to the game. It's a big game. And I love my Ravens. So, thank you and all that good stuff."

"Thank Gretchen. It was her idea. And I'm sure you'll find a way to thank her. *A proper way.* Eh?" He winked at Luke and smiled a devilish smile.

Is he trying to encourage me to have sex with his sister? I think so. That's the second time now he's kind of alluded to it. Is he setting me up for a shotgun wedding?

Dino started to walk out the door but turned around and said, "Hey, Luke."

"Yeah, buddy?"

"You can drop the cow off anytime you want. And I'll send a tractor trailer over to pick up your maze harvest. And once that's all taken care of, I'll be dropping Gretchen off. Right at your doorstep. And once the transaction is complete, that's it. Done. *Fini.* Can't be undone. And if you try to undo it, our families would have to go to war. And you'd still have to keep Gretchen."

Dino laughed.

Luke laughed, too, and shook his head. "Get out of here, you nut."

Dino turned and walked away.

Luke threw a piece of pizza crust at him, and it hit him in the back.

Without turning around, Dino called out, "The suit, bro. The suit. Don't break the suit. It was more expensive than your first car."

CHAPTER FIVE: HARD TO SAY I'M SORRY

Tuesday night, 7PM. Hope sat at the desk in her bedroom. The TV was tuned to The Disney Channel. She looked out the window at the snow. *It's going to be one of those winters.* She had time to kill before she called in to *The Midnight Ranger Show.* Greg Norman had asked her to call at ten-thirty. He said ten-thirty because that would give them a half-hour to set the stage and recap for any listeners who hadn't heard her original call. She suspected that they wanted her to call earlier in the evening to play to a larger audience.

She took a shower and then a pain pill. She wanted to time the medication so that by ten-thirty, she'd still be relatively pain-free but not messed-up. After fifteen minutes, the combination of her Scooby Doo snuggie and the Percocet made her feel all warm and fuzzy. Her hair was in a ponytail. A cup of black coffee sat on the desk. She got on her desktop and surfed Amazon, searching for DVDs. *If I'm going to be off work for the next two months, I'm going to have something to watch. I'm going to treat myself a little.* She selected *WrestleMania: The Complete History. I'm getting it. I love pro wrestling. It's like a soap opera with body slams.* She completed her transaction and clapped her dainty hands when the screen came up confirming her purchase. *Yay.*

Next, she went to YouTube and looked up 104.5's channel. They had uploaded the clip from the previous night's show. And it wasn't just the audio, either. They actually had cameras in the studio to go with the sound. She got to see what The

Midnight Ranger and Stormin' Greg Norman looked like. The Ranger had long, dark hair in a ponytail and was thin. He had a goatee and wore a white cowboy hat. And he was smoking cigarettes. *What? They allow him to smoke in the studio, with all that sophisticated equipment? That's just the craziest thing I've ever seen.* She shook her head. *Unreal. He must have that in his contract.* Greg was heavyset and balding. At one point, he smiled to reveal a Michael Strahan-like gap between his two front teeth. She shook her head again and did a doubletake. *It's crazy. You have this idea of what they look like from hearing their voice on the radio. But they really don't look anything like your image of them.*

She glanced at the view counter. *Can't be right. Are the painkillers messing with my vision?* She closed her eyes, rubbed them, and opened them again. *Nine thousand three-hundred and twenty-eight views. In less than twenty-four hours. And over a hundred and fifty comments.* She read a sampling aloud to herself. "Hope's a bitch! Luke saves her life, and she doesn't even say thanks? Hope is hopeless...Hey Hope—if you don't want him, pass him on to me, please. I need a Luke in my life...Hope is a good person. Just hurting. Badly. Leave her alone, people. Show some respect...I had a loaded 9 mil by my side early this morning because my girlfriend cheated on me and we broke up. My radio just happened to be tuned to 104.5 during The Midnight Ranger Show. And Hope's story made me realize that there's always hope. I put the gun away...Hope, you had a beautiful experience, a close encounter of the angelic kind. Luke was literally an angel, an angel sent by God to be there for you in your moment of crisis...Hope and Luke—your story made this eighty-year-old woman cry...Lifelong Baltimore resident here—God's not dead. He's working His Magic on the mean streets of West Baltimore. This story warmed my heart...Never happened, people. Hope is an actress and Luke does not exist. 104.5 pulled off the biggest fraud in the history of Baltimore radio last night. Shame on you 104.5. Worse than the moon landing hoax! Will never listen to your station again....Why so many views in such a short period? Because this is a message that the world hungers for. *Miracles* do *still happen. I think both Hope and Luke are angels, human angels, whom God chose to use to show us all The Way, The Truth, and The Light...Accepted Jesus Christ into my life tonight because of this story. Thank you, Hope, Luke, and 104.5...Hope already loves him for the same reason I love him, too. He didn't have to stop and wonder what was right or wrong. He just knew. Wow! He just knew. But I guess that's what makes heroes heroic, isn't it?"*

Hope shook her head in disbelief. *Wow. This is heady.*

She set her phone alarm for ten. Then she lay down on her bed and took a nap.

When her alarm when off, she got up and sat back down at her desktop computer. She went to the 104.5 website, clicked on *Listen Live*, and turned up the speakers. *The Midnight Ranger Show* was just starting. The intro music was David Bowie's *Heroes.*

After the music faded, The Ranger announced. "All right, Baltimore. Really big, shew, tonight, people. Really big."

Greg asked, "By the way—before I forget—how was your root canal? You had your root canal today, right?"

"Sure did. And it went great. Didn't even need any drugs afterward. Doc Jacobson offered me ten Tylenol number threes, to help me deal. But I declined. Flat out declined. Didn't need them. I was already so high off this story. This whole Hope and Luke thing. Turned down some feel-goods, peeps. How about that? That was a first, I can assure you."

"The clip of last night's show has garnered over nine thousand views already. That's two percent of the entire population of the city of Baltimore. In just twenty-four hours. That's a record for us, for our station. Pretty impressive," Greg proudly announced.

"Yeah. My understanding is that *The Baltimore Sun's* picking up this story. They're going to do a write-up on it. I have a source down there and I'm told they want a piece of this action, too," The Ranger said.

"It's great stuff. There were a couple of comments on

our YouTube channel to the effect that the commenter was contemplating hurting themselves, and that this story caused them to put the gun down or set aside the pill bottle or what have you. I don't think it's too much to say that this story's actually changing our community for the better," Greg added.

"I can tell you right now, Greg, this might be the best story I've ever been a part of. It's just so positive. And it couldn't come at a better time. The rest of the country's telling us that we're the nation's *worst city*, the *most dangerous city.* And out of this so-called ugly city, comes something exquisitely beautiful."

"Fur sure. Fur sure. We're getting tons of requests for songs with a hero theme, too. Ah, let's see…one just came in for Peter Cetera's *Glory of Love*, the old-school song from the second *Karate Kid* movie. Remember that one? That's the song where the dude tells the girl—*I'm the one who'll fight for your honor*, etcetera, etcetera. And we're also—"

The Ranger interrupted. "Let me stop you right there, Greg, and pose the query—do you think women still want guys to fight for their honor? Are they still down with that? Or did we outgrow that? Did the world grow up at some point and leave that behind?"

"No. Women still like it when guys fight for their honor. This story is proof of that. Because this story is, in part, about good old-fashioned chivalry. And all these centuries later, chicks still dig it. It's still okay to be a knight in shining armor. More than okay, in fact."

"I think so, too. So, bottom line—this story is kind of a big deal here in our fair city. It's developing a *following,* as they say. And I predict that it could really blow up after tonight's show because, people, we have some real news. There's been a break in this story."

Greg chimed in. "Correct. But it's not that we're going to have Luke here, on air. But kind of the next best thing."

"Right. Right. But we did put a bounty on Luke. A grand. If Luke, *thee* Luke, shows up here at the station, goes on-air with us, and blesses us with some of his precious time, the guy gets a freaking grand. A thousand bucks. Okay, peeps? We kind of had to draft him. It's as if this guy has become communal property. He's not a private citizen anymore. He belongs to the entire city of Baltimore now, to the entire state of Maryland. We've invoked *eminent domain* on his gorgeous buttocks. But I'm telling you, Greg, he wouldn't take the G. Not our Luke. Nope. He'd donate it, probably to the cats or something."

"I concur. I do."

"Now, Greg, let's put on our deer stalker hats. Our Sherlock Holmes caps, if you will. Because you dug up a very interesting comment from our YouTube channel that sheds *boo koo* light on this story. But it requires some analysis, correct?"

"Right. You are correct. Soooo, I had to sift through a lot of social media posts and comments to find this little nugget of gold. This comment, however, is unique. Because most of the comments and messages are just folks who have no inside knowledge. They're just voicing an opinion."

"Exactly. And that's great. Nothing wrong with that."

"Certainly not," Greg agreed. "That's what we want folks to do. But this comment purports to have detailed inside knowledge. And I'm going to read it, in its entirety, because it's not real long. And we do not know the identity of this individual. Okay? The username he or she used, however, was —IHaveADreamMLK1980. And—"

The Ranger interrupted. "And stop right there because we have to dissect this username. Obviously, it's a reference to Doctor Martin Luther King Junior, God rest his soul. Need more Doctor Kings out there, that's for sure. The nineteen eighty bit? I'm going out on a limb and say—birthyear. So, I hypothesize that this commenter is an admirer of Doctor King and approximately forty years of age. Okay, Greg, continue. Please."

"Okay, so, here's the comment itself, verbatim—

I know the full identity of Hope. I was listening to the show last night and recognized not only her name but her voice as well.

I can't say how I know her. But I do. I absolutely do. Hope, I heard you cry when The Midnight Ranger talked about his daughter. You finally cried over someone else's pain. That's where the healing starts. I've been hard on you lately, I know. Maybe too hard, given all that you've been through. But that's only because I know that beneath all the hurt, there lives a human being who is as beautiful on the inside as she is on the outside. Give Luke a chance. He likes you likes you. *And he's earned it. Two wounded, purple hearts* can come together and heal one another. Peace, Baby Girl. *Blessed are those who weep. #KeepTheDreamAlive."*

The Ranger remarked, "Wow. Okay. First impression—totally legit. This is not someone messing with us, folks. Not somebody who wants their fifteen minutes of radio fame. IHaveADreamMLK1980 knows whassup."

Greg agreed. "No doubt. Completely legit commenter. If this were *Pawn Stars*, Rick's expert would authenticate and gush over what a find it was. Totally. And here's what I think, too—this is definitely a woman talking. No dude is going to write this way. It's way too pretty to come from a guy. There's, like, a ninety-nine percent chance this commenter is female. A female about forty years of age. And let me pose this question—who would be *hard* on a person?"

The Ranger offered a guess. "I'm saying your employer. I think this is Hope's employer. Her boss. Bosses are *hard* on their people. That fits."

"Agreed. Totally. And here's another tidbit—this person purports to know that Luke *like likes* Hope. That's seventh grade-ese for—Luke has the hots for this girl."

"Exactly. And, frankly, I'm relieved. I left the air yesterday wondering—*what if Luke's gay?* Not that there would have been anything wrong with that, mind you. Hey, I don't care who you go to bed with so long as they're at least eighteen and don't have paws or hoofs, you know? But it would not have been great for this story if it turned out that Luke's favorite vacation spot is a dude ranch. That would have killed any romantic dimension to this story. I mean, am I right or am I right? And no offense whatsoever, Baltimore gay community. Love you guys. *Muah.* Okay? *Muah.*"

"The gay community won't be upset. They love a good romance as much as anyone else. But there undoubtedly are some individual gay men who are going to be very bummed when they find out Luke's not interested in men's bums," Greg noted with a chuckle.

"That's what I'm saying. Now, moving along—the whole *Peace, Baby Girl* thing. Very maternal. This is a maternal figure in Hope's life. A very strong maternal figure. She ain't no meek and mild Harriet Nelson, either. More like Florida Evans from *Good Times*. For sure. But I'm stumped on the—*Blessed are those who weep.*"

"It's one of the Beatitudes, one of the blessings Jesus bestowed on certain categories of people. Mostly poor people. And people who, for lack of a better word, had lots of baggage that they were trying to carry. And guess where it comes from? This is great because you just can't make this stuff up, folks. It comes from The Gospel According To Luke."

"Damn. I'm Catholic and I did not know that. I'm embarrassed that it took Stormin' Greg Norman, a Jewish man, to tell me that."

"Well, I had to look it up. They never covered that at Talmudical Academy, so I had to Google it."

"Gotta love that Google. It sure makes life easier, doesn't it? I used it the other day to find out whatever happened to Urkel from *Family Matters*. He's over forty-years-old now, by the way. Any-who, the other thing that this comment implies is that Luke has a wounded heart, too. So, according to IHaveADreamMLK1980, both these kids have significant issues that they're dealing with, some type of heartache. And, by the way, I'm amending the title of the book and the movie. I know I said last night that they'd be called *The Miracle At Mondawmin*. That was just kind of an okay title. But IHaveADreamMLK1980 got it right. She nailed it. Here's what the book and subsequent movie's going to be called—*Purple Hearts*. Much better title, peeps. And the book will be a romance novel. And whoever writes it will be like—*now, this is just a work of fiction.* And then they'll whisper—*but it's true. It's not a work of fiction. It really did happen.*"

"Makes it even better."

"I know, right?"

Hope looked at the time on her phone. She called the direct line number. Greg answered immediately and put her on hold.

Shortly thereafter, the Ranger announced, "I've just been handed a note from Norman. We have Hope on the line. She didn't stand us up, thank God. Unlike my senior prom date, Shannon Robinson. Never forgave her. Nineteen ninety-one. Catonsville High senior prom. Had the mullet and everything. Perfect mullet. Billy Ray Cyrus was jealous of my mullet, okay? But I had to go to prom with my French Poodle, Fifi. My emergency date. All because Shannon Robinson stood me up. It was humiliating. I was mortified. Not because I went to prom with a dog, but because Fifi was a better dancer than I was." A laugh track played before The Ranger continued. "Ah, all right, kids, it's that time. We're going to go to commercial break—have to do a little business with you. Gotta pay those bills, right? It does cost money for this station to indulge my shenanigans. And when we come back, we're going to talk to the Star-Spangled Girl herself. Her name is Hope and she's gonna give us the straight dope. But before we go to break, we're going to give a little shout out to IHaveADreamMLK1980. I hope you're listening tonight. The Midnight Ranger's gift to you—U2. Bono. Nineteen hundred and eighty-four. *Pride (In The Name Of Love).* Keep that dream alive. And keep that dial tuned to 104.5, *thee* greatest station in the nation."

Hope heard the opening strains of *Pride*. She got nervous, and her palms got sweaty. *Oh yeah. Turn down the volume on the speakers. And, tonight, don't call him Richard Nixon. Ronnie Nixon. His name's Ronnie, not Richard. God, that was embarrassing.*

She set her phone to speaker mode, turned down her computer's speakers, and waited.

After the commercials, The Ranger greeted her. "Hope! Thanks for joining us, kiddo. You're a woman of your word. You said you'd call back, and you did. Ah, how are those ribs feeling tonight?"

"Um, it still hurts. Thanks for asking Richard—I mean—Ronnie. Thanks for asking, *Ronnie.*"

"Sorry to hear that you're still hurting. Healing takes time though. But you do feel well enough to talk, right?"

"Yeah. I feel well enough to talk."

"Great. We're not going to rehash it all. We've already done all that. People listening know the story. We want to get into some new stuff. Now, Hope, did you hear Greg when he read the YouTube comment written by someone who purported to know you?"

"Yes."

"Was it the real deal?"

"Yes."

"I'm going to be bold, have some gall. I'll come right out and ask—who posted it? And can you tell us if our educated guesses were accurate?"

"I'm not at liberty to say who posted it. I know, but I can't say. Also, I can't confirm nor deny the accuracy of your guesses. I suppose I'll just have to say *no comment.*"

Greg interjected. "And that speaks volumes. Tells me that we're spot-on. Just saying. *No comment* generally means—*why do you need comment from me? You already have it figured out yourself.*"

The Ranger concurred. "Yeah. I agree. I agree. Now, Hope—last night you disclosed that you did not thank Luke for saving your life. Let's get into that a little because there are some folks out there in Radio Land who are upset with you over that one. Some people are really taking you to task over it, in fact. Can you elaborate on your reason for not thanking him?"

"It's complicated. Something bad happened a couple of years ago. Very bad. And I'm angry about it. And I hurt. And I take it out on people. I took it out on him."

The Ranger probed. "Fair enough. Would you like to talk to us about the bad thing that happened? Or is it too painful? Too private?"

"No. I'm not prepared to talk about it now. It's hard to talk about."

"And I totally respect that. So, moving forward—I'm going to come right out and ask the Sixty-Four Thousand Dollar Question that everyone's curious about—do you have feelings for this guy? Romantic feelings, perhaps?"

"Again, it's complicated."

Greg chimed in. "That's a yes. That is *so* a yes."

The Ranger admonished him. "Let her talk, Greg, will ya?"

The Ranger then turned his attention back to Hope. "Now, we know you didn't thank him but what did you say when the man saved your life?"

"He was on top of me in the ditch. My exact words were—*get off me, jerk.*"

The Ranger said, "*Ouch.* And he did nothing to deserve that type of verbal abuse, correct?"

"Correct."

"So, this behavior, this total rudeness, was the result of your issue, your baggage?"

"Yes. I believe so."

"But you are sorry you mistreated the man?"

"Yes."

"How can we make this right, Hope? Tell me. I'm here to help. I want to help."

"I don't know. I'm not good at apologizing. It's hard for me to say *I'm sorry.* I'm not good with words. I'm not eloquent. I went to college, community college, for two semesters. That's it."

"You don't have to be a Rhodes Scholar to tell someone you're sorry. It's not the six syllable words that pact the punch. It's the simple words, put together right, that do that.

And those words don't have to come from the *Oxford English Dictionary*. More often, they come from the heart, kiddo."

"I know, but it's still hard. See, there's the person that *I Am*. And then there's the person that *I Want To Be*. And those two are fighting over Me. Trying to influence Me. Trying to *be* Me. I don't know. That probably made no sense."

"No, it did make sense, actually. Perfect sense. Tell me, Hope, do you want to tell him that your sorry?"

"Yes. And I have to. It's mandatory."

"Okay, what does that mean—*mandatory*?"

"Can't discuss, except to say that I have to contact him."

"Now, do you have means of contacting him?"

"Yes. I have his full name, address, email address, phone number, Facebook page. The works."

"Wow. That's good. That was one of my concerns, by the way. I was all like—*how is she going to get in touch with this guy?* How do you come by so much info?"

"Um. I hate to keep saying this but I'm not at liberty to discuss it."

"Okay. Fair enough. So, when are you going to contact this dude?"

"Tonight."

"*Tonight?*"

"Yes. See, what I thought I'd do is request a song, a song that would help me to apologize. And ask you to give me time to call him before you actually play my request. That way, I could tell him to tune in."

With mock concern, Greg asked, "So, do you mean to tell me that Luke doesn't listen to our show?"

Hope giggled. "I doubt it."

The Ranger laughed. "I think we finally found a chink in Luke's armor. He doesn't listen to *The Midnight Ranger Show*. Shame on him. But we can work with that. That's not a deal-breaker. Now, if he were a card-carrying member of the Aryan Brotherhood or wrote-in David Duke for President—*that* would be a deal-breaker."

She didn't appreciate the attempt at humor. *"No*! He *is not* a racist. He admires Martin Luther King Junior, too. I know that for a fact. Please don't even joke about that."

The Ranger apologized. "Well, of course, he's not a racist, honey. And I probably should not joke about those kinds of things. Sorry. Didn't mean to hurt your feelings. But I have to say—I love how you jumped in and stood by your man. You went all Tammy Wynette on my keister just now and I loved it. I *so* respect that. So, you're really going to hit him up, huh?"

"Yeah. I just hope he doesn't get angry with me for calling him so late. It's after ten-thirty and Miss Manners always said that you shouldn't call anyone after nine, unless you know them well. But I feel like I should do it now, while I have the courage."

The Ranger offered assurance. "This guy isn't going to be upset. Now me? I'd be upset. When those damn sales calls start coming in at The Ranger household at night, sometimes I pick up just to go off on them. I mean it. I go Mel Gibson on those people. Drunk Mel Gibson, no less. Nothing but expletives. But Luke? Something tells me this guy is so nice that the Moonies could call him at two in the morning—on a work night, no less —and he'd sit there and listen to their spiel for a half-hour. At least. Just so he didn't offend them. And another thing— the guy's got a thousand credit cards, you know that, right? Because he picks up the telemarketing calls and feels so bad for the reps, who are just trying to make their quota, that he signs up for the cards. Doesn't use any of them. He pays cash for everything. Bought his house with cash. Bet the guy has zero debt. Zero. Just signs up for the cards. He has so many of them that he doesn't have a wallet. He has a freaking backpack. Like the ones college kids use. A little North Face backpack for his thousand credit cards. Luke walks around Baltimore with his backpack, looking like he belongs over at the Johns Hopkins Student Union. Oh, and he has a pair of Heelys, too. He does Heelys outside the library. And he knows all these Heely tricks. And one more thing—he walks around with his Starbucks.

Okay? Always has his Starbucks in hand because, you know, who *doesn't* want to pay nearly three bucks for a small cup of joe?" The Ranger and Greg both laughed hysterically and clapped their hands.

Greg added, "The image of him doing Heelys will keep me smiling all day. We know the guy looks like Elvis. So, in my mind's eye, I'm now conjuring up this picture of Elvis in all his jump-suited glory, with big old gold rings on every finger and huge tinted sunglasses, doing Heely tricks. But I also imagine Luke being a member of The Columbia Record and Tape Club. Yeah, I'll bet you anything he got all caught up in that crap. I just hope he's not sending money to the Nigerian Prince. You know, the one who's always dying and wants to make you the sole heir of his substantial estate—but first needs you to send him five grand to cover taxes." Greg laughed heartily.

The Ranger chuckled and added, "Yeah. That son of a gun has been dying for decades now. Die already, will ya? There are people wanting to collect. And let's also hope Luke's not ordering those Kevin Trudeau books from the infomercials. Trudeau's in prison for fraud, yet, somehow, his infomercials live on. Go figure. So, anyhow, Hope, when you call Luke, you're going to tell him to tune in the show because you're dedicating a special song to him—is that it?"

"Basically. Yeah."

"Are you going to say anything else?"

"Um. Yeah. I'm…I'm actually going to kind of, sort of, maybe… ask him to have breakfast with me tomorrow morning."

There was excitement in The Ranger's voice. "You're going to ask him out on a date?"

"Well, it wouldn't really be a *date*. It would just be a way for me to say *thanks* and *I'm sorry*."

"Uh-huh. Uh-huh. This is good. This is very good. This is progressing nicely. All the stars are lining up. At this pace, we'll have a baby by next year. Ah…where you kids going? For breakfast, that is."

"I'd rather not say."

"Understand. Had to ask. Had to ask. They'd have never forgiven me if I didn't at least ask. But suffice it to say that you two will break bread together at some fine eatery here in the greater Baltimore metropolitan area, correct?"

"Assuming he accepts."

"Oh, he will. How could he not? You're adorable, Hope."

"You don't know how mean and nasty I can be. Like I said, I hurt bad and it comes out sometimes. And that's an understatement. I'm a lot different talking to you guys on the phone than I am talking to people in person. In a true one-on-one relationship, it's hard for me. Real hard. I'm actually a lot more comfortable talking to strangers on the radio than I am talking to the people of my life. You guys probably think I sound sweet and mild-mannered. Trust me, though, it's different in person. I can be a real monster when I have to deal with real people in real situations. I just can't help it. I know it but I still can't help it from happening. I turn into a monster. I wish it didn't have to be that way. But it seems like it always is."

"A monster, huh? Hopeenstein. Are you Hopeenstein? Or are you Countess Hopeula? Countess Hopeula actually sounds kind of sexy."

She giggled. "Ah, probably Hopeenstien. Either that or Hurricane Hope. And I'm always a Cat Five storm."

Greg laughed. "Dang. Cat Five? Evacuate the trailer parks."

The Ranger agreed. "Seriously. *Seri-ous-ly*. Those trailer parks don't survive even Cat One storms. Hell, some don't survive a gentle spring rain. Ah, anyway, getting back on topic —you have a song you want to send out to Luke, an *I'm sorry* song, correct? What song is it, sweetie?"

"Um, yeah, um, I want you to play *Hard To Say I'm Sorry* by Chicago."

"Perfect. Per. Fect. The single greatest *I'm sorry* song of all-freaking-time. Lots of couples kiss and make up—and do some other things—to that song. I kid you not, and I speak with firsthand knowledge. Chicago. Mister Peter Cetera. How great is he, by the way? The man's a national treasure, that's what he is."

"I like him. He has a beautiful and very distinctive voice," she offered.

"You bet he does," The Ranger agreed. "So, we're going to play this gosh darn tune for you. But we'll wait, give you five minutes to give Luke a buzz, and get him tuned in. How does that sound, sweetie?"

"Sounds great."

"Good enough. Now, can we ask you to call in tomorrow with an update? Let us know how this this-is-not-a-date-date went?"

"Um…well…"

"Hope, we're invested now. The city of Baltimore is invested. And, who knows? Maybe the rest of the country will start following this story. The rest of America perhaps will start paying attention. Because this story is a very *American* story. It's very Capra-esque. Do you love America, Hope? Do you *believe* in America? Do you?"

"Um. Yes. Yes, I do."

"Then you have a patriotic duty to call us. Don't give the red, white, and blue a black eye, kiddo. Please don't do that. Call us tomorrow. Your country needs you."

Hope heard *The Battle Hymn of the Republic* hummed by someone in the background.

"Okay. Sure, sure. I'll call tomorrow. I mean, I want to be a good American and all."

"Beautiful. Beaut-tee-full. Okay, honey, we're going to let you go. Five minutes from now, we'll play your song. If you need more time, call that direct line number, and let Mister Greg know. Kay, babe?"

"Yeah. Kay."

"Talk to you tomorrow, Hope. Thanks for joining us tonight. Feel better real soon."

"I hope to. Thanks."

CHAPTER SIX: I KNEW YOU HAD A PRETTY NAME

Hope retrieved a yellow Post-It note out of her purse. She looked at it, picked up her cellphone, and dialed the number written on the note. She took a deep breath. *Here goes nothing.*

On the third ring, he picked up. "Hello?"

"Hi. It's…it's me…Hope."

"Who?"

"Hope."

"I think you have the wrong number, ma'am. I don't know anyone named Hope. If you give me the name of the person you're looking for, maybe I can go online and try to help you find the right number. These days, you can pretty much find anything on anyone on the internet. Not sure that's always a good thing, but, hey, it is what it is, right? Technology's a double-edged sword, you know?" He chuckled.

God. This is what he does when he thinks someone has the wrong number? He Boy Scouts that, too? "It's Hope. You know—Hope Kennedy. *Officer* Hope Kennedy…of the Baltimore Police Department. Officer Kennedy."

There was a long, awkward pause on the line. *He's probably debating whether to hang up. Can't say I'd blame him if he did.*

Finally, he tentatively asked, "Your name's Hope?"

"Yeah. Hope. Uh-huh. That's my name. Don't wear it out."

"How'd you get my number?"

"I'm a cop. We kind of have access to information."

There was another pause. After a few seconds, he asked, "Well, what do you want? I've been cleared of all your false allegations."

"Yeah, well, do you have a radio?"

"I have a computer."

"Right. Well, go to the 104.5 FM website and click on their Listen Live option."

"Why?"

"Because you're going to hear a song, okay? A song that's kind of, sort of, for you. It's meant for you. All right?"

"What song?"

"Just tune in and listen, okay?"

"Ah…sure. Yeah. Okay. I can do that."

"Then after the song's over, call me back at this number because there's something that I need to ask you."

"Ah…Oh…oh…oh-kay."

"They're going to play the song real soon. So, hang up and just listen. Got it?"

"Yeah. Got it."

She hung up and turned the volume on her computer speakers back up.

After a lengthy commercial for a local business called Morrie's Hair Emporium, an establishment that sold expensive toupees, or as they called them—*Scalp Confidence Systems*—The Ranger came back on air and announced, "To Luke from Hope—she's sorry, dude. It's that simple. She wants to make it better between you and her. How about letting this catchy little tune from nineteen eighty-two start the healing? Chicago. Peter Cetera's Chicago, no less. *Hard To Say I'm Sorry.* It's fifteen minutes from the top of the hour. And you're listening to *The Midnight Ranger Show* here on 104.5. And that's no jive. Let's keep hope alive. What do you say, gang?"

The song played. *Such a pretty little song. God, that's pretty.*

After the song, she turned down the speakers and waited

for Luke to call. *Wonder if he'll even call back or just say the hell with it?*

Almost immediately, however, her ringtone—a chiming bell—went off.

"Hello?"

"Hey. It's Luke. Um. Thank you. For that song. Thank you for that song. That was beautiful. I love Peter Cetera. He has such a beautiful and distinctive voice. That really touched me. It, ah, it put tears in my eyes, in fact. That was a really nice way to say what you had on your mind."

She found herself falling into old habits. "Yeah, well, don't thank me. It was the DJ's idea. He pushed that song on me."

"Oh. I see."

"Look, I'm only doing this because I have to. I have to reach out to you and apologize for the way I dealt with you. My supervisor, Sergeant Harris, thinks that maybe I wasn't one-hundred percent right in terms of how I interacted with you. So, she required that I touch base with you. So, I'm touching base."

"Hmm. So, your supervisor didn't think you were a hundred percent in the right, huh? Well, what percentage right were you? Ninety percent? Seventy-five? Fifty percent? Half right, half wrong? What percent, Officer Kennedy? I really want to know. I want you to assign a number to it."

"What difference does it make?"

"All the difference, to me. Now, Officer Kennedy, tell me, what percent right were you?"

She loudly exhaled her frustration. "Fine. Zero. Okay? You happy now? *Zero*. According to my supervisor, I was zero percent right in my dealings with you. I shouldn't have given you a hard time that night in the alley. I shouldn't have pulled you over. I should have tested the catnip before accusing you of transporting drugs. And I should have…I should have… I should have thanked you, for, you know, what you did when the van rolled up on us. Which is why Harris made it mandatory that I contact you. So, I'm doing it. This is just about me doing what I need to do to avoid a suspension. That's it. Nothing more. It's not even about you. It's just about me."

"It seems like everything is just about you, huh? Me. Me—me—me. Those drill instructors at Parris Island would PT that *me* right out of you, lady. Believe that."

"You don't know anything about my life."

"I don't see how anyone is supposed to know anything. You're so nasty. Why would anyone want to stick around long enough to get to know you?"

"I didn't call you to get insulted. Things aren't easy for me right now. My rib is hurting. I have one that's broken. I'm going to be off work for a while, too. Plus, I'm on pain medication—Percocet. That's some heavy duty stuff to be on."

"You're lucky you're not *on* the embalmer's table. Now, *that* would be some real heavy duty stuff. And I'm on a pain med, too, because I have two fractured ribs. How about that? Yeah, because of you, I'm going to miss roughly four weeks of work myself. I do carpentry and construction work, and they're telling me that I'll have to be off for about a month. A whole month. Thank God for FMLA and Aflac."

"Yeah? Well, they're telling me that I'm out for two months."

"By all rights, you should be out for good."

"Look—just to show that I'm going above and beyond, I was going to ask you to breakfast tomorrow morning. My treat. At the hospital, they told me that I shouldn't just lay around. They don't want me to do anything strenuous, but don't want me laying around, either. So, I figure going out for breakfast is probably okay."

"Yeah. The doc I saw said the same thing. Ah, where? Where did you want to have breakfast?"

"Tiffany's Diner, on Loch Raven Boulevard. Diner food. Nothing fancy. If you're looking for brunch at The Brass Elephant, you're barking up the wrong tree. I'm a cop. Not rich. Not on food stamps, either. I get by. And the only reason I'm even doing this is that I have a two-for-one coupon. Buy one breakfast, get one free. BOGO. That's the only reason, buddy."

"I like Tiffany's. I eat there a lot. It's good food for the price. And it's great that you have a q-pon. Nothing wrong with using q-pons. I use them all the time to buy cat food."

"No. I have a *coupon*. Say it right. Come on. Say it right—coupon. Cou...pon."

"I am saying it right. Q-pon. Q. Pon. Q...pon. Q-pon."

"No. Coupon. *Cou. Pon.* Say it with me, Luke. *Cou. Pon.* Don't talk like a hillbilly, like somebody from Dundalk. That's my pet peeve. Come on, now."

" Q-Pon. *Q-pon*! There. I got it right that last time."

She stuck her tongue out at the phone before continuing. "Forget it. By the way—you probably also say *I could care less* when what you really mean is *I couldn't care less.* Yeah. You're probably one of *those* people."

"Not going to lie—I've said it before, but the incongruity isn't lost on me. And I have a pet peeve of my own. Yeah. I do. I can't stand the person who you get behind at that one red light—you know, the one that takes forever to change and only stays green for five seconds. And that person doesn't realize it's green because they're too busy texting. So, you beep your horn and they finally wake up. Just in time for *them* to make the light, but not in time for anybody else to. Yeah. That gets on my nerves. So, maybe *you're* one of *those* people."

"Am not. That irritates me, too, as a matter of fact. Anyhow —do you want to go or not?"

"Yeah. I'll go. Free meal? Yes, please. I won't turn down a free meal. I haven't had too many free meals since I left the Marine Corps. So, what time do you want me to pick you up and where do you live?"

"Pick me up? No, sweetheart, you ain't picking *me* up. We'll meet there."

"Well, I just figure if you're paying for our date, the least I could do is spring for the transportation. My SUV's in the body shop. It was almost totaled. They said they can fix it, but it's going to take a while. But the insurance company set me up with a big, sweet Lincoln Town Car. It's like riding on a magic carpet. The ride's as smooth as a baby's bottom."

"Date? *Date?* This is not a date, pal. This is not a candlelight dinner at the Oregon Grille. That would be a date. This is just breakfast at Tiffany's. And, honey, I'm not Audrey Hepburn and you *sure as hell* aren't George Peppard, so don't get any ideas."

"Well, George Peppard had blond hair. I have black hair. And you look more like Demi Lovato than Audrey—"

She cut him off. "Listen—we'll meet there, or I withdraw the invitation. And the whole damn thing will be off. *Capisce?*"

"That kind of hurts. I saved your life, after all, and yet you don't even trust me enough to let me pick you up. Of course, the night of the accident, I was good enough to pick you up, wasn't I? I was good enough to literally pick you up that night. It just kind of makes me feel bad because you obviously think I'm some kind of creep. But, hey, you know, that's okay. That's fine. I'll just—"

She again interrupted and talked through clinched teeth. "Fine. *Fine.* You want to pick me up? Pick me the hell up. Lincoln Town Car? Freaking awesome. I've always wanted to know what it feels like to be a seventy-year-old married couple cruising the streets of Sarasota, headed back to Serenity Towers. Anyway, I live at two-nine-five Bolton Place. That's in Mount Royal. Near the Maryland Institute of Art. Can't miss it. When you get close, you'll see a bunch of damn hippies from the Institute milling around. Loitering and such. Hell, if you're lucky, you might even get to see one of their freaking drum circles, where they all sit around and sing *Kumbaya.* They'll probably be smoking dope, too. I swear, you don't see them anywhere else in Baltimore. After all, why should they ever venture out of Mount Royal? It's become their own little paradise. They've taken over, playing their Bob Dylan music all loud. Burning their Costco cards and whatnot. It's the Maryland version of Woodstock. Anyway, my place is a townhouse. White with green trim. There's a big Minion flag and an American flag in the front yard."

He laughed. "Minions? You don't seem like someone who'd appreciate the Minions,"

"Not that it's any of your damn business, but I like the Minions. Okay? Bob's cute, with his little teddy bear and all."

"Sure. He's cute. I agree. See, we finally agree on something. Our relationship's progressing nicely."

"Yeah—yeah—yeah. What time you picking me up?"

"How about eight? Is eight too early?"

"No, that's fine. Eight's good."

"Hey, Officer Kennedy… can I just call you Hope? Calling you Officer Kennedy at this point would be kind of weird. We stared down death together, so I figure we should at least be on a first name basis, you know?"

"Sure. What the hell. Yeah. Call me Hope. Fine. Whatever."

"Okay, well, Hope…"

"What? *What?* What do you want now? Huh?"

"I just want to tell you that you have a really pretty name. I knew you would."

There was silence on the line for a few seconds.

Finally, she softly answered. "Yeah. Well. Whatever."

CHAPTER SEVEN: OUR TIME IN HELL

Luke got up at six thirty the following morning and immediately took some Ibuprofen for his pain. Despite the discomfort, he was excited. He showered, shaved, and applied his go-to cologne, CK Euphoria Intense.

Now, what to wear? What to wear on this non-date? He decided to go with blue jeans, sneakers, a white long sleeve polo shirt and a baby blue V-neck sweater. Everyone always said baby blue brought out his own blue eyes. He looked at himself in the mirror. *This is good. Not overdressed, but I don't look like a bum, either. Just right for the occasion.*

He fed the cats and scooped their litterboxes. It hurt to bend over.

It was still cold. The day's high was forecast to be only twenty, with a windchill that would make it feel like single digits. He grabbed his red, satin Marine Corps jacket. It was quilted on the inside and sported a yellow Marine emblem with the Marine Corps Motto—*Semper Fidelis* stitched below. He walked out the front door and the wind immediately smacked him in the face.

He drove his light blue Town Car rental slowly along Bolton Place, looking for Hope's house. He saw two guys in their early 20s with long hair. They both had on headbands and John Lennon glasses. Both were smoking. *Must be getting close. There's the hippies she was talking about.*

Finally, the car's GPS system alerted him—*destination ahead*. He saw the Minion flag and pulled into the driveway. *That Bob*

The Minion really is cute. It's his teddy bear that puts him over the top on the cuteness meter.

He walked up to the front door and rang the bell. She tentatively opened the door. He looked at her and smiled. She wore a white turtleneck underneath a pair of light blue denim overalls and white leather sneakers. Her hair was in a ponytail. She wore makeup but not a lot, just a little eyeliner and mascara. *Works for me. I like the natural look.* He caught a whiff of her perfume. *She wears Angel. Love it. Angel's the best. It's such a sexy fragrance.*

Her eyes were pools of blue, sky blue. They were nearly the same color as his own. *I love that combination of black hair and blue eyes. Very exotic looking.*

The next thing he noticed were her breasts. He could tell they were large. *Yes, indeed. She's stacked. I knew that bulletproof vest was hiding a significant amount of boobage.*

She had a new pair of glasses, too. They were identical to the ones that got trashed during the accident. *She must have a backup pair. That's good. She plans ahead. She's prepared. Good trait to have.*

She was holding a black leather jacket in her arms, along with her purse.

He cheerfully greeted her. "Hi there. You all full of life today, are you?" His misty breath cloud followed the words from his mouth.

She meekly waved and gave him an unemotional, "Hey. What's up?"

"You look really pretty. I love those overalls. They're adorable. It's like you have a little *Hee Haw* thing going on there. I like it. It's cute."

"Uh-huh. Let's go." She put her jacket on, slung her black leather purse over her shoulder, and started to walk out the door.

"Hey, wait a second. Don't I get a little tour of the old homestead, the Ponderosa Ranch?"

"No."

"Why not? Is it a pigpen in there? Is that it? Is it like *Hoarders* on steroids?"

"*Is not*. I'll have you know my house is immaculate. I'm very particular."

"Why then?"

"Because I don't want you to come in, that's why. Trust me, buddy—this is as close as you're ever going to get to the inside of my house. After this morning, I will have fulfilled all of my obligations to you, and we'll never see one another again."

"Well, never is a long time. And Baltimore's not that big of a city."

She walked out the door, closed it and locked up.

"Well? You ready or what?" she asked as she threw up her hands.

"Yeah. Sure. Let's go."

They walked to his car. There was plenty of snow still on the ground.

"Watch your step now. You don't want to slip," he cautioned.

"I know how to walk, thank you very much. I learned when I was eighteen months."

"Wow. Took you that long, huh? I was running marathons at eighteen months. Climbed Mount Everest when I turned two. Without supplemental oxygen, no less."

He laughed. She stared.

When they got to his car, he walked over to the passenger's side and opened it for her.

"What the hell do you think you're doing?"

"Opening a car door for you. Why? What's wrong?"

"I can open it myself."

"I realize that. But I wanted to do it *for* you."

"Why?"

"Because that's what a gentleman should do for a lady."

"You're weird, you know that? I've never had any guy open a door of any kind for me. Never."

"So then maybe they're the ones who are weird. These guys who don't open doors for ladies, that is. Ever think of it that way?"

"Don't do it anymore. I mean it. I don't like it."

"Look, I'm not trying to repeal the Nineteenth Amendment or your right to equal pay or anything like that. I was just trying to do something nice for you. That's all."

"Whatever. Let's go. Let's get this over with."

Once they were on the road, he announced, "We have a couple of little stops to make before Tiffany's."

"Stops? What kind of stops? I didn't sign up for *stops*"

"Won't take too long. Besides, Tiffany's serves breakfast until eleven."

"Well, I was planning on being home by eleven."

"And do what?"

"Watch *Maury.* That's one of my shows."

"Here. I'll give you a synopsis of today's episode—it's guys taking paternity tests so they can be told, on national television, whether they fathered a child. That's every damn episode of *Maury*. He's beat the topic to death. He really needs to move on. It's played. *So* played. And I really don't think it speaks well of our society that guys have to rely on Maury to tell them whether they're going to be a dad."

"So, where are we stopping?"

"Two places. We're going to Mondawmin, to feed the Mondawmin Seven. Those are the seven feral cats who you harassed me over that one night. I have some dry food and bowls for them in the trunk. I found out that dry food actually works better in this extreme cold. It doesn't freeze as fast as canned food. Then were going to stop over at The Mission. That's the soup kitchen, food bank, and shelter that the Little Sisters of the Poor run over on Piedmont Street. The homeless community refers to it as *Paradise* because it's one of the few places where they can go without having a ton of questions asked. The sisters don't care about someone's past—their criminal record, etcetera, etcetera. So, folks can get a hot meal and a warm bed without being hassled."

"So, in other words, these nuns are basically excusing a lot of bad behavior?"

He shook his head. "Not their place to either excuse or condemn it. They defer judgment all together. They defer to Someone Else. In the meantime, they try to help. Anyway, I have some canned food and pancake mix in the trunk. And I want to drop it off. I've been meaning to do it for a long time now."

He glanced over at her. She shook her head in disgust and told him, "If I'd known that I was going to have to help you earn your Eagle Scout Good Samaritan Merit Badge, I never would have invited you."

"It won't take that long."

She threw her hands up. "You're driving, so—whatever. I'm basically a hostage at this point."

He laughed. "Boy, you sure can be a drama queen when you want to be. A real diva."

She stared out her window. "I'm not talking to you at the moment."

He laughed louder. "You're only proving my point. Right now, you're like something right out of *The Real Housewives*. I'll bet anything you just love to throw drinks on people at cocktail parties, don't you?"

She didn't respond, but he noticed she turned a bit red.

After they got on the Jones Falls Expresway, she turned into a backseat driver. "*Slow. Down.* You're doing nearly seventy. We're going to get pulled over, and how will that look on me?"

"You know, the night of the accident you pulled me over because I was going too slow. Now, I'm going too fast for you. A little consistency would be nice."

"Just slow down a little. That's all I ask."

"Look, I'm an excellent driver," he assured her.

"Ah, *yeah*. That's exactly what Rain Man said, and he didn't even have a license."

He laughed. "Oh, good one. Wow. She actually has a sense of humor. How a-bout that, sports fans?"

She shot him a dirty look.

When they got to Mondawmin, he parked along Fulton Avenue, right next to the alley that the cats called home.

"I'm staying in the car," she announced.

"Why don't you help me feed? It won't bother your ribs. It's not physically challenging."

"I'd rather not. It's against the law. I could get into trouble. And I'm not throwing my career away. Besides, what if these cats have fleas? Or what if they have *rabies*?"

He rolled his eyes. "They do not have rabies or fleas. We humanely trap them, vaccinate them, and give them a flea and tick treatment while we're at it. Come on, Hope. Feeding them only takes a few minutes."

She crossed her arms and emphatically shook her head. "Nope. No can do. You can do it, that's fine. And I won't even make a big stink over it. But me help? No. Not going to happen."

"Geez. A fella saves your life, and you won't even help him feed a few cats. How's that for gratitude?"

She loudly exhaled. "Fine. I'll to it. You guilted me into it. Happy now?"

"It's only right. You tried to deny those cats their treats that one night."

"They got their treats."

"Still, you were mean. So, I say you're obligated to help feed them once. No one's asking you to do it every day. Just this one time."

"I already said I'd help. You've manipulated me into it."

"You know, you might actually enjoy it. It might be good for you."

They got out of the car. He intended to open her door for her, but she made it a point to quickly exit.

He put both hands in either pocket of his jeans, searching for change.

"What are you looking for? Huh?"

"Change to feed the meter." He pulled his hands out of his pockets empty. "Hey, um…can I borrow a quarter?"

She rolled her eyes but nonetheless dug into her purse,

found one, and handed it to him.

He inserted the coin into the parking meter. "Thanks. I'll get ya next payday."

He popped the trunk and retrieved a big bag of dry cat food and some foam bowls.

A few of the cats were already there, hanging out. Patiently waiting.

He shook the bag.

"They know this sound," he told her. "This sound means—breakfast is served. Cats are like that. They learn real quick what sounds are associated with food. Like can openers, for example. When you feed canned food at home and they hear that can opener they come run—"

She cut him off. "Yeah. I know. Okay? I know all about the can opener thing. It's called Pavlov's response"

"How would you know? You don't like cats. You said so yourself."

"Forget it. Let's just get this done. It's freezing out here."

He retrieved a gallon jug of spring water from the trunk. He handed it to her and issued instructions. "Give them some fresh water. You can use those old Cool Whip containers that are already sitting there. Those are our makeshift water bowls. The water will freeze in no time, but what are you going to do?"

Hope filled the water bowls.

It took a few minutes, but the cats all showed. Luke took a head count. "All present and accounted for." He felt relieved.

He told her the cats' names and a little something about each one as they ate. "That orange tabby over there—that's Daniel Striped Tiger. He got his name from the character on *Mister Rogers' Neighborhood.* You know, the little tiger who lived in the clock. He kind of looks like him." Luke smiled and called out to the cat, "Daniel. Hey, Daniel. Hey, DST. Oh, Danny boy." He quietly sang the opening bars of *Danny Boy* as the feline wolfed down his food.

Next, he called her attention to the gray tabby. "The one with the gray stripes—that's Basilone. I named him, named him after John Basilone. He was the famous Marine who won the Medal of Honor on Guadalcanal. Yeah, John Basilone—he actually lived right here in Baltimore before he joined the Corps. Bet you didn't know that, did you?"

She didn't answer.

He pointed out the large black and white short-hair. "Now, be careful around Sassy. She can be downright aggressive. Sometimes, you don't even have to do anything to provoke her. Looking at her the wrong way can trigger her. She'll just launch herself at you, like a little fur missile. Mind you, all these cats have trust issues. They've all been mistreated in some way. But something *really* awful must have happened to Sassy. And she's never gotten over it. And she takes it out on people, even ones who've done nothing to her."

He gave her a hard stare, their eyes met and for a few seconds there was silence, except for the sounds of the traffic on nearby Fulton Avenue.

Finally, he broke the quiet by pointing to Bunky, the young, handsome gray and white long-hair. "Now, Bunky here has the potential to become a lap cat. The rest of these guys—they've been feral too long. They'll probably never become domesticated. The reality is that they'll almost certainly die on the street. One-by-one, they'll disappear. One day they just won't show up for feeding. And we'll know. It's sad, tragic, in fact. Tragic that they'll never know what it feels like to receive love because they can't let their guard down. See, love requires trust. And these guys can't trust. That happens when something is isolated for too long, when something goes too long without attention, without affection. But Bunky? Bunky's shown promise. He's been letting me touch him a little recently. Not a whole lot, mind you. Just a quick pat on the head. Why don't you reach out and try to pet him, Hope? See how he likes you. He's an elite cat, after all. In fact, he's so elite that he actually *catches* the red dot. How about that, huh? So, you know, why not show him the love?"

She shook her head and crossed her arms. "No. No way. And

I'll bet anything *Bunky* smells *funky*."

Bunky walked up to Hope and rubbed up against her leg.

"Go away. Shoo. Go on. I'm not your mom. So… *shoo*."

The cat looked up at her and meowed.

Luke smiled. "Aw. He likes you. He's marking you as his person. That's what they're doing when they brush up against you like that. And he is most definitely marking you. Like it or not—Bunky's crushing on you. Big time."

"Yeah, well, I guess I'll have to get a restraining order against his creeping little butt, huh?"

"He'd be a lot of company for you."

"*What?* You think I'd even entertain the idea of adopting him? Ha! Never. Not on your life."

"Fine. Forget that I even mentioned it. I just thought that maybe you guys could help each other. After all, life is best managed as a team sport, at least that's how I see it. You could give him a good, warm home, with lots of love. And he, well, he could maybe help you find your humanity again."

She said nothing but glared at him for a few seconds.

They waited for the cats to finish eating and picked up the bowls.

He went back to the car and retrieved a green plastic bag from the trunk and started picking up trash.

She threw up her hands in disgust. "*Now* what are you doing? That's not even your trash. We picked up all the bowls. Why the hell are you picking up other people's garbage?"

"Because trash makes the place look trashy. Nobody likes trash. The cats don't like trash. I'm beautifying the city."

"You can't beautify this city, especially this part of the city. It's impossible. It's filthy. They call it *America's worst city* for a reason. And this is the worst neighborhood in the worst city. Hell, if America needed an enema, they'd stick the tip of it right into Mondawmin. And picking up a few liquor bottles in this alley isn't going to change that."

"No. You're wrong. Everything is beautiful, in its own way. Everything. Everything except for sandals on men. Those are really ugly. I've never owned a pair of sandals. Don't want to, either. Seriously, the only guy who ever had any business wearing sandals was Jesus. And you have to cut him some slack because he didn't have a car or anything. Heck, he couldn't even afford Uber. So, he was walking all over Palestine. It got hot and so forth. He needed something comfortable, something that breathed. So, I'll give him a pass on the whole sandal thing."

She shook her head but said nothing, just stood there with her hands on her hips.

Just then, an old man pushed a shopping cart into the alley. The cats scattered at the sound of the cart's wheels pushing their way along the pavement.

Hope announced, "Oh, Gawd. A bum. Straight ahead. And I've seen him around here before. He's an alcoholic, and I know I've seen heroin tracks on his arms. And I probably have even locked him up before. But I can't remember his name. Don't even make eye contact. Come on, Luke. Let's get out of here so we don't have to talk to him. It's already nine in the morning so I'm sure he's been drunk for quite a while now."

Luke stopped picking up trash and set the bag down. "Maybe I *want* to talk to him."

She sighed an exaggerated sigh, crossed her arms, and impatiently tapped her toe on the pavement. There was a pouty look on her face. *That look—it's actually kind of sexy.*

The old man approached them. He appeared to be in his 70s. He wore a pair of jeans riddled with holes. On his feet, were a cheap pair of white sneakers that were falling apart. His hair was gray, and he needed a shave. He wore a very lightweight red jacket.

In the top bin of his shopping cart, sat a near-empty bottle of Cisco along with a small boombox. On his head, he wore an old red ballcap that said—*The Few. The Proud. The Marines.*

Luke waved to him. "Hey there. How you doing, buddy?"

"Cold. That's how I'm doing. Ain't fit for man nor beast out here today, that's for sure." The old man looked at Hope, tipped his cap to her, and nodded. "Ma'am."

The old man smiled at Luke. He was missing most of his teeth. "Your girlfriend's very pretty, by the way."

"I am *not* his girlfriend."

Luke decided to have some fun with it. "Nope, not my girlfriend. My wife. Yes, sir, my wife. And we've got one in the oven, too."

She scowled at Luke. "In your dreams, pal. In. Your. Dreams. Your cake mix will never get into my oven, dear."

Luke laughed a nervous laugh and told the man, "This gal's a great little kidder—gets a real charge out of pretending that she doesn't even like me. Awesome sense of humor. And I, for one, adore that. She's a cute little thing, that's for sure. I always say—*she's no taller than a shotgun and just as noisy.* Yep, that's what I say, all right. But that's just one of the ten million things that I love about this lady."

There was awkward silence for a few seconds. Luke could tell that the old man didn't know what to make of them.

Luke took out his wallet and pulled out a twenty. He handed it to him. "I know it's not much, but I hope it helps."

Hope snatched the bill from the old man's hands and handed it back to Luke.

"He's a bum. And if you give him this twenty, he's just going to buy more booze. Hell, the liquor store's right next door, for God's sake. He can buy six or seven bottles of Cisco with a twenty. You're not helping him. You're enabling him. You're part of the problem."

He handed the bill back to the old man. "Don't mind her, sir."

He then turned his attention towards Hope and spoke sternly. "What he does with that money is between him and The Man. You understand me? Maybe he'll buy himself a sandwich and a cup of coffee. You don't know. Neither do I. But I do know this—it's my damn money, honey. My money. My choice. After all, we don't have a joint account just yet. Don't you ever do that again. Understand? That was beyond rude.

But I guess I shouldn't expect anything better from you, huh?"

"I'm just trying to help you. I'm sure you work hard for your money. I don't want to see you throw it away, that's all."

"It's none of your business. You didn't want me in your house? Well, I don't want you in my wallet."

Luke smiled at the old man. "Don't you pay any attention to her, buddy. She's got her own issues. Forget everything she just said. Now, you get yourself some chow with that twenty, okay?"

The old man nodded and put the bill in his pocket.

There was a period of silence. He and Luke stared at each other, as if they were two long-lost brothers being reunited.

Finally, the old man pointed to Luke's Marine Corps jacket. "You were in the Corps?"

"Yeah."

"Where abouts?"

"Afghanistan. Sangin. Twenty-ten."

"Oh, that was bad."

"Yeah, it was. Real bad. Lost a lot of friends over there. Good friends. Good men."

"Amen."

For several seconds, no one spoke. It was quiet, except for the wailing sirens of emergency vehicles in the background.

Finally, with tears running down his cheeks, Luke recited a verse. *"And when I get to the gates of Heaven. To Saint Peter I will tell. One more Marine reporting, sir. I've done my time in Hell."*

There was more silence.

Then the old man pointed to his cap. "I was in the Corps, too, you know."

"Oh yeah? Where abouts?"

"The Big Puddle. Hue City. Sixty-eight."

"Oh, that was bad."

There were tears in the old man's eyes. "Yeah, it was. Real bad. Lost a lot of friends over there. Good friends. Good men."

"Amen."

The old man spoke in a voice choked with emotion. *"And*

when I get to the gates of Heaven. To Saint Peter I will tell. One more Marine reporting, sir. I've done my time in Hell."

Luke stared at him, directly at him.

With his eyes still fixed on the old man, he heard Hope complaining. "Let's get out of here. I, I just want to go. Okay? Now, let's go. It's not safe here, even in daylight."

Luke stood at attention and smartly saluted him. The old man stood at attention, as best he could, and returned the salute.

"Semper Fi, buddy," Luke told him.

"Semper Fi, buddy."

Luke and Hope started to walk away. And the old man continued to push his cart down the alley.

Luke stopped, turned around, and walked back over to him. He took off his warm, quilted Marine Corps jacket—his favorite jacket.

He tossed it to the old man. "Here you go. You need it more than I do. And you've earned the right to wear it."

He caught it and immediately put it on.

"God bless you, son."

"God bless you, my friend."

CHAPTER EIGHT: THE GOOD THIEF

When they got back to the car, he rushed to the passenger's side and opened the door for her. She loudly exhaled her disgust but said nothing. Once they were both in the vehicle, she started on him.

"Well, you just fed that bum's drug and alcohol habit. You gave him fifty dollars, and I suspect he'll split it fifty-fifty between booze and dope."

"I did not give him fifty. I gave him a twenty."

"Yes. And you gave him the jacket. A nice jacket. Satin and nice embroidery. Obviously, had a lot of sentimental value. Well, honey, to him it's just drug or booze money. The way this will go down is—he'll sell the jacket at some makeshift, street corner rummage sale. He'll get a fraction of its value. I'm saying that jacket is worth a buck, maybe even a buck fifty. Yeah, well, he'll get twenty-five for it. Add that to the Jackson you gave him and that's forty-five. But let's just make it a nice round number, shall we? So, that puts it at fifty."

"Your math makes a lot of assumptions. I could just as easily say he'll keep the jacket to stay warm. And that the Jackson buys him maybe three or four meals."

"You don't know how the streets work. I do. I deal with these people every day. Addictions are powerful things. And you indulged his. You're not even helping him. You're just giving him more bullets for the gun that he's playing Russian roulette with."

"We see the world very differently, Hope. You ask—*why?* I

ask—w*hy not?"*

"You're foolish. I recognize the way the world works, that's all. And it's not pretty. It's ugly. Very ugly. You know, I'm not even convinced that he was in the Marines. He could have gotten that cap anywhere."

"You're full of shit, and pardon my language, but you are. He's a Marine. And you never stop being a Marine. Once you earn the title, it's yours for life. So, he still is one. I know he is. He had The Stare."

"What's The Stare?"

"The Thousand Yard Stare. Marines get it once they've been in The Shit. You're living so close to death that you can almost see into the next world, into eternity. It's real, and he had it. And you can't fake it."

She dismissively waved her hand at him. "Yeah. Well. Whatever."

"We're not going to agree on this. Let's stop trying, okay? Fair enough?"

She shrugged and spoke curtly. "Yeah. I guess."

He reached up onto the dashboard and retrieved a CD case. He held it up for her to see. "Check this out—*Sounds of the Eighties*. I dig eighties music."

"It's kind of ancient history. We weren't even alive in the eighties, but I do like some of it."

"My dad got me into it. He said it was the best time to be alive because they had modern conveniences and such, but technology didn't dominate people, like it does now. It was just kind of a happy medium."

"I've never really thought about it. I try to accept the terms of the time that I live in. You, however, seem to want to live in the Middle Ages, the time when knights rode their fiery steeds, and rescued the damsels in distress from the clutches of fire-breathing dragons. And righted all the wrongs. You were born about a thousand years too late for that. There are no knights. No damsels. There never were fire-breathing dragons. It was really all a myth to begin with. All of it. But you want to make dirty, filthy Baltimore into some modern-day Camelot. Ever heard of Don Quixote?"

"Yeah, I've heard of him. I've never read the book, though."

"I did. Eleventh grade. AP English. Saint Paul's School For Girls. It was a satire, not an homage. Cervantes was making fun of him, showing that he was a fool. Not a hero but a fool. He was a fool because he couldn't accept reality. Neither can you."

"Whatever. Let's just listen to some tunes. Let's move on, shall we? It's over. Done with. If that old guy scammed me, then he scammed me. He'll have to answer for it. But I don't think he scammed me at all. I think he was tickled that someone cared about his wartime experience. Back when it was fresh, nobody cared, that's for sure. Those Vietnam vets got treated like shit. It was wrong. Beyond wrong. Anyway, let's not talk about it anymore. It's getting my blood pressure up. I can tell because I'm starting with a terrific headache."

"Fine. I was just trying to help, but you obviously don't want my help, so I won't bring it up again."

"Let's just relax to the classic sounds of the eighties. Soothing sounds."

"Sure. Why not? Put the damn CD in."

He started the car and inserted the disk. The opening notes of the first song played. As they did, he glanced over at her, smiled, nodded, and raised his eyebrows. "*All I Wanna do is Make Love to You.* What do you think about that, huh? What do you say?"

"Ah. *Excuse me?*" *What the hell?*

He repeated himself. "I said—*All I Wanna do is Make Love to You.*"

Huh? Is he serious? She looked at him with her mouth wide open.

He laughed. "The song, Hope. The song. By Heart. It's called *All I Wanna do is Make Love to You.* And, technically, it was recorded in nineteen-ninety. So, I guess they weren't real sticklers for the dates on this CD."

"Oh, you jerk. You did that on purpose, just to mess with

me." She reached over and playfully smacked his arm.

"Maybe." He started to drive. "By the way, I need a cop. I want to press charges because—what you just did—that's assault." He cackled.

She pulled out some pepper spray from her purse and held it up. "Yeah, well, here's your pepper to go with that assault. You want a spray?" She stuck her tongue out at him and blew raspberries.

He laughed.

"I'll get back at you, buddy," she promised.

"Go for it."

"I will. You can count on it. And when you least expect it—expect it."

"What would you have said if I hadn't been joking?"

"Yeah. Well. Whatever."

"You say that a lot when questions are posed that you're not comfortable with. I've noticed that. See, I'm a keen observer of human behavior."

"Yeah. Uh-huh. I'm sure."

He continued to make his point. "And the whole *yeah—well—whatever* thing is something that you say whenever something is said that you don't want to address. It doesn't even have to be a question. It could just be a statement. You know all this, don't you? That's like your version of *no comment.* That's what the politicians always say when they don't want to talk about something. *No comment.* But you say *Yeah. Well. Whatever.* So, I guess you're not going to share what you were really thinking during those two or three seconds that I had you going, huh? Because, surely, some things were going through your mind."

She said nothing but felt warmth on her cheeks. *Oh, great. I'm blushing.*

She hung her head, hoping that he wouldn't notice or at least wouldn't say anything.

No such luck.

"Aw. She's blushing. Hope's blushing. That's cute."

She raised her head and looked straight ahead. "Leave me alone, please."

"It's all good. I won't put you on the spot anymore. I promise. Now, on to the Piedmont Street Mission."

When they arrived at the soup kitchen, Hope crossed her arms and declared, "I'm staying in the car this time. I mean it. I am."

"No. Come on. Come in. It'll be good for you."

"I feel like you put pressure on me to be someone I'm not."

"The first thing I ever learned in the Marines was that you don't grow as a person without pressure. That's what Parris Island is all about. Those guys in the Smokey The Bears putting enormous pressure on you twenty-four-seven. But it really does work. In thirteen weeks, childish boys are transformed into men. Into Marines."

"Well, I'm not trying to be a Marine. And are you saying I'm childish?"

He shook his head. "I'm saying that I accept you for who you are. But I want to see you be the person who I know you can be. And maybe you can help me be the person that I can be, too. Maybe we can help each other. Now, please come in with me. It won't take long. Please."

He flashed her his puppy dog eyes.

Those eyes. Those eyes get to me. They just do. I can't help it. "Fine. In and out, right?"

"Yep. In and out. We'll just drop off the food and then be on our way to the diner."

He retrieved the donations from the trunk, and they walked in through the front door. Outside the main entrance, a large crowd milled around smoking, despite there being a large *No Smoking* sign on the front of the building.

In the lobby, there was a large mural of Jesus feeding the multitude. Above it, were the words *Blessed Are Those Who Hunger, For They Shall Be Filled.*

It was an old building. Dingy and even a little dirty. It smelled of strong coffee, pancakes, and sausage. Hope took a big whiff. *Pancakes and sausage. Smells good. I think that's what I'll have at Tiffany's.*

There was a long line to pick up food. Donation drop-offs were self-service, but Luke wanted to wait until one of the nuns freed up.

"These nuns—they make cookies during the holidays. They're great. Wonderful Snickerdoodles. I think they use a little bit of rum in them, too. I'm not a drinker at all but it does add a nice little kick. And they put them in these really nice decorative tins. Anyway, I've heard they're going to start making them year round. I want to ask about that. I want to see how I can go about ordering. You mind if we wait?"

She shrugged. "You're driving, so I have no control. Why are you even asking?"

"To be polite."

She threw her hands up. "Fine. We'll wait so you can get your freaking cookies. Maybe you can even go out and get yourself a dairy cow, so you can enjoy some nice fresh milk with those cookies."

"Don't be silly. I can't have a cow. My property isn't zoned for agricultural use. At least it wasn't the last time I looked into it."

She ignored him, crossed her arms, and looked down at her shoes. She was disappointed to see that her new, expensive sneakers had acquired their first scuff mark. *Damn. Well that sucks. But it was bound to happen. They can only be perfect for so long.*

She looked up, and then she saw him. No more than thirty feet away. Sal Rossi. He was a mobster. A member of Tommy Tennuchi's crew. Sal was the designated thief of the outfit. He'd steal anything of value. Anything. Sal even looked the part. He just looked like a mobster. He had a dark complexion and a prominent Roman nose. His hair was black and lush—no sign of gray, despite the fact that he was in his fifties. Hope was certain he dyed it.

She whispered to Luke. "See that short little guy in the pickup line? The one wearing the baggy track suit and the Pumas. All the gaudy jewelry. Toothpick jutting out of his mouth. Looks like a mafioso. You see him?"

"Yeah, I see him. He does look like a wise guy. And he has very nice hair. Most mobsters do, in fact. John Gotti—a fine head of hair on that man. Tommy from *Goodfellas*—great hair. Michael Corleone—marvelous hair. Bugsy Segal—pretty fair hair. Paulie from *Goodfellas*—again, good hair. For whatever reason, a lot of them seem to have that Stalin hair going on. Of course, Tony Soprano was bald. Still, I'm going to call him an outlier. Yeah, it's very rare that you see a bald gangster. That's the only good thing you can really say about them. Mostly, they're just jerks...except that they tend to have nice hair."

"Yeah, well, this guy's the jerk of all jerks. Name's Sal Rossi. And he doesn't just look like a mobster. He *is* one. A made man, no less. Works for Tommy Tennuchi, Two-Time Tommy, as they call him on the street. Tommy says everything twice, repeats all of his orders because he lacks even the most basic confidence in his own people. He worries that they won't hear him right or whatever. Anyhow, Sal's a member of his crew. And Sal steals. It's that simple. He just steals. It's what he does. And he will literally steal anything of value. Anything. No scruples about it, either. He once stole a blind man's guide dog because the dog was a Keeshond. A purebred Keeshond. And somebody was looking for one and was willing to pay big bucks. So, Sal stole a blind man's dog. He's a walking, talking piece of shit. He even stole from me."

"Stole from you?"

"That's right. A year ago, I was in Donnie's Donuts getting some coffee and donuts—okay?"

He chuckled.

"What's so funny?"

He shrugged. "I don't know. It's just...a cop...in a donut shop...getting donuts and coffee."

"We have to eat like everyone else."

"Right. But it *had* to be donuts and coffee? I just find it a little amusing. You couldn't have stopped at a burger joint for a burger and fries? No. That would have been no good. Had to be a donut shop. It's just funny, that's all. But, anyway, continue with the story. Please."

She shot him a dirty look. "Right. So, I dropped a twenty. Sal was right behind me. I'm sure he pocketed it before I even knew it was on the floor. He was that fast about it. Literally, within two seconds of that Jackson hitting the floor, it was home in Sal's pocket. He has a talent for swiping things. He's good at it. He is. Anyway, I know other customers saw him do it, too. But who's going to rat on one of Tennuchi's boys? Nobody. That's who."

"Are you sure he's the one who got it?"

"Sure I'm sure. I'm a cop, a cop who has great instincts."

"Yeah. Great instincts. Instincts that told you catnip was pot."

"How many more times are you going to throw that up in my face, huh? I was wrong. I admit it. I should have tested it first. I screwed up. I got cocky. Okay? There you go. Happy now? And I got chewed out by my boss. And I've been chewed out by you. And I am being punished because, after all, I'm only here with you right now because I screwed up. Being out with you today—that's my punishment."

He turned serious. "Okay. I won't mention it again. It's in the past. And I'm trying to let go of the past. Really trying. And, ah, if you're only here with me because of that little unfortunate incident, well, then, maybe I'm kind of glad that you messed up."

She crossed her arms and wrinkled her nose. "What? What are you even talking about?"

He ignored her question and looked at Sal. "This Rossi guy—what's he doing here?"

She shrugged. "How the hell should I know? I actually haven't seen him on the street in a couple of months. I've locked him up a few times over the last three years for various things but he always beat the rap. Ritchie Bonnaselli, Tennuchi 's mouthpiece, always got him off. Always found some loophole. And when he couldn't do that, they'd just buy people off. Judges, cops. Jurors. Sal's a big earner, so they've always been more than willing to pay to keep him on the streets."

"You mean to tell me that the mafia can still buy people off? I thought that ended decades ago."

She shook her head in disgust. "So naïve. Do you still believe in the Easter Bunny? The Tooth Fairy? You know, I'd bet anything that if the freaking Moonies called you, you'd sit there and listen to their sales pitch, so as not to offend them because, God forbid, any of us should oh-fend the Moonies."

He focused on Sal's appearance. "I don't know what this guy's supposed to look like, but, to me, he doesn't look so good. Looks like hell, in fact. Like death warmed over. Look—he even has one of those portable oxygen units slung over his shoulder."

She nodded agreement. "Yeah, he does. And he's thin. Way thin. Notice how his track suit looks too big? All baggy on him and whatnot. Last time I saw him, I'd say he was at least thirty pounds heavier, maybe even forty. He's kind of frail looking, too. Haggard even. No matter—I hate him. I absolutely hate him. He's pure evil. And he hates me, too. He's made that clear. Always calling me names. Dirty, filthy names. He's nasty to his core."

"Well, don't look now but he's headed this way. And whatever you do—don't tell him to go home and get his shine box." He laughed heartily at his own joke.

She stared Sal down as he approached. *I don't care if this is a soup kitchen run by a bunch of nuns. I'm not going to back down if he starts something.*

Sal walked right up to her with a bag of groceries in one hand. He extended his free hand. "Hey, Officer Kennedy. Officer Hope Kennedy, one of Baltimore's finest. How ya doin' there, huh?"

She ignored his extended hand. He awkwardly withdrew it.

She wasted no time laying into him. "Oh, so today it's *Officer*

Kennedy? What about your usual pet names for me, Sal? You know—*pig, oinker, bitch, slut, whore, cunt.* What happened to those names? I'm getting all nostalgic for that stuff. And where you been? Bet it's been at least six weeks since I last saw you hustle. Your previous record was six seconds."

"Yeah, well, I don't work for Tommy no more. I kind of got fired. That's why I'm here, gettin' free food and whatnot."

"What? Did Tommy find out you were skimming off the top?"

"Nah, he never found out about that shit. Hell, he would have had me whacked over that. The truth of the matter is that I got sick. And, well, Tommy, you know, he don't have no sick leave or ah—oh—what do they call that thing? Government program. Oh, I know—FMLA. Yeah. That's it. FMLA. He don't participate in that program. So, when I got sick, he just cut me loose. Just like that. Worked for the guy for somethin' like twenty-five years. Helped make that bastard rich, too. But all he did was pat me on the back and say—*yeah, Sal. We had a few laughs. Made some dough. Banged a few broads. Did some good coke. But, ah, you know, good riddance to ya. Cuz business is business. Can't use ya no more.* Hey, I understand. That's how this line of work works."

"Please, Sal, tell me you're dying. That would just make my freaking day," she said.

"Yeah, well, as a matter of fact, I found out recently that, you know, that I kind of have the Big C. All that smoking. Been smoking since I was twelve. I'm fifty-two now. Three packs a day. Do the math, you know? Literally, almost a million cigarettes. So, it was just a matter of time. Anyhow, they say I have stage four lung cancer. I knew there was something wrong. Losing weight left and right. Couldn't stop coughing. Tired. All that shit. Hey, wise guys get cancer, too. That's what sent both Capone and Gotti to the Big Casino in the Sky. They give me anywhere from six months to a year. Tops. And I aint even gonna go down the route of chemo cuz, you know, it ain't likely to help much and I don't want to lose my hair. What can

I say? Among my other faults, I'm vain."

"You looking for sympathy from me? Because I honestly think that the world will be a better place once you're gone."

"Yeah. I know. I deserve that. I do. I ain't been such a good guy. And I know I made your life hell. Made you do all that paperwork. And I know how much you hate paperwork." Sal laughed before continuing. "You always told me that. You always said—*Sal, you're making me do all this damn paperwork.* And you was right."

"I can't stand you, Sal. You make me sick. You can go to Hell, as far as I'm concerned."

"And I deserve that, too. I do. I ain't mad at you for feeling that way. It's the right way to feel, under the circumstances. Did you know that I used to steal flowers off graves? Yeah, I did. Pretty sleezy, huh? But they had tremendous resale value if you got 'em while they were still fresh. Like, *right* after the service. I made a bundle off that shit. But my favorite criminal activity was fixing the horse races. Made me feel like God, which I ain't, by the way. Just in case you had any doubts. But it was like I knew something that would happen in the future that nobody else knew. That's God, right? I fixed The Million Dollar Stakes over at Chesapeake Downs that one year. Everybody had *Beth I Hear You Calling* winning. Well, he should have. He was easily the best horse in the field. I always liked his name, by the way. I believe the owner must have been a fan of that little song by that one rock band. Oh, what's their name? The ones who wear the makeup, like every day's Halloween and whatnot. I think they might still be around, actually. Is it HUG? Is that the name of the group? HUG?"

Luke spoke up. "KISS. The name of the band is—KISS."

Sal snapped his fingers and pointed at him. "Right. That's right. Not HUG but KISS. Anyhow, I fixed it so that a fifty-to-one shot named *Mister Roper's Smile* won. Fifty-to-one! Oh, Tommy was tickled over that. He was all giddy and shit after that race cuz, you know, we all won a bundle. Tommy was gigglin' like a schoolgirl who just got her first kiss. He even gave me a little bonus for my work on that one, and Tommy never gives bonuses. A brick of twenties is what I got. Also, he gave me a nice *thank you* card, a very nice Hallmark card. Must have cost five bucks. Five bucks. Just for a freakin' card." Sal paused and thought for a moment before adding, "Aw, who am I kiddin? He didn't pay for that card. Nah, that card was stolen, like everything else. But stolen card aside, it was my proudest moment. Really, it was…except, except that I ain't too proud of it now. I ain't too proud of none of that shit, now."

Sal pulled out his wallet and took out a five dollar bill. "Look, Officer Kennedy, I have a confession to make. A year ago. Donnie's Donuts. Woodlawn Avenue. You dropped a Jackson and I swiped it. I did. That bill was almost literally in my pocket before it hit the floor. What can I say? I was good at what I did, you know? Had a gift for it. A gift, I tell ya. I bought three dozen donuts with that money. And, don't you know, they were stale? Donnie swindled me. Well, it wasn't my money. So, I guess he really swindled you. I think they were day-olders. I really do. The donuts, that is. Anyway, I ain't doin' that shit no more. And I'm trying to make things right for everyone who I didn't treat so right. And, with the type of interest that Tommy charges, I really should owe you about five-hundred bucks by now. But five is all I got, on account of losing my job with Tommy and all. And it's not like I saved my money. I threw it all away, is what I did with it. But, here, Officer Kennedy, this is all I got to my name right now, but I want you to have it. I want to make it right for you. Or as right as it can possibly be under the present circumstances. And I'm gonna say two little words that I aint said nearly enough in my life—I'm sorry. Sorry for everything. Truly, *I'm sorry.*"

He held the bill out for Hope.

She grabbed it, tore it up, and threw it in the air like confetti. "Fuck. You." She flipped him the double bird.

Luke intervened. "Hey, come on, Hope. People are starting to stare."

"I don't care, Luke. I want the world to know what a piece of shit this guy is. And yet he thinks handing me a goddamn five dollar bill in some soup kitchen is going to buy him sympathy? Hell. No."

Sal shrugged. "Yeah. You're right. I hate me, too, and I think I'm supposed to be biased in my favor or something. I don't know. But I ain't been such a good guy. Never. Even when I was just a wee little wise guy, I was a knucklehead. What are ya going to do? The past is the past. I think that's why they call it *the past*. Now, I aint got nothin' so I have to come here for food and shit." Sal looked down at the rings on his fingers and held up his free hand. "These rings, by the way—fake. Made in Bangladesh. They make my fingers turn green, is what they do. I had to sell the real ones to the pawn shop. Got pennies on the dollar. They robbed me blind. But, hey, I robbed them blind, too. So, I guess it all came out in the wash. Now, I'm just another hobo. A hobo originally from Hoboken. Yeah, how about that? I was born in Hoboken, New Jersey. Moved here to Charm City in eighty-two. Kind of fitting that now I'm a hobo, right? A penniless hobo. I have to come to this place for my daily bread and so forth just like all the other bums."

She was seething. "You're lucky I don't run this place. You wouldn't be getting shit from me."

"Yeah, I wouldn't give to me, neither. I pissed away everything I had on blackjack, whores, strippers, booze, cocaine. I never was a good blackjack player, either. Played by my gut, instead of my head. Big mistake. I'd always hit on seventeen and shit, thinkin' that I'd pull a four or whatnot. It rarely never happened."

"Yeah, well, you're about as smart as Danny Bonaduce is handsome. You know that, don't you?"

"Yeah. Bonaduce's an ugly man. I used to see him in casinos. He likes to play poker. He had a restraining order against me at one point. Anyway, when I was waiting for one of the five dozen tests that they run on you to confirm you got the Big C, I found this book in the Mercy Medical Center waiting room. And I'll admit it—it was the freaking Bible, okay? Well, Sal

Rossi don't know nothin' about that book. Don't know much about any book, really. Never a big reader. Porn watcher? Yes. Definitely. But reader? Nah. Not so much. So, what the hell —I pick this book up because I got time to kill, you know? Of course, now…time's killing me. Anyhow, this book aint got no—oh—what do they call them things? When you find out ahead of time what's gonna happen in a story. What do they call them things?"

Luke chimed in. "Spoilers?"

"Yes. That's it. Thank you. Spoilers. There aint no spoilers for a guy like me, since I never read it before. And I've never even read any reviews of it on Amazon or whatnot. And it wasn't like the people who I worked with were ever gonna talk about it at the office water cooler. Technically, I was baptized Catlick, but my favorite denomination has always been hundreds. Anyhow, I ain't been inside a church since Elvis was alive." Sal chuckled, looked at Luke, and again pointed to him. "Speakin' of Elvis—you're the spitting image of that cat, you know that, right? You have to. I'm sure the ladies let you know. Yeah, you're a pretty man. And I always liked Elvis. I listened to Sinatra but, deep down, admired Elvis. He did nice things for people. Like a superhero. Right out of the blue— *Shazam.* He'd appear out of nowhere, buying old ladies Cadillacs and such. With all that dough and power, he could have been content to be a jerk. But he wasn't. He was a stand-up kind of guy. And you know, I always liked that one little song of his. The *Wise Men Say* song. Oh, what's the official name of that song?"

Luke again helped him out. *"Can't Help Falling in Love."*

"Yeah. That one. When I was a knucklehead, which was up until very recently, by the way, I was too…too macho, too full of myself, to admit that that little song kind of got to me. Then the other day, I was over at the public lie-barry, on the in-tra-net. Cuz, you know, I ain't got it at home no more. And that little song got into my head. So, I went to that YouTube thingy and looked it up. Yeah. I looked it up. Found it, too. And I listened to it. And, it was the damnedest thing because when I heard it—something got into my eyes. I think somebody must have been slicin' onions. I mean—it wasn't like I was cryin' or nothin' because Sal Rossi don't cry. That's just basic science. But somethin' happened. Yeah. Somethin' happened."

Sal looked at Hope and smiled. "So, anyhow, you did all right for yourself, girl. Bagged you an Elvis." Sal nodded. "That's what's up. That's what's up."

"Screw you. And I am *not* his girlfriend."

Luke chastised her. "Your behavior's inappropriate, Hope. Totally inappropriate."

She glared at Luke and gave him the evil eye. "My behavior? *My behavior?* The man stole a blind man's guide dog, for God's sake. And yet, you're talking about *my behavior?*"

For a couple of seconds, there was a pause, and nothing was said.

Finally, Sal cleared his voice and continued with his story. "Yeah, anyhow, this book, this Bible—I picked it up and just opened it. Just randomly opened it, kind of right in the middle portion. See, on the rare occasions when I do read, I always hate startin' at the beginning of a book. I like to give myself a head start. It doesn't seem so daunting that way. So, I opened it up and just started reading. And I find it quite in-ter-rest-ing, too." Sal pointed to Luke and wagged his finger at him. "Officer Kennedy here called you *Luke.* Well, the very story I was readin' was in this chapter written by Luke. How about that, huh? You're a Luke. The cat who wrote this was a Luke. Anyhow the story—it was about this guy, see? And he wasn't such a good guy. A lot like me— a bad guy. Terrible guy, in fact. He was a thief. Stole anything and everything. Just like me. Finally! Someone I can i-dent-ti-fy with. Anyway, he was gettin' ready to check out. Just like me. And he was bein' executed by the long arm of the law. That's what was goin' on. And he deserved it, too. He was finally paying The Man. If you wanna dance, you gotta pay the band. And if you wanna steal, one day, you're gonna have to pay The Man. See, I guess this guy didn't have no Ritchie Bonnaselli to get him off, like I always did. So, he was with these two other guys and they were bein' executed, too. One was a bad guy, just like him. But the other guy? Nah. The other guy didn't belong there. He didn't do nuthin'. Well, no, wait—that ain't really true. Let me rephrase that. Okay—he *did* do some things. He did. He wasn't just sittin' back playin' his slot machine or what have you. But, ah, the things he was doin'—not really bad things. Hell, some might, conceivably, say that he was doin' good things. See, unlike me, this guy wasn't a fool. I always put my faith in the Godfather. But this guy bet on the right horse. Because he put his faith in *God* The Father. But none of that mattered. Don't know why it didn't matter. But it didn't. What the hell. It was what it was. They had it in for him, I guess. Simple as that. Happens sometimes. Some people hate just to hate. Very true. I've been guilty of that one myself. So, anyway, this one bad guy says to the innocent guy—*listen, somethin' just kind of tells me that you have some connections. Maybe not on this side. In this world, your sorry ass is as done as mine. But, you know, maybe on the Other Side—that's where you might have them connections. And, not for nuthin', but could you kind of, sort of, cut me some slack? I ain't been such a good guy and all. Might need some slack. Matter of fact—I'm sure I do.* And, so, the guy who has no business being in that position because, you know, he didn't do *shit*—he says—*yeah, sure. What the hell? I'll cut you some slack. It'll be like you wasn't such a prick. Even though you was a prick. And I know it. And you know it. Hell, everybody knows it. But it'll be like you wasn't. Okay? And you don't even owe me nuthin' for my trouble.* And that's the story. The End. That's kind of where the credits roll and all. And, I have to tell you, I was curious about what else might be in that book. So, I, ah, I actually swiped it. I did. Please, Officer Kennedy, I'd appreciate you not breaking my balls over this one because I didn't sell it. I just use it for my own enrichment, as they say. But I did swipe it. Old habits die hard—know what I mean? What can I say? I'm good at it. But I'm just thinkin' maybe there's other decent stories in this book, too. So, I'm readin' the friggin' book. What the hell. What do I got to lose at this point? Only my life, right? But I sure hope that that one story is true." Sal and Hope's eyes met. There were tears in his. "Because it kind of gives me hope."

Sal turned his attention to Luke. "I have a question, but I aint' gonna ask your girlfriend, here. Because her and me? Well, we have this history, see? So, she's biased. She should be, too. Has every right to be, in fact. Cuz I've been a real POS and a thorn in her side. The worst of the worst—that's me. The only thing I can really say for myself is that I ain't never killed nobody. Well, I didn't have to. It wasn't my job. See, I wasn't a hitman. I was the designated thief of the outfit. We were almost like a regular company. Different departments and whatnot. Yeah, we were highly organized. Come to think of it— that might be why they call it *organized crime.* Yeah, I'll bet it is. And I always wondered where that term came from. Anyhow, other than murder and rape—I've done it all. Well, not really true. No kiddie porn, either. But, still, a real royal piece of shit. She ain't wrong about me, that's for sure, ain't makin' it up. That thing she was mentioning about me stealing the blind man's dog—true. Very true. At the time, I didn't feel the least bit guilty about it, neither. So, her and me? We have this history, as they say. But you and me? We ain't got no history. So, I'll ask you, and I'd be very in-ter-rest-ed to hear what you have to say, too, since your name is Luke, same as the cat who wrote that story I was talkin' about. And I only want the Truth. I can take it. So, what say you, Luke? *Luke who has Hope.* Where am I headed, when I check out, that is? North or South? I mean, I'm hopin' that I'm not headed South because, you know, it gets hot down there and all. Real hot. And I sweat like a pig."

Luke looked at her.

She intently stared him down. *Do not side with this asshole. You'd better not, pal.*

Luke cleared his voice. "Sal, where are you now?"

Sal looked around. "You mean right this very second? Is this some kind of trick question? Cuz I ain't good at trick questions. They tend to trick me. Just like I find that stress stresses me out. Heat makes me hot. Etcetera. Etcetera. Funny how that shit works, huh?"

"No. No tricks. I promise. Where are you?"

"At The Mission. The Piedmont Street Mission. Us bums call it...Paradise."

"Then that's where you'll be. That very day, *that's* where you'll be. You just answered your own question."

Sal smiled, turned, and started to walk away. Just as he got to the front door, he turned back around and addressed Hope. "I ain't a good guy, and I ain't known too many good guys. I was always in with the bad guys. Wore the black hat. By choice, I wore the black hat. Nobody made me. My choice. Simple as that." He pointed to Luke. "And that's why he stands out. Contrasts, as they say. He's a study in contrasts. Look at me—using these big fancy words and phrases. Anyhow, he wears a white hat. Well, he ain't wearing any hat right now. When you got nice hair, you don't really want to hide it under no hat. But I'm talking as a figurative of speech, here. I'm takin' like a learned man. Which I ain't, by the way. But back to my point. And I *do* have one. Anyhow, you two should...you know...you two should...you just *should*. I think He'd like that. I think that'd make Him happy. I feel it in my bones, and I don't think it's the cancer spreadin', neither. And when you do, play that little song, will ya? The *Wise Men Say* song. Because it's a bee-u-tee-full little song and all. Make it you alls song. And have a kid or two while you're at it. Yeah, do that. They'd be good-lookin' kids. After all, Hope, you're a gorgeous young woman. And Luke, you look like Elvis. Young Elvis, no less. I mean, we ain't even talkin' Cheeseburger Elvis, here. Ain't no way that combo's gonna produce a kid who looks like Cha-ka from *Land of the Lost*." He paused and added, "And I'll tell ya somethin' else, too—I'll leave this world with today in my eyes. Not all the years, all the decades, that I pissed away, thinkin' that bein' a made man made me a man. But *today*. So, I'll say two more words that I ain't said nearly enough in my life—thank you." He turned around and walked out the door.

They looked at one another but nothing was said.

They waited in silence for a nun to become available so Luke could talk to her about the cookies.

Hope stood there with her arms crossed, pouting. *I want him to know how pissed I am right now. I want him to feel guilty for not taking my side.*

After he talked to one of the nuns, on their way out, he announced, "Yeah, with those cookies, they're going to sell them right here. Twenty bucks a box. Totally worth it, too. They should be available starting next month."

"Uh-huh." *I can't wait to lay into you, pal. You just wait till we get in the car. It'll be on. So on. There's a price to pay for treason.*

On the crosstown drive over to Tiffany's, the eighties CD played Michael Jackson's *Man in the Mirror*.

As the opening bars played, she began her verbal assault. "You embarrassed me in there."

"You embarrassed yourself—dropping the F-bomb in a soup kitchen run by Catholic nuns. Yeah. Real classy, Hope."

She ignored his point. "I can't believe what you told that man. It disgusts me."

"I said no more than ten words to him the entire time."

"Oh, it was more than ten, that's for sure."

"Okay, fine. Maybe twenty. Are we counting words now? Huh? Are we really getting *that* petty?"

"It's not how many words you spoke to him. It's what you said. You punched his ticket to Heaven."

"Nah, Hope, his ticket was punched a long time ago. He just now claimed it, that's all."

"*God.* Sending a freaking mobster to Heaven. He hoodwinked you, Luke. He fooled you. He bamboozled you. He's a flimflam artist, and he can be very charming when he wants to be, when it serves his purpose. He works these little folksy sayings and language into the conversation. He's trying to disarm you with his words, and every word is carefully chosen. Calculated even. He's an excellent actor. I think he could have actually made an honest living that way. But my point is—he's trying to sound like the mob's version of Forrest Gump. He knows exactly what he's doing. And you bought his bullshit. I don't know whether I should be pissed at you or feel sorry for you. And I know what I'm saying. Trust me. I do. I know how these people are. He's laughing at you behind your back."

Luke just shook his head. "He's The Good Thief, Hope."

"There's no such thing as a *good* thief."

"No. Not *a* good thief, as in—one of many. *Thee* Good Thief. There was only one."

"I have no idea what you're talking about and neither do you. That's the sad part."

"I *do* know. And if you don't—Google it."

"Yeah. Well. Whatever."

There was silence for a few seconds. She gathered her thoughts and continued her barrage. She just couldn't let it go. "He even admitted that he hasn't been to church in decades."

He took his eyes off the road for a second and looked over at her. "And when's the last time you've been, missy? Huh?"

"I'm Catholic but it's been a minute. How about you, *bud?*"

"I'm Catholic but it's been a minute."

He shook his head in disgust. "Do you really think it's confined to the walls of a church? You don't think it's bigger than that? You think you'll only find Him inside a church? Might be the last place you'll find Him, Hope. Might find Him on the filthy, dingy, disgusting streets of Baltimore, the nation's most dangerous city. West Baltimore, no less. Mondawmin, even. The worst neighborhood in the worst city. There. How's that? But He can be wherever He chooses to be. It's His universe, after all. We just live in it. His Universe. His Rules. He's the Dealer. And at His Table, the Dealer always has Blackjack. *Always.* You can't beat Him, and only fools try. Sal Rossi finally realized that. The wise guy finally got Wise."

She emphatically shook her head. "Sal scammed you. One final scam in an illustrious criminal career. And he managed to get Saint Luke over here to grant him his final absolution."

"I didn't grant him anything."

"Bullshit. He left that place with a big-ass smile on his ugly puss."

"You begrudge a dying man a smile?"

"Yes. For him? Yes. Hell. Yes."

"You have to let go of this stuff. I know it's hard. I have some stuff that I need to work on myself. And I have no doubt that Sal was a total POS. He admitted to it. He confirmed everything you said. But at some point, you have to let go of the anger. The bitterness. The hatred. Now, I'm reading this really good book on Doctor King and, I'm paraphrasing here, but, basically, he said that hate loves hate. But hate hates love. And that's how you conquer hate. Love is hate's kryptonite. And I really think the guy was on to something. And I also recently watched this great documentary on Netflix called *Imagine.* It was about the life of John Lennon. A lot of people think he was anti-God because he once said that the Beatles were more popular than Jesus, but he wasn't necessarily saying that that was a good thing. He was just saying what he thought was true. He was actually interested in the teachings of Jesus and—"

She cut him off and raised her voice. "Why are you so enamored with these silly dreamers? Why? They don't change anything. They never have and they never will. The world chews them up and spits them out. Because that's how the world works. And yet they're still foolish enough to try. They're like Don Quixote. It's Devine, all right. A Devine Madness. And all these people ever get for all their trouble, if they're is a damn highway named after them. You want to be the knight in shining armor? You had the chance. You could have punched Sal Rossi in the face. That would have made me feel like you were my knight. That would have been defending my honor because that man's called me every dirty, filthy name in the book. But you decided to play God—who doesn't exist, by the way—and grant him eternal forgiveness. You gave him a seat at the table."

"Anyone who's hungry should get a seat at the table."

"Ha. I'd let him starve."

"No. You're off. Way off. And in your heart of hearts, I think you know better."

"No. I don't. I absolutely don't."

"Okay. Fine. You don't. But let's forget about Sal and the homeless dude. Put it all behind us. And enjoy a nice breakfast. Breakfast at Tiffany's. Let's make a pact. No more mention of either Sal or The Cisco Kid."

"The Cisco Kid? Who the hell's that?"

"The homeless vet. I'm dubbing him the Cisco Kid. He had a bottle of Cisco. You know—Cisco? The bum wine. I was trying to be cute, trying to break the tension. *The Cisco Kid* was an old TV show. Very old. Like, nineteen fifties old. Something only my grandfather would recall. It was a Western. I only know about it because it was a *Jeopardy!* answer once. I was trying to impress you with my wit, that's all. I guess it was lost on you because you didn't know about *The Cisco Kid* TV show. The whole joke depended on you knowing about the TV show. What can I say? I bombed. But it was worth the shot because it only took me five seconds to make up the joke."

She shook her head. "Oh, *Gawd*."

"Now, one final thought about the events of this morning. Then I'll leave it be, I promise. But I feel as though I have to say this—the anger and bitterness are taking over. It's a shame, too, because I think there's a beautiful soul buried beneath all that other crap."

She looked straight ahead. "Yeah. Well. Whatever. Any other tidbits of sage wisdom you'd like to impart?"

"Yeah. Never hire The Three Stooges to do plumbing work. I saw that episode the other day on *TV Classics*. Boy, did they make a mess."

She rolled her eyes.

CHAPTER NINE: TAKE MY WHOLE LIFE, TOO

When they got to Tiffany's, before they even got out of the car, she issued a warning. "No cheesy jokes about us having *breakfast at Tiffany's,* all right? I'm telling you now because you like to go the cheesy route. I know that much already. And every couple that has breakfast here—not that we're a couple, because we're *not*—makes this big to-do over having *breakfast at Tiffany's.* They take pictures and post them on social media and are all, like—*oh, look at us, guys. Aren't we just freaking adorable? We're having breakfast at Tiffany's.* Nope. It's such low-hanging fruit that even Captain Obvious wouldn't bother. Yes, there's a movie called *Breakfast at Tiffany's*, a silly love story that couldn't possibly happen in real life. It was not faithful to the book, either. Capote was pissed when he saw it. He didn't like it at all. So there. We've gotten the whole *Breakfast At Tiffany's* talk out of our system. That's it. No more mention of it. Okay? And do not even think of buying one of those tacky, tacky t-shirts that they sell in there that proudly announces to the world—*I've Had Breakfast At Tiffany's—Tiffany's Diner, Baltimore, MD.*"

"I already have one of those shirts and have you even seen the movie?"

"No. Not really. Just bits and pieces. But I know the gist."

"We should watch it together sometime. I like it because there's a cat in it. The love story's good, too. And it's not far-fetched at all. It absolutely *could* happen in real life."

"Yeah, whatever, dude."

"Yeah. I have it on DVD."

"Good for you. Doesn't surprise me one bit. You strike me as someone who appreciates sappiness, so you probably have *Somewhere in Time*, too."

"Sure, I do. That's another good one. That one's worth watching just for the theme song."

"Oh, I'm sure. Anyhow, shall we go in? It's getting cold in this land yacht, and I am kind of hungry."

"Yeah. Absolutely. But wait—I want to get the door for you."

She crossed her arms, turned her gaze upward, and shook her head in disgust.

He rushed out and over to her side, almost slipping on the ice. *Damn. It's slick out here this morning.*

He opened the door, extended his hand, and spoke with a faux British accent. "Here you are, milady."

She looked up at him. "What's with the hand?"

He shrugged. "I just thought that I could help you out. Offer you my hand and so forth."

"Look—you opened the door for me. That's plenty. I don't need you to help me get out of the freaking car. I know this is the type of vehicle that an eighty-year-old would ride in, but I'm only twenty-eight, and I do not need an escort out of the damn car."

He nodded. "Yeah. I know. But there's a lot of ice here in this parking lot. And you know—ice can be icy"

"You sound like Sal. He's already rubbing off on you."

"I just don't want you to fall. You don't need a broken arm or leg to go with that broken rib."

"I'm a police officer. I go to the gym regularly, and I am in outstanding physical shape."

He smiled, raised his eyebrows, and nodded. "Yeah you are."

She wagged her finger at him. "Don't you be thinking those thoughts."

"What thoughts? I just agreed with your statement. You *are* in great shape. And if I had said you weren't, that would have offended you, too, no doubt. I swear, girl, you remind me of

Staff Sergeant Valentine, my senior drill instructor from the Island. There was never a right answer with that man. He got all up in my face one morning and screamed—*do you think I'm cute? Do you want to date me, boy?* To which I replied—*sir, no, sir! Sir, this recruit does not wish to date his senior drill instructor, sir!* Truth be told, he was not an especially attractive man. Well, then he said—*oh, so you're telling me that I'm not good enough for you? Is that it, maggot?* I got my footlocker dumped and scattered all over the squad bay and had to do a hundred pushups. All because I didn't want to date the guy. Of course, if I had said that I *did* want to date him, something even worse would have happened. Way worse. Anyway—there was never a right answer with him. Same as you."

"Yeah, well, that's a charming little story. Good times—good times. Let's hope Staff Sergeant Valentine finally found his valentine amongst his pool of recruits. But my point is—I am fully capable of exiting the vehicle under my own power. Kay?"

"I just don't want you to risk life and limb getting out of a car that's sitting on a sheet of ice."

"Oh, so you're concerned about my whole life, too, now, huh?"

"Certainly, I am."

He still had his hand extended to her.

She threw her hands up in exasperation. "You know what? Fine. I give up. You win the war of attrition. I'm not going to sit an argue it with you all morning. It's silly."

She held out her hand. "Here. Take my hand. Go on—take it. And while you're at it, you may as well just take my whole life, too. Since you're such a great manager of lives and all. You set The Cisco Kid, as you call him, up with booze and drug money. You opened the gates of Heaven to Sal. Yes, sir. You're a life coach, all right. Tony Robbins, step aside. There's a new weirdo guru in town."

"We agreed not to mention that stuff anymore. You already broke our pact."

"Yeah. Well. Whatever."

"And FYI— I am nothing like Tony Robbins. I almost never use phrases like *unleash your inner power*. And I don't have bleached teeth." He smiled an exaggerated smile and pointed to his teeth. "See? See that? These babies are not bleached. That is a natural white. Okay?"

He took her hand, and she exited the car. As she did, she slipped. For a split second, she teetered. He placed his free hand around her waist, pulled her close to him, and steadied her.

He lectured. "See that? Told you it was slippery."

"Let me go. I'm fine now. So just let me go. Please and thank you."

He let go of her and they walked into the diner.

Tiffany's Diner. An old-fashioned eatery on Loch Raven Boulevard. It had been in the business of serving up some of Baltimore's finest diner food since the fifties. Something of a Baltimore legend and institution, it was decked out in pink Formica, and had an old-time jukebox that got lots of play. At the entrance, there was a wall dedicated to displaying autographed photos of celebrities who'd eaten there, the so-called Wall of Fame. Some of the famous names enshrined had Baltimore or at least Maryland connections—Cal Ripken Jr., Spiro Agnew, Kathleen Kennedy Townsend, Pat Sajak, David Hasselhoff. But many of the famous faces had no local connections at all. He guessed that those individuals had simply passed through the area on business and heard about how great the food was.

They stopped to survey the wall.

"I always like to stop and look at their Wall of Fame," he told her. "You know—to see if anyone new has been added."

Hope pointed to a picture. "Oh, look. This one's new. Elizabeth Berkley. She played Jessie on *Saved By The Bell*. Then she wrecked her career by doing *Showgirls*."

He nodded. "That's her, all right. *Showgirls*, by the way, is pretty much universally regarded as one of the worst films ever made. But for some reason, I've seen it something like thirty times. Only thirty because the DVD finally wore out on me."

She pointed to another photo. "William Hung? Who's that?"

He laughed. "You don't remember him?"

She shook her head. "The name's kind of familiar, but—no, I don't remember him."

"*She Bangs*. The *She Bangs* guy. You know, from one of the earlier seasons of *American Idol.* He was memorable because he was so bad. Then he kind of developed a cult following and parlayed that into a career as a motivational speaker, believe it or not. He really stretched out those fifteen minutes of fame, huh?"

She made a face. "Oh, God. *That* guy? Geez. They're lowering their standards around here."

He pointed to two other photos. "Not really. After all, they have JWOWW and Sammie Sweetheart. I always thought that Sammi Sweetheart really *was* a sweetheart, too. I don't think she was just faking it for the cameras."

"Oh, no. *The Jersey Shore*? Seriously?" She pretended to vomit.

"And check it out—Jim J. Bullock was here recently, too."

She turned sarcastic. "Yuuuup. Only the biggest stars."

The waitress seated them. They sat across from one another in a pink booth.

The jukebox played *99 Red Balloons*. Some teenage girls were carrying on, giggling and dancing. *They probably don't know that song's about nuclear war.*

The place had the classic diner-at-breakfast-time aroma. Strong coffee, pancakes, bacon, sausage, eggs.

He pulled out his phone. "Pardon me for a moment, but I have to do my daily shares before I forget."

"Daily shares?"

"Yeah, on Facebook. I'm a member of a group called *Death Row Cats*. It's a collection of profiles of cats who are in kill shelters. Cats who are *time stamped,* as they call it. That's a euphemistic way of saying that they're going to be killed if they don't get adopted or placed with a rescue by the date that's listed. Regardless of how anyone feels about capital punishment, I think we can all agree that when humans end up on death row, it's generally because they've done something really terrible, murdered someone and such. But the only *crime* these cats are guilty of is the *crime* of being born." He used his finger to scroll and read a sample listing to her. "Code Red. Henrietta. ID number six-seven-eight-nine-one. Five-years-old, long-haired dilute tortoiseshell. Friendly, good with kids and other animals. Spayed female. Litter box trained. Needs placement ASAP. Must be out by end of day Friday. Special note: The Devonshire County Animal Care and Control facility in Utah where Henrietta is being housed utilizes the gas chamber."

He turned his phone around to show her Henrietta's photograph. It showed the cat cowering in her litter box in a tiny steel cage. "She's cute, right?"

"Can we change the subject, please? *Please*."

He shook his head in disgust. "What the *hell* is wrong with this world? Humanity has lost its humanity, you know?"

"Okay—yes. It has. Now can we please change the subject?" A solitary tear ran down her cheek. She quickly wiped it away.

He smiled a warm, gentle smile. "Speaking of humanity—you just now showed a little. Especially for someone who said, and I'm paraphrasing a bit, but the gist of it was—*I don't have a human side, only a cop side*. Remember that?"

"I *do not* want to talk about this anymore. I've already told you that."

"Fine." He shared the listing on his timeline and put his phone away.

"How's your rib, by the way? How are you holding out?" he asked.

"I'm okay. It only hurts when I take really deep breaths or laugh."

"Mine hurts when I get out of bed in the morning. That's sheer agony."

She nodded agreement. "Oh yeah. I know. Pure torture. You are right about that."

There was a brief period of awkward silence.

"So, you do carpentry work?"

"Yeah, that's right. I'm with a nonprofit called Homes For Heroes. We build houses for disabled vets. Build them from scratch. We do work all over the state of Maryland. Plus, Delaware, southern Pennsylvania. northern Virginia, and even south Jersey. My title is Head Carpenter, but the reality is that I do whatever is needed. Masonry. Dry wall. Whatever. I can do it all. After I got out of the service, I used the GI Bill to go to trade school. Learned carpentry. And I just kind of picked up the other skills as I went along. I like building houses for other vets. When I was a Marine, I used to blow things up, destroy things. Tear things down. Now, I build things up."

She nodded and shrugged. "Yeah, well, I guess there are worse jobs." She looked at his hands. "But your hands don't look all rough. Normally, with guys who do construction, their hands are all rough."

"I wear gloves whenever possible. And I moisturize. Religiously."

She nodded. "Oh. Okay."

They looked over the menu.

After about thirty seconds, she announced, "I'm really hungry so I'm going to have the Charm City Coronary. That's supposed to be three pancakes, two eggs, two sausage links, two bacon strips, and two slices of toast. Orange juice for the beverage. It's a lot, I know, but whatever I can't eat, I'll just take home."

He nodded approvingly. "Yeah, well, that sounds good. I'll go with that, too."

They gave the waitress their order and waited.

Not long after, they were approached by a woman who appeared to be in her early thirties. A pretty blonde. She pushed a little girl in a wheelchair. The girl looked to be about eight. She wore thick glasses and a Ravens ball cap to cover a bald head. Her shirt had a picture of a kitten riding a unicorn on it. And she looked frail. Very frail. Her arms were like twigs.

The little girl tentatively waved to Luke. He waved back and smiled.

The woman addressed him. "I'm sorry to bother you and your wife when you all are getting ready to eat but—"

Hope interrupted. "I am *not* his wife. Let's all be clear on that. Kay?"

The woman shrugged. "Sorry. *Girlfriend.* Anyway, my name's Grace Madden, and this is my little girl, Charlotte. And she wants to say hello. We saw you come in and couldn't help but notice that you look like Elvis, sir. And Charlotte loves Elvis. She has all his records, has seen all his movies."

Luke again warmly smiled at the little girl. "You like Elvis, huh?"

The little girl nodded. "Uh-huh." Her voice was weak and conveyed a touch of shyness.

"What do you like about him, honey?" he asked.

"Um, I like his music. And his movies. And he did nice things for people, super-nice things. And he was really, really cute, too." Charlotte giggled.

"What's your favorite Elvis song?"

"Well, I like them all, but my favorite is the *Take My Whole Life, Too* song. I think that's what it's called." Charlotte looked at her mother. "Isn't that the name of it, Mom?"

Grace helped her daughter and explained. "*Can't Help Falling in Love,* sweetie. That's the actual name of the song. She calls it *Take My Whole Life, Too,* but she means *Can't Help Falling in Love.*"

Luke nodded. "Uh-huh. Yeah. That's what I figured. That's not only my favorite Elvis song, it's my favorite song of all-time. Period. It's just a beautiful song. You have great taste, Charlotte." He winked at her.

Charlotte nodded. "My brother, Joseph, well, God took his whole life in a car accident three years ago. And He might take *my* whole life, too." Charlotte took off her hat to reveal a completely bald, scarred head. "See, I have Medulloblastoma. Fancy word for brain cancer. I could die. And I don't want to die. I want to live. I want to stay here, with my mom and with my cat, Mikey. I *love* life, even though I have a lot of pain. And it's hard to die when you love life."

Grace cried.

"It's okay, Mom. Don't cry, Mom."

Luke felt tears welling up in his eyes.

Charlotte rubbed her head. "I used to have pretty red hair, but it's gone now. All gone. I get teased sometimes, and that makes me cry. It really does. I wish people would think before they tease." Charlotte looked at her mother. "People should think before they tease, shouldn't they, Mom?"

Grace nodded as tears streamed down her cheeks.

Hope sniffled and got up with her head down. "I have to go to the restroom. I have something in my eye. Both eyes, in fact."

Charlotte called out to her. "No, lady—don't leave. You're Misses Elvis. You're Priscilla. So, I want you in the picture, too."

Grace explained. "She wants a picture for her scrapbook. A picture of both of you with her. Would you mind? Would it be too much of an imposition? It would mean a lot to her."

Luke glanced over to Hope. He saw tears in her eyes. He told Charlotte, "We'd be honored to take a picture with you, sweetheart."

He looked at Hope for confirmation. She nodded.

They got out of the booth and kneeled next to Charlotte's wheelchair, one on each side. They smiled, and Grace took the picture.

After the photo, Luke and Hope each hugged Charlotte.

Grace got ready to push her back over to their table. But before she did, Charlotte made a plea to Hope: "Elvis and Priscilla got divorced. That's sad. So sad. Because he loved her. And she loved him. And they loved one another. And my mom and dad got divorced, too." Charlotte cried. "Don't you guys ever get divorced. Okay? Promise. Promise you guys won't get divorced. Never. Okay?"

Hope nodded. "Sure, honey. I promise. We won't get divorced. We won't. Never. *Never ever.*"

Grace pushed Charlotte away but turned her head and

mouthed the words *thank you*.

They sat back down in the booth.

Hope used napkins to dab her eyes. "God. I'm so freaking embarrassed."

"Embarrassed? Why?"

"For getting all emotional just now."

"So, you're embarrassed that you were moved to tears by a super-sweet little girl who, this time next year, might not be around? You're embarrassed that you cried over that? Because I would have been embarrassed *for* you if you *hadn't*."

"Yeah. Well. Whatever."

"See, to me, this means that there's hope for Hope." He pointed to her heart. "This means that there is, in fact, a real human being inside there."

She threw her hands up. "Can we just talk about something else? Please. Something happy. Something funny, maybe. I need to laugh. Even though it's going to hurt like hell, I still want to laugh."

"Oh, you laugh, too? Wow. The full range of human emotions, huh?"

"Stop it. Just stop it."

The waitress brought their food.

He used his fork to sever a big slice of his pancakes. "You know, I was shocked that you didn't even crack a smile over the antics of that drunk on the night of the accident. I know there's nothing funny about drunk driving, but you have to admit, some of his post-accident shenanigans were pretty hilarious."

"I was laughing on the inside," she admitted. She added, "Oh, by the way, I got the lowdown on him when Corporal Coffey took me home that night. The Maryland State Police know him well. His name's Jody Biffle. He lives in Dundalk, surprise—surprise. The state troopers call him Jerk Off Jody. That piece-of-crap van of his—according to MSP, it was a jerk off van."

Luke laughed. "A *jerk off* van?"

"Yeah. Evidently, his wife is a big-time holy roller Christian and doesn't allow porn in the house. And he's a porn addict. Great combination, right? So, anyway, he filled this van with porn. And when the spirit moves him—he takes off, parks, and goes to town. Has himself a hand job party. The kicker is—according to MSP, all the porn is on old VHS tapes. He has hundreds of VHS tapes from, like, the eighties. You like nineteen eighties music. Jerkoff Jody likes nineteen eighties porn. He has a TV slash VCR unit in the back. Oh, and he had warrants, too. And he was driving on a suspended license. And he was wasted on both booze and PCP."

"I'm shocked that someone with the nickname Jerk Off Jody would be anything other than the president of the local Kiwanis Club."

Hope laughed loudly. "Oh, God, laughing is so not good for my rib, but I can't help it. It's funny. And my favorite part was when he talked into the pack of cigarettes."

He burst out laughing. "Yeah. He was getting answers, too." He took a sip of his orange juice.

"I know, right? And I guess he didn't like some of the answers because then he started fighting with it."

They both laughed. She took a bite off a bacon strip.

Luke imitated the drunk. *"I can be the Angel of Light or the Angel of Darkness. You decide which you'd rather deal with."*

She threw her head back and guffawed. "Oh, that's right! He did say that. I guess he has the power to go back and forth."

Luke shook his head. "That van of his— it looked exactly like the quintessential creepy clown van. You know the one— there's an evil-looking clown behind the wheel, playing spooky carnival music through a PA system, and has a homemade sign on either side saying—*Free Candy For Kids. Must Be Under Ten.*"

She howled. "Oh, my God. *Yes.* Thank you. That is exactly what it looked like. *Exactly.*" She smiled at him.

"You have a really pretty smile, Hope. I like seeing you smile."

She looked down for a moment then looked back up. "Thanks. You do, too. There. Never let it be said that I didn't give you a compliment. But just remember—this still isn't a date."

He shrugged. "Yeah. Sure. Fine. I already have a date lined up for the weekend, anyway."

"W—w—what, what date? What do you mean—date? What are you talking about—*date*?"

"My best friend's a guy by the name of Dino Cavanaugh. Dino was in the Air Force, but I try not to hold that against him."

Hope just stared at him with a confused look on her face.

"That was a joke. A little military humor. Different branches of the military—we like to poke fun at one another. It's all in good fun. Nothing malicious about it."

She nodded. "Oh, okay."

"Yeah. He, ah, he flew B Fifty-twos in Afghanistan. B Fifty-twos are heavy bombers."

Wrinkling her nose, she asked,"Is there any such thing as a *light* bomber?"

"Well, it's all relative. Anyway, guys like Dino saved the butts of guys like me all the time. And he has this sister, Gretchen. And, well, it's come to my attention that the woman digs me."

"Oh, is that right?"

"Oh, yes. She digs me. Yessirree Bob—she's crazy about the Luke-ster. Yes, she is. She's very pretty. A highly successful lawyer, too, with one of the top firms in the city. Makes something like a quarter mil. Dino says she's very sweet. Likes cats as well, which, you know, for me, is a huge plus. Yep, me and Gretchen are going to the Ravens-Steelers playoff game this Sunday. Fifty-yard line seats. In a skybox, no less. Limo ride to and from. All courtesy of Gretchen's firm. Yep. Great gal, that Gretchen Cavanaugh."

Hope crossed her arms and confidently announced, "I don't think she exists. I think you're making her up."

"Why would I do that?"

She shrugged. "I don't know. I'm not you."

He got out his phone and showed her Gretchen's Facebook page. "Check out her most recent status update. See that?

Mentions me. It says that she's *looking forward to her big day with Luke Matthews. Go Ravens.* And that she's *feeling excited.*"

Hope threw up her hands. "So, you have a girlfriend. I knew it. Why are you here with me if you have a freaking girlfriend? Huh?"

He laughed and raised his eyebrows. "Thought this wasn't a date."

She leered at him. "Don't be a smartass. Nobody likes a smartass."

"So, first she wasn't real enough. Now, she's *too* real? Is that it?"

"You know what I mean. You know exactly what I mean."

"For your information—she's not my girlfriend. I've never even so much as shook her hand. This would be my first time going out with her. Dino set us up. He so wants us to fall in love or whatever. He said as much. But she most definitely is not my girlfriend. And the more I think about it, the more I think it's a mistake. I'm sure Gretchen's a great woman, but I'm just really not interested."

"Why? If her profile picture is accurate, she's quite attractive. And a quarter mil? That's about three years-worth of salary for me. So, why would you not be interested?"

"Maybe I'm into somebody else, okay?"

"Oh, really?"

"Yeah. Really. I honestly don't want to go on Sunday. I'd just as soon watch at home. It's going to be bitter cold. And my heart's not in it, anyhow. But I have to at least go out with her this one time. I don't want to upset Dino, don't want to lose a good friend over this. So, I guess I'm going."

He paused then shook his finger at her. "But know this—if I did have a girlfriend, I wouldn't be sitting here with you. Because I'm a one-woman-man, Hope. When I was in the Corps, some of the guys would make fun of me because, on down time, I didn't want to go out, hookup with some girl in a bar, and just get laid. My buddies laughed at me sometimes. I would always let them laugh. It didn't matter to me. That wasn't my style. Still isn't. See, I'm greedy."

"Greedy?"

"Yeah. That's right. *Greedy.* I'm looking for that one special woman. *The One.* And if and when I find her—I'm going to be greedy about it. I'm not going to want her for just one night. I'm going to want her for every night. I'm going to want her forever."

They stared at each other in silence for several seconds.

The silence was broken when Grace Madden came back over to their table. This time, she was by herself.

"Guys, thank you so much for taking time to talk to my little girl. You almost got her to smile when you posed for that picture with her. She was smiling on the inside, for sure. But she's very self-conscious about her teeth. The chemo caused them to fall out along with her hair. So, she doesn't have any teeth, and she really doesn't smile anymore. She's gotten used to not having hair, but she hasn't gotten use to not having teeth. It affects everything, too. She can't eat a lot of her favorite foods anymore. And people are so cruel. I would just love for her to be able to smile again someday. I'd give anything to see her smile. But even without the smile, these moments are precious because we may not have many left with her. Her prognosis is not good. They don't know how long. All we really know is that her story, most likely, doesn't have a happy ending. And that's hard, you know? That's *hard.* I hold out hope for a miracle, but I'm also realistic. The kind of cancer she has is very aggressive. Anyway, she loves Elvis—he's her favorite. Her absolute favorite. And that will never change. But lately, she's been into Peter, Paul, and Mary, too, believe it or not. She found them on YouTube. She listens to *Leaving on a Jet Plane* and says she might have to *leave on a jet plane.* That's how she talks about death. And she likes *Puff the Magic Dragon,* that song about the little boy who grows up and eventually outgrows his magic dragon and leaves him behind. The loss of childhood innocence and all, you know? That kind of thing." Grace paused for a moment."Well, my little girl will most likely never leave her magic dragon behind." Grace broke down and sobbed.

Hope and Luke cried, too.

People in the diner stared.

Grace composed herself. "Thank you so much. Both of you. May God bless you."

Luke told her, "It was our pleasure. Absolutely our pleasure."

Hope nodded. "Yes, it was. He's right about that."

"She has one more request."

"Name it," he said without hesitation.

"She wants to see Elvis and Priscilla dance. Slow dance. Slow dance to her favorite Elvis song. *Take My Whole Life, Too*, as she calls it. They actually have it on the jukebox. If I play it, would you guys dance to it? I know there's not really a dance floor here or anything, but I asked the manager and he said it would be fine, that you could just do it up near the jukebox. There's a little bit of room up there. Would that be asking too much? I know it's asking a lot. And you've already given a lot."

"Of course, we'll do it." He looked over at Hope and in his best Elvis voice said, "Won't we 'Cilla?"

She nodded, sniffled, and dabbed her eye with a napkin. "Yes. Of course. Of course, we'll do that. Anything for Charlotte."

They got up from the booth and walked to the jukebox.

"Just be careful of my rib," she told him.

"Ditto."

Grace and Charlotte stood by. Charlotte had her camera ready. Grace put a dollar in the jukebox. And suddenly, the voice of a young Elvis Presley filled the room. It got kind of quiet. Some people stopped eating, stopped talking, and just watched.

He held out his hand to her. "Here, Hope. Take my hand."

She looked him in the eye and took his hand. He pulled her close to him. They put their arms around each other.

"*Take My Whole Life, Too*," she said. She looked down and quietly added, "That's what the little girl calls the song, *Take My Whole Life, Too*."

"Yeah," he whispered. "That's what she calls it, all right."

They gently swayed back and forth. Eventually, she pressed her head against his chest.

He took in the scent of her perfume.

This feels good. Holding her feels so good. So right. I could just stay like this forever. Is this what it's like? Is this what it feels like? Can you identify the exact moment when it first starts? That precise moment? Maybe you can. And maybe this is it.

When it was over, Charlotte and Grace applauded, as did some of the other customers.

They looked at one another. He saw a single tear form in her right eye.

He took his thumb and dabbed it as it ran below the lens of her glasses. "I think you got something in your eye there, kiddo."

She put her head down and spoke softly. "Yeah. Well. Whatever."

Luke walked up to Grace, pulled out his wallet, and handed her his business card. "I'm Luke Matthews. And If there's anything else I can do for you guys, please let me know."

Grace accepted his card and took a piece of scrap paper out of her purse along with a pen. She wrote something on it and handed it to him.

He read it, looked up, and emphatically nodded. "Yes. Absolutely. I promise. *I promise.*" He folded the note and placed it in his wallet.

Grace started to wheel Charlotte away.

He thought for a moment and called out to them. "Hey wait. Hold up, guys. Please hold up."

They turned around. He walked over to them. Hope followed.

He got down on one knee, so he could address Charlotte at eyelevel. "I have something I want to give to you, honey."

The little girl was excited. "You mean like a present?"

He nodded. "Yeah. Like a present."

She clapped her hands. "Yay. I love presents."

From his wallet, he pulled out his Purple Heart. He held the medal up. "This is mine. I got it when I got wounded. I carry it in my wallet. All the time. I carry it as a reminder of what me and my buddies went through in a place called Afghanistan. What we endured. It was a hard place, Charlotte. A really hard place. But I want you to have this, sweetie. I do."

"It's pretty, but what is it?" Charlotte asked.

"It's called a Purple Heart, honey. Marines get it—well, not just Marines. I was a Marine, but anyone who serves in the military gets one when they get hurt doing their job. See, there are a lot of bad guys out there, and the people in our military have to protect us from those bad guys. And sometimes they get hurt. Sometimes they get hurt real bad doing that."

Charlotte's eyes got big. "Sometimes, they, like, even die, don't they?"

He felt himself getting teary-eyed. He nodded. "Yeah. Sometimes they do. Sometimes they do, honey. Sometimes, the people who get these only get to wear them once. But they wear them forever." He took a deep breath and paused to compose himself. "Anyway, this medal, this Purple Heart—it's a symbol of bravery and sacrifice, see? And the way I look at it, you're as brave as the bravest Marine who's ever lived. And you've sacrificed as much as those Marines who have borne the heaviest of burdens. And I'd very much like you to have this medal. I'd like to give it to you. It just sits in my wallet. But I'd like you to wear it. So that all the doctors and nurses and all your friends will know that you're the bravest of the brave."

Grace emphatically shook her head. "No. *Absolutely* not. We can't accept that. It's a lovely gesture. Beyond lovely, actually. It's downright beautiful. But that Purple Heart is special and sacred."

Without hesitation he answered, "So is your little girl."

Grace again shook her head. "No. We couldn't."

"I want her to have it, ma'am. It would mean the world to me for her to accept it."

"Oh, please, Mom," Charlotte begged. "I would wear it every day. And I would take super good care of it. I wouldn't spill chocolate milk on it or anything. I would treasure it."

But Grace was adamant. "No, honey. It wouldn't be right."

He thought for a moment and snapped his fingers. "How about this, then—how about if I give it to you temporarily? Yeah, that's it. You wear it for now, until you beat cancer. And when you beat cancer, *which you will*, then you can return it to me. How's that? How's that sound, Mom?"

Luke and Charlotte both looked at Grace, waiting for an answer.

After several seconds of silence, Grace finally relented. "Yeah. Okay. We'll do that. I...I don't even know what to say. I'm just so blown away by this. I have no words. No words. This is coming from Above. That's the only thing I'm sure of right now." She wiped more tears from her eyes.

Luke looked over at Hope. She was wiping tears from her eyes, too.

"Here, sweetie, let me pin it on you."

He pinned it to her shirt. "For exceptional bravery in the face of a tough and determined enemy, I hereby award you, Miss Charlotte Madden, the Purple Heart."

He kissed her on the cheek, stood up, and smartly saluted her. She raised a thin, frail arm and returned his salute.

"I'll never forget you guys. Never. And I promise, when I beat cancer, I'll give this back to you. *I promise.*"

"Okay, sweetheart. I'll look forward to the day when I get it back."

Grace hugged both Luke and Hope. "I just don't know what to say. I feel that we were touched by an angel today. Maybe one day, an angel will reach out and touch you guys."

They watched Grace wheel Charlotte out of the diner. They watched until they'd disappeared from sight.

Hope turned to him. "I don't know what to say. I can't say anything about that because I just don't know what the right thing would be to say. I'm speechless. Not trying to be ignorant or anything. I just literally don't know what to say."

"That's okay. You don't have to say anything. I didn't do it to have you or anybody else make a big deal over it. I did it for that little girl. *Because she deserves it.* And that's all."

For a couple of seconds, they just stared at one another.

Finally, she asked, "Before you gave her your Purple Heart, I saw Charlotte's mom give you something. She wrote something on a piece of paper and gave it to you. What did it say? Huh? What was in that note?"

"Oh, that? It was just something for later," he nonchalantly told her. And that's all he would say.

CHAPTER TEN: YES, HOPE, THERE IS A SANTA CLAUS

That evening, Hope took a shower, washed her hair, and put on a pair of aqua satin polka dot pajamas. She was starting to come down with a cold, sneezing and feeling a little achy. She even felt warm, as if she had a low-grade fever.

At ten thirty, she called in to *The Midnight Ranger Show*.

The Ranger immediately came on the line. "Hope, what's happening, kid?"

"Um. Not much. I think I'm coming down with a little cold to go with my broken rib."

"Oh, no. Sorry to hear that. Take care of that cold. It's flu season, you know. You certainly don't want a nasty case of the flu with all the other stuff you've got going on."

"I know, right?"

"So, now, let's get right into this. I'm not even going to lead in with a joke. I'm just going to ask—did you get together with Luke earlier today? Did that Happening happen?"

"Um. Yes. Yes, it did."

"Beautiful. So, you all had a meal together, correct?"

"That is correct."

"Where'd you go?"

"To a diner."

"Want to name names? Give them some free advertising?"

She giggled. "No."

"That's right, sweetie. You make them pay for it. You are hot right now. Hot—hot—hot. And if a business wants your endorsement, they're going to have to show you the money, right?"

"Well, it's not really like that. It's more because of privacy and whatnot."

"Gotcha. So, how'd it go? Is he at least a messy eater? As a guy, it would make me feel better if Luke had at least that flaw, you know? Because once you get the *messy eater* rap, it sticks to you like syrup."

"No. He's actually a very neat eater. He didn't spill anything."

"Damn. Oh, well. I'll get over it. But enough about me—tell us about this date-that-was-not-a-date."

"Um. Wow. Where to start?"

"The beginning. Genesis. I mean, it was good enough for God and all..." The Ranger laughed.

"Right. The beginning. Ah, we kind of disagreed about some stuff at the beginning."

"You had a fight? At the beginning of your very first date?"

"Kind of. See, I think he's like the kid who still believes in Santa Claus. He sees the world a certain way. He sees the good. And I see the bad, I guess. I see people for who they are. And I think he sees them for who he wants them to be. He's the little kid who still believes in Santa. I'm the older kid who finally found out that Santa doesn't exist."

"So, you're more worldly, and he's, perhaps, more naïve? Is that a fair appraisal?"

"Yes. That's how I see it, at least. And I don't like to see him get fooled and taken advantage of, so we argued over some things because I thought a couple of individuals played him."

"And who were these individuals who took advantage of him? Are you at liberty to discuss?"

"A man who's both a drug addict and an alcoholic and a second man who's a career criminal. He gave money to the alcoholic and forgiveness to the criminal."

"And you resent that?"

"Yes, because they're both con men. Neither was sincere."

"How do you know?"

"I just do. I know. Trust me."

"Okay. I'll take your word. Now, were you able to move beyond this little tiff?"

"Um. Yes. I think so."

"So, what were the good parts?"

"I felt alive. For the first time in a long, long time I really felt alive. I laughed. And I cried, too."

"What made you laugh?"

"The way the drunk from the accident behaved after the wreck. We talked about that. Laughed about it. I know there's nothing funny about drunk driving, but the stuff this drunk was saying and doing after the crash, well, it was pretty amusing."

"Drunks can be hilarious, Hope. You want to know who's funnier than even the funniest comedian? I mean, this guy's funnier than Carrot Top. Mel Gibson with a few beers in him, that's who. Seriously. YouTube it, peeps. Worth your time. Totally worth your time. He is an equal opportunity offender, too. He leaves no one unscathed during his drunken rants. Okay, ah…what made you cry? Crying on a first date—generally not a good thing, right? Typically, it does not bode well for the relationship."

"Well, you wouldn't think so, but this was kind of an unusual scenario. It involved a little girl named Charlotte."

"And what's going on with Charlotte?"

"She's very sick. She could die."

"Charlotte could *die*?"

"Yes. She's only about seven or eight-years-old, but she has cancer, brain cancer."

"Oh, my God. *Jesus*. How did you come into contact with her? And Charlotte, if you're listening, stay strong, sweetheart, okay? Stay Charlotte Strong. So, how did you meet Charlotte? How, Hope?"

"She's an Elvis fan and saw me and Luke walk into the diner. She and her mom came over to our table and asked to get a photo. You know, because Luke looks so much like Elvis and all."

"So, the Elvis connection comes into play. More than forty years after his passing, Elvis Aaron Presley is still bringing folks together, God bless him. *God bless him*! And I'm assuming Luke obliged in terms of the photo-op."

"Of course. But she actually wanted a picture of both of us. See, she said I was Priscilla."

"*Aw*. Bless her heart. Bless her precious little heart. And how did it feel, in that moment, to be Misses Elvis?"

"Good. It felt good. But I cried. I cried over Charlotte. Because that little girl was just so sweet and polite and gentle and loving. She was everything Good. It was as if all the Good in the universe gathered in one place, and the result was Charlotte. And then she made me promise that Luke and I would never get a divorce because Elvis and Priscilla got divorced. And she didn't want that to happen to us. And then she asked for Luke and me to slow dance to her favorite song."

"And what song is that?"

"Well, she called it *Take My Whole Life, Too*. But she was talking about *Can't Help Falling in Love*. And the jukebox at the diner just happened to have it."

"Hope, there are a lot of great love songs out there, but *Can't Help Falling in Love* might just be the most romantic song of all-time."

Greg chimed in. "It was my wedding song. Credit Shannon with that. I was pushing for *I Love This Bar* by Toby Keith, but she insisted on *Can't Help Falling in Love*."

The Ranger laughed. "See, now, with me and Angie, it was different. Totally different. It was the exact opposite of you and Shannon, in fact. I wanted *More Than Words* by Extreme. Lovely, lovely song. But Angie—she insisted on *Keep Your Hands to Yourself*." A laugh track played. The Ranger and Greg guffawed.

"Oh, geez. I kill myself sometimes. I do. Anyhow, did you and Luke dance for the little girl? Tell me you did. Please tell me you did."

"Yes. We did. And a lot of people stopped eating and just watched us." She coughed.

"At that moment, they were living vicariously. That's why they watched. All the gals envied you, and all the guys envied him. Of course, if the gals were lesbian, they envied him. And if the dudes were gay, they envied you. And anyone who was bi just envied both of you." The Ranger again laughed at his own joke. "I'm in rare form today, boys and girls. But, ah, please, Hope, go on. Continue with the story."

"Right. So, when the song started, Luke told me—he said—*take my hand.* So, I took his hand. And then I told him—*take my whole life, too.* And we danced the dance. And, to me, it was just the two of us. Everything else faded out. And it was just us. And I almost thought, for a split second, that I even felt God. But then I realized that I don't believe in God. God's like Santa Claus. He's a nice idea, but He isn't real. No, there's no God. No angels. They're not real. It's all just wishful thinking. The only thing that's real is our longing for them. We long for them to exist to help comfort us, to help ease the pain of life. That longing— now, *that's* real."

"Getting very philosophical on us tonight, aren't you, Hope? And, frankly, I'm not sure I can keep up. I failed intro to philosophy in college, you know. My professor told us to do a research paper on Aristotle. I thought he said *Aeropostale.* I turned in five thousand words on hoodies and skinny jeans." The Ranger and Greg laughed heartily. The laugh track played, as did the sound effect of a wolf howling. The Ranger promised listeners, "I do not have writers writing this material for me, peeps. I don't. I swear—I fly by the seat of my pants, by the seat of my Aeropostale cargo pants. I really do."

He finally settled himself down. "Okay. No more clowning. I promise. Scout's honor. Now, let me ask you a question—was Charlotte real? Or was she a product of wishful thinking, too?"

"No. Charlotte was real. She was as real as it gets."

"All right. Now, we're getting somewhere. See, I think God and Santa Claus are one in the same. The same entity. Different forms of the same entity. They both give and ask for very little in return, mainly just to pass the kindness on. They both know who's been naughty and who's been nice. And they both require Faith. And if Charlotte was Real, then Reality might be more than you think. Yes, Hope, there is a Santa Claus. The Charlottes of the world wouldn't exist without Him. If you believe in Love, then surely you must simply—Believe. There's a Giving Point for all those beautiful qualities that you describe Charlotte as being. Gentle. Sweet. Polite. Loving. If Charlotte's a living doll, then there had to be a Dollmaker, right? So, I believe in Santa Claus. A world without Santa Claus? It'd be like a world without Hope. And we all know how hopeless that would be."

"I just don't know. I'm confused. I don't know what to think."

"Are you going to see Luke again?"

"I'm not sure." She sneezed.

"Don't you like him? Isn't he a good guy?"

"Yes. He's a good guy. But I have so much baggage. When he finds out, he won't want anything to do with me. I know he won't. And I don't even have the courage to talk to him about what happened to me. And I can't talk about it on the radio, either. But I'm damaged. Tainted. Ruined. I'm not good enough. And I don't want any more hurt. I think it might be best to just leave it where it's at. As a beautiful memory. A moment in time that I can always hold in my heart. A day when I felt alive and happy. But I just have too much baggage."

"Let me ask this—is he a gentleman? Is Luke a gentlemen?"

"Yes. He's a total gentleman. He opens doors for me and everything, even though I tell him not to."

"Right. Somehow, I knew he did. And a gentleman will always help a lady carry her baggage."

"I don't know. I just don't. Maybe I shouldn't call in anymore. Maybe this isn't such a good idea."

"Fine. You don't have to call in anymore if you don't want to. I know I joke around a lot, but this really isn't about ratings to me. It's about you. It's about Hope. Hope, the human being. But for whatever it's worth, here's what I think, and I'll leave you with this—complete the song."

She coughed. "Complete the song?"

"Complete the song. *Take My Whole Life, Too*, as Charlotte called it. Think of the song. The song you and Luke danced to today. What comes right after the *take my whole life, too* line? What's the next line? Get there. Get to the next line in that song. And I think if you do, all your doubts will go right out the window. And you'll see that Santa is Real. And that there is literally nothing more Real. In all the universe, there's nothing more Real, kiddo. And The Midnight Ranger wouldn't lie to you. Unless, of course, you count my endorsements. I do kind of lie in those. Like that voiceover ad I did for Paulie's Bar and Grille. Horrible place. Never go there. I know I said it was great in the commercial. Had to. But the fact of the matter is that the place is on Mace Street, and they named it *Mace Street* because you'd better have some mace handy if you're going to venture into that neighborhood. Plus, the rats are such regulars there that they have their own reserved table. Seriously, the joint needs a Jon Taffer intervention." The laugh track played

"Okay, well, I'm going to hang up now." Hope sneezed and coughed before adding, "I have a lot to think about."

"Goodnight, Hope. Take care of yourself. And remember—somethings are meant to be."

CHAPTER ELEVEN: THE FRANKENSTEIN SWEATER

Sunday morning. Game day. The Baltimore Ravens versus the Pittsburgh Steelers in the American Football Conference Divisional Playoff.

Luke got up early, around six. Immediately, he checked his phone. He'd texted Hope twice over the last two days to see if she wanted to grab dinner and a movie on Sunday evening, after the game. No response. *Should I try again? No. Don't want to make a pest of myself. I thought we had a good day the other day. Thought it went great, in fact. Especially once we got to Tiffany's. Now, she won't even respond to my texts. Disappointing. Maybe I'll never understand women. I don't even feel like going to the stupid game.*

After feeding the cats, he took a shower, shaved, and sprayed on his CK Euphoria Intense.

He looked in his closet and considered what to wear. Normally, such a big game would merit careful thought when choosing a wardrobe. But on this cold January Sunday, he simply put on a white turtleneck. Over top of that, he slipped on his purple Ravens jersey. Next, he put on a pair of Levi's. The look was completed with white sneakers. Then there was the whole matter of the face paint. The purple Ravens face paint. Dino was painting his face to show his Ravens pride. Luke had promised to do the same. But now, he just couldn't get excited.

Aw, the hell with it.

He sat on his living room sofa with Bobby in his lap reading his biography of Martin Luther King Jr. He tried to concentrate but it was hard. His thoughts were of Hope. *Why won't she even answer me? Maybe I should stop by her place later, do a little wellness check on her. Make sure she's okay.* He quickly dismissed the idea. *No. Can't do that. I'll come off like a stalker and there's nothing worse than a stalker.* He put down his book and petted Bobby.

At quarter after ten, the doorbell rang. He picked Bobby up and gently set him down. The cat mewed his displeasure. "Sorry, old buddy." *I always feel guilty when I have to make him get off my lap, like I'm a bad cat Dad.* He opened the front door. It was Dino, his wife, Kaitlyn, and Gretchen.

Dino wore blue jeans and a white Ravens jersey. Under the jersey, was a purple hoodie. And his entire face was painted bright purple. *He kind of looks like the genie from Aladdin.*

Gretchen had a white ladies-cut Ravens jersey on. Under that, she wore a black turtleneck. Her jeans looked expensive. They were tight-fitting and showcased a perfect bubble butt. Her sneakers were new and very white. *Bet they're some kind of insanely expensive designer brand.* On her head, she wore a purple Ravens stocking cap. Her glasses looked expensive, too. The frames were tortoise shell. *I like Hope's glasses better.* The outfit was capped off with a black leather jacket that was unzipped. She carried a large brown paper bag.

Dino immediately walked over to Luke and held up his hand. "High five, bro. Come on—bring the funk."

"Yeah, high five." He gave Dino an unenthusiastic high five.

Dino pointed to his face. "How come no face paint? I thought we had a pact. I thought we agreed that we were both going to don the face paint for the big game."

He lied. "Oh, I kind of remembered—that stuff makes my face break out. I think it's because it's oil-based or something."

Dino nodded and shrugged. "Oh, okay."

Luke greeted Dino's wife, Kaitlyn. She was a pretty blonde

who taught special education in the Baltimore public school system. He'd met her several times before. Luke shook her hand. *Nice lady. Pretty lady. Dino did all right for himself.*

"Hey. How are you doing, Kaitlyn?"

"Good. Doing good, Luke. How about you? How's your ribs? Dino told me the whole story. It's a shame. Some of these cops in this city are just out of control."

"I'm doing okay. I'll live. Thanks for asking."

Dino called to Gretchen. "Come here, sis. Front and center. I want to officially introduce you two to one another."

Gretchen walked over. She smiled at Luke and shyly waved. He caught a whiff of her perfume and recognized it as Martha's Vineyard. He'd previously dated a woman who wore it. It was expensive. He'd seen it in Sephora for two-hundred dollars an ounce. *It's not bad stuff. Kind of smells like the beach. Little bit of an odd choice for a cold winter's day, though. I like Hope's perfume better.*

"Look, I know you two kids have kind of, sort of, met before at my cookouts and parties and whatnot, but let me formally introduce you. Luke—this is my baby sis, Gretchen, the future Attorney General of the great state of Maryland."

Gretchen extended her hand to Luke and they shook. In her high, little girl voice, she said, "Attorney General, mah butt. I'm starting at Governor. And from there—the Presidency. I could be the first woman to be President of the United States. And right after I'm inaugurated, my first official act will be to make love to my man right on top of the Oval Office desk." She giggled.

Luke chuckled. "Well, just be careful. You don't want to push the darn nuclear button whilst in the heat of passion and blow up the world."

Gretchen teeheed and playfully tapped his arm. "Oh, you are so gosh darn funny. But in all seriousness, I totally admire your concern for humanity. That is, like, *so* Gandhi of you. But, ah, yeppers—making love on the Oval Office desk is my kink. It might be a little naughty, but that's my fantasy." She looked at Luke, winked, and smiled a devilish smile. "And you know about *fantasies,* don't you, Luke?"

He smiled and shrugged. "I know about fantasy football. Oh, and the old TV show, *Fantasy Island.* I know about that, too. I watch it on the *TV Classics Network* sometimes. It's a sweet show."

Dino nodded agreement. "It really *is* a sweet show."

Luke imitated Tattoo. *"Look boss—De plane...De plane."*

She laughed and again tapped his arm. "Oh, don't you ever stop, mister? You're funnier than Uncle Nate that time he tuned-in *RuPaul's Drag Race.* See, he thought it was *Rand Paul's Drag Race,* and that it was literally a show about drag racing hosted by Senator Rand Paul. He was drinking Johnnie Walker that night, and once he realized that it was a show about drag queens, he put a nine iron through the TV." She tittered.

God. Listening to that voice on a regular basis would drive me nuts. She sounds like me and my Marine buddies back in the day, when we'd drink on the weekends and huff helium because that was the only entertainment we could afford. Hell, she sounds so young that I'd feel compelled to card her before I even so much as put my arm around her, lest Chris Hansen should pop out from some dark corner and be like, hey there. Whatcha doin'? Go ahead and have a seat for me. Why'd you come here tonight? What were you expecting to happen?

"So, are you excited about the game, Luke?" Gretchen asked with a big smile and a nod.

With all the enthusiasm he could muster, he told her, "Yeah. For sure. Been looking forward to it all week. Go Ravens and all that good stuff."

"I know, right?" She thrust her fist in the air and cried, "Go Ray-vans! Wooooo!"

Oh, no. Not only does she have the litte girl voice, but she's a Woo Girl, too. And Woo Girls are so annoying. It'd be like dating Ric Flair.

Dino informed him, "Oh, and just so you know—not that it'd be a problem or anything—but Gretchen doesn't curse. And she doesn't like being around profanity, either."

Gretchen emphatically nodded and elaborated. "That's right. When a guy shows interest, I always tell him right from the get-go—*if your lips are profane, your overtures are in vain.* Because I do not swear, and I do not want to be subjected to it. I'm a Christian woman, after all. A very hot, foxy Christian woman, but a Christian woman, nonetheless. And I just started a cuss box at home. Yep. Every time Dino curses when he's over visiting, I charge him a dollar. It goes right into that cuss box. I'm going to put it towards a good cause. And with the way expletives fly out of my brother's mouth, in another month or so, I'll be able to pay off Wesley Snipes' tax debt." She laughed and continued. "Now, there are two places that are exempt from my *no cursing* rule."

Luke smiled. "And what, pray tell, would those two places be?"

"The boardroom...and the bedroom. There are no rules in either of those two places. *None.*" She smiled a naughty smile, nodded, and raised her eyebrows.

Luke nodded and forced a smile. "Right."

Gretchen held out her arms and twirled around for him to see. "Well? You think I look cute today, babe, or what? You didn't compliment me yet."

He nodded. "Yeah. Totally cute. You look really nice."

"And just think, you can't even get a full appreciation for my fantastic boobs because of this big, bulky leather jacket I'm wearing." She giggled.

"Well, we'll want to save something for the wedding night, right?" Luke quipped.

She casually handed him the brown bag she was carrying. "This is a little present for you, babe. I made it myself. Took me months. Hope you like it."

Dino interjected. "Oh, wait until you get a load of this, buddy. You are going to *love* this. Come on, now—open it. I want to see the look on your face."

Luke peeked inside the bag. *What the hell?* He slowly pulled out what appeared to be a green sweater.

"I took up knitting about six months ago because, you know, having domestic skills increases the value of my stock. Anyway, I made that for you. It's real mohair, too."

Great. Mohair. I'm allergic to mohair. He unfolded the sweater and held it up. There was an image on the garment. *What in God's name is this supposed to be?*

Dino was all smiles. "Look at that, will you?"

Luke was unenthusiastic. "Yeah. Look at it."

"How about the design, huh? You like that design on the front, babe? That took me, like, forever to do."

"Yeah. It's…ah…it's a Halloween sweater, right? Sure, it is." He held up the garment with one hand and pointed to the image. "And that's old Frankenstein himself on that sweater. Yeah. A Halloween sweater, for sure. With Frankie baby on it."

Gretchen gasped and stared at him for a few seconds with her mouth open in shock. She placed her hands on her hips, and finally asked, "Frankenstein? You think that's *Frankenstein*?"

Luke nodded. "Yeah. Look at him. He's all green and whatnot, has those big bolts coming from his neck. The top of his head's all flat, flatter than Mariah Carey's live voice. And he's got an ugly old scar on his forehead. No doubt about it. It's a Frankenstein, for sure. Might even be Herman Munster."

Gretchen wrinkled her nose and made a face. "Ah, excuse me? That's Baby Yoda. You know—The Child."

Luke looked at the image again, briefly reconsidered it, and shook his head. "Baby Yoda? Nah. That's a Frankenstein. I know a Frankenstein when I see one."

Gretchen rolled her eyes. "Well, then, you're blind, mister, because that looks *nothing* like a Frankenstein. But it does look *everything* like a Baby Yoda."

Dino lied. "Well, he *is* almost legally blind, sis. Those flash grenades in Afghanistan did it. Isn't that right, Luke?" Dino shot him a dirty look.

"Oh…yeah. Yeah, right. That *is* true. I really need to make an appointment at the VA to get my eyes checked. They're getting worse every day."

Gretchen covered her mouth. "Oh my gosh. I am so sorry. I didn't even know. My bad. Yeah. My bad, babe."

"It's okay. And thanks. Thanks for the sweater, Gretchen. That was really sweet of you."

Dino added, "And that was made with love, too, buddy. Can't buy that. Not even out of the Patrick James catalog."

"Uh-huh." He started to fold the sweater up to put it back in the bag.

Gretchen frowned. "Aren't you going to wear it, babe?"

He nodded. "Eventually. Next Halloween. If I want to scare the neighborhood kids."

"No. I mean—today. As in—right now. To the game."

Again, Dino involved himself. "Well, of course, he's going to wear it, sis. He's going to wear it to the game. Aren't you, old buddy? After all, this is a lovely garment. Made by a lovely lady. Any guy would be proud to wear it."

Luke handed him the sweater. "Here. Then you wear it. *Old. Buddy.*"

Dino handed it back. "Don't be silly, Luke. It was made for you—your measurements and everything. Remember when I borrowed that one sweater of yours last fall? Well, that's what I wanted it for. So that Gretchen could use it as a size guide."

"You never did return that sweater, by the way. And that was my favorite sweater. Very comfy. Nicely broken in, too. It was a tremendous all-around sweater."

Gretchen matter-of-factly announced, "I donated it to Goodwill after I was done with it. I would have thrown it out with the rest of the trash, but why not get the tax write-off, you know? I saw the tag. It was the Walmart brand. Seriously? Walmart? Do people really buy clothes there? You couldn't swing Macy's? Or even The Gap?"

Luke glared at Gretchen.

Nonchalantly, she issued an order. "Put the Baby Yoda sweater on. Come on, babe. Make Mama happy. Put it on. Put. It.

On. Putiton."

He shook his head. "It's not going to fit over my jersey." *She sounds like she's twelve and now she's referring to herself as my mother. If Hansen doesn't get me, Springer will.*

Dino said, "Don't be silly. Of course, it'll fit. See, Gretchen gave you some room to grow. You're too thin. And when you start to eat her cooking on a regular basis, you'll fill out some. So, you know, go ahead and slip it on. Slip it right on."

Luke put the sweater on over his jersey. He immediately sneezed.

Dino sized him up, smiled, and pumped his fist. He laid it on thick. "*Yeah*! Right on, man. Dy-no-mite. Yeah, dude. That is righteous. I dig it. Oh, I *so* want one. That looks amazing, by the way. Doesn't even need more cow bell. Oh, buddy—you are going to get yourself noticed *to-day.* They might even put you on TV. Make you a big star." Dino gently punched him on the shoulder. "The whole town's going to be talking about you, my boy. You and that gorgeous Franken, I mean *Baby Yoda,* sweater."

Yeah. Getting noticed. That's what I'm afraid of. "I'll be the belle of the ball, all right."

Gretchen shifted gears. "Oh, and before I forget—I was looking at your Facebook page. You need to delete that one post about the lady cop who harassed you."

Luke shrugged. "What was the problem with the post?"

"Well, besides grammar, sentence structure, punctuation, and spelling—two things. First, if I didn't know better, I'd say that you had a thing for her. Which I know you don't because you're, like, *so* into me. But that's one reason it needs to go. Second, when we sue, it could hurt our case. See, the city's lawyers will scour your social media accounts looking for anything to weaken our case. A sympathetic post on Facebook is just the type of thing they'd love to find. Now, I talked to old man Jenkins on Friday, and we think the case is worth about ten mil, based on comparable cases around the country. That cop violated your civil rights. She trampled on the Constitution. It was egregious. Nefarious. Scandalous. And you were physically injured as a result of her actions. She'll be fired as part of the settlement, by the way. I'll personally see to that. Trust me, it's not even going to get to court. They'll be happy to settle. Jenkins said we could take the case on contingency. The firm gets twenty percent. That should leave about eight mil. You'll be a rich man when it's all said and done. And I'd personally be representing you. Of course, that means we'd have to spend a lot of time together working the case." She winked at him, licked her lips, and kissed the air. "Maybe even some overnighters."

"I'm not suing. I don't want to sue. It was all a misunderstanding. And it's been addressed to my satisfaction."

She dismissively waved her hand at him. "Look, we'll talk about it later. For now, just delete the gosh darn post."

Dino assured her. "He'll delete it, sis. He will. That's the beauty of Facebook. You can always delete. Delete—delete—delete. When in doubt, delete. Just like when Uncle Nate posted that rant that detailed his political manifesto by quoting Archie Bunker. Remember that one, sis? Huh? And how he said that anyone who didn't *like* his post was a communist stooge? He was on Mad Dog Twenty-Twenty that night. Yes sir. The big ole Mad Dog." Dino imitated a dog. "Woof! Woof! But Aunt Helen made sure it got deleted. Until the next time he got drunk...which was the following morning. But for a good seven hours, that post *did* disappear. Any-who, he'll make it go away, sis. He will."

Gretchen started looking around the living room. She perused a shelf with CDs and DVDs on it.

"You have a lot of pro wrestling DVDs. What's up with that? Huh, babe?"

"I like pro wrestling. It's like a soap opera with body slams."

She wagged her finger at him. "Luke, you live in Roland Park, not a trailer park."

She pulled a CD off the shelf and held it up. The album was

KISS Alive II. "And what's with this? Huh?" She made a face.

He shrugged. "I like KISS."

"Yeah, well, news flash—KISS stands for *Knights In Satan's Service*. They play the Devil's music. They're satanic."

"Satanic? Their biggest hit was *Beth*, for crying out loud."

"Satan lures you in with a soft ballad, to get you hooked. Then he drops the hard rock right on top of your head. But, hey, if you want to take a dip in the lake of fire that is Hell, I guess that's up to you." She casually tossed the CD back on the bookshelf and muttered something about needing to "wash Satan off" her hands.

Dang. This woman's as nutty as Kanye.

Gretchen paused for a moment and tentatively spoke. "Oh, and another thing. And this is kind of a delicate subject, I know, but I feel it has to be discussed because it's grating on me."

Luke threw his arms up and again sneezed. "What needs to be discussed? Tell me."

"Your uncanny resemblance to Elvis Presley."

"So?"

"Again, trailer parky, babe. Elvis was a good example that you can't buy class. Elvis was trailer park chic personified. The man had all that money and what did he do with it? Did he buy blue chip stocks? Did he join a classy country club? Nope. He spent his money on gaudy jewelry, gaudy clothes, gaudy cars, and gaudy women. Ever see the getup he wore when he met President Nixon? I saw a documentary on his meeting with the President. Now, this is the President of the United States, mind you. And Elvis was meeting him in the Oval Office. That's as official as it gets. It's an honor. Especially meeting a great man like Richard Nixon. And what did Elvis wear? Did he observe decorum and protocol? Ha! Dream-the-heck-on. He wore skintight purple velvet pants. A high-collared white silk shirt unbuttoned to his waist. More gold than a Vegas pimp. Huge, amber tinted sunglasses. And to top it all off—a purple cape. Yes. A gosh darn cape. Now, who the heck wears a cape?"

Luke laughed. "Three people. Three people in history have been Constitutionally authorized to wear the cape. Superman. Dracula. And Elvis, baby."

She rolled her eyes. "Oh, good gosh almighty. And then there's his eating habits. The man could have eaten caviar at the finest five-star restaurants. But what did he do? He ate fried peanut butter, banana, and bacon sandwiches. He ate Moon Pies. And to drink? Dom Perignon? Try RC Cola. Hillbilly juice. That's the number one selling soft drink in Kentucky, for goodness sake."

Luke threw up his hands. "He was down-to-earth, Gretchen. And what's your point, anyway?"

"My point is—it would be great if you didn't have to look so much like him. It could hurt my career. When we would go to cocktail parties, which is one of those events where careers are advanced, it would look silly. The people who I socialize with, the movers and shakers of Baltimore, would point and laugh. And when I run for Governor, it could really be a problem. It'd be major campaign fodder for my opponent. *Yeah*, my candidacy would be looked at with lots of *suspicious minds*, that's for sure."

"Well, it's not like I've had cosmetic surgery to look like him, like some of the impersonators—oh, sorry—I mean *tribute artists*—do. They say everyone has a doppelganger. I guess I'm Elvis'."

"Yeah, but, ideally, you'd look like Hugh Grant, circa nineteen ninety-five. And if you could work on a British accent, that'd be great. British accents are very debonair and classy. And a change is definitely needed. Because, truth be told, the whole Elvis thing is driving me freaking crazy."

Sounds like a short ride to me. He forced a smile and spoke pointedly. "Look. Gretchen. I'm not British. Don't wanna *beeeee* British. Now, don't misunderstand me—England has gifted the world some pretty awesome things over the centuries. Benny Hill. The Spice Girls. Driving on the wrong side of the road. But a little war was fought nearly two-hundred and fifty years ago. Ever hear of it? They call it The Revolutionary War. The *American* Revolution. And the British lost. Yeah, that's right—they lost. You see, their powdered wigs, and fancy-pants red coats, and fine tricorn hats couldn't beat the guts and determination of regular, run-of-the-mill Americans. The mutts beat the pedigrees. They kicked His Majesty's royal ass. And I, for one, am proud to be a mutt. I watch pro wrestling. I listen to KISS. And I look like Elvis Presley. And I'm proud of it. Hell, before we get married, you really ought to know that I have some Billy Ray Cyrus CDs, too. Yeah. More than one. In fact, I have them all. I have the man's entire career on CD. And I've line danced to *Achy Breaky Heart*. I drink RC Cola. And the restaurants where I eat always inform you—*for another fifty cents, I can supersize that for you.* And that, Gretchen, is the greatness of America."

Gretchen gasped and covered her mouth. "Oh, sweet Jesus, my Lord and Savior. Billy Ray Cyrus? He's worse than KISS. That hideous mullet, that hideous music, and half of the DNA behind Miley. I think I'm going to faint."

Good grief. He hasn't worn the mullet in at least twenty years. This woman's actually worse than Kanye. She's reached the rarefied air of Charlie Sheen-like nuttiness.

Dino whistled and applauded. "Woo! Praise the Lord and pass the ammunition. Guess he told you, huh, sis? Now, let's just go to the game, shall we? Once we get to the game, you two lovebirds will sing your sweet song to one another. I know you will."

Gretchen put her hands on her hips. "You know what? I don't think I'd be comfortable going to the game with *him*." She accusingly pointed to Luke. "And seeing how they're *my* tickets and it's *my* limo, I really think Luke should do the decent thing and bow out."

"Are you dumping me, Gretchen? If so, I really shouldn't go. I'll watch here at home."

She wrinkled her nose and emphatically nodded. "Yeah, I'm dumping your keister, mister. You're not good enough for a

Cavanaugh. And I'll bet you're not even Republican."

"I'm Independent, baby, which is what you're going to be for the rest of your life because nobody short of Hugh Grant circa nineteen ninety-five is ever going to be good enough for you."

She stuck her tongue out at him and turned to her brother. "Come on, Dino. Let's go to the game."

"Yeah—yeah. Give me just a sec, sis. I want to talk to Luke here right quick."

"Make it fast." Gretchen and Kaitlyn started to walk out the door. Gretchen stopped and turned around. "Hey Luke—"

"Yeah?"

"Knock—knock."

"Who's there?"

"Fuck you! That's who!" She flipped him off and continued her verbal assault. "You're a bum. You know that? A *bum*. And you're content to be a bum. You're nothing but a carpenter, for God's sake. I thought I could make you into something more, something worthwhile, but I was wrong."

She turned back around and walked out.

"I thought she only curses in the boardroom and the bedroom."

Dino shrugged. "There's a third exception. When she's feeling vindictive. Then, she unleashes a potty mouth that rivals even Bobby Knight's. That was kind of your own fault, though. When she said *knock—knock*, you should have known better than to have even answered the door at that point."

He wagged his index finger at Dino. "You know, Dino, she should count her blessings. She has her health. She should be grateful, but instead, she walks around being Little Miss Nasty Head to everybody."

Dino emphatically nodded. "I know—I know. I tell her every day, I say—*sis you have your health. You should be thankful. You shouldn't be walking around being Little Miss Nasty Head to everybody.*"

Luke extended his hand to Dino. "Yeah, well, anyhow—this thing between me and Gretchen, it's not your fault. So, you know, no hard feelings on my end. And I hope you don't have any either."

They shook.

Dino dismissively waved his hand. "Nah. No hard feelings, man. After all, she dumped *you*. And it's better for you that she dumped you now. Frankly, she would have taken you to the cleaners in the divorce settlement."

They both laughed.

Dino patted him on the shoulder. "Enjoy that sweater, dude."

"That's the ugliest sweater I've ever seen."

"Tell me about it. She made me one for Christmas. I looked at it and thought to myself—*oh, wow, what a sweater. It has a picture of a walrus on it. A big, silly walrus with a huge shit-eating grin on his face.*"

"Was it at least supposed to be a walrus?"

"Nah, man. It was supposed to be Grumpy Cat."

Gretchen screamed into the living room. "Dean-noooo! Get your ass into this limo! Now! I want to get to the tailgate area before all the decent spots are taken."

"Gotta go, before she uninvites *me*. Right now, she's madder than Uncle Nate was when he found out his MAGA hat was one of those knockoffs made in Mexico. Anyhow, I'm going to scalp the extra ticket. It should bring at least a thousand bucks. At least. Should cover about two weeks of my damn cussing fees."

Dino turned and started walking away.

"Hey Dino—"

He turned back around. "Yeah buddy?"

"That narrative—*she dumped me*. Not really accurate. I think it was more like we dumped each other, you know? It was a mutual dumping."

Dino shrugged and threw up his hands. "What can I say? Maybe the tabloids will be fair to you. You know, let you tell your side of the story and all. In the meantime, the Gretchen PR machine, via any and all social media outlets, will run with the story that she dumped your sorry ass." Dino laughed.

Luke laughed and waved goodbye. "Get out of here, you nut. Enjoy the game. I'll be watching from my couch. Where it's warm."

After they left, he took off the sweater, rolled it into a ball, and talked to it. "I didn't wear *you*. You wore *me*, you ugly thing. And I don't care what she says—you *are* a Frankenstein sweater." He threw it to the floor in disgust.

CHAPTER TWELVE: THE HELLO KITTY ONESIE

Luke watched the game on his couch, with Hannah curled up in his lap. Baltimore lost, 37-34, on a last-second field goal. He looked on as the game-winning kick sailed through the uprights. He was nonchalant, stoic even, about the defeat. "Oh, well. Better luck next year," he said to the cat as he gently rubbed her under the chin.

Normally, he would have been devastated. But this day, he found it difficult to care. *Hard to find either joy or sorrow in the outcome of a football game right now. I'm just bummed.*

He wasn't hungry so he skipped dinner. After he fed the cats and scooped their boxes, he settled in for a movie. He picked *An Officer and A Gentleman* from his DVD collection. *Somebody may as well have a happy ending around here. I guess it'll be Richard Gere and Debra Winger.*

An hour into the picture, the phone rang. He recognized the number. It was Hope. He was excited. "Hey there. What's up?"

Her voice was hoarse. "I think my temperature."
"Say again."
"I'm not feeling too hot. In fact, I'm sick as hell."
"Sorry to hear that. A cold?"
"I guess. I'm coughing, sneezing. Achy. My chest hurts a little. Headache. Bad headache. Nauseous even. I feel really

bad." She coughed and wheezed.

"When'd this start?"

"I don't know—a couple of days ago, I guess. I...I was wondering if you have any cold medicines. I don't have anything, and I feel too crappy to go out and get some. Do you have anything that might help? I'd pay you for them, and I'd also pay for your gas to bring them over and all."

"Yeah, I have some stuff I could bring over. But I won't take any money from you. Give me, maybe, a half-hour or so."

"That'd be great. I appreciate it. How was your big date? I had the game on here in the bedroom. I saw where the Ravens lost. Sorry about that."

"Yeah, well, my date didn't really happen."

"*What?*"

"I got benched before the game even started. When they came to pick me up in the limo, Gretchen and I had a big falling out. Right here in my living room. I was promptly uninvited to the game."

Hope coughed some more. It took her a moment to compose herself. "What happened? What'd you fight over?"

"Oh, let's see. There was Billy Ray Cyrus. Pro wrestling. Elvis Presley. The American Revolution. The rock band, KISS. An ugly-ass sweater that's supposed to depict an image of Baby Yoda, but I still say it's a Frankenstein. Um...oh yeah—Richard Nixon and Hugh Grant both showed up at the party. Both uninvited. But what the hell, you know? There were no bouncers to keep them out, so they just waltzed right in. How 'bout that? Quite a cast of characters, huh?"

"Bizarre."

"Yeah it was. The bottom line—I'm not good enough for her. Not good enough for the future Governor of Maryland. The future President of the United States, no less. Not good enough for a Cavanaugh."

"I don't like this woman."

"Yeah, well, even I, myself, am highly unlikely at this point to hire a skywriter to draw a big heart in the atmosphere whilst she and I ride through Patterson Park in a Hansom cab, arm-in-arm, sipping hot chocolate, and being serenaded by the driver with a medley of Burt Bacharach tunes."

"So, you're single again, huh?" She rapid-fire sneezed three times in a row.

"Bless you. And I know you don't believe in God, so I hope me saying *bless you* didn't offend you. And I was never not single. You and I have more of a history than me and Gretchen ever had."

"We don't have a *history*."

"We do. We stared down death together on a highway. That's a history, baby. Matter of fact, that jumps us ahead to, I'm going to say, at least the tenth date. Yeah. That sounds about right. Tenth date. We're on the tenth date now."

"Yeah. Well. Whatever. The front door is unlocked, and the lights are all on. I'll be upstairs in bed. Just come on up. And, yes, I know I vowed that you'd never see the inside of my house, let alone my bedroom. So fine. There. You win. You win again. Happy?"

"I wasn't even going to mention that. That's the past. And I'm trying not to live in it. It's a real struggle, but I'm trying. Now, just sit tight. I'll be over in a little bit." He hung up, put together a makeshift medical bag, and headed out.

◆ ◆ ◆

It was another brutally cold night. The low was forecast to be in the single digits, right around six degrees. It was windy, too. When he left, he had to retrieve his metal trashcan from his neighbor's yard. *Damn wind. Must be blowing at least thirty miles per hour.*

When he got to Hope's house, he turned the knob on the front door. Sure enough, it was unlocked. He walked in, carrying a light brown plastic bag. The lights were on. He could smell the aroma of the Angel air freshener. *Wow. That is such a great fragrance. So feminine. Love it. Can't get enough of it.*

He felt strange being in her house, being downstairs by himself. *She must trust me to let me in like this. Despite what she says, she must really trust me.*

As he started up the stairs, a framed photo on the wall caught his eye. It was a photo of Hope tenderly holding a handsome gray tabby cat with one hand. The cat had a child's paper birthday hat on. In her other hand, she held up a cake which had lettering on it. It read—*Happy Birthday, Desi.* Hope was making a silly face at the camera. He smiled when he saw it. *She* does *like cats. I knew it.* As he continued to ascend the stairs, there were more framed photos of Desi on the wall. The pictures showed the cat at various stages of life. He studied one that showed him as a tiny kitten. Hope was sprawled out on the floor next to him with some toys. In the background, sat a cardboard cat carrier that proclaimed *I'm Going Home.* He found it poignant. *Must have been the day she adopted him.* There was another photo of the feline wearing a tiny Santa hat and sitting next to the Christmas tree. He smiled again. *This cat was a big deal to her. So, what happened?*

When he got to her bedroom, he knocked on a partially open door. He could hear a TV playing inside.

"Come on in," he heard her say in a froggy voice.

Tentatively, he entered.

She was in bed but wasn't under the covers. Her hair was messed up and her nose was red and chapped, obviously from tissue burn. She wore a pink Hello Kitty onesie.

Aw. She looks so cute in her onesie. It even has the little built-in feet.

She was in mid hack. The floor was littered with used tissues near a small trashcan, which sat about five feet from the bed. *She must not be good at basketball. No touch on her shots whatsoever.*

As she coughed, she raised her hand to greet him. "Hey." She tried to sit up.

He looked her up and down and shook his head. "You look like hell."

She smiled a toothy, sarcastic smile. "Gee. Thanks. You sure know how to flatter a girl."

He set his bag down on the bed, which was covered with a pink comforter. "I didn't mean for it to come out that way. Sorry. I just meant that it's obvious that you don't feel well at the moment, that's all."

"Tell me something I don't know."

"Just two weeks before he died in a high-speed car wreck, James Dean taped a PSA urging motorists to obey the speed limit and drive defensively."

She shot him a befuddled look. *"Huh?"*

He shrugged. "Well, that's something that you probably didn't know. But it is true. The PSA in question is on YouTube. You can look it up for yourself if you don't believe me. Oh, and it gets even more creepy because the talking head who interviewed Dean in the spot was none other than Gig Young. He was a big movie star of the fifties. Well, Gig Young ended up killing his wife and then turning the gun on himself in a murder-suicide. They never determined the motive, either. I tell ya, that was one cursed PSA."

"Yeah—yeah—yeah. Did you bring the cold meds?"

He retrieved a digital thermometer from his bag. "Before we start with any meds, I want to see if you have a fever."

"I'm sure I do."

"Yeah, well, let's see how high. And although I never thought I'd tell *you,* of all people, to open your mouth—come on, Hope, open your mouth. Open it."

He placed the thermometer in her mouth. After thirty seconds, it beeped. He removed it and read it aloud. "102.9. And that's not some new radio station channel number, either. That's a relatively high fever."

"I know it's high. I already told you—I feel like crap." She again wheezed and coughed. "Oh, God, it hurts when I cough or sneeze."

He pulled out a pulse oximeter. "Here. Give me your index finger."

She shot him an incredulous look. "You have your own little oxygen thingy?"

"Yep. It's called a pulse oximeter. Got it three years ago. And it only cost ninety-nine cents in the bargain bin at CVS. This is the first time I've ever had to use it. But this essentially makes it worth the buck that I paid. It's now more than paid for itself, in my mind."

"Yeah. Well. Whatever."

He placed the instrument on her left index finger. *Aw. She has such nice nails. Must get them done all the time. They're French manicured. And her tiny little hands are adorable. So are her tiny little feet.*

After a few seconds, a number registered on the instrument.

He read it aloud. "Ninety-three. Your oxygen saturation is ninety-three percent."

She considered it and shrugged. "Ninety-three. In school, a ninety-three on a test was borderline, right between an A and an A-minus."

"Uh-huh. Well, a ninety-three on *this* test basically means you're an eighty-five-year-old who's been smoking two packs of Lucky Strikes a day for seventy years, and you're now in the terminal stage of emphysema. It's low, Hope. Dangerously low."

"I realize that. I've had some first aid training, you know. I am, after all, a cop."

"Then I'm sure you also realize that one of the most common complications from broken ribs is pneumonia."

"I don't have pneumonia."

"I think you might."

She coughed some more. "Fine. I'll go to the doctor tomorrow. Maybe. If I can get an appointment."

"No, you're going tonight."

After another coughing fit, she told him, "It's Sunday night. All the doctor's offices are closed. So are the urgent care places."

"Yeah, but there's this great little place called the ER. It's open twenty-four-seven and you just walk right in.

No appointment needed. In fact, they don't even take appointments. They offer free cable TV and magazines. Reasonably priced refreshments, too. Imagine that."

"I *am not* going to the ER."

"You are. Pneumonia can kill. Your fever is high, and your oxygen level is low. You're going. And I'm taking you."

She crossed her arms and shook her head. "Can't make me."

"I can call nine-one-one. I can call nine-one-one on your ass. And that's what I'll do."

"You wouldn't."

"I would. And I will if I have to. We can do this the easy way or the hard way. Up to you. I think you might need to be admitted."

"They're not going to admit me. They can't hold me against my will. I know that much."

"If they want to admit you, you'll be admitted because I'll tell them I'm your husband and that you're delirious. And incapable of making sound decisions. And that I'm invoking power of attorney to admit your ass. I'd do that. I'm serious, girl. Now, come on. Let's go."

She pointed to herself. "Look at me. I look like shit. You said so yourself. And I'm wearing a freaking pink Hello Kitty onesie. And I don't have the strength to change. So, everyone in the whole damn ER will stare at me and laugh."

He shook his head. "Will not. It's the ER. Half of the people there will be in pajamas. The doctors and nurses are used to it. It does not faze them at all. And the person that everyone will be staring at is—That Guy. Okay? *That Guy.* Yeah. The one who constantly seems to be in the ER because he's always sticking things up his butt. Clothes pins. Soda bottles. Coat hangers. Tonight, he took his son's Power Ranger doll and shoved it up his ass. Just to see if he could. Plus, he thought it might, possibly—somehow—feel good. Now, it's stuck up there. And he's in the ER. And as we speak, he's lying there on his stomach, reading a three-year-old issue of *People*. And he's low priority because, you know, he's stable or whatever. And some poor son-of-a-bitch-doc is going to lose the rock, paper, scissors battle with the other doctors and eventually have to deal with That Guy. Now, *that's* who everyone will be staring at. So, let's go."

"Fine. Let's go. But it's going to be crowded as hell because it's still the weekend, so we'll probably be there all freaking night. And I do not want to hear you complaining."

"You won't. Now, where's your coat? You need a coat. It's very cold. Single digits tonight."

She pointed to her closet. "My coat's in there."

He looked in her closet and pulled out a heavy bright green Sherpa winter coat that had a hood attached.

"No, that doesn't match my onesie. And I hate that coat anyway. I don't know what possessed me to buy it. There are a lot of other coats in there."

"But this one's the heaviest, the warmest."

"But it doesn't match."

He shook his head. "Not a fashion show, Hope. The ER, that is. It's not a fashion contest. They most likely are not going to have a runway for you to sashay down while the guys from *Queer Eye* sit there and judge your look on a scale of one to ten. Eighty-five percent chance that's not going to happen. I'll be very surprised if we walk in and Carson Kressley is strutting around with a clipboard, clapping his hands, saying—*all right, people. Places everyone. Places. We can finally get started now that Hope's here, rocking her onesie. Oh! It is so on, bitches. This is going to be absolutely savage.* That little scenario is not all that likely to unfold. Okay? So, let's get the jacket on, shall we?"

He helped her put the jacket on and pulled the hood up over her head.

She frowned. "Oh, *no*. I have to wear the hood, too?"

"Yep. That's where you lose most of your body heat. Through your head. I learned that in the Marines. Got to bundle you up, you know."

He pulled the drawstrings on the hood tight and tied them into a bow. The hood then closed in on her face.

She shot him a look of horror. "Oh, good Gawd. With these drawstrings pulled tight, I look like Kenny from *South Park*. People are going to make fun of me. They *are*."

He shook his head and wagged his finger at her. "No. Now you listen to me—Kenny's cute as the dickens. Okay? He's the cutest kid on that show. Love that Kenny. It's a damn shame they always killed him off in the earlier seasons. I don't know why they did that. Just for the sake of gratuitous violence, I guess. But, ah, Kenny—that kid's all right in my book."

He looked at her closely, smiled a big smile, and proclaimed, "*Aw*. Now, look at you. Bee-you-tee-ful. You're all bundled up and you really do look like someone who's ready to go to the ER. You look exactly like an ER-goer. Yes, you do. A cute little ER-goer. Now, let's go. Go—go—go."

"Before we go, I want my J-Lo glasses. They're on my desk."

"Your *what?*"

"My J-Lo glasses. Grab them." She pointed towards the desk. "They're the big, oversized, light blue tinted glasses. I call them my J-Lo glasses. They'll distract from my sickly appearance."

He found the glasses and held them up. "These? These what you're talking about? These big old things? Holy crap, Hope. They're bigger than MacArthur's. He, ah, he was a famous five-star general, by the way. Douglas MacArthur. His trademark was his big, gaudy sunglasses. Well, that and his corncob pipe. *I shall return* and all that jazz. He wanted to nuke communist China. That was his strategy for winning the Korean War. In a very controversial move, Truman fired him. Long time ago. I learned about him in the Marines."

"Uh-huh. Bring them over here and put them on me, will you? Yeah. Put my J-Lo glasses on me."

He put the glasses on her, stood back, and gave her a hard stare. "Whoa. *Hello*. Instant diva. You're J-Lo. Lord have mercy! You are *Jay-Low*, girl. J-Lo in da hooooouse, y'all. May I have your autograph, Miz *Low-pez?*" He stuck an imaginary microphone in her face. "And I have a follow-up, as well—what was Matt McConaughey like to work with? Is he really as zany as he seems on all the talkies?"

He tucked her hair inside the hood and casually noted, "You know, you really don't have to worry about looking like Kenny anymore. With the combination of the hood and the glasses, you look more like the Unabomber. Just like the Unabomber's FBI composite sketch. Yeah, no doubt— I am definitely seeing more Unabomber now that we've added the big, dark glasses. If you had the mustache, you'd actually be a dead ringer for him."

She giggled and shook her head. "You're the zany one, you know that? Crazy is what you are. Cray-zee, boy."

"Of course, I am. After all, I joined the Marines. They didn't draft me. I waltzed right into my local recruiter's office and said—*thirteen weeks at Parris Island? Communal showers with seventy other dudes? Drill instructor screaming that you make him a believer in reincarnation because nobody could possibly get that stupid in only one lifetime? Yes, please. Give me those enlistment papers and a pen.*" He laughed.

She again giggled. "You're in rare form tonight, bud. Are you on cocaine or something?"

"Nah. I just stopped at Starbucks on the way over and got their sixty-four ounce cup of coffee. Extra caffeine variety. I had to take out a second mortgage to afford it, but what can I say? I love me some Starbucks."

She pointed to a mahogany dresser on the other side of the room. "Can you get me my purse? It's sitting right there on the dresser. I'll need my insurance card."

He retrieved her purse and she slung it around her left shoulder.

She looked up at him with exasperation. "I think I'm too weak to walk, Luke."

"Then I'll carry you. Yeah. I'll carry you. No problem. I might be a little gimpy, but I can still carry you."

She threw up her hands and sneezed. "Great. Even more humiliating."

"Well, how are you going to get to the car, then? Is God, who you don't even believe in, going to miracle your little butt into the front seat? Huh?"

He didn't wait for an answer. He scooped her up. "Come on, lass. Everyone needs a little help now and then. There should be no shame or embarrassment in it, either."

"You better not drop me, mister. If you do, I'll kick your ass." She coughed and placed her arms around his neck.

He chuckled. "You will, will you?"

She emphatically nodded. "Damn right."

"My dear, at the moment, I don't think you could kick Richard Simmons' ass."

He stopped and looked her in the eyes. His blue eyes met hers.

"Look, I'm not going to drop you. Or hurt you. Or let anything bad happen to you."

"Promise?"

"Yes. I promise."

Her voice was hoarse. "Kay then."

CHAPTER THIRTEEN: OUT OF THE MOUTHS OF BABES

They arrived at the Mercy Medical Center ER at eight that evening. He carried her in. As expected, it was crowded—typical weekend. He set her down in a chair and signed them in. She took off her coat. The triage nurse got her a wheelchair and assessed her in a small room near the registration desk.

The nurse was in her 50s. She wore a lot of makeup and perfume. Hope took a deep whiff. *Tommy Girl, and Tommy Girl always gives me a headache. Not that it really matters tonight because I already feel like my head's in a vice.*

The nurse chewed gum obnoxiously and asked some questions as she took Hope's vitals.

After a couple of minutes, she announced, "Temp's 103.1 and oxygen saturation is only ninety-two. BP's way up—one sixty-five over ninety-five. You're sick, honey."

Hope coughed then talked through gritted teeth. "No shit, Sherlock."

Luke chastised her. "Hey, what's the matter with you, huh? Listen to yourself. Gettin' all mouthy with the nurse over here. Shame on ya. It's not her fault you feel bad. Why don't you do us all a favor and let that cut under your nose heal for a while?"

He apologized to the nurse. "Sorry. Normally, she's not like this at all. She's really a very upbeat, cheerful person. She's just irritable because she's sick."

"Oh, believe me, I'm used to it. I've seen far worse than your wife."

"I'm not his wife. Everyone thinks I'm his wife. I'm not. Kay?"

The nurse shrugged. "Fine. Girlfriend. Anyhow, you two have a seat in the waiting room and we'll get to you as soon as possible. Might be a while, though. As you can see, we're very busy tonight. Par for the course on a Sunday night. So, get comfy." The nurse pointed to her. "By the way, I love the onesie. Got my granddaughter the exact same one for Christmas. She's six."

I knew people were going to talk about the onesie. I just knew it.

He wheeled her into the waiting room. "Where do you want to sit?" He pointed to empty seats near the TV. "How about over there?"

She whispered. "No. There's hippies sitting over there. And hippies stink. They smell like a combination of dope and patchouli."

"Fine. Then over by the magazines. There's seats open over there, too."

"Yeah. That'll be fine."

He wheeled her over to that area and took a seat.

She draped her coat over the back of her wheelchair and placed her purse in her lap. Badfinger's *Day After Day* played from the phone of an older man sitting three seats away. *Oh, I love this song. So pretty.*

He took some change out of his pocket and started to sift through it.

She coughed. "What? You need some change for the vending machines? Because I might have some in my purse."

"Oh, no, no. I'm examining my quarters. Here's a nice little *get to know you* type thing—see, I'm something of a coin collector. I'm just an amateur, at this point. Haven't turned pro yet. Anyhow, the U.S. Mint—the Mint makes all of our coinage—it screwed up recently. You know how all our coins bear the motto—*In God We Trust?* You've seen that on money before, right? I'm sure you have."

She nodded. "Right. Sure."

"Okay, so anyway, they screwed up. I read about it in my online coin newsletter, *The Coin Chronicle.* Yeah, so, they made what they call an *error coin.* With these quarters, instead of putting *In God We Trust* on them, they put *In Goo We Trust.* The government was right on top of it, though. They only struck a little over two million of them before it was caught. But if you happen to have an *In Goo We Trust* quarter in your possession—well, they're quite valuable. Yeah. Those quarters fetch a pretty penny. On eBay, they're going for at least a grand. So, I always check my change because if I find one, I'm going to sell it and donate the proceeds to Recycled Love. See, I was just reading on our Facebook page that Beatrice—she's a Persian whose person recently died—well, we just found out that she's diabetic and is going to be insulin dependent. And a thousand bucks would buy her, maybe, four months-worth of insulin. Insulin's really expensive, by the way."

He finished checking the change. "Nope. No *In Goo We Trust* quarters today. Better luck next time, you know?"

Before he put the coins back in his pocket, he handed her a quarter. "Here. That's the quarter I borrowed from you to feed the meter that day in Mondawmin. I always pay my debts, no matter how small."

She held it up and examined it. "Gee. Thanks. What does a quarter even buy these days?"

"Sometimes, the supermarket marks their day-old donuts down to twenty-five cents each."

"*Mm.* Day-old donuts. Because who doesn't want to bite into a baked good that's so hard that you run the risk of chipping a tooth?"

Before she put the quarter in her purse, he pointed to the portrait of Washington on the coin. "Riddle me this: what do you call George Washington's false teeth?"

She didn't answer, but instead rolled her eyes.

"Presi-*dentures*." He cackled.

"I think the pneumonia already killed me and I went to Bad Joke Hell," she muttered.

He handed her a magazine from the magazine table, a gossip rag called *Tattle Tales*. "Here. Here you go. Use this time to do something constructive. Educate yourself." He pointed to the headline on the cover. "See that? Good article—*A Star Is Porn: Find Out Which Tinsel Town A-Listers Are Secret Smut Addicts*. There. Read that for yourself. Which stars are porn fiends? Read and find out. Sounds like they're going to name names and everything. Always good info to have. Beautiful info to have, in fact. You always want to know who's a porn creep so you can steer clear of them. Okay?"

She threw the magazine back down. "I'm not interested in reading about guys' disgusting porn habits."

"Okay. Um. How about a game? Yeah, let's play a little game while we're waiting. It'll both pass the time *and* help us get to know one another better. I call it *Fun Facts*. We tell each other interesting, quirky facts about ourselves. Sounds like *fun*, right? And we're dealing in the realm of *facts*. Has to be factual. Can't make stuff up. Hence, *Fun Facts*."

She coughed. "Whatever, dude."

"Good. Now, my fun fact is that I own a pair of Heelys. You know, the sneakers with built-in wheels. Got them a long time ago, when I was in the Marines. They were expensive, too, because they were a big fad back then. Haven't used them in years, but they're still in my closet. Yeah, they are. Back in the day, I could do tricks with them and everything. On my days off, I'd go to the Camp Pendleton base library and do stunts outside. See, the base library was kind of the hub of the community. Everybody went there. People would watch me and take pictures and video. They'd post them online and whatnot. There's still a clip on YouTube that shows me doing Heelys at Pendleton. It's gotten something like a thousand views, too. Of course, that's since twenty-ten. Some comments, as well. Mostly positive. And the haters are just jealous."

Damn. The Midnight Ranger's good. Starbucks? Check. Heelys? Check.

"So, what's your fun fact, Hope?"

She thought for a moment. "Um. Well, I always kind of had a crush on Bill Hader."

"Bill Hader, huh? You know, you're not the first woman to tell me this. My cousin, Lauren, who back in twenty-twelve was third runner-up in the Miss Maryland Pageant, wants to marry the guy and have eight kids to him. He apparently has quite a female fandom. I'm going to go ahead and give you all a name. I dub you, the female admirers of William Hader—Hader Heads. Like Jimmy Buffet's fans are Parrotheads. You guys are Hader Heads. Kind of surprising, though. When you think male sex symbol, he's not the first name that generally comes to mind."

She shrugged and coughed. "He's funny and sweet. That's a winning combination. Funny and sweet will get you a shot at, I'm going to say, about seventy-five percent of all single women. Even if you look like Baba Booey from *The Howard Stern Show*. For example, there's this woman—Katie Hendricks. She is this absolutely stunning blonde who works at the nail salon that I go to. Okay? Well, she thinks that Radar from *MASH* is a total hottie. Why? He's funny and sweet. Hence, the explanation of the Bill Hader phenomenon. Us chicks dig him."

He nodded approvingly. "That's cool. Hopefully, he's not one of the stars named in the tabloid article." He pointed to the magazine and laughed.

"Yeah. Because that would just ruin it for me. How about you? Do you have any celebrity crushes?"

"Yeah. Matter of fact, I do."

"Who?"

"Several, actually. I have a huge crush on Carrie Underwood's legs. Oh, and that one congresswoman from New York, the one they call AOC. Sure, I might not agree with her on the issues but—*dang*—AOC is A-O-Kay. She's a lawmaker and a heartbreaker. And don't even get me started on Jenna Fischer. Oh, Lord—Jenna Fischer. She was just cuter than a bug's ear on *The Office*. That Jim Halpert was one lucky dude. And then there's the woman from the Progressive insurance commercials, and—"

She interrupted. "Wait—wait—wait. You have a crush on Flo?"

"No. Not Flo. The cute little one. Kind of has reddish hair. Smallish. Real tiny little thing, in fact. I don't know her name. I'm not sure she has one. Doesn't say much. She's just kind of a supporting character."

She nodded. "Yeah. I know the one you're talking about. I don't know her name, either."

"I'll have to look it up one of these days. Anyhow, my number one celebrity crush is Jo from *The Facts of Life*. When I was coming of age, like twelve, I'd watch the reruns of that show on the *TV Classics Network*. And, up until that time, I had always kind of thought that you guys—girls, that is—were just little monsters with pigtails. Back then, in my mind, you all really weren't good for anything. Couldn't play football with a girl. The first time she got tackled, she'd complain about her hair getting messed up and run off bawling. And if I tried playing baseball with one of you—well, you just kind of threw like a girl. But when I saw Jo—let's just say things changed. Suddenly, I thought that maybe, just maybe, these strange creatures called girls weren't useless after all. That maybe there were things that girls were good for. And the crazy thing was that I didn't really like the show that much. Just liked watching her. She was pretty, but feisty and tough, sassy even. And I liked that. Still do, in fact. There. I said it. I like my women a little on the sassy side. A little spicy. And I'll let you in on something—the first time I ever voted for President, I didn't like either of the two main candidates, so I wrote in—*Jo, from The Facts of Life*."

"You wrote in *Jo, from The Facts of Life*? That's literally what you wrote on the ballot? *Jo, from The Facts of Life*?"

"Yep. That's what I wrote. I couldn't remember the actress's name, but they knew who I meant. I'm sure if you check the official stats from that election, they will reflect that at least one vote was cast for—*Jo, from The Facts of Life."*

Hope put her head down, shook it, and laughed. "I don't know about you sometimes. But it is kind of, sort of, in a very goofy way...cute."

"Oh, so you're admitting that I'm cute?"

"I didn't say *you* were cute. I said *it* was cute. Your *vote* was cute, not *you*. Two totally different statements. Kay?" She wheezed.

"All right. Well, that's a start. So, here's another cool *get to know you* kind of game. It's called *I Believe*. We each tell one another three things that we believe in, and you do so with short, pithy sentences. You don't elaborate on anything, either. Just stick to brief statements. And you have to start each sentence with the phrase—*I believe.* So, again, I'll start —I believe Oswald acted alone. I believe the United States of America is the greatest country on the face of the earth. I believe the best pizza comes from the little mom and pop pizza joints, as opposed to the big national chains. There. Now, what do you believe?"

"Um. Let's see. I believe there's nothing fun about those little, tiny *fun-sized* candy bars. I believe there was enough room for Jack on that floating door. And I believe happiness is for other people...but not for me." She frowned.

Just then, a little boy approached them. Hope thought he looked to be between six and eight. He had dirty blond hair, wore blue jeans and a red Paw Patrol shirt. In his hand, was a pack of strawberry licorice.

"Hi. I'm Stewie." The boy spoke with a lisp. "But they call me Booger."

Hope took a whiff of Stewie. *Damn. The kid reeks. He smells like cigarettes, like the Pagans' clubhouse. We would have been better off sitting next to the hippies.*

"Hey there, little man. I'm Luke." He pointed to her. "And she's Hope. And what brings you here on this cold, frigid night, with old man winter bearing down on us?" He pretended to shiver. "Brrrrrr."

"Well, I ain't sick, but my brother, Petey, is."

Luke frowned. "Aw. That's too bad, buddy. I hope it's nothing serious."

"Chicken Pox. *Chicken. Pox.* Mom says I might get 'em, too, on account of me and Petey share a bedroom."

"Back up, kid," Hope told the little boy. She used her two index fingers to make the sign of the cross, the way one would in order to ward off a vampire. "I've never had Chicken Pox, so I have zero immunity. Six feet. At least six feet away from me, boy. I do not need Chicken Pox on top of pneumonia and a broken rib."

Luke agreed. "Yeah, back up there just a wee bit, okay, Stew-Meister?" He imitated a truck's back-up warning beeper. "*Beep. Beep. Beep.*"

Stewie backed up.

Luke smiled at him. "There. There you go. Perfect, dude. Ah, *gracias, senor, gracias.* Oh, and by the way—love the name. *Stewie.* That name's more righteous than The Righteous Brothers and there were two of them."

Hope rolled her eyes and shook her head. "He's a kid. He's not going to get your stupid jokes that make reference to pop culture."

Stewie pointed to Hope's feet. "You got little feet, lady. Tiny little feet. They ain't much bigger than mine. What's up with that?"

Hope glared at Stewie. "It's not uncommon for women to have small feet. *Stewie.* Okay?"

Stewie nodded. "I know why you guys are here."

Luke chuckled. "You do, huh? So, let's hear it, Psychic Friends Network Stewie." He looked at Hope, smiled, and winked. "Lay it on us, dude. Tell us why we're here."

"A baby," Stewie confidently announced. "See, my nanna says that when a man and a lady wanna have a baby, they go to the hospital and look at a catalog and order whatever kind of baby they want. Then it takes nine months for the hospital to build the baby, see? Then, when the baby's ready, the man and the lady come back and get their baby. And that's how babies happen. So, are you guys ordering or picking up?" Stewie picked his nose.

"Ah, no. No. And *hell no*," she declared. *And now we know why they call him Booger.*

"Don't curse in front of the kid, Hope."

"*Hell* is not really cursing."

"It is. A little bit, it is. It's cursing." He turned his attention back to the boy. "And we're not really here for a baby. Ordering a baby—that's a pretty major step for a man and a lady. Me and Hope—we're not quite at the baby-ordering stage just yet."

Hope coughed. "And we never will be, either."

Stewie stared at Hope's breasts. He pointed to them. "You got big old bumps, lady. How come you got big bumps? Because I don't got bumps like that." He pointed to Luke. "And he don't got bumps. Now, my mom, she does have bumps. But they're little, especially compared to yours. So, why are yours so big? Why, lady?"

"My *bumps*, as you call them, are none of your damn business, kid. Buzz off." *This kid's getting on my nerves. Big time.*

Stewie picked a wedgie. "I know what those bumps are. They're mosquito bug bite bumps. You got bit by mosquitos and their bites made those bumps, right?"

Luke nodded emphatically. "That's exactly what happened. That's why we're here, in fact. We have to get those mosquito bite bumps checked out."

"Those were some big fuckin' mosquitos, too. They must have been to make bumps *that* big," Stewie declared.

Luke chastised him. "*Whoa.* Hey, little buddy—what's with the language? Where did *that* come from? Huh? No need to sound like a Dave Chappelle HBO special over here. Let's try to keep it G-rated, shall we? Heck, I'd settle for PG-Thirteen."

Stewie shrugged. "That's how my mom talks." He thought for a moment and added, "Now, my dad's new girlfriend, Debbie, she talks a lot better. She's real religious, see? When I go to my dad's trailer every other weekend, her and my dad go into his bedroom, and I hear her praying. In the middle of the night, I hear her praying. Real loud, too. Screamin' in fact. She's all like—*oh ,God! Oh,God! Oh, Jesus! Oh, my God! Oh, Jesus Christ!*"

Luke nodded. "Yeah. It's awesome that she gives all the glory to God."

Stewie again fixated on Hope's breasts, ogling them.

"Don't be staring at me like that, kid. I mean it."

Luke intervened. "Let me handle this. Please. You're only going to make it worse. He needs to hear this stuff from a guy. It will resonate more coming from a guy. Okay? So, allow me to address this situation."

She wheezed and dismissively waved her hand at him. "Fine. Then handle it. Just make sure he doesn't try to get all touchy-feely with those little rat claws of his."

Luke gave Stewie a stern look and shook his finger at him. "Stewie. *Mis-ter Stewie.* Time for a consultation. A power convo. A little man-to-man. A meeting of the minds, if you will. So, here's the thing—it's not polite to stare at a lady's bug bite bumps. It understandably makes a lady feel uncomfortable. Okay?"

"My dad does it all the time. He did it just the other day to the waitress at Olive Garden."

Hope chimed in. "Your dad's a jerk, kid."

Luke shot her a dirty look. "Stop that. What is wrong with you? Huh? For Heaven's sake. Do not tell the kid that his dad's a jerk."

"Well, he is."

"Okay, so maybe he is. Still, the kid doesn't need to hear that from you."

Luke turned his attention back to the boy. "Good rule of thumb, Stewie—don't stare at a lady's bug bite bumps."

A confused look crossed the child's face. "So, you can never, ever, *ever* look at them? No matter what?"

Luke laughed a nervous laugh. "I wouldn't necessarily go

that far. It might be a bit extreme to say *that*."

"Well, how do you know if it's okay to look? Oh—and how about touching? Can you ever touch them?"

Luke emphatically shook his head. "Touching them is a much bigger deal than looking. *Much* bigger. Touching is a no-no. Biiiig no-no."

Stewie was still confused. "So, mister, you're trying to tell me that no man has ever touched a lady's bug bite bumps?"

"No. I'm not saying that at all, son. It does happen."

"Well, why is it okay sometimes and not okay other times? Huh, mister?"

Luke looked over at Hope.

She coughed and giggled. "Don't look at me for help. You wanted to handle it. So, handle it. This is your Ward Cleaver moment here, bud. Rise up to it."

"Right. Yes. Fine. I'll handle it." He nervously smiled at the boy. "Look, Stewie—you're a little dude. It should be several years before you're really even interested in women's bug bite bumps. Right?"

"Shit, boy, I'm interested right now. Somethin' just tells me that they're fun as hell. More fun than Play-Doh." Stewie wiped his runny nose on his shirt.

Luke and Hope just stared at the boy in silence.

Stewie loudly passed gas.

Hope admonished him. "Ah, *excuse you!*"

Looking at her with utter confusion, Stewie wrinkled his nose. "Huh?"

Stewie cracked his knuckles, pulled a cigarette out of his pocket, put it in his mouth, and talked with it dangling. "All right, then. Guess I'm gonna go out and have me a smoke."

Luke gave him a steely stare. "Where'd you get that cigarette, boy?"

"My mom. Sometimes, if I'm a *super good boy*, she lets me bum one of her Virginia Slims. I keep telling her that brand's not strong enough for me. I need a man's cigarette. Something like unfiltered Camels."

He snatched the cigarette from boy's mouth, crumpled it up, and tossed it into a nearby trashcan.

"Hey, what gives, mister? Those things are expensive."

Luke shook his head. "No, sir. Not on my watch, son. Uh-uh. Not gunna happen."

Stewie accusingly pointed at him. "You owe me a cigarette."

"Don't worry. I'll buy you a whole carton to make it up to you."

The child's eyes got big. "You will?"

"Sure will. The day you turn fifty."

"Aw, you're no fun."

"Neither is lung cancer, COPD, and heart disease."

"Whatever. Anyway, I guess I'm gonna watch a movie on my iPad. Maybe I'll watch *Despicable Me Three.* Or maybe I'll watch *Jerry Springer Uncensored.* Yeah. One of those two."

Hope coughed. "Yeah, run along, you little rug rat. Bub-bye." She waved a Miss America wave.

Luke waved, too. "All right. Take care, little buddy. *Au Revoir*, as the French say. That's not *goodbye*, but rather—*until we meet again.* Oh, and, ah, you know—quit smoking, too. Yeah. Do that. It's just a shame that human beings ever invented smoking. I've often wondered how smoking got started. I mean, what made the first smoker pick tobacco, roll it up, light it on fire, puff on it, inhale, and exhale? There's a lot of steps in that process. I'm amazed that primitive Man was capable of such sophisticated thought. But it was truly one of the worst innovations of all-time. Right up there with pop-up ads and Asbestos. Not only is it bad for your health, but it'll wreak havoc on your appearance, too. Do you want to end up looking like Keith Richards? Huh? That what you want? Because he's a lifelong smoker. You want your face to look like an old, worn-out leather catcher's mitt, like some relic from the early days of baseball that they keep on display at the Hall of Fame? Keep on puffin' and that's what'll happen. Now, the Y has a really good smoking cessation class. They might even offer a discount for smokers under the age of ten. Not sure. I'm a former smoker myself, back when I was young and foolish. I smoked when I was overseas, in the Marines, because of the stress and all. But I took the Y's class and have been tobacco-free since June fifteenth of twenty-eleven. It *can* be done."

"Yeah. I'll think about it. But that nicotine's really got ahold of me. Like a demon possessing my very soul. Anyhow, so long." Stewie waved, turned and walked away.

After a few steps, he turned around and walked back over to them. He emphatically pointed to Luke. "I have a question for *you,* mister."

"Sure, Stewie. As long as it doesn't have to do with women's bug bite bumps."

"Nah. It's not about that." Stewie pointed to Hope. "Are you gonna fall in love with her? Are you, mister? Huh? Are you gonna fall in *luuuv* with her?" He giggled, puckered his lips, and made kissing sounds.

"What makes you think he might fall in love with me, kid?"

Stewie shrugged. "Well, he's here with you on a Sunday night when he could be home watching *America's Funniest Home Videos.* And it's cold as hell out. It's so cold that when the bums piss in the alley next to my apartment building, it freezes. Plus, I know you're, like, pretty in real life and all, but right now, you got a red nose, redder than Rudolph's. And your hair's all messy, too. And he puts up with your sass." He emphatically pointed and shook his finger at her. "You have a sassy mouth, lady." He paused and looked at Luke. "So, are you? Are you gonna fall in love with her?"

There was silence for several seconds. Finally, Stewie nodded and answered his own question. "Yeah, I think you're gonna fall in love with her. I *know* you are." He giggled, turned, and skipped away. As he did, he shouted, "He's falling in love with her! He's falling in love with her! He's falling in love with her!"

The entire ER looked at him. And at Luke and Hope.

Luke looked at her, shrugged, and laughed.

Hope shook her head but laughed, too.

He brushed the hair out of her eyes. She shot him a leery look.

"I just don't want you to be like that one breed of dog. You know—what do they call those dogs? The ones that always have the hair in their eyes." He thought for a moment and snapped his fingers. "Oh yeah— Tibetan Terriers. The Tibetan Terrier. Yep. I have no idea how those dogs pass the eye exam for their driver's license."

"God. Your jokes are lame, boy. Lame." But she was laughing as she said it.

He pulled out his phone. "While we're waiting, I'm just going to catch up on my show. It's this new Netflix series called *Hail to the Neanderthal.* It's a very interesting, edgy concept. I'm addicted to it. It's about this caveman, see? His name is Proud Ax. That's it. No first name. No last name. Just *Proud Ax.* And he originally lived during the time of the cavemen. Back in the olden days. I don't know—maybe, like, three hundred years ago, might have even been closer to four hundred. Yeah. Let's go with four hundred. That sounds about right. He got frozen during the last Ice Age. Well, modern scientists found him and thawed him out, see? They revived him and he came back to life. And darned if the son of a gun didn't get himself into Harvard and earned a degree in political science. Summa cum laude, no less. Then he went into politics and somehow got elected President of the United States, God love him. America really *is* the land of opportunity. Anyway, the whole show focuses on how he struggles to come to terms with modern times while simultaneously serving as the leader of the Free World. And he does struggle, too. When he reads the daily intel report on his Oval Office computer, he thinks that, surely, what us moderns call email must be *tiny demons inside magic box carrying messages from Netherworld.* And Air Force One is *giant flying lizard with bad onboard movie.* Oh, and a solar eclipse? That's *moon eating sun.* And the teleprompter he uses is— *Great Oracle of the gods.* Hell, once he almost ordered a nuclear attack just to pay homage to said gods by *painting pretty pictures on sky."*

She laughed and playfully smacked his arm. "Stop that shit. It hurts to laugh. And it's not even a real show. You just made the whole thing up."

"Sure, I did. To make you laugh. I made it up to make you laugh. I thought that's one of the reasons you crush on Bill Hader—because you like guys who are funny."

"I do like guys who are funny. Funny and sweet. Yeah, I do."

CHAPTER FOURTEEN: DOCTOR MIKE

They finally took Hope back for a chest x-ray. Afterwards, she was brought back to the waiting room where they sat for another hour and a half. It was closing in on midnight.

Finally, a nurse came out, looked at her clipboard and called Hope back to an exam room. "Kennedy. Hope Kennedy."

Luke looked at her. "Um. Do you want me to go back there with you?"

"You don't have to, no. I'm a big girl."

"Well, I realize that, but I just wondered if you, maybe, wanted me to. I know I don't *have* to."

"If you want to come back with me, you can. That's fine. But I do not want you to go back there with me and then, later, complain about it, and say I made you do it."

"I wouldn't say that, but I don't want to go back there with you and have you, later, say that you didn't really want me back there with you. And that I was pushy about it."

"And I don't want you to say that I pushed you, either, because I am not a pushy person."

An elderly man reading a magazine sat in front of them. He wore a gray cardigan and a yarmulke. Without so much as even looking up, he told them, "*Oy vey.* She wants you to go back with her. You want to go back with her. So, go back with her, already. I'm trying to read this good article in *Conspiracy Theory Magazine—Saturday Night Live: It's Never Live.* So, both of you—go on. Get. Because I'm going to be very honest here—

and I think I speak for the entire ER—you two are getting on everyone's nerves."

Luke and Hope both shrugged. He went back to the exam room with her.

There, they waited some more.

Hope loudly exhaled and coughed. "I love how they make you wait forever. Just so you can finally get back here to an exam room…and wait forever."

"Hurry up and wait. That's what we always did in the Marines."

There was a life-sized skeleton in the corner of the exam room. She looked on as Luke walked over to it. He touched it.

She coughed. "Leave it alone. Those things are fragile. It doesn't take much for them to fall apart."

He ignored her warning. "Well, if he falls apart, then he'll just be…Napoleon Bone-apart. Besides, they want you to play with these things. That's why they put them in the room."

He held up the skeleton's left hand and shook it. "Pleased to meet you. You know, for somebody who's dead, you look pretty good. Just a little on the thin side, that's all." He laughed.

The skeleton's hand came off.

"I *told* you not to touch it." She wheezed.

He casually tossed the left hand on the counter and shrugged. "He'll be *all right*."

She snickered and shook her head. "Oh, Gawd. Cheesy."

A few minutes later, the door opened and in walked a handsome, young-looking African-American doctor. He wore a white lab coat, blue corduroy jeans, a blue and white checkered shirt, and a navy blue knit tie. He carried a manilla file with him. And he was humming *Can't Help Falling in Love*.

Hope looked him up and down. *He looks like John Legend.*

The doctor opened the file and glanced at it. He was still humming. After about ten seconds, he stopped humming but still looked at the file. Without looking up, he said, "Hope my humming didn't annoy you all. I saw *Crazy Rich Asians* the other day and now I have this pretty little song stuck in my head. I think Elvis originally did it. It's called something like *Fools Rush In*."

Hope rolled her eyes. *God. Doesn't anyone know the right name of this song?* With a bit of attitude, she corrected him. "*Can't Help Falling in Love*. That's the name of the song. Not *Fools Rush In*. Not *Wise Men Say*. It's called *Can't Help Falling in Love*. Okay?"

Still focused on the file, the doctor nonchalantly replied, "Yeah. Right. That's it. Real pretty song." He pulled out his pen and made some notations.

Finally, he closed the file, looked up, and warmly smiled at Hope. "Hey there. And how are you doing tonight?" Before she had a chance to answer, he hit himself on the forehead with his open palm. "What a stupid thing for me to ask, right? If you were doing well, you wouldn't be here, now, would you? Duh. My bad, guys, my bad." He laughed.

Luke jumped in. "I think our society just needs to get rid of all these meaningless phrases and questions. Let's get real —does that cashier in the supermarket really care if you *have a nice day?* I doubt it. Just like when people say you're in their *thoughts and prayers*. You're not. It's the biggest throw-away line of all-time. It's downright silly. People who say that aren't thinking about you nor are they praying for you. It's a totally meaningless phrase."

The doctor nodded. "I hear you, man. But right now, my pet peeve is the use of the phrase *at the end of the day*. Everyone seems to be on that bandwagon. There's a proctologist here who's in love with that phrase. And it's like nails on a chalkboard to me."

Luke agreed. "Right, doc. And how about when celebrities talk about cultivating their *brand?* I hate that. Brands are for bread and soda, not people."

"Exactly. That irritates me like fleas in my undershorts. It comes off as very pretentious and self-important, you know? And most of the ones who talk that way are nothing more than reality TV C-listers. I just want to scream at the TV—*sorry,*

Snooki, but you're just not that important. So, get over yourself."

Luke laughed. "Tell me about it. And speaking of reality TV, I think it's so silly and hypocritical how when someone gets voted off the island or kicked out of the house, the very people who plotted, schemed, and conspired against them sit there and bawl their eyes out. And I'm thinking to myself—*stop with the crocodile tears, already. You wanted them gone so you'd have a better chance of winning. At least be honest about it."*

The doctor again nodded. "*Yes.* A very insightful comment. Thank you. A little honesty would be nice. But I'm convinced that there's very little that's *real* when it comes to reality TV. I think it's mostly scripted and—"

Hope loudly cleared her voice to get the doctor refocused. She then forced a nasty cough. *I'm right here in front of you, doc. Yeah. I'm the one who's sick. I'm kind of a big deal right now.*

The doctor turned his attention back to her. "Sorry. Didn't mean to get distracted. Any-who, I know that you're Hope. Well, technically, to Mercy Medical Center, you're patient number five-four-zero-two-nine-seven. But, to me, you're Hope. And my name is Mike. You can just call me by my first name, if you want. Or, if you really want to be formal, you can call me Doctor Mike."

Luke nodded approvingly. "Mike. Good name. Good solid name. Lots of good Mikes out there. Mike Ditka. Mike Douglas, the old talk show host. I saw some clips of the *Mike Douglas Show* on YouTube. He was a very good interviewer, always got the big celebs to really open up. Oh—and Mike Myers, Mister Austin Powers himself." Luke did an Austin Powers impression: "Oh, behave, baby. Yeah, baby, yeah! Anyway, I like the name Mike. I do."

"I like it, too. I'm told it was given to me because it's strong but gentle."

"Strong but gentle, huh? Sounds like an ad for a laxative," Hope quipped.

Doctor Mike pointed at her and laughed. "Hey, good sign. You haven't lost your sense of humor. And nice J-Lo glasses, by the way. Oh, and I hope my informality doesn't bother you. I try to be human to people. You see, I believe that one of the problems with modern health care is that we've stripped it of its humanity. Patients are just numbers. *Get em' in and out,* they say. I call it *assembly line medicine.* I try to tell these new interns—*you're not putting cars together on some GM assembly line. You're putting people back together. Real people. People who have families, jobs, dreams, fears.*" He looked directly into her eyes. "And hopes. They have hopes, too. So, I hope you don't mind, Hope, if I call you Hope. Cool?"

Hope shrugged and nodded. "Yeah. Sure. Fine by me."

Luke chimed in. "You know, I think it's refreshing to hear a doctor talk like this. With most doctors, they not only see the patient as a number, but they see themselves as God. It's like they know everything. They come off as being arrogant, too, at times. Some of them can be total a-holes, in fact."

Doctor Mike agreed. "Yeah, don't get me started on the whole God complex thing that so many of my esteemed colleagues are inflicted with. Again, I try to tell these kids fresh out of med school—*there are two things you need to do before you can be a good doctor. And they come before any of the technical knowledge and skills. They literally come before any of the stuff you learned in med school. One—you need to be bold enough to accept the Reality that there is a God. And two—you need to be humble enough to accept the Reality that you're not Him.* Do they listen? Nope. Most of them don't. And they suffer for it. And their patients do, too, by the way." He shrugged. "But what are you going to do? You can't force people, you know?"

Luke laughed. "Unless you're in the Marines. Then they can force you. They can force you to do pretty much anything in the Marine Corps."

"Oh, you were a Marine?"

"Yep."

"Well, then thank you for your service."

Luke nodded. "Welcome, doc." The two men shook hands.

Doctor Mike again briefly looked at Hope's file. "Well, I've reviewed the results of your tests. And I can confidently say that in addition to rocking that sweet Hello Kitty onesie, you're rocking a pretty nasty case of pneumonia, almost certainly as a complication of your broken—"

Luke interrupted and exclaimed, "Ah-ha! Pneumonia. Just as I suspected. Good job, doc. That was my diagnosis as well."

Doctor Mike raised his eyebrows. "Oh, so you're a physician, too?"

"Well, no. Not, not exactly. But I have seen every episode of *ER*. Twice."

"*ER*. Right. Ah...anyway, like I was saying—you have pneumonia, Hope."

"You're not going to admit me, are you? I don't like hospitals. I had a real bad experience associated with a hospital stay a couple of years ago."

He nodded his understanding. "I get that. I do. But here's the thing—what you have is dangerous. Pneumonia kills, and not just the elderly. I think your case is very borderline. Now, what kind of support system do you have at home?"

She pointed to Luke. "Well, aren't you going to be like everyone else and assume that he's my husband, or at least my boyfriend?"

"No. Why would I do that? That would be presumptuous of me. I'm just trying to find out if you have anyone who, for lack of a better phrase, can take care of you. Because that's what you need. Someone to monitor your vitals, especially your temp and oxygen saturation. Someone who can bring you back to the hospital if things take a turn for the worse. If you have that kind of person in your life, I can give you some oxygen and send you home with meds. You would need round-the-clock care and monitoring for at least a few days. Probably closer to five days, actually. If you don't have an individual like this available to you, well, I'm afraid you'll have to be our guest here for a little while."

Luke spoke up. "Look, doc, I have some time on my hands. I'd like to take care of her. I want to do that. I really want to...if she's okay with it, that is."

They both looked at her for a decision.

"What do you say, Hope? This handsome Marine just volunteered to be your own personal security detail. It would keep you out of the hospital."

She sneezed and emphatically shook her head. "No. I don't want him to do it because then he might come back later and say it was a burden and that I messed with his life. And I don't want anyone to be able to say—"

Doctor Mike cut her off. "Fine. No problem. Your prerogative. I'll get the admission paperwork started."

She loudly exhaled her exasperation and coughed. "Fine. *Fine.* He can take care of me. I'll let him do it." She glared at Luke and shook her finger at him. "But I don't want to hear any complaining. If I start vomiting at two in the morning, I don't want to hear—*I didn't know it was going to be like this*. I don't want to hear it, mister."

"You won't. I promise."

Doctor Mike looked at them. "Do we have a deal here?"

"Deal," Luke said.

Hope tentatively nodded. "Deal."

"Well, go ahead and shake on it then. Go on. Go ahead. She's not contagious. I promise, she's not."

They shook hands. *His hands are big but soft and gentle.*

Doctor Mike smiled a big smile. "Great. Outta sight. I'm going to send some prescriptions down to our pharmacy for you. I can send them electronically. And it's open twenty-four-seven, by the way. So, you can pick them up on your way out. Also, we'll give her an oxygen treatment before she's discharged."

He issued Luke instructions. "Check her vitals every few hours during the day. Make sure she takes her meds. Make sure she drinks plenty of fluids. Make sure she gets lots of bed rest. No exerting whatsoever. She probably won't want to eat much. Chicken broth is best. Keep her nice and warm, too. Once you get her home tonight, she should not be out in this weather at all. Any change for the worse—bring her back in ASAP. At that point, she'll have to be admitted. Any questions?"

Luke spoke up. "Yeah. Is the gift shop still open?"

"Yeah. It's open twenty-four-seven, now, too. Unfortunately, business is that good around here."

Hope shot Luke a confused look. "Gift shop? Why do you care about the gift shop?"

"I want a candy bar."

"They have vending machines with candy bars right here in the ER."

"Okay, so I want…a magazine. Yeah, I want to read a magazine while we wait for all this stuff."

"There are plenty of magazines in the waiting room," she reminded him.

"Fine. Then I want a…romance novel. Yeah. That's it. A romance novel. I love a good love story. I'm thinking about writing my own, you know. I'm going to call it *Gentle Rogue*. It'll be a bodice ripper." He proceeded to give a brief synopsis. "In Victorian England, a saucy lady of the court forgoes an arranged marriage to a proper, politically-connected nobleman and, instead, chooses the handsome, sexy, brooding scoundrel—the *Gentle Rogue*."

Doctor Mike laughed and patted Luke on the back. "You're too much, Luke. Too much, man. Great sense of humor. The world needs more laughter. The crazy thing is that if you pitched that idea to publishers, you might actually get a few bites."

Luke smiled. "I know, right?"

Hope shook her head in disgust. "He never quits with these cheesy jokes, doc, and you only encourage him when you laugh."

"Hey, now—wait a second. I saw you snicker, too."

She held her thumb and forefinger close together. "Maybe just a little."

"Any other questions?"

Luke shot him a leery look. "Yeah. How'd you know my

name? I didn't tell you and neither did Hope."

"You signed in. At the main desk, you signed in, as per our security requirements."

"I did. That's true. But it was just scribble. Are you telling me that you could actually read my chicken scratch?"

Doctor Mike threw up his hands and a big cheesy smile came over his face. "*Heeeey,* who you talkin' to here? Huh? I am a doctor, after all. I'm fluent in both scribble and chicken scratch. It's actually a mandatory class in med school. You need it to graduate. It's true. I can both read and write in scribble and chicken scratch. How about that?"

Luke looked at him with suspicion. "Right. I guess I should have known that. So, you mean to tell me that you actually get that info? The info from the sign-in sheets, that is."

"I get all the information I need to do my job."

Luke nodded. "Right. Evidently, you do."

Doctor Mike looked at them. Stared at them. Smiled at them. "Now, one more thing. And this is for both of you. You can think of what I'm about to say as a *referral,* I guess. So, here goes—I'm here to heal. Whenever possible, I heal. It's what I do. But I don't heal hearts. I'm not a heart specialist. And that's what you both need. The good news is that you each have access to one. And you wouldn't even have to go out-of-network. You guys can figure out the rest. There. Now we're finished."

Hope and Luke looked at one another but said nothing. It was quiet in the room for a few seconds.

Finally, Doctor Mike told them, "I have to go now. I have a guy in room fourteen waiting. He shoved his daughter's Barbie doll up his butt and now it's stuck up there. When I asked him why he did it, all he said was—*I just wanted to see if I could, doc.* Well, he could, all right. And yours truly lost the rock, paper, scissors battle with the other doctors. So, I get the privilege of digging that thing out. But I still say my rock should have smashed right through Doctor Quang's paper."

Hope coughed and shook her head. "No. Paper covers rock."

"That's what Doctor Quang claimed, too. The worst thing is that this same guy was here on Thanksgiving night, not even two months ago, with the same problem. Only that night, it was his wife's turkey baster that was stuck up there."

They all laughed.

Doctor Mike winked at them and walked out. As he did, he told them, "All right, then. Goodnight, y'all. God bless and keep warm. That wind's brutal out there tonight. It's so strong it nearly blew my mind."

They gave Hope her oxygen. Luke went to get her prescriptions filled.

When he got back, she was still taking her treatment.

She removed the mask. "Did you get your romance novel at the giftshop?"

"Nah. They didn't have any that I liked. I only read Civil War romances where the hero is from the South, preferably Texas, and the heroine is from the North, preferably Maine. You know—they're just trying to be together, but the world is doing its darndest to keep them apart, what with the war and all. And it must be written in such a way that you get both protagonist's points-of-view. Not just one. And it should be set during the early years of the Civil War, when the outcome was still in doubt. Makes it more dramatic that way. Oh, and one more thing—the hero should not have sideburns but should be fond of exclaiming—*damnation!* Unless the novel meets that simple list of basic criteria, I don't waste my time because it obviously wouldn't be a good read."

"Uh-huh."

"Oh, hey, while I was out, I picked up this form." He held it up for her to see. "They have a really cool contest here at the hospital for the employees. It's called the Touched By An Angel Excellence of Service Award. If you think one of the hospital's employees went above and beyond for you, you can nominate them for the award. You just have to fill out this form. And you don't even have to put your information down. It can be anonymous. They just need the details of your *angelic encounter,* as they call it. A winner is selected each month. If your nominee wins, they get a cool pair of angel wings to pin onto their uniform, a day off with pay, and a one-hundred dollar gift certificate to Cracker Barrel. And they're also eligible for the Angel of the Year Award. I think we should nominate Doctor Mike. He was great. He cared. I've never met a doctor like him. He was a regular guy. So human, you know? Not arrogant, not full of himself, like so many doctors nowadays. Others could learn from watching him. What do you say? You think we should nominate him? I really think we should. It's only right."

She blew her nose and nodded. "Yeah. Definitely. He was a very nice man, very sweet. I actually agree with you. He was, by far, the most compassionate doctor I've ever met. Once, I was in the hospital and the doctors were really callous. They didn't care. The way they asked some of their questions—it wasn't right. They didn't know how to talk to a woman who had just…well, they just didn't know how to talk to people, that's all. Here. Give me the form and I'll fill it out. I'll give him a really nice write up. Maybe he'll win."

She filled out the form and asked him to look it over.

He read it and liked it. "It's good. And so are you. You're good. And you're pretty. Very pretty tonight."

"Liar."

"Yeah. You're right. I lied. It's not *tonight* anymore. It's now *this morning.* But you're still pretty. Look at you. Who do you think you're fooling? Huh? You're a total heartbreaker, that's what you are."

She put her head down and shook it. "Even the kid thought I look like hell."

He laughed. "He also thought your boobs were *mosquito bug bite bumps* and that babies get *ordered* from catalogs."

They laughed.

She looked up at him. "You're either the world's smoothest player…or the real deal. I don't know which. And both of the possibilities scare the hell out of me."

He reached over and gently squeezed her hand.

She put her mask back on and finished her oxygen.

It was three in the morning. They were finally ready to leave the hospital. He pushed her in a wheelchair. On the way out, they stopped at the ER Department's nurse's station to turn in Doctor Mike's nomination form.

There was an attractive young nurse sitting at the desk. She had red hair and blue eyes. Her light blue scrubs had pictures of kittens on them.

From her wheelchair, she held up the form for the nurse to see. "Hi. Excuse me. Can we turn in this Touched By An Angel award nomination form thingy here?"

"*Aw.* You were touched by one of our angels tonight, huh?"

"Uh-huh," Hope replied. "I was."

"That's sweet. Of course, I'll take it. And we forward them to HR."

Hope gave her the form.

"Let's see here. Who did you nominate? Says here—*Doctor Mike.* You're going to have to help me out. Who's Doctor Mike?"

"Ah, *Mike* is his first name. We didn't get his last name. He said he's informal. He said he just likes everyone to call him by his first name and whatnot," Hope explained.

"And you saw this gentleman in the ER? Our ER? Today?"

"Well, technically, it was yesterday."

"Right. But within the last twelve hours or so?"

"Within the last couple of hours. He was very nice. So sweet and kind. Funny, too. We just would like him to be recognized for his service," Hope said.

"Uh-huh. Right. The problem, ma'am, is that we don't have any doctors named *Mike* or *Michael,* for that matter, in this department."

"No. You do. You definitely do. He just saw me tonight. He, ah, looks like John Legend. You know—John Legend. The legend, John Legend."

"Okay, now I'm certain you're mistaken." The nurse held up her left hand and wiggled her fingers. "Single gal here.

Okay? And if there was a freaking doctor running around this hospital looking all like John Legend, I would know about him. Trust me, honey. Now, there have been three providers in this ER over the last twelve hours. Doctors Quang and Simeon, and a physician's assistant named Williamson. None have the first name Mike or Michael. And none of them even remotely resemble John Legend. Were you, maybe, at another health care facility before coming here?"

"No. It was here. Everything happened here. Not that long ago. We saw him. We did."

"I don't know what to say. I don't think you could have seen him here, in our ER."

Hope lost her patience. "Excuse me? Are you calling us liars? Hmm? Because If you are—"

Luke intervened. "Don't get all angry. That doesn't help. Here. Let me talk to her for a sec."

Hope coughed and threw up her hands. "Fine. Go for it."

"Okay, lady—are you calling us liars? Because if you are, you're making a big mistake."

"No, I don't think you guys are lying. Why would you lie? It's just a nice little contest to have fun with, not a Third World election between two rival warlords. I don't think anyone would lie or stuff the ballot box. I just think you're confused. Look—I've been here for five years. And I have never, ever seen anyone like the individual you're describing in this entire hospital, let alone in the ER Department. I'm sorry, guys. But I don't think your Doctor Mike or Doctor Michael or whatever his name is, is going to be able to get his angel's wings."

Hope snatched the form from the nurse, tore it up, and threw it in the air. It rained down like confetti. "Fine. Whatever. Let's go, Luke. I'm tired as hell. I just want out of here. I guess Doctor Mike doesn't get his wings."

Luke kneeled down beside her wheelchair. He spoke softly. "Yeah, let's get out of here. It doesn't matter. Really, it doesn't. Doctor Mike doesn't need a set of cheap, plastic, clip-on angel wings. Now, let's just go home."

"I just wanted his boss to know he did good, that's all. I wanted Doctor Mike's boss to know that he was human to us."

"He was human...*to us. To us*, he was human. And his Boss knows, Hope. His Boss already knows. Okay? Now, let's go home. It's late...I mean early. And we're both tired. So, let's go home."

They stared at one another in silence for several seconds. He just nodded to her. And she nodded back.

As they left the ER, a nurse came running out and raced ahead of them. She was a heavyset brunette. Her hair was up in a bun. She wore pink scrubs and looked to be in her 40s.

The nurse waved. "Hi. I'm Nancy."

Hope put her head down. *God. What now?*

Luke nodded and smiled. "Hi-ya, Nancy. That's a very pretty name, by the way. How goes it? You all full of life tonight, are you? Cold enough for you out there? Personally, I'm ready for spring, you know? I've had enough of this winter weather. Of course, in July, when it's ninety-eight in the shade and humid, we'll all be talking about how we can't wait for winter, right? That's how it always works here in Baltimore. We complain when it's cold and we complain when it's hot. I guess us Baltimoreans just like to complain, huh?" He laughed.

Why are you engaging with this woman?

Nancy pointed at them. "I know who you guys are. I saw Hope's name on the paperwork. And I noticed that you, sir, look like Elvis. See, I listen to *The Midnight Ranger Show* religiously. So, I know who you two are."

Luke nodded. "Great. Lovely. We know who we are, too. Now, if you'll excuse us, we've been here a very long time and—"

Nancy interrupted. "I don't have my phone with me now. We're not allowed to have them on our person anymore. We have to keep them in our lockers because of the whole Pokemon fiasco from a few years ago. So, now, we can only have them out on break. And I go on break in twenty minutes. Could you hang around that long? I'd like to get a picture."

"Why would you want a picture?" Luke asked.

"I'll be honest—*The City Paper* is offering two fifty for a picture. I'd offer to split it with you, but I'm sure you guys are above profiting off this. Love is its own reward and all that jazz. Besides, you both already know you'll probably get a book deal, a movie, and maybe a reality show out of this. So, what I'd do is donate half to charity. One twenty-five for me. One twenty-five to charity. What do you say?"

Luke shook his head as if to clear cobwebs. "Charity? *Now* what are you talking about?"

"Yeah. Charity. Let's say it goes to, oh, I don't know… maybe…Jerry's Kids. Okay? One twenty-five to Jerry's Kids."

"*Jerry's Kids*?" he asked with a quizzical look.

"Sure. Don't you think Jerry's Kids are worthy?"

"Ignore her, Luke. Let's just go. Come on. I want to go. *Now*."

He took his hands off her wheelchair, put them in his pockets, and nodded emphatically. "Yeah. Of course, I think Jerry's Kids are worthy. Certainly, they are. No one is worthier. Come on—Jerry's Kids? That's a total no-brainer."

"And when's the last time you gave to Jerry's Kids?" Nancy asked.

He shrugged. "It's been a minute. I'll admit it."

"Have you ever given anything to Jerry's Kids? Huh? Have you?"

"I…I don't recall. I, ah, don't recollect at this time."

"Oh, now, you sound like a politician who's gotten himself into trouble and finally has to answer to it. *I don't recall. I don't recollect.* Funny how that works, huh? Once they've been busted, suddenly, none of them can recall anything. Guess you're the same way. They don't have the telethon anymore to help them. You know that, right? And Jerry's gone. He's dead, God rest his soul. The Kids don't have Jerry to lean on anymore. That means you and I have to step up. Don't you support Jerry's Kids?"

He rolled his eyes. "I already said I do. You're making it sound like I'm anti-Jerry's Kids, lady, and I'm not. Like I sneak up behind them, dump them out of their wheelchairs, and laugh about it. I don't do that crap. Come on, now. I love both Jerry and his Kids. Let's just make sure we're all clear on that, shall we?"

"Well, if you support Jerry's Kids, you'll hang around and let me get a picture."

Hope coughed and shook her head. "I am not having my picture taken. No picture for you! We've been here since last night. We're going home. Goodnight. And, by the way—get a life. Come on, Luke, let's go. Now, please. I want to go."

He pulled a twenty from his wallet and handed it to Nancy. "Here. This was going to be my Starbucks money for the week, but, ah, you know, Jerry's Kids need it more than me. So, go on and donate that twenty to them and make it a donation in your own name. I don't care about getting the credit for it." He shook his finger at her. "And I'm putting you on the honor system with that money. I do not want it going for Power Ball tickets. Now, we're leaving. No pictures. Still don't know why you'd want one. And no further questions. This presser is over. Good. Day. Madam."

He wheeled Hope away and Nancy shouted down the hallway at them. "It's already gone to your heads. You're both beyond difficult. The tabloids will eat you alive. Eat. You. Alive. You all might be bigger than Harry Hamlin and Lisa Rinna, but you are *not* bigger than Prince Harry and Meghan Markel. And you never will be. They have class, and you two are both just a couple of low-rent Balti-*morons.* Just remember that. And Jerry's Kids could have done a hell of a lot better than a measly twenty bucks if you guys had just cooperated."

CHAPTER FIFTEEN: WAR STORY

On the way home, she told him about her calls to *The Midnight Ranger Show*, detailing the whole thing. "You're not mad at me, are you? For bringing you up on the radio and all, that is."

"Did talking on this radio show help you?"

"Yeah. It did. It was kind of therapeutic, actually."

"Then I'm not angry. Not at all."

They decided she would stay at his place during her convalescence. It was easier since he had the two cats at home to look after. He'd give her the master bedroom and move into one of the spare rooms.

They stopped at her place so she could pack some things

He sat on her bed as she put items in a pink suitcase. "Say, are you, by any chance, related to the Hyannis Port Kennedys? You know—JFK, JFK Junior, Bobby, Ted, Jackie, Ethel, Rose. Etcetera, etcetera. The only reason I ask is that you spell your name the same as they do. K-e-n-n-e-d-y. Just wondering."

"Yep. You got it. You found me out, blew my cover." She sneezed. "Yeah. I'm one of the Hyannis Port Kennedys. One of *those* Kennedys. And that's why I work for the Baltimore PD. They set up my trust fund so that I have to work until turn thirty. You know, just so I get a taste of what life is like for the commoners. Once I hit thirty, I can retire and live off the trust fund and family name."

"I sense some sarcasm, so I'm going to assume you're not related to the Hyannis Port Kennedys."

"Boy, you Marines sure are smart. Next thing I know you'll be telling me that water is wet."

He chuckled. "Good one. But I don't care about your last name. You could have some crazy last name like Wigglesworth. You could be Hope Wigglesworth and I'd still like you. Hell, you could be Myrtle Wigglesworth and I'd still like you. You know, there was a guy in the Corps who had that last name. Wigglesworth. Chris Wigglesworth. Poor son of a gun. Man, did they ever ride him over that. The drill instructors called him *Wiggle Worm*." He imitated a DI's harsh, gravelly voice. "*Get your ass over here, Wiggle Worm*. He said he was going to change his last name because he had to literally walk around with that name—*Wigglesworth*—on his uniform for the whole world to see."

He glanced up at a shelf above her bed that displayed a Beanie Baby collection. He pointed to it and chuckled. "Beanie Babies, huh?"

She wheezed. "Yeah. Beanie Babies. I collected them as a little girl, back in the day. The ones on that shelf are all originals, from the nineties."

"Cool. It was a big craze, swept the whole nation. I remember it well."

She coughed. "Yeah. I love them. They have such cool names, like Alacazam and Patti the Platypus."

"Yeah, well, they might have given them those *cool names* to distract you from the fact that you shelled out twenty bucks for a bag of rice." He laughed.

"You never quit, do you?"

"Nope. Marines never quit. We really don't. We press on until the mission is accomplished because failure is not an option. There's just too much at stake."

She neatly folded a pair of black lace panties and placed them in the suitcase. "And what's your mission now, huh? Tell me."

"My mission is to get over my missions."

"Yeah?"

"Yeah. That and to be a wrecking ball."

"Wrecking ball?" She hacked and spit some phlegm up into a tissue. "Oh, God, it's all green. That's gross," she noted.

"Right. I want to knock down walls."

"What walls?"

"Yours. You have them, and I want to knock them down. So that there's nothing left standing between us. So that it's just you and me. Just the two of us. Just Hope and Luke. No more walls separating us."

"I don't know that I want my walls knocked down. It took a long time to build them. And they've been up for a minute."

"Ever hear of the Berlin Wall? It was a very famous wall. Ever hear of it? I actually have a piece of it. A little tiny piece. No bigger than a small rock. Got it off eBay, like, five years ago. Paid something like thirty bucks for it. I sure hope it's legit because they do counterfeit that stuff. Although it did come with a certificate of authenticity, but those can be faked, too. Gee, now I'm worried. I sure hope it's the real deal…anyway, ever hear of the Berlin Wall?"

"I've already had this history lesson. Harris gave it to me. So, you're wasting your time."

"Yeah? Well, you must have failed. So, I'll give it to you again—that wall existed to imprison people. And those who built it used fear and intimidation and even violence to keep it up. To keep people from being free. And that wall stood for decades. But it fell in a matter of hours. *Hours,* Hope. Because people decided that they were tired of living as prisoners. Prisoners to the past. They didn't wait for freedom to come to them. They took it for themselves. And they only took what God Himself had already given them as a birthright. They tore down that wall and threw its rubble on the trash heap of history, another testament to the evil and arrogance that can live in the human heart.

"I want you to be free. But the walls have to come down first. Everyone has a war story to tell. You have one. I know you do. You give me this bullshit about how you don't like cats. I saw the shrine you have downstairs to that gray tabby. All those pictures. I saw them. Some kids don't have birthday parties as elaborate as the one you had for that cat. So, what's *your* war story? Huh? I'll tell you mine if you tell me yours."

There were tears in her eyes. She shook her head. "I'm not ready to tell mine."

"Fine. Fair enough. Then I'll go first. Okay? Yeah. I'll tell you mine. How's that? And you can tell yours whenever you're ready. No pressure. All right?"

She nodded and wiped the tears from her eyes. "Yeah. Kay."

He looked at his watch. "First, I need to get your temp and oxygen. Doctor Mike said it's important to regularly check your vitals."

He took her temperature and oxygen saturation. "Temp is down. 102.7. O2 level is up to ninety-four. That's up a little, maybe only because of the oxygen they gave you in the ER. But whatever the reason for the mild improvement—I'll take it."

She lay down on the bed.

He sat on its edge and began. "Everyone starts at the beginning, right? At Genesis. I'll be different. I'll start at the end. At Revelation. So, here—I'll *reveal* something to you." He placed his left leg up on the bed and rolled up his pant leg. He pointed to a scar. "There. See that scar? That big, ugly scar?" She nodded. "That's why I got the Purple Heart. And that's why I have a little hitch in my giddy up. I'm sure you probably noticed my limp, right? You're a cop, so I'm sure you're observant. It's subtle but it's noticeable. Yeah, well, I got shot with an AK-Forty-seven. It felt like someone hitting me in the leg as hard as they could with a baseball bat. A searing hot baseball bat. And I used to like to play baseball, too. I can't do that anymore. I won't ever be able to again because I can't really run too well. And that's just the physical scar. Now, if you want to talk about the emotional scars—I sometimes have trouble sleeping at night. And I take, oh, let's see—Paxil, Ativan, Ambien, Buspirone, and Ambilify. And I have to go to counseling every week. Yeah. That's right. I see a psychiatrist. And I can't listen to the song *Rainbow Connection* without freaking out. You know—*Rainbow Connection*? That pretty little song that Kermit The Frog sings, about the lovers and the dreamers. Yeah. Can't listen to that. More on that later. You were telling me how people who listen to that radio show think I'm some kind of angel because of what I did that night on the highway. Well, no angel would harbor the kind of demons that I do. So, that's the prelude. Or I guess it's actually part of the epilogue.

"Anyhow, here we go—War Story. *Based on actual events,* as they say. And no names have been changed." He took a deep breath and loudly exhaled. "So, have you ever heard of a place called Sangin?"

"No."

"Virtually no one else has, either. And that pisses me off. It really does. Because a lot of blood was shed in that shitty little place. And yet nobody knows. Except those of us who were there. Those of us who were there on Saint Crispin's Day. Anyhow, Sangin's a little acre of Hell in the Helmand Province of Afghanistan. The fighting was tough there, Hope. Very tough. The enemy was highly motivated and well-equipped. They had Russian stuff. Okay? Our casualties were high. The price of victory, steep. Quite a few young Marines who fought there never got the chance to become old Marines.

"In the fall of twenty-ten, I was a machine gunner with the 3rd Battalion, 5th Marine Regiment, Alpha Company, 1st Platoon. I was responsible for the *deployment and operation of the M2 Browning fifty caliber machine gun in combat operations against military assets belonging to the enemy.* That was the official Marine Corps job description. That's a fancy way of saying—*your job is to kill, kid.* I was a lance corporal. So, I was only junior enlisted, an E-3. Pretty low on the totem pole. And I was just twenty-years-old.

"We were commanded by a butter bar. That's military parlance for a brand new, inexperienced second lieutenant. They call them *butter bars* because the lieutenant's bars that they wear are a gold, butter color. The guy's name was Danny McKay. Lieutenant Danny McKay. From anywhere and everywhere because his dad was a Marine officer, a lieutenant colonel at the time. So, they moved all around. I think he was born in North Carolina. Danny McKay is important to this story, so you have to know a little bit about him.

"Lieutenant Danny McKay was one good-looking son of a bitch, okay? I'm confident enough in my masculinity that I can admit that. He was a beautiful man. Blond hair, blue eyes. Soft, delicate features. Rosy cheeks with high cheekbones. A pretty man. And he had graduated from Dartmouth, an Ivy Leaguer. He was a drama major, and he wanted to write screenplays which he would star in. He had this gorgeous girlfriend named Stacy. Beautiful girl. So, Danny McKay was headed to Hollywood. But he got lost somewhere on the way to Tinsel Town, see? And he ended up in Quantico, Virginia, at Marine Corps OCS. Now, was that because he really wanted to be a Marine officer? Nah. It was because he was expected to fulfill his family's tradition of service to the Corps. Every male McKay had honored that tradition since the Halls of Montezuma, or maybe it was the Shores of Tripoli. Not sure. One of those two. Anyway, LT was a nice guy. A real nice guy, in fact. Maybe too nice. But LT didn't belong in the Marine Corps. Nor did he belong in Afghanistan. And he *sure as hell* didn't have any business commanding a Marine infantry platoon operating in a combat zone. But no war is perfect, you know? It was what it was. LT was a gentleman, but he was no officer. He didn't make decisions. Decisions made him. He wanted to mull everything over, wanted to take a half-hour and write down pros and cons to everything on a sheet of yellow legal paper. In combat, there's no time for that stuff. And indecision can be worse than bad decision.

"He carried this spiral notebook with him because he was writing a screenplay for what he said would be *thee definitive war film*. Better than *Saving Private Ryan*, so he claimed. Naturally, he would star in it. He even had a name for it—*War

Story. He said it was *beautifully simplistic*. See, he thought that filmmakers got too cutesy with titles. Simplicity was key, in his mind. He said it was going to be *a story about war*. Ergo, the title should be *War Story*. That simple. So, that was LT.

"So, we were in Sangin, and our job was to control this road, a main artery, into the town. We set up a roadblock. And we put up all kinds of signs ahead of the roadblock. In Pasto, in Dari, in English. To let anyone traveling that road know that it was not open for business. And, moreover, that anyone who got too close was subject to being fired upon because the Taliban could pack a vehicle with explosives and kill a lot of Marines by running a roadblock. The Marine Corps learned its lesson about vehicles harboring explosives in Beirut way back in nineteen eighty-three. Well over two hundred dead Marines in The Root. All from one car bomb.

"I had my fifty cal set up behind some sandbags. Gunny Nichols was there with me. And LT brought us some brownies that his girlfriend had sent him in a care package. They were good brownies. They didn't have nuts in them. I don't like the ones that have nuts. Anyway, LT was all giggly and shit because he'd recently seen the episode of *Friends* where Ross wears the leather pants on a date and can't get them off because they're so tight. He just thought that was funny as hell. *Funnier than a turd in a punchbowl*, as he was fond of saying. He rehashed the whole episode even after we told him we'd seen it.

"And I lit up a Camel because I smoked back then, and looked down the road and damned if there wasn't a vehicle headed towards us. Some type of black sedan. Found out later it was an old Chrysler New Yorker. Headed straight for us. I'm going to say it was about a hundred and fifty meters away. The vehicle had already ignored some of our signs. So, I looked at LT, and said—*what are your orders, sir?* Nothing. LT had frozen. So, I repeated myself—*come on, sir, I need an order. The vehicle's still advancing on our position.* Still nothing. So, Gunny Nichols reached over and smacked him hard on the side of his Kevlar and told him—*hey! Wake the fuck up, LT! Time to earn your goddamn money! Sir.* Still nothing. So, Nichols tells me—*warning shots, Elvis. Fire some fuckin' warning shots.* So, I fired warning shots, just to let them know they were pissing us off. I fired well over top of them. Well, not only did it not stop but somebody in the vehicle started shooting back. The fire wasn't too accurate, but somebody was shooting at us, all right. We could tell it wasn't anything heavy but, hell, regardless of the caliber, any piece of hot lead flying through the air faster than the speed of sound can kill, even a little twenty-two round. So, again, I asked for an order—*LT, they ignored the warning shots and we're taking fire. Now what? I need an order, sir.* LT was shaking, sweating. So, finally, I screamed at him—*LT, I need a goddamned order! Sir!* Now, at that point, the rules of engagement said that that car was fair game. It was in a secured area. It had ignored both signs and warning shots. And we were taking fire from it. So, in the eyes of the United States government, the occupants of that vehicle represented a hostile enemy force. But we were the good guys, right? So, we gave everybody the benefit of the doubt. And, sometimes, we did so to our own detriment. Marines definitely died over there because they were so conscious about wanting to avoid civilian casualties. We truly didn't want to kill anything that didn't require killing.

"So, I pressed LT to make a decision. And, finally, he says, real tentative like, *light 'em up, Elvis. I guess we should light 'em up.* And I told him—*guessing's not allowed. Sir! Guessing's not a fucking order! Sir.* And finally, with more confidence, he said—*light 'em up, Elvis. Light 'em the fuck up. Do it* now!

"So, I said—*aye, sir!* And I lit 'em up. I lit 'em the fuck up. And I poured at least fifty rounds of fifty cal into that car. Maybe more. And it stopped, all right. Sure, it stopped. And then we went to check it, and there was smoke and shit still coming from the engine block. And we looked inside." He paused and started crying. "And it was a family, Hope…it was Dad, Mom, and Baby, Baby Girl. And Baby Girl looked to be no more than two. All just as dead as they could be. Of course, they were.

Nobody gets wounded with a fifty cal round. Only killed. Dad's head was sitting in his lap. And they had this boombox in the back with the kid. And, somehow, it manage to survive without getting hit. How? I don't know. It's war. Random shit happens. And they had a CD in, and the disk was still playing. And the song that was playing was *Rainbow Connection,* that sweet little song about the lovers and dreamers. Yeah. That's what was playing. For the kid, I guess. And it was so eerie, so spooky, to hear that music playing and then have to look at all that carnage inside the car. Surreal is what it was.

"And, as it turns out, they didn't have any explosives in that vehicle. They did have a couple of handguns, a Glock and a Makarov, probably for personal protection. But there was no evidence that they were Taliban. In fact, the speculation was that they were fleeing the Taliban."

"Why didn't they obey the signs? Why did they shoot at you guys?"

He shrugged. "Who knows? You can only speculate. They might have ignored the signs because they were illiterate. The literacy rate in Afghanistan is not high. They don't have a good educational system. Real estate agents in Afghanistan can't use the old *this neighborhood has a great school system* hook when they show properties. And as far as why they shot back—they may have thought that *we* were Taliban. Or, it could have been as simple as the fact that when someone starts shooting in your direction, and you have a gun handy—well, the most natural thing to do is to shoot back, I guess. Bottom line—the only people who could answer those questions are all dead. The *fog of war,* Hope. When the fog of war rolls in, it can get very thick. And it's impossible to see things clearly. And in the fog of war, anything—literally *anything*—is possible. And as long as war, with all its chaos and confusion, exists, the fog of war will exist. No, we'll never have all the answers. I wish I could know. But what I do know is that I killed an entire family that day. *An entire family.* They were ruled legal, justified kills because we adhered to the rules of engagement. But just because something's legal doesn't make it right. It was a tragic accident. But I can't help but wonder if, maybe, there was something that we—*that I*—could have done differently. Maybe if we had waited just a little bit longer before opening up on them, given them a little more time. But, then again, what if that car had been packed with C-4? I don't know. I just don't know. But what I do know is that, in my mind's eye, I replay that day in Sangin constantly. Literally, not a day goes by when I don't think about it, when I'm not haunted by it…when I don't see that dead family." He shook his head and wiped tears from his eyes.

"Oh, and in case you're wondering—where are they now? Danny McKay was killed two weeks later. And he didn't die heroically, didn't die diving on a live grenade or charging a Taliban machine gun nest. No. He died because he did something stupid. We were on patrol and he saw a Maneki-neko Cat on the ground. You know—those cute little ceramic cats with the one paw raised in the air. They're supposed to be lucky. Yeah. Lucky. LT's last words were—*oh shit, boys. Looky here. A lucky cat, and we sure as hell could use some luck.* He picked it up. I guess he wanted a keepsake. But it was booby trapped. The damn thing blew up in his face. Keepsake—lose life. And as pretty as that man was, his parents had to give him a closed casket funeral. That was the scuttlebutt, anyway. And Gunny Nichols—well, he ended up in a wheelchair. A bullet severed his spinal cord about a month after LT bought it. He made out all right, though. We exchange Christmas cards every year and email one another once every couple of months. He has a great wife, Christine, and that makes all the difference. Having someone, that is. Yeah, that makes all the difference. He does motivational speaking now. He calls his presentation—*To Hell and Back: One Marine's Battle to Win the Peace.*

"And that's my War Story, Hope. And it eats me up inside, especially at night. Late at night. In the quiet and darkness of the night. When I first came home, before I got on meds and into counseling, I went out and bought a nine millimeter and some ammo. And one night, I loaded it and put the barrel in my mouth. I did. And the TV was on, tuned to Animal Planet. That saved my life, by the way. Yep. My life was saved because the TV just happened to be tuned to a particular channel. Talk about serendipity. Anyhow, Animal Planet was playing this documentary called *Pets For Vets*. It was about how animals were helping veterans with PTSD, how animals were actually part of the therapy. So, I put the gun down and sold it back to the gun shop the next day. And I got involved with Recycled Love. And that helps. *A lot*. Animals really have helped me, and that's an understatement. Sometimes, I look at Bobby and Hannah and wonder—who rescued who? An animal's love is unconditional and that means that they live much closer to God than most humans. But I still have bad days. Yeah, there are plenty of times when I hate myself for that day in Sangin. I literally *hate* myself. But I can't go back. I can't change it. I can't bring that family back. I'd trade my life for theirs in a heartbeat. Jesus Christ, I would! But I can't. And I don't know how to make it right. And I don't think it even can be made right. So, I do my best to live with it. And I pray each day that God will forgive me for my mistake. I guess that's all I *can* do. But it's a helluva thing to live with."

They both had tears in their eyes.

She patted the mattress. "Come up here with me. Lay down with me for a little while, okay?"

"Lay down with you? Are you sure?"

"Yeah. I want you to. So, just lay down with me. Okay?"

He lay down next to her, on the right side of the bed, leaving about a foot between them.

"You can be closer than that. Come on. Doctor Mike said I'm not contagious. So, come on, scoot over closer."

He moved closer, until his shoulder touched hers.

She coughed and rolled on her side, so she was facing him. "I'm so sorry. I'm sorry for the way I treated you. I'm sorry for everything. Can you forgive me? *Please* forgive me."

"Of course, I do. It's over. Forgotten. Forgiving means forgetting."

"Here. Give me your hand," she told him. "Yeah. Give me your hand. Come on."

He gave her his hand. She held his hand and interlocked their fingers. "Look at that. You have this huge hand. Like a lion's paw or something. And I have a tiny little hand." She coughed.

He chuckled. "Yeah. There's definitely a little bit of a contrast there."

She squeezed his hand. "Let's just stay like this for a while. All right? Can we just take a little nap together? Then when we wake up, we'll go to your place." She wheezed.

"You okay?"

It took her a couple of seconds to catch her breath. "Yeah. I'm okay…I think."

He reached over and brushed her hair with his hand. "Remember, I won't let anything bad happen to you."

"And you promise, right?"

He nodded. "I promise."

"Kay then. Now, I can sleep."

She put her hand on his chest and drifted off to sleep. But he didn't sleep. Instead, he stayed awake to keep an eye on her breathing.

CHAPTER SIXTEEN: CRAZY FOR YOU

Later that morning, as they got ready to leave her house, she picked up her suitcase. He took it from her. "Nope. You are not carrying that."

"I don't want to ask you to do everything for me."

"I'm going to carry it for you. Okay? Let me do it. Please."

She nodded. "Kay."

He insisted on warming up the car for her, too.

On the drive from Bolton Hill to Roland Park, he stopped at Giant supermarket to get some chicken broth and orange juice for her.

When they got back on the road, the *Sounds of the Eighties* CD played Madonna's *Crazy for You*.

He looked over at her, smiled, and raised his eyebrows. "*Crazy for You*. How do you like that? *Crazy for You*."

"Crazy for *me*?" A confused look crossed her face.

He laughed. "The song, Hope. Madonna. *Crazy for You*. I like it. Love it, in fact. It's a sweet song. Do you like it?" He sang along.

"Oh, yeah. The song. Right. The song. Madonna. *Crazy for You*. Yeah, it's great. Pretty, pretty little song." *Oh, God. I think I just made a fool out of myself. But he really does have a nice voice. I'd love to hear his interpretation of* Come Monday.

"It's a great slow dance song."

She nodded approvingly. "Yeah. I guess it is." She hacked.

"When you feel better, maybe we could dance to it."

"Yeah, we could do that. We could totally do that. I don't see why not."

He looked over at her and smiled. "I'm going to hold you to that. I am. You look very beautiful today, by the way."

She put her head down. "I know I look awful…but thank you."

"You know, Giant has some good sales going. Their bakery has a BOGO thing going on with pies. I noticed that when I was in there getting your broth and orange juice. I wouldn't have minded having both a huckleberry and a boysenberry pie."

"You should have gotten them. I could have waited a couple extra minutes."

"Nah. It's too cold to make you wait. Plus, I lost my Preferred Customer Card. You have to have the card to get the deal. Although, I have to tell you, if anyone and everyone can get the card, are you really a *preferred customer*? I. Think. Not."

She coughed. "Yeah. Good point. I've wondered the same thing about those supermarket discount cards. They try to make it sound like you're all special, but in reality, those cards are handed out the way Jehovah's Witnesses hand out Bible tracts. I have my Preferred Customer Card in my purse. We can swing back around if you want."

"Oh, no— don't be silly. I'll just bake my own pies."

When they got to his place, he showed her to the master bedroom.

She took a shower and washed her hair. She shaved her legs and used her bikini waxing strips. *Sick or not, I hate body hair. Don't even like it on men and certainly don't like it on myself.* After blow drying her hair, she put on a pair of gray sweatpants and a grey t-shirt with the Baltimore Police logo on it. Her hair was up, and she wore pink and white ankle socks. She sprayed herself with a single pump of Angel perfume.

She plopped herself down on his bed. *Pretty comfy bed. More comfortable than mine, actually. I already like it here. I like it better than my house. So many bad memories in that house.*

She turned on the TV and watched *Family Feud*, playing along during the fast money round. *Name a celebrity who wears a wig.* "Most any of the Real Housewives," she muttered.

After a half hour, she heard a knock on the door.

"Come on in." Her voice was hoarse.

He walked in with one hand behind his back. He wore a pair of blue jeans and a red sweatshirt with the Marine emblem on it.

She couldn't tell what he had in the hand that was hidden, but she sensed it was for her.

"How are you feeling?"

"A little better, actually. I don't feel quite so drained. I think that nap earlier helped." She pointed. "What, ah, what's that you have behind your back?"

He brought his hand around to reveal a bouquet of red roses, walked over to the bed, and presented them to her. "For you." He smiled.

She smiled back and hacked. "Aw. They're beautiful. God, Luke, no guy has ever given me roses before."

"What? Seriously?"

She coughed and nodded.

"You've been dating the wrong guys. Thee. Wrong. Guys."

Tell me about it.

He expanded on his thought. "That's crazy—that's what that is. No roses for Hope? That ought to be illegal. There needs to be a law that says that you get a dozen red roses at least once a week. Seriously, it needs to be in the Constitution. They need to amend the dang Constitution and put that in. I'm calling my congressman about that."

"This is so incredibly sweet of you. Thank you."

"I got them at the hospital gift shop and then put them in the trunk of the car. That's the real reason I wanted to visit the giftshop."

She chuckled. "Yeah. I wasn't buying that whole *romance novel* thing."

"Yeah. See, I don't want to read a romance novel. I want to live a romance novel. I want to live it out with that one special person. And I want a happy ending."

"You want your very own HEA, huh? That's what they call them, you know—HEAs. It stands for *happily ever after*."

He turned his gaze upward. "Right. So, if there's a Writer up there writing this story, please give me a little piece of Heaven because I've already had a heaping helping of Hell. I want to live happily ever after."

She added, "With the luck I've had, I'd settle for living happily ever after—every now and then."

They looked at each other and it was quiet for a few seconds.

Finally, she told him, "I need to put these in water."

"I'll do it."

He left the room and came back a couple minutes later with a green vase. He took the roses from her and placed them inside. He set the vase on the dresser.

"Are you hungry?"

"No. Not yet."

"Let me know when you are, and I'll make up some broth for you. And in the meantime, I'll excuse myself and let you get some rest."

"No. Don't go. Please don't go. Stay here with me. I'm lonely. Stay and talk with me. Please."

He sat on the edge of the bed. "What would you like to talk about?"

"I saw some wrestling DVDs on your bookshelf."

He shrugged. "Yeah. I hope that's not a problem for you because I like it. Pro wrestling, that is. I like pro wrestling."

She nodded. "I like it, too, actually."

At the same time, they both said—"It's like a soap opera with body slams."

They laughed.

"You know, that's one of the things that Gretchen Cavanaugh held against me, that I like pro wrestling. That was one of the many things that made me unworthy."

"Yeah, well, she's an idiot."

"Thanks. She made me feel inadequate. She's all about breathing that million air. Me? I'm just trying to breathe. I don't care if my air comes from the dollar store, so long as I can breathe. Because sometimes I think I'm suffocating."

"Yeah. I know the feeling." *Boy, do I know the feeling.*

"You smell good," he told her.

"Thanks. The fragrance is Angel. You smell good, too, by the way. I haven't lost my sense of smell yet."

"Intense Euphoria. It's by Calvin Klein. I hope I didn't overspray. I was trying to get that *Stewie* smell off me. That kid had a horrible stench associated with him. Cigarette smoke—that's what it was."

She laughed. "Oh, I know, right? He reeked. He wasn't shy, either. After all, it's not every day that you have a seven-year-old gawk at your chest." She coughed.

"And how about his talking points and questions? Awk. Ward."

They laughed.

"I know. Seriously. I noticed, towards the end, you just kind of stopped answering his questions. For example, you never answered his last question. You know? That last question he had for you," she said.

"Oh, I answered it. Just not out loud." He quickly changed the subject. "Say, let's play more Fun Facts. I'll start. I have *boo koo* credit cards. Probably, literally, like, fifteen of them. That's just a guess. Could be more. I have so many I need a second wallet to accommodate them. And the reason I have so many is because when the sales reps call, I can't say *no.* I feel bad for them. They're just trying to eke out a living, right? So, I sign up for the dang cards. But I almost never use them. I carry very little debt. So, they're not making any money off me. I'm just helping the sales reps out. You know, doing them a solid."

The Midnight Ranger's uncanny. Scary, is what he is. The guy should be picking stocks.

"Your turn, Hope. Tell me your Fun Fact."

"Um. Okay. Um…I like fruitcake. And the fruitier the better."

"Goodness. Quite a bombshell. I'll try not to hold that against you." He smiled, winked at her, and turned serious.

"Tell me something that makes you cry."

She sneezed and blew her nose with a tissue. Then, she took a deep breath, smiled at him, and said, "Boy. That's a tough one."

"Why is it tough? What makes it tough?"

"Because tears make you vulnerable, I guess."

"They do. They also make us human, make us real. I'll tell you what—I'll start with this one. I'll tell you what makes me cry, besides all the stuff that happened in Afghanistan. And what makes me cry is the book, *The Velveteen Rabbit*. Specifically, the part where he becomes real, when the rabbit becomes real. Makes me cry every damn time. And guess what? It's a tear that brings the rabbit to life. Once he sheds a tear, he becomes real. So, what makes you cry? What makes you real, huh? I want to know."

She answered tentatively. "The...the ending of *Planes, Trains and Automobiles*, when you realize that John Candy's wife is dead, and he has nowhere to go for Thanksgiving." She started to tear up. "See? Just thinking about it gets me misty-eyed."

He nodded approval. "Yeah, I love John Candy. There was just something about him. A genuineness. Something you can't fake. No Hollywood PR machine could concoct what he had."

"Yeah. He was a sweetheart. Gone way too soon."

"Hey, do you want to watch the film? I have it on DVD. I know it's basically a Thanksgiving movie and here we are in January, but a good movie's a good movie."

"Um. Yeah. Sure." She held up her box of tissues. "I have my box of Kleenex all ready." She giggled and wheezed.

He administered her medication and took her vitals. Her temperature and oxygen saturation were about the same.

Her ribs were hurting.

"God, I'm having a lot of pain from these ribs today."

"You have your pain meds with you, right?"

"Yeah. But I've been trying not to take them. I've been skipping doses. I guess maybe, because I'm a cop and see what those drugs can do to people, I'm hesitant. But I'm really in a lot of pain right now."

"Take one, then. Taking them short-term, as directed, is highly unlikely to result in dependency. The people that get into trouble with that stuff are the ones who exceed the prescribed dose or take it long-term. You have the right to be pain free. That's why the doctor prescribed them."

She nodded. "Yeah, I guess you're right. Um, my purse is on your desk. Can you hand it to me?"

He retrieved her purse and she fished out a pill bottle. "You have any water? I can't take these dry. They're fairly large pills and they get caught in my throat."

He went downstairs and came back with a bottle of water and handed it to her. He sat down on the edge of the bed.

She popped the large blue pill and took a swig of water. "La-la Land here I come."

He turned the TV on, put the DVD in, and sat down on the foot of the bed. "Want some popcorn? I can make some."

"No. I still don't feel much like eating."

"Okay, but you should eat something soon, even if it's only broth."

"Yeah. Okay. I will. But for now, let's just spend some time together. Like we did this morning, at my place. That was nice, wasn't it?"

"Yeah. It was nice."

"You were such a gentleman, too, when we laid down together. I loved that. This officer likes gentlemen. Gentle. Men. Gentlemen are sexy."

They watched the previews on the DVD. He told her, "I always like to watch these. It makes me feel like I'm actually in the theater. The only thing missing is the four dollar box of Milk Duds."

Towards the end of the previews, she could feel the opioid kicking in. *Yeah. This feels good. Mellow. Relaxed. Pain free. Worry free.*

She patted the mattress with her palm. "Come on. Get up

here. With me. Up here with me. Please." *I feel loopy, but confident. Sexy even.*

He lay down next to her but left a good foot or so between them.

"No. Come on, Luke. What's wrong with you, huh? What? Do I smell like Stewie, like stale cigarettes? Closer. Closer please."

He moved closer so that his shoulder pressed up against hers.

She looked at him and smiled a big smile.

He smiled and waved. "Hi there."

"Hi yourself, boy." She reached out and caressed his arm.

By now, the drug was hitting her full force. "Oh, I feel so good. So freaking good. Hell-to-the-yeah. I feel like shit, don't get me wrong. But I feel *good*." She coughed then giggled.

"I think you might be a little bit high."

"I am. Percocet's a hell of a drug, baby boy." She reached over and gently pinched his cheek.

"*Baby boy*, huh?" He chuckled. "I'm on Vicodin for my ribs and you know what it makes me do?"

"What's that, huh? What's. That? Whatsthat? Wazzsup?" She giggled, reached over and brushed his hair with her hand. "Cute boy," she mumbled.

He paid no mind to her silliness. "Yeah. Anyhow. Vicodin turns me into a spendthrift. I spend money left and right when that stuff kicks in. The other day I took one because it was really bothering me. Mind you, now–I always take it exactly as directed but it still affects me. So, I took one and fifteen minutes later I was on this super mellow high. *Chasing the dragon*. I think that's what they call it on the street. And I found myself online, on this website called Dapper Dan's Pet Boutique, ordering Bobby and Hannah cashmere sweaters. Bobby got baby blue and Hannah got pink. And neither of them will wear clothing. I've tried to get them to wear clothes before and they just won't. The stuff hasn't arrived, but I already know it was a waste of two-hundred dollars. Oh—and Vicodin makes me itch, too. Does Percocet make you itch?"

She ignored his question but intently stared at him. "What kind of girls do you lick, boy?" She coughed, burst out laughing, and shook her head as if to clear the cobwebs. "That sounded dirty. Dir. Tee. I meant to say *like*. Like. Yeah, that's what I meant."

She turned on her side, so that she was facing him, and rested her chin in her hand. "So, what kind of girls do you lick? Huh? What kind? Inquiring minds want to know."

He laughed. "I don't think you have to worry about crying at the end of this movie. Something tells me that you're never going to make it that far. I think the Sand Man's going to pay you a visit real soon and throw some of his magic dust into those pretty eyes of yours, those pretty glazed over eyes, and you'll be down for the count."

She occasionally slurred her words. "All the more reason to answer my quess-shun right now. Yeah. You're pretty tall and all." She snickered. *"Tall and all.* I made a rhyme, and I wasn't even trying. I'm a poet and I don't even know it. I am one talented little gal." She got back on track with her thought. "Does she have to be, like, a freaking model, all tall and whatnot, to have a chance with you, Luke? Sir Luke."

He laughed. "Oh wow. You knighted me, huh? Now, I'm right up there with Elton John and Paul McCartney. I think I like you stoned."

She emphatically nodded her head. "You are a knight, a freaking knight in armor shining." She talked baby talk to him. "Yes you are—yes you are—yes you are." She paused, coughed, and continued. "And those skanks who have been calling and emailing the radio station about you are going to keep their filthy paws to themselves, too. Damn sluts. Finders keepers. That's how it works, dude. But you still didn't answer my quess-shun, honey. *Hun. Knee."*

"Oh, right. I didn't. Ah, no, she does not have to be tall. In fact, I like short, petite women."

She opened her mouth wide. "Oh, reel-lee?"

He laughed. "Yeah. Really."

She intently stared at him without blinking.

"Why are you looking at me like that, Hope?"

She coughed and shrugged. "Ah ont know. I'm just really... *hearing* you right now. Yeah. I am *so* hearing you."

"Uh-huh. Uh-huh. The only reason I ask is because that look on your face kind of suggests that you're a witch who's contemplating turning me into a lawn gnome."

She laughed loudly and playfully tapped his arm. "Oh, my Lore. You're funny, too. Cute and funny. Cuter than Bill Hader and funnier than...I ont know...Kanye."

"Thanks. That's always been my goal in life."

For several awkward seconds they just stared at one another.

My eyes feel heavy. But I'm going to fight it as long as I can because I feel so damn good.

She yawned and hacked.

"What's the matter? You running out of interesting topics? Here. I'll give you one—The Era of Good Feelings was neither an era, nor good, nor about feelings. Discuss amongst yourselves and be prepared to defend your thoughts in front of the entire class tomorrow."

"Say whaaat?"

"Forget it. That was just me being *funnier than Kanye*. Or at least trying."

"What about hair color? Huh, boy? You probably like blondes because, you know, the whole *gentleman prefer blondes* thing. Right?"

"No. I actually prefer brunettes. I like black hair." He pointed to her head. "Kind of like yours."

She put her left arm up and pulled it down the way the driver of a semi would in order to sound the horn in the rig. "Cha-ching." That was immediately followed by a, "Woot—woot." And that, in turn, was followed by a coughing fit.

"Let me see that pill bottle. What dosage of this stuff do they have you on?"

She shrugged and handed him the bottle. "Ah ont know. The

happy dose, I guess."

He examined the label. "Oh, Good Lord. They've got you on ten milligrams, girl. That's a lot. A hell of a lot. What doctor did this?"

She again shrugged. "Ah ont know. Whoever was there the night of the accident."

He squinted to read the small print on the label. "Let's see here—which doctor was it? It probably *was* a witch doctor… oh, here we go…*Henderson, PA.* A damn physician's assistant. Not a real doctor and probably doesn't even play one on TV." He shook his head in disgust. "I'm no medical professional but this is way too much for you. Five milligrams would be plenty. You might even be able to get by with two and a half. Next time, why don't you cut one in half? At least try it that way. Okay? That's why you're so wasted. Ten mil is too much for a woman as tiny as yourself."

She shot him and incredulous look. "Tiny? *Excusez-moi?*" With her index fingers, she pointed to either breast. "Uh-uh. No sir. Big. I kin ass-sir you—big. Big—big—big. *Biiiig.* Thirty-four double D big. Katy Perry big. Real and big. Real big."

He nodded. "Yeah. Okay. I get it. They're big. Real, too. You're a Hope who has quite a chest. Uh-huh. Duly noted."

"What? You don't like big? You like small? Cameron Diaz? Kate Hudson? You don't dig big?"

"I do dig big. Big time. I'd have to be a very *small* person not to appreciate *big*. There's a big place in my heart for big. Big's a big deal, okay? Always has been. Not sure why. Just is. I think it might go back to seeing reruns of *Baywatch* when I was a teenager. Those images of Pamela Anderson running on the beach always stuck with me. You see, *Baywatch* was on the first time I ever, you know, I was in my room, all by myself, at that age… and…ah…never mind. Almost TMI. Anyway, you don't have all your faculties about you right now. Seriously, Dean Martin after three martinis sounded more articulate than you do at the moment."

She went on. "What about butts? Asses. Badonkadonks. You

like them? Maybe a nice, round, tight bubble butt like mine? I spend, like, a lot of time at the gym to get this bubble butt."

"I...I do. I like bubble butts. I like boobs, butts, and legs. We'll just get the legs out of the way while we're at it because I like them, too. And I know that's going to be your next talking point. Or should I say *slurring* point. I'm a heterosexual male, Hope. Okay? I like all that good stuff. All that wild, wacky stuff. I like it. Love it, in fact. I envy you all for having those wonderful pieces of equipment. I wish I had them." He thought for a moment. "No wait. Forget that last thing I said. It didn't come out right. But suffice it to say, I am a huge supporter and fan of the female anatomy. It's part of what makes America great. No. Wait. Forget that, too, because women in other countries also have that stuff. So, that didn't make any sense at all. Look, it's like this—I like the ladies. Not that there would be anything wrong if I preferred the gents. Nothing wrong with that, if that's your bag. And although I'm definitely not gay, I think I might be somewhat metro because I do like to go to ye old tanning salon once in a while, especially during the winter months, just for a little color."

She looked at him, coughed, and licked her lips. "I want me some sugar."

"I have some chocolate chip cookies downstairs, Famous Amos. They're good. I think they're actually the best store-bought cookies you can get. Of course, they're not as good as homemade but they're pretty darn close. If you think your little tum-tum will tolerate something that heavy, I'll run down and get you some, along with a glass of organic milk to wash it down. Now, what do you say?"

"No. I want *sugar*."

"Right. Sugar. If cookies aren't your jam, I also have donuts filled with jam."

"No. Come on. Listen to me, now. Communication is key in a successful relation-shit. Now, I want me some sugar, damnit! Now, please." After a brief pause, she repeated herself. "Sugar. *Shug. Ger.*" She reached up and squeezed her breasts through her shirt.

"*Oooh.* You want some *sugar. That* kind of sugar, huh?"

She emphatically nodded. "Yeah. Right. Right on, man. *Duh.* Sugar."

He chuckled. "Aw. You're cute. You know that? Hammered, but cute."

"I not cute. I sex-say. Make luv to you, dude." She talked in a whisper. "Be the bess you ever had. Yeah. It would. Truss me, kay? Yeah, juss truss me. You down with that? Wanna do it? A little hey-hey? Huh? You *down* with getting it *up?*" She sneezed twice.

He stared at her, arms folded, and just shook his head. Emphatically, he shook his head.

She threw up her hands and raised her voice a bit. "I mean—I am *sorry* for being a sex-sue-yule cree-chur. I pol-low-gize if mah sex-sue-al-ity *oh*-fends you. But I *am* a sex-sue-yule being. That's just the way me made the Good Lord. So, what do you say? Huh, boy? Cute boy." She sneezed, coughed, and wheezed.

He again shook his head. "Nope. Wham—bam—no thank you, ma'am. Not the right time. Not gunna happen. No way."

"No? Really?"

"Really."

"Well, how about a game then?"

"Say, now that's a great idea. A nice wholesome game. What game did you have in mind? I have Monopoly around here somewhere. I also have Risk. And if you really want to go old school, I can even break out the Yahtzee."

"It's for two players. And it's called Kissy Pooh. Kissy. Pooh. Kissypooh. Kissy…Pooh! Does Sir Luke want to play Kissy Pooh with The Hope-ster? What do you say, boy? You down for some Kissy Pooh? Huh? It's just Kissy Pooh. Not like I'm trying to get all sex-sue-yule with you. Dang. Why you so difficult, man? Sure, it might poss-a-bee, conceive-a-bee, get sex-sue-yule. And whatnot."

"I can't play Kissy Pooh with you under the current circumstances. And the rea—"

She cut him off. "Oh yeah? Well, there are a lot of dudes out there who would love to play Kissy Pooh with The Hope-ster. But they're assholes. Because, up until now, that's what I've always attracted. *Assholes.* I'm not good enough for anybody else. You don't want me. Only douchebags want me. I am freaking tainted. Okay? I know that. But do you have to throw it up in my face?" She cried.

He spoke tenderly. "Hey—hey. Listen now—you didn't allow me to finish. First of all, do not talk about yourself like that. Ever. Second, the reason I can't kiss you is that you're, shall we say, tipsy. And you're pretty darn sick, too." He used his thumb to wipe away her tears.

She shot him a leery look. "Me? Tipsy? Surely you jest." She sniffled and coughed.

"Yes, you're tipsy. A wee bit." He held up his thumb and index finger close to one another. "I think you're a wee bit tipsy, lass. And a gentleman doesn't take advantage of a lady when she's a wee bit tipsy. It's not right. That's part of the gentleman's code of honor. I wouldn't do that to any woman. And I certainly wouldn't do it to you because I respect you. Now, hopefully, you can understand why I can't play Kissy Pooh with you. Do I want to? Yeah. You bet, I do. In the worst way. Just not with you like this. It wouldn't be right. It's just that simple."

"What about later? Play Kissy Pooh later?"

He took a deep breath. "I don't think playing Kissy Pooh is really a good idea while you're sick."

"Why? I not contagious. Doctor Mike said so."

"Yeah. He did say that. Listen, if you want to play Kissy Pooh when you're feeling better and not under the influence of painkillers, I'll gladly play that game with you."

"Can I get it in writing?" She pulled a tissue from the box and loudly blew her nose.

"Writing? You want it in writing?" He chuckled and shook his head. "You women want everything in writing, huh?"

"As Yoda would say—*in writing must be it.*"

"Right. Because I'm all about following the edicts of fictional characters." Without even getting up, he reached over to the nightstand and grabbed a pad of Post-It notes and a pen. He wrote on the pad. After he finished, he peeled off the note and handed it to her.

"Here. An IOU. Or a q-pon, if you will."

"*Coupon.* Say it right, damnit."

"Right. Sorry. Q-pon. I signed it and everything. It's all legal-like. I'm no lawyer, but I'm pretty sure it would stand up in court. It can be redeemed at a later time."

She read it aloud. *"Let it be known—Sir Luke owes The Hope-ster one game of Kissy Pooh. This may be redeemed at the place, date, and time of The Hope-ster's choosing, so long as she is not under the influence of her pain medication and is feeling better. Sir Luke. No expiration date. No refunds. No exchanges."*

He nodded. "There. It's in writing. Happy now?"

"But it's not notarized."

"Well, since there's no notary on duty here in my bedroom, you're going to have to let me slide on that, okay?"

"Kay." She folded it up and stuffed it down her bra. "Into the vault it goes."

"Right. The vault."

She coughed, reached over and picked up her iPad from the nightstand, and started typing.

"N—n—now, now what are you doing?"

"I on the World Wide Web, the information superhighway." She dismissively waved her hand at him. "Chill out, dude. Lee me alow. Don't worry about it. *Gee-sus.*"

"What are you doing on the World Wide Web?"

"On social mia. Facebook."

"What are you doing on your Facebook page? Huh? What?"

"Not doing it on mah page. Doing it on yer page, dude."

"What are you doing on my page?"

"Posting on yer timeline." She coughed.

"What are you posting on my timeline?"

"Jess that we're gonna be playing Kissy Pooh."

"No—no—no. *No.* Come on, now. Give me that iPad. You should not be online while under the influence. Nothing good ever comes from being on social media while high or drunk. Rosanne can vouch for that. So, let me hold onto that device for now. You don't want to Kissy Pooh and tell, right? Come on, I'm serious. Give it up, girl." He reached for the iPad.

She turned so she was still on her side but facing the opposite direction and clutched the iPad close to her chest. She squealed. "Nooooe! Lee. Me. Alow. God! Jerk!"

"Come on, Hope. Give me the damn iPad. You're being a little bit of a brat."

She hid it under her shirt and rolled back over so she was again facing him. She giggled like a schoolgirl and coughed. "You want it? Come-n-get-it. Comeon." She puckered her lips, coughed, and kissed the air. *"Come. On."*

He threw his hands up in defeat. "You know what? I'm not going to play these games. The hell with it. I don't have that many Facebook friends anyway, a few hundred. Tops. And it's not like people check my timeline to see what I'm posting. I'm not one of these silly so-called influencers. So, I'm not going to obsess over it right this second. When the Percocet wears off, you can delete it for me. Not going to worry about it right now." He shook his finger at her and lectured. "But I'll tell you something right now, missy—all this carrying on and tomfoolery is not good for your pneumonia."

She ignored his point. "So, we'll still play Kissy Pooh, right? You're not gonna cancel it just cuz I'm being a little ornery. Right?"

"The Kissy Pooh hasn't been cancelled. I'm cutting you a lot of slack here because you're so smashed and, bless your heart, it's not really even your fault. It's the PA's fault for having you on such a high dose of the medication. But I have to ask—is it always like this every time you take one of those pills?"

"Well, no. Cuz normally there isn't anybody to talk to. But now, I got somebody—a boy—to talk to. And to play with, a boy to play with."

"Right. A boy to talk to and play with. That would be me."

"Um. Can I ask another quess-shun?"

"Yeah, sure, why not? Shoot."

She just looked at him for a few seconds. She started to cry again. "I almost did. Oh, God. I almost did. I'm sorry. I'm so sorry."

"*Shhh.* Okay? Listen—you didn't. You didn't shoot me. It's okay. Don't cry. Please, don't cry. We talked about not living in the past. Remember? Well, that's the past. I don't want you to cry over it anymore. All right? Please. Can you do that for me?"

She nodded. "I'll try."

"Good. Now, what's your question, sweetie?"

"Um. Well, I know you can't kiss me now because of the gentleman's code of honor. Is there anything in that code that says you can't hold me in your arms while we lay here? Real tight. Can you hold me real tight? I don't know anything about how that code works because I've never had a gentleman before. Never. *Ever.* And I guess I'm higher than a hippie in a hot air balloon right now, but it would mean a lot to me to have a man hold me that way. And let me know that I might actually be worth a damn because I've never had that before. Is that against the rules of the code? Huh? Is it?"

He had tears in his eyes. "*Oh, Hope.* You're breaking my heart. You know that, right? And I'm pretty sure you're breaking God's Heart, too. But to answer your question—no, that's not against the code. It's not. I'd love to hold you."

"Honest?"

He nodded. "Come here." He opened his arms to her. "Come on. Bring it in. Circle the wagons, Hope."

He put his arm around her and pulled her into him.

"Tighter, please. Hold me tighter. Please."

He held her tighter.

She placed her head on his chest and draped her arms over his midsection.

He softly kissed her on the forehead. She coughed then sniffled.

She gazed up. "That's not our game of Kissy Pooh. That doesn't count because it was only on the forehead."

"That was a free one. You're right, it doesn't count."

They lay there together and after about a minute, he whispered to her. "Don't quote me on this or anything, but I think this is how it's supposed to work between two people. Aside from the fact that you're stoned and sick and all. I think this is right. I do. I think this is how it was intended to be. I think this is the *right way.*"

"I'll have to take your word for it. I don't know anything about the right way. I only know the wrong way. I know a lot about the wrong way, the messed-up way."

The movie was still playing.

He spoke softly. "Let's watch the picture. And we'll laugh at the funny parts. And we'll cry when we find out that John Candy's wife is dead, and that he has nowhere to go for Thanksgiving. We'll cry at that part, okay? Because that makes us human, right?"

She nodded. "Right." He brushed her hair with his hand.

He reached over to the nightstand and picked up his phone.

"I'm going to give us a little bit of background music."

He made his selection. "Here we go. Listen…and enjoy."

Vanilla Ice's *Ice Ice Baby* played.

She giggled.

"Oh, dang. *Oops.* Not that one. I don't even know how that song got into my playlist. I really don't. This technology—it's literally developing a mind of its own. Because I *did not* place that song in my playlist. I've never even heard it before. What's the dude's name? Vanilla Spice? Is that it? Sounds like an air freshener. I think his real name's Robert Van Winkle. Isn't that crazy? That's a crazy name for a rapper, right?"

She shook her head and laughed. "You're nutty, boy. Coo-coo is what you are."

He fiddled with his phone some more and then looked at her. "Ah. Here we go. This is the song I had in mind."

Crazy For You started to play.

He looked at her and tenderly brushed her cheek with the back of his hand. "Crazy for you. Right?"

She nodded. "Yeah. Madonna. *Crazy For You*. It's a good song."

He shook his head and warmly smiled. "No, Hope. This time I wasn't talking about a song."

CHAPTER SEVENTEEN: YOU'RE JOHN CANDY

She'd fallen asleep in his arms as they watched the movie. He lay with her for about a half hour. When he got up, he was careful not to wake her. At the kitchen table, he made a shopping list for later. Hannah walked up and rubbed against his leg. He briefly glanced at her, reached a hand down, and scratched her chin. "Well, hello there, sweetie. Do you and Bobby realize yet that we have a houseguest? Do you? Yep. We sure do. A very special house guest because that's the girl that I'm going to—" He abruptly stopped. *Don't get carried away. You don't know how she really feels about you. That Kissy Pooh stuff might have just been the drug talking.*

He made his shopping list on a piece of yellow legal paper. After he finished writing, he read it back to himself aloud. "Pop Tarts, dry and canned cat food, soda, bread, lunchmeat." He thought for a moment. *Oh yeah. Kitty litter. Need kitty litter, too. Always seem to need kitty litter. They are, after all, little peeing and pooping machines.* He added it to the list and again thought for a moment. *Wouldn't mind having one of those t-shirts that show the cat dressed as a gangster rapper. One of the volunteers at Recycled Love has one. They're cute.* He wrote it on the list.

Later that afternoon, at five o'clock, he knocked on her bedroom door. "Hey, Hope, are you awake in there?"

No response.

He knocked again, harder. "Hey, come on—I just want to make sure you're alive and okay."

Through the door, he heard her say, "No, I'm not alive. I died of embarrassment. Now—go way!"

He opened the door and walked in. She immediately pulled the covers over her head.

"*Ugh*! I don't want to have to even look at you right now."

He heard a sneeze from under the covers.

He sat on the edge of the bed. "What's wrong? Hmm? Talk to me."

She kept her face covered. "What's wrong? I made an ass out of myself when I was on the Percocet high. And now I am freaking mortified."

"I wasn't even going to mention it." He pulled the covers down, so they no longer covered her face. "Having your head covered—that's not good for your breathing. Come on, now. I have to get your vitals. Plus, it's time for your medication."

Her oxygen saturation was up to 95, and her temperature was down to 101.9.

"Overall, how are you feeling?"

"Hanging in there. A little better, I guess."

Her medication and a bottle of water sat on the nightstand, next to the bed. He got her pills out and handed them to her, along with the water.

She swallowed the pills, took a swig of water, and handed the bottle back to him.

The iPad was still under her shirt. She pulled it out.

"I know I posted crazy crap on your timeline."

"You actually remember doing that?"

"Yeah. I remember. Unfortunately, I pretty much remember everything."

"Wow. That surprises me."

"You already deleted that post, right?"

"No. It was *your* post."

"Yeah, but you could have deleted it."

"You can delete someone else's post?"

"If it's on your timeline, yeah." She coughed.

"Really?"

"Yeah. Sure. You control your own timeline."

He shrugged. "I'm not real social media savvy. I didn't know that."

"So, that post is still on your page?"

"Yep. It's gotten some attention, too."

"I'll bet it has."

He moved up to the head of the bed and pointed to the iPad. "Go to my Facebook page."

She brought up his page and found the post.

"See that?" He pointed and read aloud. *"The Hope-ster is gonna play Kissy Pooh with Sir Luke. I want some sugar, damnit!* I got a whole bunch of *likes,* some *ha-has,* a few *wows,* even a couple of *loves.* And look at the comments. My friend Dino wrote, *Bicardi 151 strikes again. LOL.* My friend Dana, who I volunteer with at Recycled Love, posted, *I'll have whatever she's having.* Hell, even Gretchen Cavanaugh had something positive to say. I forgot to unfriend her after we had our blowout and I guess she forgot to unfriend me, too. She saw the post but was nice. She actually said, *Looks like Luke finally got the woman he deserves. Hope you two are happy together. Smh.* Now, I'm guessing the *smh* must mean— simply...marvelous...and heartwarming?"

She rolled her eyes. "Boy, you really are a social media novice. My neighbor's six-year-old knows what *smh* means. *Shaking my head,* Luke. That's what it means. As in—*shaking my head in disgust.* She was being a sarcastic smartass. It was a diss. She was dissing both of us."

"Oh wow. And here I thought maybe she was being nice."

"Well, here—let's delete it. It'll take all of two seconds."

"You go ahead and delete it, if you want. But, frankly, I'm not ashamed of it."

"You're not?" She wheezed.

"No. Of course not. I got to thinking about this while you were asleep. A beautiful, sexy woman posted that she wanted to kiss me. I'm not married, and I don't have a girlfriend. So, why should I be ashamed of that? You tell me."

"Not saying you should." She sneezed. "I'm a single girl. And if I want to kiss a handsome, sexy, sweet guy—why should I be ashamed?"

He threw up his hands. "No reason to be. No reason for either of us to be embarrassed by the post, if you ask me."

"You think we should just leave it? Is that what you're saying?"

He nodded. "Yeah. Sure. Let's leave it."

"But what will people think?"

"Who cares? The only negative reaction was from Gretchen. Do you think I care what Gretchen thinks? Let's not be like her. Let's be more authentic than her. She lives her life obsessing over what everyone else thinks. She really obsesses over it. I don't want to live my life that way."

"Yeah. Come to think of it, you're right. So, we'll leave the post?"

"Yeah, we'll leave it. And I guess my only question is—with the Kissy Pooh stuff—how much of that was the drug talking? And how much was real?"

She laughed, coughed, and shook her head. "You don't spend a lot of time around people who are drunk or high, do you?"

He chuckled. "Nah. Not anymore. I used to see my share of drunks when I was in the Marines, though."

"Yeah, well, in my job, I see drunks and stoners every day. Every day. Hell, part of my job is to babysit those people."

"And?"

"And here's the truth about drugs and alcohol—people think that when someone gets drunk or high, they say things that they don't really mean. Wrong. Booze and dope both act as truth serum. When you get drunk or high, you say things you *do* really mean but generally don't have the balls to say. There. There's your answer. Happy now?"

"*Soooo*...you're saying that that Kissy Pooh stuff was real?"

She snapped at him a bit. "What did I just tell you? You want me to come right out and say it? Is that the game we're playing here? Fine. You win. Yes—I want to kiss you. Okay? There. You got me to say it."

He shrugged. "It's not a game or a contest. It does make me happy, though."

"Yeah?"

"Yeah. Sure, it does. You still have the q-pon I gave you, right?"

She patted her chest. "It's still in the vault and I'm not even going to correct your pronunciation anymore. I give up on that."

"Once you start feeling better, you can redeem it anytime you like, so long as you're not on pain meds at the time of redemption."

"Thank you for being a gentleman, for not taking advantage of me when I was stoned. Even though I was throwing myself at you. Not many guys that I've known over the years would have been so decent."

"You've known the wrong guys, Hope."

"Tell me something I don't know."

"Clark Gable suffered from severe halitosis."

She shook her head as if to clear the cobwebs. "*What*? What are you even talking about?"

He shrugged. "Again, that's something you probably didn't know. But I read all about it on the *Tattle Tales* website, in the Golden Oldies section. His breath was so bad that when he was making *Gone With the Wind*, Vivien Leigh actually confronted him about it because, you know, she had to kiss him and all. She came right out and told him his nasty breath was making her nauseous. And do you know what his reply was?"

"Oh, Gawd. Here we go."

"Come on, Hope. What was his reply? Come on. Don't make me waste this joke. It's too good to waste."

She rolled her eyes but nonetheless asked, "Fine. What was his reply?"

He imitated Gable's voice. "*Frankly, my dear, I don't give a damn.*" He laughed and added, "That's where that iconic line, that little piece of Americana, came from. The director overheard him and decided he had to work it into the script somehow."

She looked at him with suspicion.

"Okay. So, I made that last part up. But Gable did have an issue with bad breath. It's very well documented. All of his leading ladies complained about it. They'd all be like—*should I offer this guy chewing gum or toiler paper?*"

She laughed but quickly turned serious. "I never really talked to you about what you did for Charlotte, about you giving her your Purple Heart."

"There's no need to talk about it. Like I told you—I didn't do it so that you or anyone else would fuss and make a big deal over it."

"I know you didn't. But it was a big deal. It was nice." She paused, took a deep breath, and loudly exhaled. "God, what am I saying? *It was nice.* Such an understatement. That's like saying September Eleventh was *kind of sad.* The problem for me with that gesture is that there's no words for it. None. I've racked my brain trying to come up with words and there aren't any. So, I'll just say this—you're John Candy."

He looked down at his waist. "John Candy? Hey, I weigh a buck seventy-five. That's the same weight that I was in the service. I've kept my girlish figure. And John Candy, well, he was a great guy and all, but let's face it—the man liked his candy."

She shook her finger at him. "Stop that. Stop it right now. Not everything has to be a joke. I am trying to be serious here and tell you something. Something important." She hacked.

"I'm sorry. I'll behave." He imitated Austin Powers. "I'll behave, baby."

She scowled at him.

"I'm sorry. The word *behave* is what triggered that. It's out of my system now. I'll be serious from now on. I promise. Go ahead. Continue. Proceed."

"Right. Anyway, remember when we agreed that John Candy had something that you can't fake? A genuineness. A sweetness. A kindness. Remember when we said that?"

He nodded. "Yeah. I do."

"Well, you're just like John Candy. Exactly like him. And believe it or not, this cynical, jaded cop has a real soft spot in her heart for the John Candys of the world. Because they're super rare. Rarer than unicorns. And maybe if there were more John Candys walking around, this cynical, jaded cop wouldn't be so cynical and jaded."

He lay down next to her and put his arm around her. "That's the nicest thing anyone has ever said to me." She snuggled up close to him and buried her head in his chest. He kissed her on the forehead.

"I guess we'll never see Charlotte again, huh?" she asked.

"Baltimore's a little big town. So, you never know. Our paths might cross again. You just never know."

She gazed up at him. "What was in that note, the note Charlotte's mom slipped to you in the diner? I'm dying to know what it said."

"The information in that note—it'll be *disseminated on a need to know basis,* as we used to say in the Marines."

"So, in other words—you won't tell me?"

"Not right now, no."

"Well, while we're on the topic of medals— what did you get your Bronze Star for? Will you at least tell me that?"

"How did you know I got the Bronze Star? I've never mentioned that to you."

"I'm a cop. I have access to information."

He shot her a confused look.

"Harris told me, okay? She did a little research on you the night of the accident. I got a complete briefing on your background. It was part of my tongue lashing. So…will you tell me?"

He nodded. "Yeah. I'll tell you." In his mind, he took himself to another time and place.

With a deep breath, he began: "There was this kid, and that's really what he was, too. A kid. His name was Michael Lambert. He was eighteen. And he was from Lullaby, West Virginia. Yeah, that was the name of the town. Lullaby. He had just graduated from high school. Some kids go to the beach after they graduate. Mike went to Parris Island. Well, I guess that's a beach of sorts. They have plenty of sand fleas there, at least. Anyway, eventually, he ended up with my unit, in Afghanistan. He was a good kid. Truth be told, a great kid. A special kid. Michael Lambert loved animals. I mean—he *really* loved animals. And he would send money to the ASPCA each month. Something like nineteen ninety-nine, he'd send them each month. It was to sponsor a dog in their shelter. The dog who he sponsored—I still remember, even after a decade—was a brindle Pitbull named Waldo. They sent him a picture of Waldo and he carried it around with him. He put it inside his helmet. He'd show anybody and everybody that picture, too. He was proud of that. His ambition in life, beyond the military, was to do two things. One—he wanted to start his own funeral home for animals, with an adjacent pet cemetery. He thought they deserved the same dignity as humans. He even had a name picked out. It was going to be called *Rainbow Bridge Memorial Chapel and Gardens.* The other thing he wanted to do was write a book, a coffee table book. It was going to be a book full of pictures of headstone inscriptions from pet cemeteries. And there was going to be accompanying text that would delve into the story behind that animal's life, that inscription. You see, he saw a headstone at a pet cemetery once that really moved him. I so vividly remember him telling me this, like it was yesterday. The marker was for a cat named Charlie Chaplain. There was a photo of the cat on the headstone. Mike said he was black and white. A tuxedo cat, kind of like Sassy. Anyway, the marker simply read—*I Knew Love—I Had This Cat.* Yeah. That really got to him. He thought it was *so* simple but *so* beautiful, and that there had to be wonderful stories behind those headstones. He even had a title picked out for the book. He was going to call it,

If Love Could Have Saved You, You Would Have Lived Forever. So, that's what he wanted to do with his life. Mike was also funny as hell. He could have been a stand-up comic. He did a great Owen Wilson impression. Spot on with it. But more than anything else, Mike Lambert wanted to fall in love. He was in love with the idea of being in love. We'd talk about it sometimes, about what it would feel like. He'd talk about wanting to take long walks on the beach with a girl, holding her hand. Oh, and it had to be at sunset, too. Yeah, at sunset. I'm not making this stuff up. That's what the kid wanted. Just like the picture on the front of a Hallmark card. And if anyone thinks that's corny and wants to make fun of him—well, that boy—*that man*—earned the right to be corny. He was a good Marine, too. Not a shitbag. That's what we call Marines who don't live up to the title. *Shitbags.* Well, Mike Lambert was no shitbag. But Mike Lambert knew that he was going to die. He knew, okay? He had a premonition. And he talked about it, too. He told me one day, he said—*Elvis, the only way I'm ever going home will be on an angel flight.* I told him he'd seen too many war films. But he insisted that there was something to it, that some guys *just know* that they're not going to make it. And there's nothing that anyone can do about it because it's written in the stars or whatever. Well, one day, we were in this vil, and we were pinned down by a Taliban machine gun nest. And Mike tried to flank it, so he could throw a frag— that's a grenade, by the way—at it to take it out. But they saw him, and he got cut to pieces. They lit him up. They shot him full of holes and filled him full of lead. And he was dead. Mike was dead. We all knew it. But Marines don't leave their dead behind. No matter what. Literally, no matter what. Okay? One way or another, everyone comes home. Even if it's on an angel flight. Now, this was after McKay got killed, so we had a new lieutenant. A guy by the name of D'Amato, from Yonkers, New York. A Naval Academy man. So, I told him—*LT, we have to go get Mike. We can't leave him. We can't let those monsters get ahold of him."*

He cried. "So, everybody laid down some suppressing fire. And I went out and I got Mike. So he could go home. And that's when I got shot. The machine gun missed me, but another one of those sons of bitches got me with an AK, but I managed to drag Mike's body back to our position. I got my Bronze Star and Purple Heart for the same action. And when I got Mike back to our lines, our medic, he was a Navy corpsman—Doc Washington—came over. He looked at Mike and he screamed at me—*don't look at him, Elvis! Don't even look at him! If you do, it'll fuck you up in the head.* Well, I looked at him. They shot him in the face, Hope. A lot of times, the enemy would try to do that because we had pretty decent body armor. So, that was the one place where we were totally vulnerable. It didn't even look like a human being anymore. It's crazy how much damage a small piece of hot lead hurtling through space can do. And Doc Washington was right. It fucked me up in the head."

He broke down and sobbed.

She put her arms around him and squeezed him tight, and they stayed just like that for a while.

Finally, after an hour, he had himself composed. He got up, cleared his voice and told her, "I have to go feed the Mondawmin Seven. It's my turn. Then I have to stop at Walmart to pick up a few things. Do you need anything?"

"Yeah. I do, actually. Could you pick up the new Nathaniel Dunn book for me? I think it's called *The Scrapbook*. You'll see it. They'll have a big display set up in the book section. I want the hardback, too."

"*You* read Nathaniel Dunn?"

"I do. I have every book the man's ever written. He writes so beautifully. I live vicariously through the characters in his novels. And I've seen all of the movies based on his books, too. And if he ever comes to Baltimore for a book signing, I'm going. I don't care how much it costs or how long I have to wait in line."

"I wouldn't have pegged you as a Nathaniel Dunn fan."

"Well, I am."

"Huh. I've always heard he's kind of a jerk."

"*Who* is?"

"Nathaniel Dunn."

"He most certainly is *not*. And where'd you hear that anyway?"

"Can't remember specifically. It was on the internet—I do know that much. Look, if you don't believe me, just Google *Nathaniel Dunn is a jerk*. Stuff *will* come up."

"You don't even know the man."

He shrugged. "So? I didn't know JR from *Dallas*, but I think it's safe to say he was a jerk. I didn't know Mussolini either, but I think it's safe to say he was a jerk, too."

She shook her finger at him. "Hey—hey. My name might be Kennedy but I'm half Italian here. On Mom's side. Her maiden name's Morelli."

"Oh, so you're I-talian?"

She wheezed. "I am. And us *I*-talians, as you say, are very sensitive about references to Mussolini. It's a chapter we'd rather forget. And the easiest way to get an I-talian girl to go all Old Country on your ass is to mention Benito Mussolini, okay? Because, Pisan, you ain't been properly cussed until you been cussed by an I-talian girl, in I-talian. Which I could easily do, by the way."

"Dang. Just the suggestion of it turns me on."

She laughed, dismissively waved at him, and coughed. "You're impossible. You know that, right? And you have major issues with pronunciations, too. I'll bet you call McDonald's *Mac*-Donald's."

"I was just teasing, except about Nathaniel Dunn. I have heard he's a jerk. All full of himself and whatnot. He thinks he's the new Hemingway and such. But, nonetheless, I'll still get the book for you. Anything else?"

"Um. As a matter of fact, yeah. Some potato chips. I've been craving potato chips."

"I have chips. A brand new bag, in fact. It hasn't even been opened."

"What brand?" She coughed.

"Utz."

She made a face and stuck her tongue out.

"What's wrong with Utz? It's a local company, you know. Their factory is right up the road, in Hanover, PA. And they're decent, hard-working Americans who make quality products *for* decent, hard-working Americans."

"What can I say? I only like Herr's. I'm a Herr's girl."

"So, what you're telling me is that we're going to have to become a two potato chip household? His and Herr's? Is that how it's going to be?"

"Yeah, I guess so because I'm not eating Utz. But do me a favor—don't get me any weird-ass flavors. I noticed that, when it comes to chips, the flavors are getting more bizarre all the time. Not long ago, I saw ones that were French toast flavored. I'm sorry, but if I want French toast, I'll go to IHOP. I just want my potato chips to taste potato-ey. Is that too much to ask?"

"Not too much to ask. I hear ya. But, just as an aside, for French toast, Denny's is better than IHOP. Denny's makes theirs light and fluffy. The ones at IHOP are too dense for my liking. But, anyway, with the chips, I'll get the old-school Herr's. Herr's Classic. Anything else?"

"Yeah. One more thing—a Pick Three lottery ticket for tonight's drawing. I buy one every week. That's the extent of my gambling—a buck a week."

"A whole buck a week, huh?" He whistled and added, "Damn, girl, you've got it worse than Jordan."

She scowled.

He nervously smiled. "That was a joke, by the way. A reference to Michael Jordan. He likes to gamble. *A lot.* Matter of fact, the guy's blown millions in casinos over the years. It was kind of funny because you only gamble a dollar a week, so, in reality, you're *nothing* like Michael Jordan. See what I did there?"

She maintained her scowl.

"Any-who…so, ah, you want a random, computer generated

number?"

"Oh, no. No—no—no. Since I've been a cop, I play my badge number. Nine-seven-three. And I box it. A six-way box. You don't win as much that way, but the odds are better. And which Walmart are you going to?" She sneezed and hacked.

"The one on Edmonson Avenue."

"Great, because they have a self-service lottery terminal at the entrance, right next to the Redbox. So, you won't even have to go out of your way."

"Cool. But even if I did, I'd do it. I'd go out of my way for you." He smiled.

"You want me to write down that number?" she asked.

"Yeah. You'd better."

She reached over to the nightstand and grabbed a pen and notepad. She wrote the number down, tore off the slip of paper, and handed it to him.

He glanced down at the paper, looked up, and smiled. "You have nice writing. It's very girly. I like that. It's cute. Even kind of sexy."

"Thanks." She reached into her shirt and pulled out a dollar bill and handed it to him. "Here. This is for the ticket."

He laughed and pointed to her chest. "Boy, you like keeping things down there, don't you?"

"Well, it's basically like a little storage area. I usually keep a dollar bill or two in there. Sometimes, business cards. Your coupon. Things like that."

"Uh-huh. Those items are very lucky." He smiled a sly smile and winked at her.

He put the slip of paper and the bill in his pocket and started to walk away.

"Wait. Let me get my purse and give you some more money because the book alone will probably be over twenty bucks."

He turned around and waved her off. "Fugetaboutit."

She shook her head. "No. I won't. I won't forget about it. I don't want to owe you anymore than I already do, which is a lot. A hell of a lot."

He walked back over to the bed. "Wait—wait—wait. You think that's what this is about? Who owes who? And how much? Is that what you think? Because that's not what it's about to me."

"What is it about then? What's it all about?"

He sat back down next to her. Gently, he brushed her cheek with the back of his hand. "It's about me being the luckiest guy on the face of the earth."

She shook her head. "I don't think I deserve any of this. For so many reasons, I don't deserve any of it. And you don't even know why. And even though I'm trying very, very hard not to—I can't help—" She stopped abruptly.

"What Hope? What can't you help?"

"I can't say. I'm not ready to say."

"Okay. That's fine. You don't have to say."

He took his phone out of his pocket and went through his playlist. "Here. I'm going to play another song for you. Here we go. This is my way of saying *thank you.* Thank you, Hope, for bringing hope into my life."

Right Said Fred's *I'm Too Sexy* played. He quickly paused it, nervously laughed, and told her, "That's not the song I was talking about. That's another one that I didn't put in my playlist. There must be little, tiny gremlins inside my phone that do this crap. They must put these crazy songs in my playlist because *I am not* doing it, that's for sure." He fiddled around more with the phone.

Finally, he announced, "There. Now, we're set. Here. This is the song."

Wayne Newton's *Danke Schoen* played.

He took her hand and interlocked their fingers. "Hear that? *Danke Schoen.* It's German. *Thank you very much.* That's what it means. Pretty song, right? Sang as only The Midnight Idol himself can. Wayne Newton. I love his music. And that's what I say to you—*Danke Schoen.* For making me feel alive again. *Danke Schoen.*"

"*Danke Schoen,*" she told him. "*Danke Schoen* for being like

John Candy…for being Luke Matthews."

They stared into each other's eyes and smiled as the song played.

CHAPTER EIGHTEEN: LUKE'S LOVE EMPORIUM

four days later

She was starting to feel better. Her fever had broken, and she was less congested. It was easier for her to breathe, and she wasn't sneezing as much. Her oxygen saturation was up to 97, almost normal.

It was about noon, and they lay in bed together watching an episode of *Blossom* on the *TV Classics Network*. The show had just started.

She wore a white t-shirt and a pair of pink terrycloth shorts. Her feet were bare, and her hair was up.

He wore grey sweatpants, a red sweatshirt with the Recycled Love logo, and white athletic socks.

He shook his head. "Oh no. This is the one where Blossom gets her first period. I'm sorry, but I can't watch this." He turned the TV off.

She laughed. "What? What's wrong? It's a coming-of-age episode. There's nothing wrong with it."

"Oh, yes, there is," he insisted with great conviction. "That stuff doesn't need to be thrown in our faces. Like the ads for tampons and Vagisil. Those kind of commercials are not necessary—the darn products are going to sell, anyway. No need to advertise them."

"So, those commercials offend you, do they?"

He emphatically nodded. "Yes. Absolutely. I am officially *oh*-fended. Hell, everyone else in this society is offended by something, so I may as well join the party. Therefore, I demand a safe space from feminine hygiene ads." He cackled.

She threw up her hands. "What is it with guys and periods? What's the issue? Why are so many of you squeamish about them, especially a guy like you? You've been to war, seen lots of blood."

"Yeah, but not *that* kind of blood. Blood from a sucking chest wound is one thing. But blood from *down there*—well, that's something else entirely. I'm sorry, but I just don't want to turn on the old telly to be entertained, and have to be reminded of women's menstrual cycles, that's all. Truth be told—I'd rather not think about women's periods. *Period.* And another thing while we're on this topic: they don't need to be putting tampons in the boy's bathrooms in public schools because boys *do no*t have menstrual cycles. The fact that they're spending taxpayer dollars to do that is literally insane. And if saying so makes me intolerant and narrow-minded, then so be it. Because as I'm sure you know by now, I'm far from perfect."

"You're silly, is what you are. But if being queasy about women's periods is your biggest flaw, I can live with that. And I do agree with you about the whole tampons-in-the-boy's-bathroom thing. And you may have—conceivably— noticed that I'm not quite perfect, either."

"So, I guess we're just two imperfect people then, huh?"

"We're perfectly imperfect."

There was a period of silence.

He loudly exhaled and looked over at her, gazed down at her smooth, silky, shiny legs.

Smiling, he asked, "How are you doing over there? How's your life?"

She laughed. "Okay. I'm doing okay these days. How *you* doing?"

"Oh, fair to middling, I suppose."

He looked back down at her legs, smiled, and pointed to

them. "You're wearing shorts in the winter."

"Yeah, well, I'm inside. And it's kind of one of my little idiosyncrasies, wearing shorts in the winter, that is. Of course, I wouldn't wear them outside. But it's not cold in here. It's nice and toasty."

"Uh-huh. That's because I've got the heat on. Yeah. The heat is on, all right."

She laughed. "It is, is it?"

"Yep. Most definitely. The. Heat. Is. On."

"Well, do you like my legs?"

"Huh?"

"I *said*—do you like my legs?"

He nodded. "Yeah. Oh yeah. Most definitely. I'll bet they really get you from point A to point B. You could do some traveling with those legs. Those legs were made for walking. And that's just what they'll do. I really get a *kick* out of your legs."

Aw. I think he's nervous. That makes two of us. "Look, do you… do you want to… touch them?"

"Touch your legs?"

"Yeah. Touch my legs."

"Sure. I'll touch them. You know, just to make sure you have good blood flow, proper circulation…and whatnot."

"Right. Because sometimes it's better to have someone else check the circulation in your limbs."

"Yeah. Right. So, I'm going to check you out now." He quickly amended his statement, "What I mean is—I'm going to check your circulation."

He reached over with his right hand and pressed it against the area just above her knee. He gently ran his hand down past her knee and then up to the area near her thigh.

"How does it feel?" she asked with raised eyebrows.

"Good. It's soft. Smooth. Very smooth. Creamy. Warm. So, I'd say your circulation is good. Quite good. Of course, I'm no doctor."

He gently patted her leg, removed his hand, and smiled.

That went pretty well. It didn't freak me out.

She felt a sudden weight on the bed. At the bottom, she saw a black cat kneading the comforter with great vigor.

He called out, "Hey, there's Bobby, the Bob-ster. *Robert.* I call him Robert sometimes. I think he prefers that. It's more dignified. He and Hannah have been laying low these last few days. They're not used to having someone else in the house. But Bobby's curiosity finally got the best of him. I imagine Hannah will eventually venture in here to check you out, too."

He patted the mattress to beckon the cat to the top of the bed. "Come here, buddy. Come meet Hope."

The black cat walked towards them, tail in air.

He settled between Luke and Hope, plopping himself down. He purred and drooled.

"As you can see, he has a pretty bad underbite, and that causes him to drool."

Hope stared at the cat.

"Why don't you go ahead and pet him? He's a very nice cat. He doesn't bite or scratch. He's gentle. I think he'd like it if you gave him a little pat on the head."

She looked over at Luke.

"It's okay, sweetie. You can pet him."

He took her hand, her right hand, gently squeezed it, and moved it to the cat's head.

Bobby meowed.

"He's talking to you, Hope. He's talking to *you.* How about that?"

Oh, God. I don't know if I can do this without falling apart.

She tentatively ran her hand along the cat's head and down his back.

"He's missing part of his left ear, as you can see. I think he's kind of self-conscious about it, too. I really do. He's a former street cat."

She smiled as she continued to gently stroke Bobby.

"You know, I got an email from my friend, Dana. She's the one who volunteers with me at Recycled Love. She feeds the

Mondawmin cats, too. And she was saying that little Bunky is really starting to come around. Remember him? You saw him that day you helped me with the feeding, before we went to Tiffany's. He liked you. Remember that?"

They looked at one another, but she didn't respond to his question.

"Yeah, anyway, she was able to pick him up the other day. He's becoming tame. That's pretty amazing, huh? He's come a long way. Dana was saying that he really shouldn't be on the streets and she's right. Well, none of those Mondawmin cats should be. No animal should be. But now that he's becoming domesticated, he really needs to find a home. If there was any room at the Recycled Love shelter, we could take him there and put him up for adoption. But it's a small facility and we're at our legal capacity right now. Hell, I'd take him in a heartbeat, but the Roland Park Homeowners Association only allows for a maximum of two pets. And they enforce it, too. The president of the HOA is a jerk with way too much time on his hands. He's known for his *pop-in* visits where he actually does head counts. Still, Bunky needs a home. He has to get off the streets. I'm afraid that, eventually, something bad will happen, and now that he's becoming domesticated, he's more at risk than ever. Trusting the wrong person can be deadly for a street cat."

She still said nothing, just stared at him.

He cleared his voice. "Do you, ah...do you have any thoughts on that?"

She stopped petting Bobby and withdrew her hand. "I hope he finds his home, but it won't be with me, if that's what you're hinting at."

He nodded. "Okay. All right. I just kind of thought you two would be good for one another. But if you're not ready, that's fine."

"Let's just talk about something else. Please." *I'm not ready to talk about things yet. But I'm going to have to eventually, I suppose. How will he react? How will he feel once he knows? How will he look at me? How will I look at myself?*

He brushed her hair with his hand. "You okay?"

She nodded. "Yeah, but let's just get off this whole topic."

"Sure. No problem."

He turned the TV back on. The *Blossom* episode was still playing. "Oh, Good Lord," he declared as he changed the channel. "Got to find something normal to watch." He looked upwards. "TV gods—is that too much to ask? To find something normal on television?" He flipped through the channels and finally settled on one.

He pointed to the screen. "Oh, here we go. Good movie—*Kung Fu Hillbilly*. It's about this guy who takes a drink from a magic bottle of moonshine and instantly becomes an expert in the martial arts. He then uses his power to fight crime in trailer parks. Kind of a superhero-type film. A poor man's *Superman,* if you will."

"Uh-huh."

Bobby jumped off the bed and into his padded window perch.

She reached over to the nightstand and picked up her phone and the lottery ticket he'd purchased for her.

She held up the ticket. "While this is on my mind, I'm going to check it. I almost forgot about it."

"Yeah, you definitely want to check it. I've always heard that billions of dollars in lottery winnings go unclaimed each year in this country, including some really big jackpots."

"I know, right? I don't get it, either. If you're going to spend the money on the ticket, at least check it. It's fast and easy. They have an app for it. All you have to do is scan the barcode with your phone."

She scanned the ticket and waited for it to register. "It's thinking..." She coughed.

After a few seconds, a message flashed on her phone's screen. "Oh, my God. It says—*congratulations, you're a winner.*"

"You won?"

"That's what it says. I've never won anything in my life. Nothing. Nada. I'm so unlucky that when we had field day in elementary school, I didn't even win a participation trophy."

"Wow. That's pretty bad."

She flashed him a dirty look and then looked back down at the screen. "Anyhow, it looks like the winning number was three-seven-nine and because I boxed it, I won. I always knew boxing was the smartest way to play. It says here that I can redeem the ticket at any lottery retailer."

"How much did you win?"

She fiddled with the phone and went to the page that listed the prize structures. "Um...let's see here...oh—here it is—eighty bucks."

He laughed. "Eighty bucks, huh?"

"Hey, eighty bucks isn't bad for a one dollar investment."

He nodded. "Right. But you play a dollar a week, correct?"

"Yeah. So?"

"And how long have you been doing that?"

"Seven years."

"And this is your first time winning anything, right?"

"Yeah. Right."

"So, a buck a week, times fifty-two weeks in a year, times seven years. I'm no Stephen Hawking, but I believe that, overall, you're still approximately two-hundred and eighty bucks down."

She rolled her eyes. "Thanks a lot. You had to go and ruin it for me, didn't you?"

He shrugged. "Just crunching the numbers."

"Yeah, well, maybe this is the start of a good luck streak for me. I haven't had much luck in my life, that's for sure."

She turned on her side, facing him. "You know, I still have another ticket of sorts. My IOU for that game of Kissy Pooh."

"Your *q-pon*, you mean?"

"I swear, you're mispronouncing that word just because you know it gets on my nerves."

He put up his hands and laughed. "I plead the Fifth Amendment, officer. And I want my lawyer present before any further questioning."

She laughed and playfully smacked him on the arm. "Stop that. I hear that enough at work. You sound like an actual perp. That's just how they talk."

"So, what are you telling me, lass? That you want to redeem your voucher—I'll call it a voucher so as not to get on your nerves, even though I think either pronunciation is acceptable—at Luke's Love Emporium?"

"Luke's Love Emporium, huh? You selling love, boy? Because if you are, I might have to call the station and let the vice squad know. Because that would make you a gigolo, honey."

He howled and sang the opening bars of *Just A Gigolo.* "Now, see, I could never be a gigolo. The overhead associated with it is just tremendous. I'd have to go out and buy all kinds of gold rings, chains, and bracelets. And gold is around nineteen hundred dollars an ounce right now. Plus, I'd need a whole new wardrobe. Silk shirts. Leather pants. *I*-talian shoes. I'd have to buy all kinds of crazy lotions and oils, too. Also, I'd have to get one of those silk kimono robes, preferably one with a big fire-breathing dragon on the back. And I'd definitely have to install a jacuzzi. Oh, and the big ticket item—I'd have to get a new set of wheels. Yeah, I'd have to upgrade to a Porsche, or at least a Corvette. Yup. I'd have to charge, like, a grand a night and it'd still take me forever just to break even."

She laughed. "Oh, Lord. You're silly."

"No, seriously, Luke's Love Emporium is a very special business. It's there to serve one customer and one customer only. And customer satisfaction is the top priority. And if I don't get it right the first time, I'll do it over and over and over and over. Until you're happy with the work. And there's no charge for any of the services rendered."

"No charge, huh? Well, how's it going to be profitable if you don't charge anything?"

"It's not going to turn a profit. When it fails, I'll just call old Tommy Tuttuchi and have him send one of his crews over to torch the place after hours and then put in the insurance claim." He chuckled.

She corrected him. "It's Tommy *Tennuchi*, not *Tuttuchi*. Better not ever let him hear you mispronounce his name. That's a whackable offense, dude. I'm serious, he's whacked guys for less. The word on the street is that he had one of his capos, Don Piano, whacked for using his private bathroom. And nobody is supposed to use his private bathroom. But the guy really had to go. The story that I heard is that he had had Taco Bell a few hours earlier. Tommy went to take a leak, found the guy in the john, and had him whacked the next day."

"So, I guess we can finally say that Taco Bell's food was responsible for someone's death, huh?" They laughed.

Then he turned serious. "But you do want to play Kissy Pooh?"

"Yeah. Is there a problem with that?"

"No. None at all. You want to do it now?"

"No. Let's wait until tonight. See, to me, you're like pizza crust."

"Pizza crust? Can't wait to hear the explanation behind this one. It has to be a doozy."

"Well, it's just that I like pizza. But my favorite part is the crust. Now, some people don't like the crust. I know people who throw it away. Not me. I love the crust. It's the best part of the pie. So, I always save the crust for last. That way, I have something to look forward to. So, you're like pizza crust. I want to save you until the end of the day. So I can look forward to it, anticipate it. Anticipation makes everything better. Don't you agree?"

"Yeah. I can see your point. Makes sense. So, we'll play Kissy Pooh tonight?"

"Right. Tonight."

"It might be kind of tough for me to concentrate, though. It's going to be hard to think about anything else."

She shrugged. "That's kind of the idea."

"Yeah, I'm going to be thinking about how soft your lips are going to be. Soft and yummy."

She laughed. "Soft and yummy, huh? If you want them to

literally be yummy, I can put on some strawberry-flavored lip gloss for you."

He smiled and raised his eyebrows. "That'd be great. I'd totally dig that."

"So, Luke's Love Emporium is set for its grand opening?"

"Absolutely. And I think, to celebrate our first kiss, our first *make sesh* as the cool kids used to say in high school, we should get a pizza for dinner tonight. It's only fitting since I'm your pizza crust."

CHAPTER NINETEEN: FIX YOU

Luke walked in the front door carrying a white box with takeout pizza inside. He took off a red ball cap with the Marine logo on it and angrily threw it down in the recliner.

He walked to the kitchen and set the box on the counter. Bobby and Hannah both came out to greet him, brushing up against either leg. But he didn't reach down to pet them, to dote over them, as he normally would have.

He walked up stairs and into his room. The door was open. Hope lay in bed, reading her Nathaniel Dunn book without her glasses on.

"Hey," she called out as she briefly looked up from her book.

He didn't respond. Instead, he walked to his bookshelf and selected a DVD. He turned the TV on, put the disk in, and forwarded past the previews.

The feature started. He sat at the bottom of the bed. Intently, he stared at the screen, as the film's opening scene played, an opening scene he'd watched many times. The cemetery scene in *Saving Private Ryan*.

"Why are you watching that?"

He turned around to look at her. She'd put her book down. He didn't answer, didn't say anything.

"You don't need to be watching that."

Still, he said nothing.

She got up and sat down on the foot of the bed, next to him. She held her palm out. "Here. Give me the remote. Please give me the remote because you do not need to be watching this movie."

He stared at the screen, didn't even acknowledge her. For a couple of minutes, there was silence, as they both watched.

The D-Day scene started. Tears filled his eyes as the onscreen battle— the slaughter—played out.

"Why are you watching this? Why?"

Finally, he spoke quietly and calmly. "The best war films are the ones that don't preach a message. They aren't pro-war or anti-war. They just show war and let war speak for itself. And then it's up to each individual to decide if it's worth it. And they got this one right. Spielberg got it right. God Almighty, he got it right, Hope! The sights. The sounds. The chaos. The randomness. The insanity. The *death*."

She spoke tenderly, in a whisper. "Okay, so they got it right. Fine. But you do not need to be watching this. Okay? It's not good. It can't be. God knows, I'm not a psychologist, but it can't be good for you."

Again, he ignored her point. "Caparzo reminds me of Michael Lambert. They both had a heart of gold. They even kind of look alike. Gentle giants. And they both died."

They continued to watch for several minutes.

Onscreen, the desperate fight for Omaha Beach was reaching its crescendo. A soldier wandered the beach, looking for his lost arm that had been blown off. He finally found it and picked it up off the sand. And then wandered around some more.

She grabbed for the remote. "Enough. No more. Give it to me."

He clutched it tight. "No. I'm going to watch it all the way through."

"No. You're not."

She got up and walked over to the DVD player, opened it, took out the disk, and bent it until it broke in two.

"It's time to break with the past." She threw the two pieces to the floor.

"Why'd you do that? It's *Saving Private Ryan,* for God's sake. What you just did is nearly sacrilege."

She raised her voice a bit. "I don't give a damn about Private Ryan. Tom Hanks saved Private Ryan. I'm trying to save Lance Corporal Matthews. That's all I care about."

"Yeah, well, maybe he's not savable."

"What happened? You were in a good mood when you left to get the pizza. So, what happened?"

"I went to Lefty's Pizza, over on Hanover Street. They give a veteran's discount."

"Something happen there?"

He nodded. "Yeah. Something happened."

"What? What happened? Come on—tell me. I can't help if you don't tell me."

"There were some kids in there. College kids. At least they had U of B hoodies on. One of them saw my Marine Corps cap and overheard me talking to the cashier about the military discount. So, this kid—couldn't have been any older than twenty—asked me, *where you in the USMC—Uncle Sam's Misguided Children?"*

"I nodded and told him I served in Afghanistan, and I tried to laugh the insult off. But then he said—*you know that you didn't accomplish anything other than exporting Imperialism, right?* I told him I wasn't there to debate American foreign policy, that I was just there to get a pizza. But the kid wouldn't let it go. He told me that we were just a bunch of murderers. And that he wished that the Taliban had killed more of us."

He cried.

She put her hand on his shoulder. "You ran into an asshole. A very cruel person. There are cruel people in this world. There are. Lots and lots of cruel people, people who can't feel good about themselves unless they make someone else feel bad."

"But I did kill. I killed that family. Maybe the kid was right, at least about me."

"No. He wasn't. He was an ungrateful, snotty-nosed brat who probably lives in his parent's basement and spends all day jerking off to online porn. But he wasn't right."

"Don't bullshit me, Hope. I killed that family. I did."

"It was an accident, though. A horrible, tragic accident. It was nobody's fault. Like you said—it was just the fog of war."

"Why does He let stuff like that happen? Huh? If He's really in control, how does that stuff happen? I don't get it."

"I've asked myself that same question a million times. I don't know. I don't have an answer for you. I wish I did. I think that literally—*God only knows.* There are a lot of things like that in life. Maybe, one day, it'll all make sense. Maybe, just maybe, when we die—maybe that's when it all suddenly makes sense. And all the Mysteries, all the whys and wherefores, are solved. And we finally Know."

"You sound like a believer. I thought you were an atheist."

"Maybe I gave it up for Lent."

"Lent's several weeks away."

"So, maybe I want to avoid the holiday rush." She playfully stuck her tongue out at him.

He laughed.

"There. See? You always make me laugh. Now, I finally made *you* laugh."

He smiled at her. "It hurt me. The way that kid talked. It really hurt me. It dredged up all those old feelings, the ones I've been trying to put behind me. It's painful. And this kind of pain can be worse than physical pain."

"I know. I know psychological pain is hard. I do. Believe me—I do."

He started rocking back and forth. "I want this feeling to go away, but I don't know how to make it go away."

She put her arm around him, and he stopped rocking. "I'm going to help you. This relationship has been very one-sided. And I'm sorry for that. I've been taking from it. Now, I'm going to give because that's what a relationship is—it's taking, but it's giving, too. And it's my turn to give."

She got up and lay down on the bed and patted the mattress to beckon him. "Come on. Up here with me."

He lay down with her. She put her arms around him and pulled him in to her bosom. He felt the warm fullness of her breast and it comforted him.

He spoke softly, in a near whisper. "Sometimes, I don't feel like such a good person. I feel like a bad person. A bad guy. Gretchen Cavanaugh said I'm a bum. Maybe she's right."

"Gretchen Cavanaugh's an idiot. And you're certainly no bad guy. I've seen plenty of bad guys. I know bad guys. I know them all too well. You're the exact opposite. Like Sal said—you're one of the good guys. That's one thing the man was right about. Do you know that you've been like an angel to me?"

He turned his gaze up to her.

She nodded. "Yeah. It's true. You put up with all my bitterness and nastiness. All my anger. My rage. And you still treated me with kindness. You made me feel like I mattered. Like I was worth something. No guy has ever made me feel like I was worth something, Luke. Guys have always wanted me for one thing. They've just wanted to get under my shirt and into my pants. And now you've got me starting to believe in things that I haven't believed in for a long, long time. You did all that. And I didn't deserve any of it. I think I was lost. And now I'm found. I'm lousy at picking guys. You don't even know how lousy. So, I'm glad that you picked me. And, maybe, just maybe, Someone picked both of us. I don't know."

She reached across his body. Her breasts brushed up against his face. She picked her phone up off the nightstand.

"Here. I'm going to play a song for you. For us, actually. For both of us. Okay?"

He nodded.

She dialed up Cold Play's *Fix You*.

Kissing him on the top of the head, she whispered, "Maybe we can fix each other. All right? How's that sound?"

"I'd like that."

She held him tight. "Here. Let's take a little nap. And when you wake up, you'll feel better. I promise you will."

"Yeah. A nap sounds good."

He settled in and nuzzled his head against her breasts. She gently stroked the top of his head with her hand.

After a minute or so he called out to her. "Hey, um, Hope, are you still awake?"

"Yeah. What is it?"

"I noticed you weren't wearing your glasses when you were reading. It's very important to wear your glasses when you read because, you know, I don't want your eyes to go bad or anything. And they're pretty little glasses. They accentuate your face so well."

"Okay, I'll wear my glasses when I read from now on. I promise. All right?"

He nodded and drifted off to sleep in her arms.

CHAPTER TWENTY: REDEMPTION

That night, they sat at the kitchen table and ate their pizza. She saved the crust for last.

"One of these days, I'm going to cook you a homemade dinner. I promise," she said.

"You cook?"

"Yes, I cook. I enjoy it. I find it helps relieve stress. I like to think I'm pretty good at it, too. In fact, I'm going to go ahead and say that if there were a Nobel Prize for delicious, I'd win."

"Yeah, well, the last woman I dated wasn't a good cook. She was such a bad cook that I always prayed *after* the meal. She was such a bad cook that whenever she made chocolate mousse, I'd always get an antler stuck in my throat." He laughed and added, "In the interest of full disclosure, I can't take credit for those last two lines. They were both part of an old Rodney Dangerfield bit."

She rolled her eyes. "Oh, Gawd. Here we go."

"No, but seriously, I'd love a homecooked meal."

"You could use one, too. You're thin, boy. Way thin."

"What would you make?"

"Spaghetti and meatballs, garlic bread, tossed salad. Red wine. I don't normally drink, but I'd make an exception for our special dinner."

"Sounds good. And since you made a promise, I'll make a promise to you, too."

"And what's that?"

"You remember how I was telling you that I like Wayne

Newton?"

"Yeah."

"Well, I'm going to take you to see him one of these days."

"Does he tour? Does he ever come to Baltimore?"

He emphatically shook his head. "Oh, no—no—no. Wayne doesn't come to you. You have to go to him. He's Mister Las Vegas. And he only performs in Vegas. Currently, he's in residence at Caesar's Palace."

She raised her eyebrows. "Oh, so you're going to take me to Vegas, are you?"

"Yeah, but Wayne isn't getting any younger. Don't get me wrong—he's still kicking it and all, but he's closing in on eighty. So, you know, we'd have to do it sooner rather than later."

She nodded. "Yeah. Sounds like fun."

"Ever been to Vegas?"

"Nope. You?"

"Sure have. When I graduated from Parris Island, I got what's called boot leave. It's ten days off before you go to Marine Combat Training. All new Marines get it. I guess they figure you need time to decompress after three months of constantly being yelled at. Anyhow, I came home for a few days and then flew out to Vegas. I had a little dough that was burning a hole in my pocket because, in boot camp, you don't really have a chance to spend money. I was going to play craps. Craps and blackjack. I was just nineteen at the time. But what I didn't know is that to gamble in the great state of Nevada, you have to be at least twenty-one. So, when I tried to walk into the Mandalay Bay casino, security stopped me and ask for ID. Once they looked at my military ID card, they turned me away. I asked the security guy—*so, I'm old enough to go to war and pull the trigger on an M16, but I'm not old enough to pull the leaver on a slot machine?* He shrugged and told me—*take it up with the Nevada State Legislature, kid.* Fortunately. there's a lot to do in Vegas other than gamble. I went to the Hoover Dam. The Mob Museum. The Liberace Museum. The *Pawn Stars* pawn shop. Didn't see any of the Pawn Stars themselves, though. That disappointed me. I had my heart set on getting the Old Man's autograph. Anyhow, I did all of that good stuff."

"Whenever I think of Las Vegas, I think of that old Nicholas Cage movie, *Honeymoon in Vegas.* Didn't like that film. Didn't like it at all. He basically whores his girlfriend out to a gangster to erase a gambling debt. How is that even remotely romantic? And yet, somehow, Sarah Jessica Parker still loves the guy after all that? Stupid, stupid plot. Really messed up, in fact. And I would never marry a guy who tried to do that to me. Don't ever try to do that to me, okay?"

"I would never, ever even think about doing something like that. Never. Seriously, I would put an ornery, inquisitive chimpanzee named Joe Bananas in charge of the nuclear button before I'd do that, all right?"

She shook her head and laughed. "You're too much."

They did the dishes together. He fed the cats.

Then they went back up to the bedroom.

"Let's put in a movie," she suggested. "A nice movie. A movie with a happy ending. And absolutely no war films."

She perused the DVDs on his bookshelf, picked one, and held it up for him to see. "Here. This one. *The Wedding Singer.* Good movie. It has a happy ending."

"Not a very plausible one, though. Adam Sandler and Drew Barrymore just happen to be on the same flight to Vegas? How convenient. And then, Billy Idol, of all people, is on the flight, too? And he agrees to run interference on the asshole fiancé, so that Adam Sandler can profess his undying love to Drew Barrymore? A lot of serendipity at work there."

"Serendipity's a real part of life. And if you don't like the movie, why do you even own it?"

"I think it was in the bargain bin at Walmart. Five bucks. I took a flier on it. And it's not a bad film, *per se.* But it's just that, well—how is it that a nice girl like Drew Barrymore gets mixed up with an asshole to begin with? Not realistic."

"No, that part is realistic. People do get mixed up with the wrong people. All the time. Everyday. It happens. Believe me."

"It sounds like you're speaking from experience. Do you… do you want to talk?"

"Not right now, no."

"You sure?"

"Yeah, I'm sure. You'll know when I want to talk."

She put the disk in, and they sprawled out on the bed together.

"Thank you for earlier tonight, by the way. I feel better now. You made it better for me. Back in the old days, it would have taken me several days to get over something like that."

She smiled. "Maybe I can make it better still."

She put her hand under her shirt, into her bra, and pulled out the voucher he'd written for her.

Pretending to be a customer, she presented it. "Um, yes, I have this coupon. I'd like to redeem it, if I could."

They both sat up and got on their knees, facing one another.

He took the piece of paper and examined it."Hmm. Let's see. A redemption, eh? Well, I'll have to scan it. Everything gets scanned these days, you know." He pretended to scan the paper with an invisible scanner and made a sour beeping sound. "Huh. Says *invalid.* Is this a counterfeit q-pon? Did you make this at home on your computer? Because, ma'am, trying to pass a fraudulent q-pon is a federal offense. A felony, no less."

"No. I got this *cou*pon from the proprietor himself. I suggest you scan it again."

He again pretended to scan the paper. This time he made a more pleasant sounding beep. "Ah. Here we go. Yes. It's coming up now. Must have been the scanner. Or maybe the barcode. Sometimes, the barcodes get all messed up. All bunched up and whatnot. Makes it hard to scan. Anyhow, yes, everything appears to be in order. As a courtesy, I'll sign you up for our Elite Customer Card. You can earn bonus points. Of course, you'll have to complete many, many, many transactions before your eligible for any prizes. Eventually, though, you might earn enough points to get a stylus or a Grinch snow globe or something of that nature."

She spoke sarcastically. "A Grinch snow globe? Whoopee."

"Okay. No more clowning," he promised.

She licked her lips. "Kay."

He caressed her cheek. "You are an extremely beautiful woman, inside and out. I'm lucky to be here with you. Do you understand that? I want you to understand that. I want you to believe it because it's true."

She nodded. "I believe you. I do. I know you're the real deal."

He reached into his pocket, pulled out some Binaca, and sprayed some in his mouth. "After all, I did just have that pizza."

"Oh, hey, give me a hit of that, too, will you?"

"Open up."

She opened her mouth, and he gave her a spray.

Licking her lips, she told him, "Wow. That's very refreshing. Peppermint, too. Cool. Smooth. Clean."

"Yeah. It really is. It's a good product. A quality product. Made in the good ole USA, too, by the way. That's always a plus, you know?"

He placed the Binaca back in his pocket and pulled out his phone. She watched as he went through his playlist.

Kissing's not going to freak me out. Kissing should be fine. Should be.

After a few seconds, the sound of *Lost In Your Eyes* filled the room.

He leaned forward and whispered to her. "I get lost in your eyes, Hope. Hope has given me hope."

I feel like I've been lost, too. Lost these last couple of years. But now I feel like I'm found.

The smell of his cologne became more pronounced as he leaned in. The vetiver and amber notes were particularly nice. She looked at his eyes, glacier blue and kind. She closed hers and waited. *I almost killed this guy and now I'm getting ready to kiss him. God, life is so strange. Real life is stranger than fiction.*

She felt his lips press against hers. His large, soft hands caressed her cheeks. She took a deep breath and gasped, but quickly recovered. His technique was soft and tender, not at all aggressive. She felt relieved. *This is exactly how I need it to be.* She kissed him back with gusto and flung her arms around his neck to the sounds of their lips smacking and thrusting at one another.

They just kept kissing. And kissing. And kissing. She smelled his cologne and tasted the Binaca. And she felt emboldened by the fact that she was actually able to passionately kiss a man. That's when she opened her mouth wide. He followed her lead. Their tongues wrestled and he put his arms around her, gently squeezing. *Oh, wow. It feels so good to hold someone and be held. That's so underrated.* And at that moment, she felt the rest of the world and all its troubles fade away. Her universe became a universe of two.

She leaned forward and inadvertently caused him to lose his balance. They broke off the kiss. He fell and ended up on his back. She fell, too, and ended up on top of him.

A grimace came over his face. "Ouch. My ribs. You landed on my ribs."

"Oh, God, Luke, I'm sorry." She repositioned herself. "There. Is that better?"

"Yeah. That's fine."

"I didn't hurt you again, did I?"

He shook his head. "No, you didn't. I'm fine, so don't even worry about it. And let yesterday go. Okay?"

"Yeah. Kay."

There was silence for a few seconds. They smiled at one another.

Finally, she asked, "Could you taste my strawberry lip gloss?"

He licked his lips and nodded. "I did. Very nice indeed. The combination of peppermint and strawberry was fantastic. Maybe it could be a new flavor of potato chip. Strawberry-peppermint. You'd like that, wouldn't you?" He chuckled.

"You're going to make me sick at my stomach, boy. And I'm going to hurl right in your face. How's that for sexy and romantic?"

She brushed his hair with her left hand and softly bit her own lower lip.

"Here. Tilt your head back a little and expose your neck to me," she ordered.

He tilted his head back and laughed. "You're not a vampire, are you?"

"Hey, lady vampires are sexy, right?" She looked up at him and winked.

"Right. But I'm not really a night person. I'm much more of a day person. It'd be tough for me ever to join the ranks of the undead. I don't look my best when I'm really pale, either. I look much better with some color. That's why I go tanning once in a while. I do kind of like garlic, as well. And sleeping in a coffin would really creep me out because I *am* mildly claustrophobic."

"Uh-huh." She gently blew on his neck.

He took deep breaths. "Oh, wow. That feels amazing. Cool but not cold. I've never had a girl do that to me before."

She giggled, pressed her lips to his neck, and started kissing.

"Oh, good God, woman. *Day-um.* I don't care if you are a vampire at this point. Do what you will. Have your way with me, girl. It feels all tingly and so forth."

She gazed up at him and cooed, "You're going to *love* this."

She flicked her tongue at his neck. And then she stuck her tongue out and ran it up and down his flesh, painting it with her saliva.

"Oh, wow. Wow. Wow. And wow. Just wow," he said.

She kept at it.

After a few seconds he added, *"Whew.* If I were a woman, I think I'd be orgasming right about now. It is true that you all can have orgasms without actually having sex, right? That's what I read in an issue of *Cosmo* that one time I was waiting in my doctor's office. I had to read *Cosmo* because they didn't have *Sports Illustrated.* It was either *Cosmo* or *Southern Living,* and I had absolutely no interest in learning how to make pineapple cobbler. I hate pineapples. But anyway—is it really true that woman can orgasm without having intercourse?"

She didn't stop to answer but just nodded.

After a couple minutes of licking, she pulled another skill out of her repertoire. Gently, she sucked on his neck.

"Woah. As Gomer Pyle was fond of saying—*shazam*. Shazam, girl, shazam."

She momentarily paused to inform him, "I'll try not to give you a hickey."

"Don't even worry about it. That's what turtlenecks are for. In fact, in high school, Rachel Watson gave me several hickeys and I wore a turtleneck all semester. Of course, it got a little uncomfortable because that was during summer school. See, I failed calculus that year, and Mom and Dad made me do the whole summer school thing. But, ah, yeah— suffice it to say that it's really no fun wearing a turtleneck when it's ninety-eight degrees with ninety percent humidity."

She stopped sucking and looked up at him. "Speaking of your mom and dad—tell me about your family. I want to know. What are your parents like? They must be special people to have raised such a great guy."

He put his arm around her and held her tight. She put her head on his chest and listened.

"My folks live up in Cecil County, in a little town called North East."

"Oh, hey, I've been up there before. I took my sister to that crab house up there. What's the name of that place? I think it's pretty well-known."

"Woody's. You're thinking of Woody's. It's supposed to have the best crab cakes and steamed crabs in the state."

"Yeah. It was good. I liked it. My sister, Jules, enjoyed it, too."

"Yeah. It's good. A little pricey, but good. Anyhow, my mom's name is Linda. She has her own business, an antique shop right on Main Street called The Last Yankee. My dad's name is Greg and he, ah, he's... a..." He paused and laughed.

"He's a what?"

"He's a...cop."

She playfully smacked him on the arm. "Nah ah."

"Ya ha."

"No way."

"Yes way."

"What agency is he with?"

"Maryland State Police. He's a lieutenant. He's the commander of Barrack F. And he's getting ready to retire. He says he's going to play golf, help Mom with the business, and volunteer at the local animal shelter. He aims to be a dog walker and cat cuddler. Oh, yeah—he has a bucket list item to try for, too. He wants to get on *The Price Is Right*. Yep. That's his dream. To get on the show and win both showcases during the Showcase Showdown."

She again playfully smacked him. "You jerk. Now, why didn't you tell me your dad's a cop?"

"You didn't ask, and I didn't want you to think that I was trying to use it as an *in* with you. Now, mind you, had my natural charm not won you over—rest assured—I would have eventually used that information to my advantage. That was my ace in the hole."

"Any siblings?"

"No human siblings, but my parents have three rescued cats who are like kids to them. Dada, Mark, and Gypsy." He thought for a moment and added, "When I joined the Marines, my mom had a fit, a real conniption. She had this fear that her only son was going to get sent overseas and get killed. She actually tried to bribe my recruiter. Yeah, she sure did. She called the guy and said she'd write him a check for five grand if he'd find a reason to DQ me. Technically, she committed a felony—*attempted bribery of a federal official*. Fortunately, my recruiter was cool about it. He said it wasn't the first time a parent had tried to bribe him into disqualifying their kid."

"Well, your mom was almost right. You did get sent overseas. And you did get shot."

"Yeah. I guess the only thing that kept her worst fears from becoming a reality was the fact that the Taliban fighter who shot me wasn't a good marksman. In the Marine Corps, he wouldn't even have gotten the dreaded pizza box."

"Pizza box? What the hell?"

"The pizza box, the Marksman Badge. It's the lowest rifle qualification badge you can earn. It's square, like a pizza box. So, that's what we call it. And it's not something anyone is proud of."

"You guys have your own little language. And, hopefully, in that language, you're better with your pronunciations. Mister Q-*pon*." She stuck her tongue out at him.

He smiled. "What about you? What about your family? I'd like to know about them."

She took a deep breath. "Well, my mom's name is Marie. She's a teacher. She teaches social studies to middle school kids in Baltimore County, in Towson. I have a sister named Juliet. We call her Jules. She has Down Syndrome, so even though she's twenty-six, she still lives with Mom. Her life is harder than it should be. People are cruel, you know? She was crying not long ago because she hardly has any Facebook friends. Basically, it's just me and Mom. Nobody ever sends her any friend requests. She so wants to be like everyone else." She paused for a moment. "Would you mind if Jules hung out with us some time? Maybe someday we could take her somewhere. Maybe to the zoo. She loves animals. Would you have any problems with that?"

"Of course not. I'd love to meet your sister. Why would there be a problem?"

"Some guys have issues with it. I once had a guy tell me he didn't want Jules hanging out with us because he didn't like being around *re-tards*. Needless to say, I broke up with him on the spot."

He kissed her forehead. "Good for you. He was an asshole. A total asshole. I'd love for Jules to hang out with us. And I'll send her a friend request, too."

"You mean that?"

"Absolutely. What name is her Facebook account under?"

"Juliet Sophia Kennedy, Towson, Maryland. Her profile

picture is a photo of her cat, an orange tabby named Mimsie. She named Mimsie after the little orange kitten who meowed during the end credits of *The Mary Tyler Moore Show.* Jules loves that show, even though it went off the air almost twenty years before she was even born. When she found out the real Mimsie died way back in the late eighties, she bawled her eyes out."

"Aw. Bless her heart. We'll definitely do stuff with Jules. Anyone who is important to you is important to me."

"Thank you."

"Of course, going to the zoo might be a problem, though"

"And why is that?"

"Come on. Are you kidding me? The zookeeper would take one look at yours truly and try to make me one of the exhibits. He'd have his little khaki shorts and shirt on. He be wearing his little tan pith helmet. And he'd be running after me with his big old net. It'd be like two beauties and one beast." He yelled a Tarzan yell. "*Auhuaaa Uaaa Uaaaaaaaa!*" He laughed.

She playfully punched him in the shoulder. "Don't you ever stop with the silliness?"

"Not really. I swear, one of these days, I'm going to audition for that talent show that airs on WJZ Saturday morning, *Baltimornings.*"

She cleared her voice and turned serious. "You know, if anything ever happened to Mom, I'd have to take custody of Jules. She'd have to live with me. Of course, Mom's only in her early fifties, but you never know…and, well, if Jules had to live with me…well, would that be an issue for you?"

"No. Not at all. That's what I'd want you to do. That's the only right thing to do."

She gently patted his chest with her hand. "I wish I could have met you a long time ago."

"Now, what about your dad? You didn't even mention him."

She stared up at the ceiling and shook her head. "Frankie Kennedy is dead to me. That's his name—Frankie. And I can't stand the SOB. So much so that I refuse to use the noun *father* to describe him. Because he wasn't a father. He was a sperm donor. Nothing more."

"What'd he do?"

"He's an alcoholic for one thing. I swear, the man has Jim Beam running through his veins. He never had any time for us. And he ran out on us when I was six and Jules was four. He left to chase his whores. Because that's what he did. Chased whores. Still does, from what I understand. He loved strip clubs, too. He had a gorgeous wife at home, but he just had to have those strip club skanks. He wouldn't buy me or Jules a birthday present, but he buy the damn pole cats diamond rings and necklaces. He screwed around on Mom every chance he got. Case in point— Christmas Eve, nineteen ninety-seven. The man had a wife, a five-year-old, and a severely developmentally disabled three-year-old at home. And what was he doing? Putting up the Christmas tree? Taking us all to Christmas Eve Mass? Helping Mom with the presents? Nope. He was at Sherry's Show Bar, the strip joint in Canton. And he was *whoring*. And when he finally stumbled in on Christmas morning—or should I say Christmas afternoon, because it was after twelve o'clock—he reeked of cheap booze, cheap cigars, and even cheaper women. And guess what he does now?"

"What's that?"

"When he left us, he went down south, to Norfolk. And a few years ago, he finally made his dream a reality. He opened his very own strip club. It's called Frankie's Fantasia. And—get this, now—the man's fifty two, okay? Fifty *freaking* two. And he's living with one of his dancers. She's eighteen. And, according to the grapevine, she just turned eighteen four months ago. Yeah, well, he's been living with her for something like a year now. And, in Virginia, the age of consent is eighteen. So, you do the math on that one. And I'll tell you something right now—and I'm just putting it out there—if, by some miracle, I ever get married, the jerk is not invited to the wedding. And if, by an even bigger miracle, I ever have kids, he's not seeing them. Ever. I don't care if he's on his death bed. He didn't want the responsibility of being a father. So, he doesn't get the privilege of being a grandfather. That man singlehandedly ruined my childhood."

"I'm sorry."

"And this is one sinner that you're not going to turn into a saint. Sal Rossi was one thing. That was personal, too. But this is my so-called father, so this is real personal. Stand by me on this one. Please. Be on my side. You have the right to remain silent on this one. And I suggest that you do because anything you say can and will be used against you. And if you do say something, be supportive. Okay? That's all I ask."

He patted her hand. "Okay. I'm on your side. I am. And I'm certainly not going to make excuses for him."

"Thank you. I hate strip clubs. You know, I was standing in line at Walgreen's one day about a year ago, minding my own business. It was my day off, so I was in street clothes. And this sleazebag came up to me, handed me his business card, and was all like—*hey, pussycat, you've got a great face and body. You could make good money dancing at my club. I can make you a star. You'd be the girl of every guy's dreams. Wet dreams, that is. What do you say, babe? You willing to shake it to make it?* According to his card, he was the proprietor of Tony's T and A Palace. Hadn't heard of that one. Evidently, it had just opened. I flashed him my badge and told him the Baltimore PD vice squad would be paying a visit to his establishment, to make sure he was in compliance with all the rules particular to businesses such as his. He disappeared real fast when he heard that. So, yeah, I hate those places and everything about them." She gazed up at him. "You're not a *strip club guy*, are you? I'm sure you're not, but I just want to hear you confirm it."

"Nope. Not a *strip club guy*. Could never be a *strip club guy*. They all use money clips. I guess because it's easier to access the dollar bills that they're going to stuff into the dancers' G-strings. But I prefer a wallet. Also, I'm not a fan of lowriders with big woofers in the back. Plus, I don't like wearing my ball cap turned around backwards. Additionally, I take the tags *off* my clothing. And I could never, ever wear my pants so low that they drooped down past my butt. Nah, I'm not a *strip club guy*. Definitely not."

"Be serious, please."

"No, Hope. I'm not into strip clubs. I was in one once, when I was nineteen and in the Marines. There was one near Camp Pendleton. The place didn't serve alcohol so anyone eighteen or over could get in. I still remember the name, too. It was called The Gentleman's Gold Club. My Marine buddies dragged me in there one night. Didn't like it. I didn't really see any *gentlemen* in there, either. Truth be told—it was kind of a sad, depressing place. It was mostly a bunch of middle-aged guys throwing money away because they deluded themselves into believing that, somehow, a beautiful twenty-year-old would be interested in them. And the girls were just hustling. It was a very phony place. I'm sure there was probably some prostitution going on there, too. And I wouldn't want my sister, if I had one, doing that stuff. And I would never want my girlfriend doing that stuff. So, why would it be okay for me to watch someone else's sister or girlfriend do that stuff? No. I didn't like it at all. And I've never been in one since."

"Good. I'm glad to hear that."

"I do kind of have a stripper fantasy, though."

"Oh yeah? Do tell."

"Well, it doesn't involve seeing some woman who I don't even know taking her clothes off in some seedy strip joint. This involves a certain super-sexy policewoman. And my fantasy is seeing her wearing the blue uniform top with her badge on. No pants on, but the uniform shirt would hang down past her thighs, so everything would still be covered. Of course, I'd have a nice view of her gorgeous little legs. Oh, yeah—she'd also have her hair up and her cute police hat on. Underneath her shirt, she'd be wearing a sexy Victoria's Secret matching lace bra and panty set. Preferably blue, royal blue. And there'd be music, too— maybe *She's Got The Look*."

"Yeah, well, I don't know the first thing about performing a striptease, so I guess you're out of luck, dude."

"There are tutorials on YouTube…so I've heard. That's what Dino was telling me, anyway."

She again stuck her tongue out at him.

"You know what else I'd really like to do with you sometime?"

"What's that?"

"Take you ice skating."

"*Aw.* I love ice skating. I'm half-way decent at it, too."

He chuckled. "I'm not. I can't skate at all."

"Then why would you want to go?"

"Because I think you'd look really cute in those little white skates. But me? I wouldn't even attempt it. I'd be like Rocky. Remember in *Rocky*, the original *Rocky*, when he takes Adrian ice skating? That's their first date—they go ice skating. And he can't skate so he's just out there on the rink sliding around in his street shoes. Remember that scene?"

"Yeah. I do remember that part. That was cute." She thought for a moment and frowned. "But Rocky lost. He lost the fight."

"Yeah. He lost the fight. But he went the distance, and that's all he ever really cared about anyway. And, most importantly, he got the girl. He lost the fight but got the love of a good woman. So, Rocky won. *Rocky was a winner.*

"Life is like a high-stakes prizefight, Hope. And I think going the distance and finding love at the end of the fifteenth round is reward enough, you know? More than enough. In fact, I'll go so far as to say it's the ultimate Victory. But you have to answer the final bell to get there. When that bell sounds for the start of the last round, and you're tired and hurt—hurt bad—you still have to answer it. But if you do, you can find redemption."

CHAPTER TWENTY-ONE: BUNKY

one week later

It had gotten a little warmer. Luke pressed the button on the Town Car's dashboard that displayed the outside temperature. *Thirty-four and it's not even noon yet so it should get warmer. The cats' food and water won't freeze, at least not until tonight.*

He wore a black leather jacket over top of a purple Ravens hoodie, a pair of blue jeans, and white sneakers.

When he got to the feeding location, he parked along Fulton Avenue. He fed the meter, broke out the food and water, and carried it along with the bowls into the alley.

He shook a bag of dry cat food, and, one-by-one, over a period of about five minutes, each member of the Mondawmin Seven appeared. He filled seven foam bowls with dry food and set them down. The cats started to eat but momentarily scattered when a fire truck raced by on Fulton Avenue, with its sirens blaring. After a few minutes, they gradually returned and resumed feeding.

He gave them some fresh water. Next, he opened the canned food, scooped it into bowls, and set it out. As they ate, he talked to them. "This is really good food, guys. It's Iams. A nice person donated it to the shelter. It's nutritionally balanced."

Slowly and deliberately, he approached Bunky, the gray and white long-hair. The young cat vigorously chowed down on the canned food. Luke kneeled down next to him. Bunky didn't run but continued eating.

He tentatively reached out and placed his hand on top of the cat's head. He flinched a bit but still didn't run.

Slowly and softly, he ran his hand along the length of Bunky's back. He still didn't run. Luke talked to the cat in a gentle, falsetto voice, as he'd read an article that suggested cats pay more attention and respond better to high frequencies.

"Hey, look at you, buddy. You're really coming along. Yes, you are. You're a handsome boy, aren't you?"

The cat briefly stopped eating, looked up at Luke, meowed, scratched his ear with his back leg, and went back to eating.

After a few minutes, Sassy, the large black and white tuxedo, finished her food and walked over to Bunky's bowl. She lashed out at the smaller cat with a thunder paw. Bunky immediately backed away, and Sassy pillaged his food.

Bunky looked up at Luke and meowed a pitiful meow. *Aw. He has such a sad, disappointed look on his little face. Nobody can tell me that these guys don't have feelings, don't have souls.*

Luke gently admonished the bossy feline. "Hey, Sassy—that wasn't nice. If you want more all you have to do is ask, but you shouldn't just steal from the other cats."

He opened a fresh can of food, scooped it into a new bowl, and set it down in front of Bunky, who immediately resumed his meal. "Don't worry, dude. I won't let Sassy steal from you this time."

An old man stumbled into the alley. He wore a straw cowboy hat, a tan trench coat, and brown cowboy boots. He appeared to be in his 60s. Where the trench coat ended, his bare knees were visible. *Oh. Geez. Is he naked under that coat? I'll bet he is. I'll bet he's a flasher.*

The man waved and called out to Luke. "Hi-ho. *Hola.*"

The cats scattered.

Luke was frustrated but nonetheless tentatively waved and managed a monotone, unenthusiastic greeting. "Hey. How's it going?"

The man smiled a snaggletooth smile. "I'm watching

a movie next door, at the porn joint. They sometimes play movies for their customers' satisfaction. Today, they're showing *Saving Ryan's Privates*."

Luke nodded. "Uh-huh."

The man opened his coat to reveal that he was nude. *Damn. He has to be freezing. It's still only in the thirties, after all.*

He urinated in the alley. "Don't mind me, boy, I'm just taking a piss. Beer makes me do that."

"Right."

As he urinated, he expressed relief. "Oh, *shit*. That feels good. I thought my bladder was gonna bust. That ain't such a good feeling, either. Know what I mean, chief?"

"Yep. Been there."

"Say, you don't know anywhere in the city where a fella can score some good Krokodil, do ya?"

"Nope. Afraid I can't help you." *What the hell is Krokodil?*

"Well, how about Penicillin? Got any of that? I got this bad sore on my lip." He reached up with his free hand and touched it. "I'm thinking it might be herpes."

"Sorry. Can't help with that, either."

"Well, then what good are ya? Huh?" The man laughed a belly laugh and wheezed. When he recovered, he assured Luke, "Aw, I'm just joshing, just breaking your balls a little, that's all."

"Right." *You'd better stay away from my balls, pal.*

When he finished urinating, he launched into a joke. "Say, Holmes, what happens to your computer when it gets the Viagra virus?"

Luke shrugged and threw up his hands. "I, I don't know. You've got me. What happens?"

"It turns your three and a half inch floppy into a hard drive." The man laughed hysterically.

Luke forced a smile. "Right. Good one." *Three and a half inches? Speak for yourself, buddy.*

"Say, you got an extra smoke on you, Hoss?"

"Sorry. I don't smoke." *Go back into the porn shop, already, will you? You're probably missing the big orgy scene.*

The man belched. "You know, I screwed Lucille Ball last night. And good God, man—she was good. What a dish. Big ole boobs on that woman, and they're real. Reasonable prices, too."

Luke chuckled. "Lucille Ball? She's been dead for a very long time now. Decades, I believe."

The man snapped back at him. "No—no! What's wrong with you, boy? Not *that* Lucille Ball. The Lucille Ball who dances at Escapades, the strip joint off Perring Parkway."

"Oh, okay. Gotcha. That makes more sense."

The man scanned the ground. After about thirty seconds, he picked up a cigarette butt that contained some unsmoked tobacco. He held it up and smiled as if he'd just found a rare gold doubloon. He put it in his mouth. "There. This one has at least a few hits left on it. Now, I got me a smoke." He lit it and stumbled away. As he did, he waved to Luke and told him, "See ya in the funny papers, boy."

Huh? I have no idea what that was supposed to mean. Note to self—Google it.

With the man gone, the cats returned.

Luke apologized. "Sorry your meal got interrupted, guys. You all deserve better than this. It stinks. You're living in garbage. And nobody likes garbage."

He walked over to Bunky, who had his face again buried in the bowl. Gently, he stroked his head. *Wonder if he'll let me pick him up?*

Luke positioned himself so that he stood over the cat, with his legs on either side of the feline. Slowly, he reached down with both hands. He gently talked to him. "Easy does it, little guy. I just want to pick you up. Not going to hurt you. I would never hurt you."

When Luke's hands touched the cat's sides, he flinched, but he didn't run away. Luke grabbed hold of him and slowly, gingerly lifted him up. When he got him chest high, he slipped his right hand under the cat's back feet to support him. And he pulled him into his chest and stroked his head. He talked to him in a whisper. "Hey, how about that? Huh? You let Dana pick you up and now you're letting me pick you up. You're doing great, pal." Bunky began to purr. "You like being held, huh? People aren't so bad after all, right?" He looked down, into the cat's green eyes. "Well, some people aren't. You just have to be careful about who you trust, that's all. Hey—you remember that pretty lady who was with me when I fed you guys that one day? Real pretty lady. Well, I think she's a good candidate to be your human. Your mommy. I'm working on it, too. I am. It just takes time." The cat yawned, meowed, and gently extended his paw so that it touched Luke's nose.

He reached into his pocket, pulled out a grey toy mouse stuffed with catnip, and held it up to the cat's nose. "You like catnip, buddy? I'm giving this toy to you. Yeah, this is yours. Your very own toy. How about that? I'll bet you've never had a toy of your own before, huh? I bought this at the pet store, especially for you. So, this is yours. All yours. And don't let Sassy steal it from you."

Gently, he set the cat back down and put the toy mouse between his front paws. Bunky batted it around. Then he plopped himself down, on his side. He grasped the toy with his front paws and used his back feet to rabbit kick it.

Luke laughed. "That's right, little Bunk-A-Roo. You show that mouse who's boss."

Suddenly, the man in the trench coat was back. Bunky ran away. *Oh, good grief. Come on, dude. What do you want now?*

"Hey, Hoss, you got any extra rubbers on you?"

"No, I don't. I really don't. I'm sorry. I'm just here to feed the cats."

The man shrugged. "All right then. I'll just do it raw tonight. What the hell, you know? Ain't like I'm going to catch anything that I don't already have, right old chap?"

Luke rolled his eyes. "Yeah. Right. There you go. That's the spirit."

The man walked away.

Luke's phone rang. It was Hope. She was still staying with him. He answered the call by excitedly telling her about his breakthrough with the cat. "I picked up Bunky. He actually let me pick him up. How about that? And he'd probably still be laying at my feet, playing with his toy, if it wasn't for the old pervert from the porn shop who's paying to have sex with Lucille Ball."

She ignored his news about Bunky and didn't even ask about the pervert and Lucille Ball. "Can you, like, come home right now?" She sounded upset.

"Why? What's wrong?"

"I was taking a nap and I had a bad dream. And it was one of those dreams where, when I woke up, I couldn't tell whether it was just a dream or it really happened." She started to cry. "It was a replay of the accident. Only this time, I shot you. Please come home right now. So, I can see that you're okay."

"I'm fine, Hope. I'm perfectly fine."

"I know. But I have to see you. I have to touch you to *really* know that you're okay."

"Okay. I'm coming home now. Give me fifteen minutes. All right?"

"But you're coming home, right?"

"Yes. I'm coming home. Right now. I promise."

"Okay. Hurry. Please. Because I'm kind of freaking out a little."

CHAPTER TWENTY-TWO: CAT'S IN THE CRADLE

Hope looked out the living room window. Her hair was up, and she wore a pair of gray sweatpants and a blue hoodie. She nervously chewed on the hoodie's drawstring. *Where is he? He said he'd be home in fifteen minutes, and it's been nearly a half hour. Should I call him again?*

Five minutes later, she finally saw the car pull into the driveway. She took a deep breath and even crossed herself. *Thank God.*

He walked in the front door carrying a package. She immediately rushed over to him and tried to throw her arms around him, but the package got in the way. He dropped it in a tan armchair that sat by the door and they embraced.

She buried her head in his shoulder. "Thank God you're okay. When we talked on the phone, you said you'd be home in fifteen minutes—and that was a half hour ago. I was getting really worried."

"They were doing roadwork on the Jones Falls Expressway and had a lane shut down."

She closed her eyes and squeezed him as tight as she could. "If you didn't already think I was crazy, I'm sure you do now. But I just had to make sure you were all right."

He gently stroked her hair. "No, I don't think you're crazy. Don't even say that."

"It was just such a vivid dream. I was so scared. And, at first, I couldn't tell if it was real or just a dream. I'm sorry I freaked out, but I can't help what I dream, you know?"

"It's okay. Nobody can help what they dream. I know that. Believe me—I know that." He kissed her on the forehead.

She gazed up at him. "It didn't bother you that I called you like that?"

"Nope. I'm flattered, actually."

"Flattered?"

"Sure. A beautiful, sexy, sweet woman was worried about me and wanted me to come home to be with her. You think that's a problem? Because if that's a problem, then I know a lot of guys who'd love to have that problem."

"Really?"

"Yeah, really. Listen to me—since I left the Marine Corps, I've never had anyone, except the cats and Dino, to care about me. It feels good to have someone care. Real good. It feels good to hold you like this, too. You feel good. You smell good. You sound good, too, by the way. Yeah. You have that perfect feminine voice. I'll bet you can sing, can't you? You look a little like Demi Lovato and I'll bet you sing like her, too. Can you sing a few bars of *Sorry Not Sorry* just so I can verify that you sound like Demi Lovato?"

"Ha. I sound more like Demi Moore."

"What? Is Demi Moore a really bad singer or something?"

She shrugged. "I don't know, but that's the only other Demi I could think of."

He threw his head back and laughed. "Yeah. There aren't too many famous Demis out there. Lovato and Moore—that's pretty much it."

Her glasses slid down on the bridge of her nose. He pushed them back up.

"They've been sliding down on me lately. I think I need new nose pads."

"Those glasses are very cute. You're very cute."

They shared a quick kiss.

"Oh, before I forget, what's Krokodil?"

"It's a narcotic, an opioid. And it eats away at your skin. It comes from Russia, and it's becoming popular in Baltimore. Why do you ask?"

"When I was feeding the Mondawmin cats, some pervert from the porn shop asked me where he could find Krokodil. I had no idea what it was. So, you're saying it comes from Russia?"

"Yep. From Russia with love," she said sarcastically.

"I swear, nothing good is coming out of Russia these days. And if you think about it, it's been a minute since anything good's come out of that country. The Taliban always seemed to magically come up with Russian arms and equipment. Kind of made one wonder at times. It almost seemed like a proxy war. I'm going to go ahead and say that the last good thing to come out of Russia was Anna Kournikova and that's been a while."

"Is she another one of your celebrity crushes?"

"No. From that part of the world, my preference has always been Lilly from the AT&T commercials. She was born in one of those *stan* countries not too far from Russia. At least that's what her Wikipedia page says. But the interesting thing is that since I met you, I haven't binge-watched any of her commercials on YouTube. Just not interested anymore. Compared to you, Lilly just seems silly. Matter of fact, compared to you, Lilly is about as attractive to me as the guys from Milli Vanilli." He sang the opening bars to *Blame It On The Rain*.

She shook her head. "You're too much. You're a character and a half. You know that, right?"

He turned serious. "I mean it, too. No other woman compares to you."

She put her head down. "Thank you. You make me feel good about myself."

He placed his hand under her chin and gently tilted it upwards, so she was looking at him again. "I'm just telling you the truth."

There was silence for a few seconds. They just smiled at one another.

Finally, he broke the quiet. "Hey, look over in that chair." He motioned towards the armchair with his head. "That package—I think it's for you. It was left on the front porch. I think it must have been old San-ney Claus who left it. Yeah. Had to of been. He was a little late this year but, hey, better late than never, right?"

She tilted her head and shot him a suspicious look. "San-ney Claus, huh?"

"Yeah. Sure. You still believe in San-ney Claus, don't you? I sure do."

"Boy, you really struggle with pronunciations. But, yes, I'm beginning to think it's actually possible that *Santa* Clause exists."

"Well, that's a start. Now, why don't you open your present?" He picked up the package and pointed to the label. "See that? It's even addressed to you."

He handed it to her.

"I need a box cutter or something. I don't want to break a nail trying to get this tape off."

He went to the kitchen and returned with a steak knife. Carefully, he sawed through the brown shipping tape and opened the box.

"Go ahead. Look inside. Yeah, look inside."

She reached into the box and pushed aside packing peanuts and tissue paper. Finally, she pulled another box from the shipping box. She held it up and read the writing on the box aloud. "Hasbro's Joy For All Interactive Virtual Cat."

The box showed the image of what was inside—a silver gray tabby virtual feline.

"His name's Joey, but you can change it, if you want. Here. Let's open the box. Let's get him out. What do you say? I'll show you how he works."

He opened the box and pulled Joey out along with a slip of tan parchment. He held the paper up for her to see. "This is his birth certificate." He read from the paper. "Let's see here... says he was *born to love you*. And that he enjoys being *scratched under his chin* and likes to *purr* and give *gentle head bonks.* And he should already have batteries."

He pulled the robotic cat out of the box and offered it to her. "Here, Hope. He's for you. Joey's for you."

She took the toy but told him, "Oh, God. I can't believe you did this. Do you know who gets these things given to them?"

He said nothing.

She answered her own question. "Old People. Old people, Luke. When old people are forced into nursing homes and their children take away their real cats and turn them into a shelter, they give them one of these. Because they're trying to somehow make it right for them."

He threw up his hands. "I...I just thought that this, maybe, could be something that could help you transition to a real cat. A real cat like Bunky, for example. He's coming around. Big time. And he needs a home. But this could be a start, you know? Baby steps. But if you don't like Joey, I can send him back."

She found the power switch and turned him on. "I didn't say I didn't like him."

Joey immediately opened his eyes and meowed. After a few seconds, he started purring. Then, he kneaded with his front paws.

She smiled and gently stroked Joey's head. The machine purred louder.

"These things are expensive," she noted.

"How would you know?"

"Because I almost got one for myself about a year and a half ago. How stupid is that?"

He embraced her, with the virtual cat between them. "It's not stupid. Totally not stupid."

"You shouldn't have done this. Why did you do this?"

"I already told you—it's a Christmas present. You know how everyone always says—*make every day like Christmas.* Well, I'm trying to make this day like Christmas. Who knows? Maybe he wasn't even born in December anyhow. Nobody really knows. So, as far as I'm concerned, today is as good a day to celebrate as any. So there. Merry Christmas, Hope."

She softly kissed him. "Merry Christmas, Luke. Our first Christmas together, I guess, huh?"

"I hope it's the first of many." He smiled at her and winked.

"We're making memories, aren't we?" she asked.

He nodded. "Most people don't have the presence of mind to think that way. Rare is the person who has the wisdom to know that they're living out a special time in their life. To be *in the moment* and actually have that knowledge—well, that's a gift."

She kissed him again and then kissed the top of Joey's head. "Would it be crazy to love him?"

He shook his head. "No. Of course not. You go right ahead and love him, honey."

She looked down at Joey's eyes. "His eyes are so expressive. They look real. Almost real."

They broke off their embrace and she cradled the cat in her arms, like a baby. She talked to the toy and gently rocked it. "Cat's in the cradle, baby. Cat's in the cradle." She sang *Cat's in the Cradle* to the machine.

CHAPTER TWENTY-THREE: WORKS IN PROGRESS

three weeks later

They'd just gotten back from Hope's townhouse. He'd run her over to Bolton Hill to get more of her stuff. Even though she'd made a full recovery from her pneumonia, she'd asked if she could continue to stay with him. "I just don't like my house. There's nothing for me there. I like it better here. I feel more comfortable here," she'd told him.

It was getting cold again. The city had just received three inches of snow.

They lay together in his bed. She wore a pair of blue jeans, a white fisherman's sweater, and pink and navy argyle socks. Her hair was in a ponytail.

He wore a pair of gray sweatpants, white athletic socks, and a navy sweatshirt.

Joey the virtual cat was situated between them. At the bottom of the bed, Bobby and Hannah curled up together

They watched a movie on The Romance Channel called *Cheaper To Keep Her.* It was about a man who woos his estranged wife back in order to avoid paying alimony, only to find that he still loves her.

He gently nudged her with his elbow. "Do you think we could be a Romance Channel movie?"

"No. We're too real. According to The Romance Channel,

nobody ever swears, nobody ever has any real issues. They're all kind of silly movies about perfect couples who have some very minor obstacle to overcome before they profess their undying love. And it's usually an obstacle that could be overcome in a half-hour but gets dragged out for the full two. I don't really like Romance Channel movies. They're very fake, if you ask me."

"Can I change the channel, then?"

"Yeah. Fine with me. Go for it."

He tuned in the *TV Classics Network;* it was showing a *Brady Bunch* marathon.

He immediately recognized the episode. "This is the one where they go to Hawaii. Oh, yeah—this is a good one. Now, *this* is entertainment."

She agreed. "Yeah. Mike Brady was a great dad. I would have given anything to have a father like Mike Brady. Instead of Mike Brady, me and Jules got Frankie Shady."

He softly kissed her on the forehead.

She reached across him, to the nightstand, and picked up her Nathaniel Dunn book. As she did, her breasts brushed up against his chest. *Hello. Yes, that feels nice. Very nice, indeed.*

She opened the book to the spot that was marked and started reading.

He loudly cleared his voice to get her attention. *"Ahem."*

She looked over at him. "What? What's the problem?"

He pointed to her glasses, which were still on the nightstand. "Your glasses. You should wear your glasses if you're going to read." He reached over, picked them up, and handed them to her.

"Yes. My glasses. Of course." She put them on, looked directly at him, and smiled a big, exaggerated smile. "There. Happy now?"

"It seems like you don't like those glasses, and I don't know why. They're really cute. Adorable, is what they are. I love those black frames. They match your hair color and everything."

"I wish I had gone with contacts."

"Don't be silly. Those glasses are sexy. They're a great accessory. My eyesight is darn near perfect, but I'm thinking of getting some eyewear just as a fashion statement. Yeah, I'm thinking about getting a monocle, just like the one Colonel Mustard wore. But you really need them, so you don't get cataracts or glaucoma or eye cancer or whatever."

"I'm not sure you can get any of those diseases from not wearing glasses."

"Well, just the same, you should wear them. That's why the eye doctor prescribed them. Right?"

"Right."

She looked back down and started reading again.

"So, how's the book? Did Mister Nathaniel Dunn write another masterpiece?"

She answered without taking her eyes off the page. "It's pretty good, but I'm still waiting for the romance between Jazz and Skylar to heat up."

"Now, you see, from those names, I can't even tell who's who. I can't tell which one's the guy and which one's the girl."

She still didn't look up, but loudly exhaled. "Jazz is the guy. Skylar's the girl."

"What's with these romance novels these days? Doesn't anyone in a romance novel ever have a common name anymore? They're all *Piper* and *Joda* and *Raylon* and *Ridge*. *Eros* and *Dak*. It's stupid. I swear, you'd think no parents ever give their kids traditional names anymore. There are plenty of Johns and Marys still out there. Oh, and if it's a military romance—the dude's going to be a Navy SEAL. You can bank on it. I got news for you—there aren't that many Navy SEALs out there. It's a very small community of warriors. And you've got way more of them running around in the pages of romance novels than you do in real life. It just kind of comes off as silly and melodramatic, if you ask me."

She laughed. "How is it that you know so much about romance novels?"

"They have a display set up at the Walmart on Edmonson

Avenue, near the checkout line. While I'm waiting—which I do a lot of because they never have enough cashiers working—I sometimes browse them. Most of them are not good, either. So phony. Not real at all. Billionaires and princes—all that nonsense. Now, by way of contrast, I think you and me—we'd make a great romance novel."

"We would, huh?"

"Absolutely."

She finally took her eyes off the page and looked at him. "I don't think so. Like I was saying—we're too real. I swear too much. My dialogue would *oh-fend* peoples' sensibilities. And we don't live in some beautiful, exotic location, which is another prerequisite. We live in Baltimore. A dingy, dirty, violent city. And we don't have glamorous jobs or lifestyles, either. We're both blue-collar types. Nope. Nobody would have the balls to put us in a romance novel."

She went back to reading.

He turned his attention to the episode of *The Brady Bunch*. Occasionally, he commented. "I don't like Mike's perm. He looked better without the perm."

After a half hour, she marked her novel and grabbed her iPad. A few minutes later, she announced, "I got an email here from the radio station. In fact, it's from The Midnight Ranger himself. You know how they've been wanting us to go on the show together?"

He nodded. "Right. And we decided that we were going to keep our relationship private. At least as much as possible."

"Exactly. Well, he sent me a nice email saying he understands, respects our decision, and that the thousand dollar prize they'd been willing to pay to get us both on the show together—well, they're going to donate that to the charity of our choice."

"Oh, wow. Sweet. What charity do you want?"

"I think it should be Recycled Love."

"Are you sure?"

"Yeah."

He kissed her on the lips. "Thank you. That will do some real good for the cats. And I just got an email earlier today saying that Duncan needs to see a veterinary cardiologist. They think he has an enlarged heart. He's a long-haired black cat that we just got. His family dumped him because of a new baby. And he's really old, too. Nobody seems to know exactly how old, but I think he's so old that when he was a kitten the Dead Sea was just kind of mildly under the weather. Anyway, that thousand bucks will pay for his appointment and then some."

He thought for a moment. "But I have to confess, I feel a little guilty about keeping our story so private."

"Why?"

"Because I wonder if it's really just *our* story."

"What do you mean?"

"What I mean is that I'm starting to wonder if it's just for us. Maybe it's intended to be for more than just us. Think about it. All the stuff that's happened. The accident. The homeless Marine. The Midnight Ranger. Sal. Charlotte. Stewie. Doctor Mike. You have to admit—that's a pretty odd cast of characters. I'm starting to wonder if it's bigger than just us."

She rolled onto her side, so she was facing him. He felt the fullness of her breast brush against his forearm. *Ay—yai—yai. That feels good.*

"I don't know but I've been thinking about something."

"Oh yeah? Do tell."

"I want to do something for us. For both of us."

"What's that?"

"Well—you know—I like you a lot. I mean *a lot*. A whole lot."

He smiled. "I like *you* a lot. A whole lot."

"Right. So, we're two people who like one another a whole lot."

He chuckled and nodded. "Absolutely."

"I'd like to be closer to you, Luke."

He glanced down at the small gap between them. "Well, you have another few inches or so. So, you could scoot over a little bit more, if you want."

She smiled and gently caressed his cheek with the palm of her hand. "No, that's not what I mean."

"*Ooooh*. You mean—*closer* in the Biblical sense."

She giggled. "Yeah. Right. In the *Biblical* sense. So, how do you feel about that? You think we're ready?"

"I'd love to make love to you."

She kissed him.

"You know, I was reading an article in *Psychology Today*. The gist of it was that sex can help heal emotional wounds," she told him.

"Yeah?"

"Yeah. That's what it said."

He rolled on his side so that he was facing her. "Very interesting."

"Yeah. I thought so. So…let me ask you a question—what kind of stuff do you like? Sexually, I mean."

"Um. I'm not real kinky or anything. Pretty mainstream. Nothing too crazy. I definitely don't have the desire to put on a Moe from The Three Stooges Halloween mask, have sex with you, record it, and then upload it to a porn site. Not into that. And, before you ask, the reason I use that example is that I knew a guy in the Marines who did just that to his girlfriend. But I'll tell you what I would like to do."

"What's that?"

"I'm kind of getting a craving for those little legs of yours. I wouldn't mind licking them."

"*Reel. Lee?* That sounds fun."

"Yeah. Fun. Nothing too crazy. But nonetheless fun."

"How do you feel about me being on top?"

"I don't have a problem with that. Your being on top is the tops. From the *bottom* of my heart—I'd love for you to be on *top*."

"Cool."

"You know, I like your boobs, too. I'm really into boobs. I'll go ahead and admit it—I'm a boob man. A very dedicated, committed boob man. And do you know what the existence of boobs proves?"

She looked at him, laughed, and just shook her head.

He smiled at her and gently nudged her with his elbow. "Huh? Come on, Hope. Come on, now. What does it prove?"

"I know this is going to be another bad joke."

He delivered the punchline. "That guys really *can* focus on two things at once." He guffawed.

She didn't. Instead, she blew raspberries at him. "You know, I've heard you tell really cheesy jokes, but that was probably the cheesiest."

"No. You want the cheesiest? Here you go. *This* is the cheesiest. Ready for this? Here we go—what do you call the space between two surgically enlarged breasts?"

She looked up and rubbed her eyes. "Oh, brother. Give me a break."

"Huh? Come on. What's it called? What's it called, Hope? Huh?"

She didn't venture a guess.

"I guess you give up, right? Can't blame you. It's a tough riddle. But the answer is—the Silicone Valley. Yeah. The Silicone Valley. See, I learned that joke in the Marines."

She spoke sarcastically. "Yep. The American people's tax dollars at work. Gotta love it."

"Okay, I promise—no more bad jokes. I got it all out of my system. I swear."

She reached out and stroked his chest. "So, I thought what I would do is make you a real nice meal tonight. I said I'd make you authentic, homemade spaghetti and meatballs. Remember?"

"Yeah. I remember."

"I'll do that tonight. We can have a nice meal and then we can...you know."

"Yeah. I'd love to *you know* with you."

He thought for a moment. "I'm sorry if I sometimes joke around too much. It's just that when I was younger, when I was overseas, I had to be serious. So, I suppose I'm trying to make up for lost time."

"It's okay. I can live with bad jokes. It's kind of cute actually. Endearing, even."

He took her hand and interlocked their fingers and gently squeezed.

With her free hand, she picked up Joey the virtual cat and set him on her chest.

"You like him, huh?"

She nodded. "Yeah."

He talked to the machine. "Hey, how you doing there, tiger?"

He held Joey up and called out to Bobby, who was still at the bottom of the bed. "Hey, yo— Bobby. Check out your new housemate, your new brother of sorts."

Bobby was curled up in a ball but looked up when he heard his name called. He looked at the fake cat with great interest. Luke turned Joey's power on, and he meowed.

Bobby yawned a big yawn and arose. He crouched, stuck his behind in the air, and wiggled it. Bobby launched himself forward, landing just inches from the fake cat's face. Bobby hissed, and swatted at Joey, striking him in the head.

Luke laughed. "Aw! Look at that. That was a big ole thunder paw." He mildly chastised Bobby. "Whoa. Hey there, champ—take it easy, will ya?"

He turned the machine off. "Mister Bobby's upset. Mis-ter Bobby doesn't like Mis-ter Joey."

He explained to Hope. "It took him a good two months to get used to Hannah when she first got here. Yeah, for the first two months she was here, he'd jump up on the kitchen counter and poop in the sink. Religiously. Very true story. Yeah, he's set in his ways, all right. But he got used to her and now their best buds. Oh, and—just in case you're wondering—I put in a new sink. I did. Really."

She took Joey back and hugged him. She kissed Luke's shoulder. "I'm looking forward to being with you tonight."

"Likewise. It's kind of amazing how things have worked out with us."

"Yeah. Amazing's a good word for it."

"I knew, Hope. I knew when I saw you that first night in Mondawmin. *I knew.*"

"What...what did you see in me? What could you have possibly seen in me that night? I was mean. I was beyond mean, actually. So, what did you see in me?"

"I saw you as the first draft of a Nathaniel Dunn book."

She shot him a confused look. *"Now* what are you talking about?"

He shrugged. "Well, I assume that even the great Nathaniel Dunn's first draft isn't that great. He has to work on it. It's a work in progress. I saw *you* as a work in progress. And that's really what we all are. He sees us all as works in progress. Everyone gets that benefit. He's giving us that benefit. So, shouldn't we give it to one another?"

She smiled, caressed his cheek, and they kissed.

CHAPTER TWENTY-FOUR: VICTIM'S STATEMENT

Later that afternoon, he went shopping to get all the ingredients she would need for the dinner. He walked in with two brown paper shopping bags and a long, thin white box.

He set them down on the counter in the kitchen.

She came out to inspect the groceries. "Now, you did get this stuff in Little Italy, right? Because that's the best place in Baltimore to get authentic Italian ingredients."

He nodded. "Yes, ma'am. Sure did. Di Pasquale's on Gough Street, right smackdab in the heart of Little Italy. By the way, Don Fanucci says *hello*."

"Who?"

"Don Fanucci. He was a crime lord. Vito Corleone killed him in a flashback scene in the second *Godfather* film. Guess you didn't see that one, huh?"

"Guess not because I have no idea who you're talking about. The only thing I remember about the *Godfather* films was the awful scene with the horse's head. That made me sick."

"Yeah, I know what you're saying. As an animal lover, that's hard for me to watch, too. Unfortunately, it *was* a real horse's head. They got it from a slaughterhouse."

"I hate that."

"I do, too."

"Let's just stop talking about animal abuse, all right?"

He put his arms around her, pulled her into him, and kissed the top of her head. She gazed up at him.

"I got you something while I was out."

"Yeah?"

"Yeah." He broke off the embrace, picked the white box up off the countertop, and presented it to her.

"Here. These are for you. I wanted tonight to be special for you."

She opened the box and separated the tissue paper. "Oh, geez. More roses." She nodded. "Sweet. So sweet. Thank you." She kissed him.

He pulled out his phone. "Here. I'm going to play a song for us. Dance with me, will you?"

She emphatically shook her head. "No. No can do. I have to get this dinner started."

"What's the hurry? Huh? Where are either of us going? What? You have an audience with the Pope or something? Is that it? Or maybe you have an appointment to see The Great and Powerful Oz." He thought for a moment and added, "You know, he was downright nasty. Oz, that is. What a letdown. Not a nice guy. All angry at the world and whatnot. All full of himself. He had that poor old lion freaked out, biting his own tail and such. Then he proceeded to roast everyone. Ever notice that? Yeah. One by one, he dissed the whole bunch of them, even Dorothy. I mean, they braved flying monkeys for that man. He could have at least been polite."

She playfully smacked him on the arm. "You're silly."

He held out his hand. "Come on, I'm serious—dance with me. Sometimes, in life, you have to make time to dance. Right?"

She took his hand. "Yeah. I guess you're right."

He pulled his phone from his pocket and scrolled through his playlist. "Here. Here you go, Hope. We're going to make this *our song*. And it's coming straight from the heart." He talked in a deep, dramatic disc jockey voice. "Nineteen-hundred and sixty-one. From the movie *Blue Hawaii*. My main man, Elvis

Him-sel-vis—*Can't Help Falling in Love.*"

The song played. They put their arms around one another and gently swayed to the music.

He brushed her hair with his hand. "We can make this our song, can't we? It's such a pretty little song. It's downright gorgeous, is what it is."

She nodded. "We can make it our song."

He caressed her cheek with his palm. "Listen, I want you to know that, to me, sex is a physical expression of what I feel inside for you. I really believe that. I want you to believe it, too. Okay? I know I joke around a lot. But I'm serious about this. It's really important to me that you understand."

"I understand."

They danced their dance. And after the song was over, they held one another in an embrace. He kissed the top of her head. "Your hair smells so good. I've been meaning to ask you—what brand of shampoo do you use?"

"Wen Pomegranate."

"Nice. Now, can I ask you another question?"

"Sure. Go for it."

"Do you have a valid driver's license?"

She shot him a confused look. "Of course, I do. I'm a cop. What kind of question is that anyway?"

He shrugged. "Well, I just figured that it might have been suspended for being so beautiful that you *drive* all the guys crazy."

"Oh, It's not enough to tell bad jokes. Now, you're going to start with the cheesy pickup lines, too?"

"That wasn't cheesy. You want to hear cheesy? Here. I'll give you cheesy. This is *A Night at the Roxbury* kind of cheesy. He reached over her shoulder. She turned her head and watched as he pulled out the tag in the back of her shirt and examined it.

She laughed. "You nut! What are you even doing?"

He nodded. "Uh-huh. Just as I suspected. *Made. In. Heaven.*"

◆ ◆ ◆

After dinner, they each took a shower. He waited for her on the bed. She went into the adjacent bathroom and put on a royal blue lace matching bra and panty set. It didn't leave much to the imagination. Her large breasts were threatening to spill out. Over top of that, she put on her light blue police shirt, complete with badge. The bottom of the shirt hung down to just above her knees. She put her hair up and her police hat on. The look was topped off with a pair of mirrored aviator sunglasses. She wanted to fulfill his fantasy. *Please, God, let this go well. Let me be able to do this without freaking out. Let me be able to enjoy this.*

She sprayed on one pump of Angel and walked out the bathroom door and into the bedroom. She had her phone in hand. He lay on the bed, wearing a matching olive drab t-shirt and shorts set. The shirt and shorts each read *USMC* in black lettering and displayed the Marine Corps emblem. Bobby slept at the bottom of the bed. The lights were out but the room was illuminated by quite a few candles.

Luke picked up the cat. "I'm going to have him leave the room. After all, I'm his dad. And it would be really weird for us to, you know, *do it* with him in the room. It might traumatize him. And I wouldn't want to be responsible for that."

He opened the door and gently set the cat down in the hallway, patting his head. "Okay, Robert, the grownups are going to do some grownup things. You can come back when we're finished."

He closed the door and lay back down on the bed.

They smiled at one another.

"Well, here we are," he said.

"Yep. Here we are." She stretched out her hands over her head. "We are here."

He nodded approvingly. "You look sexy, girl. Really sexy."

She nodded back. "Thanks. I appreciate that. The truth of the matter is that I'm tense. Really tense, actually." She turned her palms upward, looked at them and nervously laughed. "My palms are even sweaty."

"You okay?"

"Oh, yeah. Yeah. I'm fine. It's just been a while since I've been with a guy."

"Same here." He thought for a moment and added, "Wait a second. Just to clarify—I've never been with a guy. What I meant was that it's been a while since I've been intimate with anyone. I mean, sure, Zac Efron's hot and all, but I certainly don't want to sleep with him...I guess I'm kind of, sort of, nervous, too."

"Yeah. It's natural to be nervous the first time you're with someone, you know?"

"Sure. Right. Totally natural."

"So, ah, let's, ah, let's just get into it. Let's start," she said.

"Yeah. Let's start. You have to start before you can finish."

She wagged her index finger at him. "Yes. Yes, you do. Finishing is almost always preceded by starting. So... that was a good point. A really good point."

She took a deep breath. *You can do this. You can.*

She scrolled through her phone's playlist and selected *I Know What Boys Like*. She danced for him. She'd looked at some of the YouTube tutorials on the art of striptease and had even practiced in front of the mirror.

Slowly, she rotated her hips to the left and her shoulders to the right. She smiled her best naughty smile and put her right hand on her right hip. Bending her back a bit, she leaned forward and waved her head sharply. Her hat fell off. She stood upright, ran her hands up her torso, and swung her hips from side to side. When her hands reached her breasts, she clutched them, squeezed them, and let out a low moan.

Am I doing this right or do I just look stupid? She looked to him for the answer. He had a big smile on his face. She could also see the classic *tent effect* in his shorts. *Must be doing something right.*

As she continued to dance, she gradually lost pieces of her outfit. First, she threw off her shades. She pulled the clip from her hair, shook her head, and her shiny black hair cascaded down. Finally, she slowly and deliberately unbuttoned her shirt. Ever so gradually, she slid it off her shoulders and let it fall to the floor. She stood before him in bra and panties. And she turned around, bent over, and grabbed her ankles, to give him a good view of her tight bubble butt. The song was ending.

He clapped and whistled a catcall. "Very nice! Lord have mercy, girl. You are a little heartbreaker, that's what you are. That was *hot*."

She could feel the heat of her face blushing. "Was that okay? Was that you're fantasy?"

He nodded. "And then some."

She climbed on top of him and straddled his chest. *So far, so good.*

Leaning forward, she passionately kissed him. As their lips met, their mouths opened. Their tongues grappled with one another. Her large, full breasts, barely contained by the bra, pressed against his chest. He ran his hands along her smooth, silky legs.

"Oh, good God, woman. Your boobs feel so good smashing up against me like that. They're so soft. And warm. And just… good. They're good. And your little legs are amazing, too."

She talked in a husky voice. "I think I need to strip search you, boy."

He threw his arms above his head in surrender. "I'm not going to resist, officer. But I should tell you before you begin that I am packing a concealed weapon."

"Yeah, and I know the penal code for that, too," she quipped.

She helped him remove his t-shirt. As she pulled the shirt up, she kissed his hairless chest. His chest was lean but not particularly muscular. She liked that. *Good. I never did care for muscle heads.*

They got the shirt over his head, pulled it off, and tossed it to the floor.

And then—she saw it.

On his left shoulder, he had a tattoo. It was the Marine Corps eagle, globe, and anchor. Below the emblem, were the Latin words, *Semper Fidelis*. She stopped and pointed to it.

She talked excitedly. "What's that, huh? What the hell's that?" *Oh, God! Why do you have to have a tattoo and why does it have to be on your left shoulder?*

It took her back to the night, two years prior, that she'd been assaulted. She replayed the attack in her mind's eye. It was all coming back again.

He turned his head to look at it. "Oh, you mean my tattoo?"

She raised her voice. "Yeah. Why did you get a damn tattoo?"

He shrugged. "Seemed like a good idea at the time. It's the only one that I have. I don't really care for tats, but I made an exception in this case."

"Why?"

"Because it's about the brotherhood. It's a tribute to all the guys who didn't make it home. Is there a problem here?"

She climbed off of him and started to cry. "Yeah. Big problem."

Sitting on the edge of the bed, she hung her head and sobbed.

He got up and sat next to her. Putting his arm around her, he spoke tenderly. "Hey, come on—what's wrong? Hmm? Talk to me."

"Put your shirt back on so I don't have to see that damn tattoo."

He put the t-shirt back on.

"You don't like tattoos?"

"No. I don't. Not at all. Okay?"

"Why not? You just think they're ugly or what?"

She put her head in her hands and talked through her tears. "*He* had one. On his left shoulder, just like you do."

"Who had one, Hope? Who?"

"Jason."

"Who's Jason? You're going to have to help me out here. I don't know Jason."

"My ex. Two years ago."

"Okay, so what about him? And what happened two years

ago?"

"I don't want to tell."

"We have to talk. Can you tell me what happened two years ago? Please. I need to know."

She lifted her head up and looked at the ceiling. "He broke into my house."

"And?"

She said nothing but just shook her head. Tears ran down her cheeks.

"Did he steal stuff?"

"Yeah. He stole things from me, all right…just not material stuff."

"What does that mean? Now's no time to talk in riddles."

"Oh, God." She paused for a second and screamed a blood-curdling scream. *"God!"*

He spoke gently, in a near whisper. "Tell me what Jason did, Hope. Tell me."

She took a deep breath. *Just say it. Go on—say it. There's no easy way to tell him so just tell him. Blurt it out. Who were you ever fooling? It was bound to come out, bound to end this way.*

She again screamed. "I got raped! *I! Got! Raped!* The son of a bitch drugged and raped me!"

"What?"

"You heard me. Don't make me say it again."

"Where is he, huh? This Jason character—where is he? Is he still walking the streets?"

"No. He's at the Jessup House of Corrections and most likely will be for the rest of his life."

"That's a good thing for him because if he were walking the streets, I'd hunt his ass down and I'd hurt him. I'd want to hurt him very badly."

There was silence—awkward silence—for several seconds. She wailed.

Finally, he spoke in a near whisper. "I don't know what to say."

She talked through her tears. "Of course, you don't. Nobody

does. Nobody wants to talk to the girl who got raped about the rape."

"It's just that it's…it's hitting me like a ton of bricks. I'm trying to process it. Right now, I'm kind of freezing up like a computer with too many windows open. The only thing I can think to say right at the moment is that I am very sorry that this happened to you. That you…that you got—" He abruptly stopped.

She glared at him. "You can't even say it, can you?"

He just stared at her with a confused, pained look on his face.

"I don't blame you, Luke. Rape. It's a dirty word, isn't it? It just sounds nasty—*rape*. Whoever came up with that word did a good job capturing the filthiness of that act, didn't they?

"Consider this my *victim's statement*. Yeah—you were right. Everybody has a war story to tell. This is mine. Now you know. And here's the worse part—after he raped me, while I was still unconscious from the Ketamine, he went into the kitchen, got an ice pick, and stabbed my cat to death. Yeah, he did. You know the cat whose pictures are all over my house? Well, that was Desi. And he was my best friend. And I loved him. Like a child, I loved him."

She turned her gaze upward and sobbed. For the first time since it happened, she totally broke down. The faucet of her anguish was turned on so as to allow for maximum flow. She talked to the deceased cat. "Oh, God, Desi—I love you. Momma loves you, baby boy. I miss you. *I loved you best. I loved you best.* You were the best boy. The day that I got you from the animal shelter was one of the happiest days of my life. You were my favorite *hello* and my hardest *goodbye*. And that motherfucker stabbed you over twenty times. And he put you on my chest. And I can never, ever forget that look in your lifeless eyes. That startled, surprised look. Like you were shocked that Momma didn't protect you. You're gone from my life but never from my heart."

Luke cried, too, and kissed her on the forehead. "God, I am

so, so sorry. I knew something really bad had happened to you, but I had no idea it was this. If I could go back in time and prevent it, I would. If I could take all your hurt away and put it on myself, I would. I absolutely would."

She wiped the tears away. "On the outside, I pretend that I don't like cats because it hurts so much. God, it hurts. Every day, it hurts. But I love them. They're innocent. They're hearts are pure. But I don't deserve to have another one. I couldn't protect Desi. I was his mom, and I couldn't protect him. I failed. I'm a failure. I'm responsible for his death. It's my fault. So, it's easier to just pretend that I don't even like them. It's easier on my mind, on my heart, that way."

"Oh, no. No—no—no. You can't think like that. It's not your fault."

"You're saying all the right things, but it *is* my fault. It's my fault that I got raped, too."

"Oh, God, no. Not you're fault. Please don't think that way. You can't think that way, Hope."

"It was. *It. Was.* He wasn't a random stranger. I knew him. I dated him. And I was already a cop by then. I should have known better. I should have been a better judge of character. I should have done a background check on him and I would have found out that he was a sex offender. But I didn't think that would be fair to him, so I didn't. I was trusting and I got burned. I should have been able to steer clear of a guy like him. But I didn't. Bottom line—I didn't."

"You can't blame yourself for the evil that other people do. It's *not* your fault, honey. Not even remotely your fault. Now, let me ask you this—are you in counseling?"

"No. I tried counseling. It didn't help."

"How long did you go for?"

She hesitated. "Two...two sessions."

"Two sessions...that's...that's nothing. It's not going to be better after two sessions. It took me a few months before I saw results. But counseling is a very important component of the healing process."

"You sound just like Harris. She told me the exact same thing."

"Well, I think she's right."

She shook her head. "Luke, this isn't going to work."

"What's not?"

"*Us.*"

"Why? Why do you say that?"

She took a deep breath and loudly exhaled. "Well, it's like this—you're the first guy I've been involved with on any level since it happened. And I thought I was ready to be intimate with a guy again. But I saw that tattoo of yours and it set me back. I had no idea it was going to hit me so hard."

"I'll get the tattoo removed. And in the meantime, I'll cover it. Okay? That's no big deal."

"You shouldn't have to have it removed."

"Yes, I should. If it makes you hurt, I should."

"It doesn't matter. This…this…*fiasco* tonight reminded me that I'm not ready to be intimate with a guy yet. After two years, I'm still not ready. I thought I was. And I want to be. I really do. It's not like I don't like sex. People think that women who get raped don't want to be intimate afterwards. Not true. At least in my case, it's not. Everyone who's had this happen responds differently. There really isn't a typical reaction. For me, I *want* to be intimate. I want to. And I thought I could. I was willing to try. I thought I was ready. But I was wrong. But I just wanted to be close to you, as close as two people can be. I wanted to show you how I feel."

"That's okay. I can wait."

"How long, huh? Because I don't know when I'll be ready. I can't tell you. Maybe I'll be ready next week. Maybe next month. Maybe six months from now. Maybe two years. Maybe *never.* He took things from me, Luke. Precious things. He took my baby away from me. Before you, Desi was the only male figure I've ever had in my life who really treated me right. So, he took that away. And he took away my ability to be a complete woman. Because a complete heterosexual woman has the ability to have and enjoy sex with her man. And I just found out that I can't do that yet. I'm still not ready. And I don't know when I will be."

"Honey, we can deal with this together."

"You say that now but what if, a year from now, we're still not having sex? Huh? What then? And what if we get married and you can't make love to your wife on your wedding night because she's nuts? Is that going to be a happy home? Is it?"

"We can take it one day at a time. I want to be with you. What you just told me doesn't change that basic fact."

She threw up her hands and yelled at him, "Don't you get it? I'm tainted! I'm ruined! I am spoiled! I'm like that ham sandwich that you put in the fridge and then forget about. And two weeks later, you start to smell this horrible stench coming from the kitchen. It smells like death itself. And you finally open the fridge and find the rotten sandwich. And it's all nasty. All greasy. And it makes you gag. Yeah, well, that's me on the *inside.* I'm not a real woman anymore. A real woman can make love to her man. And I feel like shit that I can't. Because you're a great guy. The best. Thee. Best. And you deserve better. Just like Desi deserved better. We can't see each other anymore. I'm sorry, but we just can't."

"What? You have to be kidding."

"Not kidding. You need to move on. Find a real woman, a normal woman."

"Hope, in case you haven't noticed—I'm not normal myself."

"Then all the more reason for us not to be together. It's a huge gamble. We're a longshot."

"Well guess what? He loves to gamble. And He bets on longshots. Always has. In fact, He *only* bets on longshots. The longer the better. And I'll bet He's betting on us."

"I wish I could believe that."

"So, you're just going to give up then?"

"Yeah. And I'm doing you a favor. You'll one day thank me. I'm breaking up with you. And not because I don't care about you. But because *I do.* And you deserve better. You deserve the best, in fact. So, yeah, I'm officially giving up."

"*Uh-huh. Uh-huh.* You know what I think?"

"What's that?"

He pointed at her. "I think somebody should have joined the Army."

"What? What are you *even* talking about?"

He repeated himself. "Somebody should have joined the Army. That's what Sergeant Valentine used to say when someone in the platoon wasn't putting out the maximum effort expected of Marines. He'd point out the individual in question and say—*somebody should have joined the fuckin' Army.*"

"I don't want to hear any more of the wit and wisdom of the United States Marine Corps."

"Well, you're going to because it *is* wisdom. What the DIs taught us in boot camp was that when the enemy has you surrounded you have two choices. You can surrender—give up. Or you can start working on a way to improve your tactical situation. You accept the reality of your predicament—yes. But you work to improve it. Well, what are we going to do, Hope, to improve our tactical situation? Huh?"

"Not see one another anymore, that's what."

"That's giving up and Marines never give up. And, by the way—don't I get a say in this?"

"No. You don't. Like I said—you'll eventually thank me. Go find yourself a nice, normal girl. You're a great guy. Maybe it's not too late to get with Gretchen Cavanaugh."

"I don't want Gretchen Cavanaugh. I want *you.*"

"You say that now, but sex is an important part of a relationship. It is. That's just the reality of it. It's a big part of life, too. You could argue that it makes the world go round. Without sex, the human species would die out. I can't be a real woman to you right now—don't you *get* that? And it makes me feel shame. And it embarrasses me because I can't be fucking normal."

"This fight's not over yet. It's only in the middle rounds.

Don't you quit on me, Hope. Please don't quit. I don't know much about sexual assault, but I have heard it's more about control than anything. If you give up, if you quit, he wins because that means he's still controlling you. Even from behind bars, he's in control. Don't give him that victory."

"You don't know how it feels."

"No, honey, I don't. And I am so, so, so sorry that you do. I would give anything to change that. But no one can change the past. Not even God can change the past."

"Look—I just want to go home."

"And do what? You're only twenty-eight-years old. You've most likely got at least another half century left in this world. Are you going to just be alone for the next fifty -plus years? Not even going to allow yourself the company of a cat? That's a long, long time to be alone. I knew when we first met that we were kindred spirits, that we both had a bruised, purple heart. Let's move forward. *Together.* I still want you, Hope. I do."

"No. You don't. You can't. I can't stand myself. How can anyone else stand me? I almost got you killed. You just feel sorry for me, that's all. You feel sorry for the girl who got raped."

"*Semper Fidelis*. You know what that means? Huh? It's Latin. It means—*Always Faithful*. I'm loyal and faithful to those who I care about. I want you in my life. I *want* you."

"I have way too much baggage."

"Then I'll help you carry it."

"You shouldn't have to."

"I want to."

"You shouldn't have to worry about this shit. It makes me feel guilty as hell."

"We have something good. You make me feel good. When I'm with you—I feel better about myself. I was lonely before you came along. But you made me not lonely. And I'd like to think that maybe I did the same for you. It's nuts to throw that away."

She shook her finger at him. "Bingo. *I'm nuts.* You should

have known that the first time you met me."

He tried to hug her. "You're just frustrated right now. This is frustration talking, nothing more. I know it is."

She pulled away and got up. "Take me home. Please. I want to go home."

"We need to talk some more. Let me make some coffee and we can talk this out."

"No. I want to go home. I don't want to see you anymore. And it's because I care, not because I don't. So, don't call. Don't email. Don't post on social media. Don't stop by. I'll ignore you."

"Listen, there's no pressure. For the time being—let's forget about sex. Let's just take that right off the table altogether. And let's focus on getting you some help. That's all that matters at this point. I'll go to counseling with you, if it would help. I'll sit there and hold your hand the entire time."

"And that is so incredibly sweet. And that's why I can't let you do that. I can't let you waste the best years of your life on me. That would be selfish, and it's time for me to stop being selfish."

"You know, I thought I could never feel a pain greater than what I felt in Afghanistan, when bad things happened over there. But this hurts more. You're breaking my heart."

"Better that it gets broken now than later. Now, please take me home. And if you won't, I'll call the station and get them to send a patrol car over to pick me up."

"Wait. Please wait. There's something I want to give you. Okay?"

"What? What do you want to give me? There's nothing you could possibly give me that could change my mind."

He walked over to the closet door, opened it, and pulled out a small safe. He set it on his desk.

Pointing to the safe, he told her, "What I have to give you—it's in here."

"What could possibly be in that safe that would change things?"

"There's something in here that could. You'll have to decide that."

The safe was a digital safe with a keypad on the front. She watched as he pulled out his wallet and frantically looked for something.

"I'm looking for the combination. I can't remember it, but I thought I had it written down on a slip of paper. And I'm sure I put that slip in my wallet. But that was several wallets ago. This safe only has one item in it. And it hasn't been opened since I deposited that item, ten years ago."

He walked over to the bed, sat down, took every single item out of the wallet, and sifted through it all. "Damn! It's not here. It's not here. I must have inadvertently thrown it out when I switched wallets."

Looking at her, he pleaded, "Please, just bear with me. *Please.* I'll call a locksmith. Yeah—that's what I'll do. There are ones that are available twenty-four-seven and I'll bet I could get one here within a couple of hours and—"

She cut him off. "I've already told you—it's pointless. There's nothing in that safe that will change anything. I've made up my mind. This is best for both of us. I should have realized all this right from the start, and for that I'm sorry. I'm sorry that I led you on. Now, take me home. I want to go home."

He took a deep breath, loudly exhaled, and scratched his head. "Fine. You want to go? Get dressed. I'll take you home."

"I'm sorry, Luke. I should have told you all this before tonight. I should have told you right from the get-go. But I couldn't. And there's just no easy way. How do you tell someone? Do you casually announce it at the dinner table and be all like—*hey, could you please pass the salt…oh, and by the way, I got raped by my ex-boyfriend two years ago? And he stabbed my cat to death, too.* How do you say that? How do you even broach that topic?"

"Don't blame yourself for any of this."

"Well, I do because it is all my fault. I got mixed up with a loser. And that was by choice. And, in life, we have to answer for our choices. If I hadn't gotten in with him, he wouldn't have raped me. And Desi would still be alive. And I'm sorry that I dragged you into the mess that is my life. But, even with everything that's happened, deep down, I still wanted love. Yeah—like every other human being who has ever walked the planet, I crave love. There. I admit it. And that's a hard thing for me to admit because it makes me feel vulnerable as hell. And I've said my piece. I've tried to explain things to you as best I can. So, let's just treasure the time we had. I know I will. But I have to go. I do."

They got dressed and she got her things together. He picked up Joey, the virtual cat, and handed him to her.

"You may as well take him with you. He is yours, after all."

She screamed. "Dammit! It's a machine, a robot. He was never real. It's an *it* and not a *him.* Because it's just a damn machine, a toy. But I don't even deserve to have a virtual cat."

She hurled Joey across the room. He slammed up against the wall and his left front leg fell off. The impact turned him on, and he meowed and purred.

He took her home. There was silence in the car. But when they got to her house, before she got out, she reached over and hugged him. She cried. "You've given me some wonderful memories. Memories that I will treasure. *Forever.* For one brief, shining moment, I knew what it felt liked to be loved."

She got out of the car and he called out to her. "Hey…"

She turned around. They looked at one another, looked each other in the eyes.

"I'm not going to give up—you do realize that, right? At Parris Island, the DIs used to tell us—we *will not give up on you even after some of you have given up on yourselves.* Well, that's my attitude, too. I'm not giving up on you. I still have hope, Hope. I've been searching for you my entire life, and now that I've finally found you, I'm not giving up."

She wiped tears from her eyes. "Yeah. Well. Whatever." She turned and ran to her front door.

CHAPTER TWENTY-FIVE: THE FINAL BELL

the following evening

The locksmith was named Earl, according to the embroidery on his navy, pinstriped work shirt. He wore matching Dickies workpants and black boots. He was thin and balding. Luke detected the distinct scent of British Sterling. It was overpowering.

Earl sat on the bed and worked on the safe. After a half-hour of trying various tools and techniques, he looked up at Luke with exasperation. "Sir, I can't get this thing open without drilling. This is a Sentry, and Sentry makes them right. I can get it open for you, but it'll ruin the safe. You good with that?"

"Do what you need to do. I don't care about the damn safe—only what's inside."

"As long as you don't go on Yelp or Google Reviews afterwards and say that I wrecked your expensive safe. That's all I care about."

"I wouldn't do that to you."

"Uh-huh. That's what they all say."

"Well, I won't. I promise."

Earl got his drill out and plugged it in. "You want to put a towel or something under the safe before I start drilling? Because this drill's going to throw metal shavings on the bed."

"I'll vacuum after you're done. Just open it, Please."

"Suit yourself." Earl smiled and patted the top of the safe. "Must be something pretty valuable in here, huh? You're authorizing the destruction of an expensive safe and you're paying three-hundred bucks for me to do it. Oh, and you do realize that, right? It's eight-thirty. Anything after five constitutes emergency after-hours service. That's an extra hundred and fifty. And I don't take checks, either. Cash or major credit card only. The dispatcher did tell you all that over the phone, didn't she?"

"I don't care what it costs. Just open the safe. *Earl*. And don't worry about what's inside. It's personal and private. That's why it's in a safe."

"Yeah. Sure. I'm not trying to pry or anything." Earl thought for a moment and added, "Well, actually, I am trying to pry, if you know what I mean." He patted the top of the safe and laughed. "I'm trying to pry this son of a bitch open."

Luke didn't laugh. Instead, he glared at Earl with his arms crossed. "Yeah, well then get to work because I need this open tonight."

After ten minutes of drilling, he finally opened the safe and looked inside. He pulled out a white, business-sized envelope and held it up for Luke to see. The Marine emblem was in the upper left-hand corner.

He handed it to Luke. "That was the only thing in there. You just spent three-hundred bucks to have me open a safe that contained one envelope. I don't get it, bud."

"No, you don't get it because what's in this envelope is not for you. *Bud*." *I'm probably being a little short with him, but I'm stressed and he's too damn nosy.*

Luke paid him with a credit card.

Earl lingered at the front door and loudly cleared his voice. "Ahem."

Luke threw up his hands. "Yes? Can I help you? You need something?"

Earl shrugged. "Well, it's just that, you know, it is customary, especially for the after-hours stuff, to tip your technician."

"You want a tip, Earl?"

Earl held out his right hand. "Yeah. Sure. Lay it on me. It'd help make me feel better about this job, since folks who tip are satisfied customers."

"Here. Here's your tip—at three-hundred bucks for less than an hour's worth of work, you can afford a better cologne. There you go. Now, if you'll excuse me, I have to make some plans for this evening. So, Good. Day. Sir."

Earl started to leave, looking dejected. As he walked out the door, Luke called him back, pulled a twenty from his wallet, and handed it to him. "Sorry, man. I'm a little moody right now. Here. Take this. It was going to be my Starbucks money for the week, but, you know, I'd like you to have it as a token of my gratitude. Thanks for coming out. Hopefully, you just played a role in shaping the rest of my life."

"Really? How so?"

Luke held up the envelope. "I hope what's inside this envelope will convince the woman who I love that I love her."

"Yeah? Well, if it all works out, how about naming your first kid after me? *Earl.*"

Luke put his arm around him. "Listen, bro, you got three-hundred bucks and a twenty dollar tip. Let's just call it even at this point, shall we?"

He patted him on the back and guided Earl out the door.

◆ ◆ ◆

Luke lay on his bed, petting Hannah, who was sprawled out on his chest. He wore a pair of blue jeans and a plain black sweatshirt. He looked at his wall clock. It was five after ten.

He picked the cat up and set her down next to him. "It's time for me to rock and roll, girl."

He made a call to *The Midnight Ranger Show* and requested a song. He asked that they wait fifteen minutes before playing it.

Then he called Hope. She didn't answer. He didn't leave a message. Instead, he called back. *She doesn't want to answer? Fine. I'll just keep calling. I'll blow up her damn phone.*

Finally—after the eighth call—she picked up.

She raised her voice. "What? What the hell do you want? You're driving me freaking crazy. My ringtone is a bell chiming and now I'm going to hear that bell in my sleep because you won't stop calling. You're making a pest out of yourself—you do realize that, don't you?"

"If you didn't want to talk to me, all you had to do was turn off the phone."

"I was using it to read my email, okay? Do you want me to turn it off? Because I can. And that way I won't have to put up with your BS. If you really want me to, I'll gladly do that."

"No. I don't want you to do that. I'm glad you answered. My entire plan for this evening hinged on you answering this call. Everything depended on you answering the final bell. *And you did.*"

"What *plan*? What the hell are you talking about?"

"I need you to do a few things for me tonight."

"It's after ten. What could you possibly need me to do at this hour? And what makes you believe that I'd be willing to do anything for you at this point? I told you I wanted a clean break. You make it harder for me when you pull this shit. Is that what you're trying to do—make things harder for me than they already are?"

"Look—I hate to play this card, but it's the only card I have left to play. So, here goes—you owe me, lady. I saved your life. And you owe me. And I want to cash-in now. Right now."

"What? What do you want me to do?"

"To start with—tune in *The Midnight Ranger Show.* In a little while, they're going to play a song. And it's for you. From Luke to Hope. And after you hear the song, meet me at the feeding location for the Mondawmin Seven. Right there in the alley between the liquor store and porn shop."

"Mondawmin? This late at night? You must be out of your freaking mind."

"You're a cop. Bring your gun. And I guarantee it'll be safe. I've already got the security taken care of."

"Anything you have to say to me, you can say over the

phone."

"I have some things to *give* to you. Some things that are yours."

"What? What do you have of mine?"

"For starters, you're winning lottery ticket. In your rush to leave yesterday, you forgot to take it."

"Oh, for God's sake—it's worth a grand total of eighty bucks. I don't care about it. Cash it and donate it to Recycled Love. Buy some food for the cats."

"No can do. Not my money. If you want to cash it and donate it, well, that's your business."

"This couldn't have been done earlier? When it was still light out?"

"I was busy today. I spent the day doing some research online. Then, I went down to Pratt Library to do some more research, checked out some books and such. Took care of some other matters, as well."

There was a pause.

She loudly exhaled. "Fine. I'll listen to the damn radio. And I'll even meet you in Mondawmin. But this is *it*. Really, it is. We aren't going to keep playing these games. And I'm only doing this because I owe you. But this is it. This is your repayment. After tonight, we're even. Understand?"

"Yeah. I understand. Just turn on your radio. And after you hear the song, meet me in Mondawmin."

He hung up.

Turning on his radio, he tuned it to 104.5

After a commercial for the Quigley Funeral Home, which encouraged listeners to "get laid to rest with the best," The Midnight Ranger told his audience, "Well, kids, the Hope and Luke trail has been kind of cold lately, kind of like the search for DB Cooper. I don't think he survived the jump, by the way. DB Cooper, that is. And I'm normally all-in on conspiracy theories. For example, I totally believe Tupac's still alive and living in a Tijuana trailer park, where he's employed as maintenance supervisor. Anyhow...we've just had a call from a gentleman purporting to be Luke himself. Yes, gang—*Thee* Luke. He's broken his silence. And he has a message for Hope. He said that he believes she's listening tonight. Well, Hope, if you're tuned in, here's his message—*Go the distance with me.* And in that same spirit—here's a little tune from one of the greatest sleeper hits of all-time. Sly Stallone. Nineteen hundred and seventy-six. Best Picture. I was a baby when this film was a hit. Anyway, it's the theme to one of the greatest movies ever made. I could have done without all the sequels because they never recaptured the magic of the original. You know what I'm talking about, right, folks? Well, of course, you do. It's the theme from *Rocky*. Go the distance, Hope. He wants you to go the distance with him."

He listened to the song and then headed to his rendezvous. *This is either going to be one of the best nights of my life or one of the worst. Either way, it'll be a night to remember.*

CHAPTER TWENTY-SIX: THE ONE

She drove through the streets of the city in her black, late model Jeep Wrangler. It was yet another cold night. The overnight low was supposed to be around twenty. A light snow fell. It wasn't supposed to amount to much. A coating, maybe an inch, tops.

She was all bundled up, wearing a thick pair of blue jeans and a baby blue crewneck over top of a white turtleneck. She also wore white sneakers, mittens, and a black leather jacket. On her head was a black stocking cap that had the Baltimore Police logo on it. But she'd forgotten her glasses.

When she arrived at the feeding location, she noticed two Baltimore Police patrol cars parked at either end of the alley, blocking access to it. *What the hell? What are two units doing here? Is something going down?* She parked along the side of the street.

Approaching from the north end, she walked up to the police cruiser and saw that it was Corporal Coffey, a heavyset African-American cop in his thirties. Coffey was eating an Egg McMuffin and sipping coffee. He rolled down his window. "I'm really digging this all-day breakfast thing that McDonald's has going on. They better not ever stop doing it. I'll be pissed. I'll write a letter to Mister McDonald."

"Uh-huh. What's going on? Why you here?"

Coffey shrugged. "Deterring crime."

She shot him a leery look.

"Look, Kennedy—I do what I'm told. Harris told me and

Ramos to sit at opposite ends of this alley for a little bit tonight. And that's just fine by me. It's like getting an extra break. Oh, by the way—how's your ribs?"

Hope nodded. "Coming along, I guess."

Coffey took a big bite of his sandwich and talked with his mouth full. "Yeah, well, he's already here. He's already in the alley waiting."

She tentatively walked into the alley and saw him leaning up against the porn shop's wall with his hands in his jacket pockets. He wore blue jeans, white sneakers, and his purple satin Ravens jacket.

He walked up to her and waved. "Hey."

"Hey," she said meekly.

He lectured her. "Where are your glasses? Huh? You shouldn't be driving—especially at night—without them. You know that, don't you?"

She rolled her eyes and threw up her hands in exasperation. "I forgot them, okay? I had other things on my mind."

"Yeah, well, it's dangerous. At night, you need to be able to see your best because, even though we're in the city and all, there are deer around. And they'll just dart right out in front of you. And that happens because us humans keep closing in, keep encroaching, on their territory. I saw a show about it on Animal Planet and they said—"

She cut him off. "Did you bring me here to give a lesson in wildlife conservation or what?"

"No. That's not why I brought you here." He pulled out his wallet, retrieved her winning lottery ticket and handed it to her.

She looked at it, nodded, and put it in her pocket. "Thanks… I guess."

"How do you like the security arrangements?" he asked.

"Oh, so you're the one responsible for that?"

"Yeah. I called in a favor. See, the day after the accident, Sergeant Harris called me to apologize. She said if she could ever do anything for me, to let her know. Well, tonight she could, so I did."

"You're just calling in favors left and right, aren't you?"

"Might as well. If tomorrow earth gets sucked in to a blackhole and the world ends, I'd hate to have uncashed favors still floating around out there, you know?"

"Uh-huh. Well, I got my ticket so, I guess this is it. This is goodbye. Huh?" She looked around, looked at the alley and noted, "This is where it all began. How appropriate. It *ends* where it *began*."

He took her hands in his and shook his head. "No, Hope. It begins where it began."

She pulled her hands away and shook her head. "No. We've already been through this. Just no! The answer is—*no*."

"Come on, Hope. Go the distance with me. Please. Go the distance."

"But I'm scared."

He pulled out a white envelope from the inner pocket of his jacket and held it out to her. "Here. Open this and read what's inside. If—after you read it—you never want to see me again, you don't have to. That's all I ask. Deal?"

She looked at him with suspicion but nonetheless took the envelope and tentatively nodded. "Yeah. Fine. Okay. Deal."

He told her about what was in the envelope. "It's a letter. A letter written ten years ago. It was written seven thousand miles from here, in a combat zone. And it was written by a young Marine. A young Marine who was scared, scared that he'd never make it home. Scared that he'd die. More than that —scared that he'd die without ever knowing what it felt like to be in love. That was that young Marine's greatest fear. And this letter has been sitting in a safe for the last decade. It hasn't seen the light of day since I got home. I've never even come close to giving it to anyone. And I *sure as hell* wasn't going to give it to Gretchen Cavanaugh. But, tonight, I'm giving it to you. It's for you, Hope. It's yours." There were tears in his eyes. "Open it. Read it. *Please*."

With trembling hands, she tore open the envelope. Slowly,

she unfolded it. It was on Marine Corps letterhead; the Marine emblem was at the top.

She had difficulty reading it in the dim light and shook her head in disgust. "*Gawd.* I really should have worn my glasses." She pulled out her phone and activated the flashlight feature. With her free hand, she focused the light on the paper.

On the letterhead, was a poem. A simple poem, written in black ink. It was war zone poetry. Tears ran down both of her cheeks as she scanned it. With a shaky voice, she read it aloud —

"The One
By Lance Corporal Luke D. Matthews, USMC

*If I make it home
I'm going to search for you
Maybe in your dreams
You're searching for me, too
And when the day arrives
For me to lay down my gun
I'll travel to the ends of earth
To find you, my love—The One
I'll search high and low
Until the End of Time
I'll search low and high
Until your love is mine
See, I've never found true love
And have always felt cursed by fate
Like The Fourth Wise Man, the one no one's ever heard of
Because he arrived one day too late
So, each evening in this Hell of war
I ask the Keeper of the Stars
To send me a piece of Heaven—a human angel
To help erase my scars
This letter has seen the crucible of battle
In distant, far off lands*

> *But now, this letter is back home*
> *And finally in your hands*
> *You see, if you're reading this letter*
> *It means my search is done*
> *Because if someone ever reads this letter*
> *Then, Someone...you're The One."*

"You're *The One*, Hope. The One and Only. We can get you into counseling. I'll help you find the best counselor in Baltimore, someone who specializes in sexual assault cases. And I'll go with you. I'll hold your hand the entire time. I spent the day today at the library. I checked out books on sexual assault. I did research online. I went to the Women's Health Center and did more research. I went to a tattoo parlor and they started working on removing my tat. It might take about four or five sessions before it's completely gone, but in the meantime, I'll cover it. Then I went down to the Recycled Love shelter. I put Desi's name on the Tree of Memories. It's a special tree we have that celebrates the lives of animal friends who've gone to the Rainbow Bridge. And I went on your Facebook page and found pictures of him. I used them to make a video tribute. It's a photo montage set to the song, *In My Life*. I'll let you look at it, and, if you like it, we can upload it to YouTube. So that the entire world will be able to see what an awesome, special cat he was. I did all that. To *show* you how I feel. I want to be with you. You and only you. I know some days won't be easy. I realize that sometimes it'll be hard. I'm used to hard. Parris Island was *hard*. Afghanistan was *hard*. Coping on a daily basis with what happened at that roadblock is *hard*. But I'm not going anywhere. I won't quit on you, Hope. Marines don't quit. We never give up. Never surrender. *Never*. We're Always Faithful. And I want us to work through this together. No matter what."

By now, she was crying hard. Still, she managed to ask, "No matter what?"

"No. Matter. What. That's why they call it *unconditional* love, Hope."

He pulled out a bag of cat treats from his jacket pocket and shook it. "Bunky, come here, buddy. Come here, dude." He whistled and clapped his hands.

The little feline came running out from behind the dumpster, as did some of the other cats. He sprinkled the ground with treats and picked up Bunky. The other cats scattered. He gently caressed him in his arms and stroked his head. The young cat was now completely domesticated, purring and kneading.

He held him out to her. "Here, Hope. Take him. Please take him. *Take this life.*"

She took Bunky in her arms and cradled him like a baby. She scratched him under the chin and kissed the top of his head. Though she was still crying, she whispered, "Hey, baby. I'm gonna be your mama. I'm gonna love you."

Next, he told her, "Now, take *my* life. Take my whole life, too."

Through her tears, she replied, "For I can't help…"

And in that cold, filthy alley, they simultaneously sang these words to one another: *"Fall-ing in love…wiiiith…yoooou."*

Then, finally, he told her what was in the note that Charlotte's mom gave him.

And with Bunky between them—purring—they passionately kissed as a light snow fell.

EPILOGUE: CHARLOTTE'S SONG (THIS MEDAL YOU GAVE)

six months later

Hope and Luke stood at the altar of the Cathedral of Mary Our Queen. It was a beautiful summer day in Baltimore. Blue skies and not too hot. No humidity, either. A gentle breeze blew. A good day to get married. After the ceremony, they were jetting off to Las Vegas for the honeymoon. He'd secured two front-row seats to The Wayne Newton Show for the following evening at Caesar's Palace.

She was going to counseling sessions every week, making good progress. He went with her and held her hand. They'd just bought a new house together, in the Mount Vernon section of the city. A new home. A fresh start. A place where they could have the three cats who now made up their little family.

So, there they stood at the altar.

He wore a traditional tuxedo, and she wore a lovely white lace wedding dress, complete with veil and train.

Dino was best man.

The Midnight Ranger and Stormin' Greg Norman were there, as was Sergeant Harris. They'd all been spotted before the ceremony began.

But they both wondered about the status of one particular invitation. A very special invitation.

The note Charlotte's mother had passed to Luke that day in Tiffany's Diner requested that, should there ever be a wedding, that Charlotte be invited. She'd included all of her contact information.

Luke was true to his word, his promise. He'd sent both Grace and Charlotte an invitation, followed-up with an email, and even a message via Facebook. But he'd never heard back, never received an RSVP. And they hadn't been seen in the crowd before the ceremony.

So, they stood there facing one another, about to recite their vows.

The church was quiet. Totally quiet, as the priest fumbled around, searching his Bible for the right passage.

And then they both heard it. A little girl's voice loudly called out to them—"Hey, Elvis and Priscilla!"

They turned their heads. And they saw her. They saw a smile in the fifth row. Charlotte and Grace Madden were sitting in the fifth row, in the first and second seats in, respectively.

Charlotte's hair had grown back, and she wore it braided. It was shiny and very red. Her smile revealed perfect white teeth. She wore a gorgeous pink dress. And she was beautiful. That day, she was truly Beautiful.

She waved, pumped her little fist, and shouted, "Way to go, guys! *Way to go!*"

They smiled and waved back—both had tears in their eyes.

After the ceremony, they stood at the back of the church, greeted, and thanked each person in the receiving line.

Grace tentatively approached them. She hugged each of them and offered congratulations.

Luke smiled at her. "I'm so glad you could make it. When we didn't get an RSVP, I was worried. I thought maybe something happened. But it was so wonderful for us to see Charlotte here today, looking so strong and healthy. Charlotte's a big part of our story. She'll always be a part of our life. She'll be special to

Hope and I. After all, she helped us fall in love."

Grace started to cry. "You saw Charlotte today?"

Hope nodded. "Yes. Of course, we did. She's around here somewhere, isn't she? We saw her sitting right next to you. She called out to us during the ceremony. She waved to us. You didn't notice that?"

Grace sobbed. "Charlotte left on a jet plane. She died at Mercy Medical Center three days ago. The seat next to me was empty. Empty the entire time. She so wanted to live long enough to be able to attend you guys' wedding. That was her only goal during the last couple months of her life. To live long enough to see *Elvis and Priscilla,* as she called you two, get married. I didn't RSVP because I wasn't sure whether she'd make it or not. And I just couldn't email you right before your wedding and tell you she'd died. I just couldn't do that to you. I didn't want to ruin your big day. It's hard—*so hard*—for me to be here today. But I thought I had to come. She'd want me to come, you know? And I wanted to bring your Purple Heart with me, so I could return it to you. But this morning, I couldn't find it. She wore it everywhere. She wore it as she died. She was so proud of that medal. And before they took her to the funeral home, I unpinned it from her Winnie-the-Pooh pajamas and put it in my purse. I know I put it on my nightstand. It was there just last night. I saw it. But this morning, it was gone. I don't know what happened to it. I'm sorry. So sorry."

For several seconds, there was silence. And they all just cried.

And then Dino approached them. He was holding a large white envelope.

He handed it to Luke. "Special delivery, buddy. A guy just handed this to me and said you need to open it pronto. As in— right now. He said it's a wedding present, a very special wedding present. And get this—this dude looked like John Legend. You know—the legend, John Legend. He said his name's Michael, but you and Hope know him as Doctor Mike."

Grace wiped tears from her eyes. "Doctor Mike? He was the

doctor who was with Charlotte when she died. And—yes—he looked just like John Legend. That's him! That's him!"

Luke and Hope looked at one another for a couple of seconds. Just stared at each other.

Finally, Luke took a deep breath and opened the envelope. His hands trembled. He pulled out a lovely, white wedding card. On the front was a couple walking hand-in-hand on a beach at sunset.

He opened the card, and he and Hope both looked at what was written on the inside.

It was a poem. A child's poem. Or, rather, two poems, merged together, and written in red crayon. And it wasn't Shakespeare. And it wasn't Keats. But it was something. Luke read it aloud—

"Charlotte's Song (This Medal You Gave)

I got my wings the other day
Doctor Mike was there to show me The Way

My time in this world was short,
and that makes me feel blue

But for God to take my cancer away, He had
to take my life. My whole life, too!

Now, I'm gone, and your memories are all that are left

But please guys, please remember this—promises
were made, and promises were kept

So, remember me and be happy
because our meeting was a Gift from Above

Remember me often and fondly, guys,
and remember me always...with love

Now, as for this medal: this medal you gave
—it was a source of great pride

And on this, your special day, this medal
and I were both there by your side

This medal you gave—I kept it pristine
I wore it with dignity, like the bravest Marine

This medal you gave—it stuck to me like glue

But today, this medal you gave, this precious badge
of honor, this Purple Heart, I give back to you

It was never really mine, except as a loaner

And now, like me, it's back in the hands of its original owner

Goodbye. Farewell. Amen."

The priest played *Can't Help Falling in Love* on a piano near the altar.

And as the music filled the cathedral, Luke jiggled the envelope. "There's something else in here."

He held out his right hand, turned the envelope upside down, and gently shook out the remaining contents. And into his palm fell a Purple Heart.

ABOUT THE AUTHOR

Arthur Archambeau

Know me through my writing. It's all in there. My life story is in my stories.

BOOKS BY THIS AUTHOR

Letters From 1969

Right person. Wrong Time.

An Army officer visits a mysterious antique shop and is given a hope chest containing love letters written more than fifty years prior by a nurse in Vietnam.

Mike Falco is a young Army lieutenant and 1960s aficionado. When Mike visits the new antique shop in town, the eccentric proprietors insist that he's the rightful owner of an old dust-covered hope chest.

Reluctantly, he accepts the piece, despite the caveat that, "Once you touch what's inside this chest, it will touch you back." He quickly discovers that the sole contents are love letters written in 1969 by a twenty-two-year-old Army nurse serving in Vietnam.

As Mike reads the letters, he finds himself deeply moved by them. And by the young woman who'd penned them more than a half-century before. He sets out on a quest to track her down, hoping she's still alive so he can return them. But what he discovers when he finally unlocks the Secret of the Letters From 1969 propels him on an odyssey that spans not only continents, but across Time itself. It's a journey fraught with risk and danger. But Mike's willing to go as far as necessary for love, even if that means finding his future in the past.

So, put on your bell-bottoms, tie-dye, and love beads because Letters From 1969 will take you back to the Age of Aquarius, to the music, the culture, and the events that embodied that tumultuous time. And to all the joy—and heartache—that shaped both a nation and a generation.

BOOKS BY THIS AUTHOR

Just Grace And Danny

They were two lost souls… until they found each other.

A burned-out pop diva runs away from fame and falls for a handsome Roman Catholic priest, who allows her to hide inside a Church rectory in an idyllic small town known as the real-life Mayberry.

Grace Stevens has it all. Beauty. Fame. Money. But, at only twenty-seven, all has become too much. Grace has become a prisoner to her own fame. She's tired of the crazy tour schedule, the intrusive fans, the paparazzi hounding her, and her sleazy business manager controlling her. She yearns for a normal life. And she wants to find love, true love.

Danny O'Connor is a thirty-one-year-old Roman Catholic priest and a combat veteran of the Afghan War. He suffers from severe PTSD. Danny made a battlefield promise to God that if He got him safely home from war, he'd become a priest.

Reluctantly, Danny agrees to allow Grace to hide inside the St. Mary's Church rectory, where she takes up residence with him. What he didn't count on, though, was falling in love with her. Now, he's confronted with the ultimate choice—will he choose God or the girl? Will he break his vow of celibacy in the heat of passion or abide by his commitment to the Church?

Just Grace and Danny is a slow burn but steamy romance about the power of love to mend brokenness. It's a triumph of small-town values over the bright lights of the big city. It will get into your laughter, your heart, your soul. And maybe even a little into your tears. And leave you craving penny candy from a small town five and dime store, and bubble gum kisses in the rain.

Printed in Great Britain
by Amazon